D0389795

Lestrade and the Ripper

The year is 1888, and Jack the Ripper terrorizes London. All of the brutal killer's victims are discovered in the same district, Whitechapel, and all are prostitutes. But theirs aren't the only murders to perplex the brains of Scotland Yard. In Brighton, the body of one Edmund Gurney is also found dead.

Foremost amongst the Yard's top men is the young Inspector Sholto Lestrade. It is to his lot that the unsolved cases of a deceased colleague fall—cases that include the murder of Martha Tabram, formerly a prostitute from Whitechapel, and that of Gurney.

Leaving no stone unturned, Lestrade investigates with his customary expertise and follows the trail to the public school Rhadegund Hall. It is his intention to question the Reverend Algernon Spooner. What he finds is murder.

As the Whitechapel murders increase in number, so do those at Rhadegund Hall. What is the connection between them all? As it weren't confusing enough, Lestrade is hampered by the parallel investigations of that great detective, Sherlock Holmes, aided by Dr. Watson. Who is the murderer of Rhadegund Hall, and are he and the man they call "Jack the Ripper" one and the same?

Other books in M.J. Trow's Lestrade Mystery Series

THE ADVENTURES OF INSPECTOR LESTRADE
BRIGADE: THE FURTHER ADVENTURES OF LESTRADE
LESTRADE AND THE HALLOWED HOUSE
LESTRADE AND THE LEVIATHAN

Lestrade and the Ripper

Lestrade and the Ripper

Volume VI in the Lestrade Mystery Series

M.J. Trow

A Gateway Mystery

Published in the United States by
Regnery Publishing, Inc.
An Eagle Publishing Company
One Massachusetts Avenue, NW
Washington, DC 20001

Distributed to the trade by
National Book Network
4720-A Boston Way
Lanham, MD 20706

Printed on acid-free paper.
Manufactured in the United States of America

10 9 8 7 6 5 4 3 2 1

International Standard Book Number:
0-89526-311-4

The character of Inspector Lestrade was created by the late Sir Arthur Conan Doyle and appears in the Sherlock Holmes stories and novels by him, as do some other characters in this book.

To Peter

Contents

'Ruthless red-handed Murder sways the scene,
Mocking of glance and merciless of mien.
Mocking? Ah yes! At law the ghoul may laugh,
The sword is here as harmless as the staff . . .'

'Blind Man's Buff'

Punch 22 September 1888

False Trails

The two men sat in the silence to which they had become accustomed as they waited for their breakfast to arrive. Only the rustle of newspaper and the shooting of cuffs broke the stillness. The stockier of the two, nodding in the direction of middle age and with the unmistakable stoop of a man who had been hit by a jezail, probably in Afghanistan, raised his head and flared his nostrils as though scenting the breeze.

'Eggs, I'll be bound,' he said triumphantly.

'Mmm?' the other man mumbled in distant response behind his paper.

'Breakfast,' said his partner. 'Mrs Hudson's been boiling eggs.'

The paper fell. 'Ah, no, that's my current experiment – hydrogen sulphide, Doctor. A little something you may have come across in your career. It's kippers.'

'Hydrogen sulphide?'

'No, breakfast.' The paper reader was the epitome of a man inches from neurosis, teetering on the brink, a martyr to jangled nerves. He reached elegantly for the yellowing meerschaum in the rack near his head.

The other man coughed as if to warn him of Mrs Hudson's arrival, starched and bombazined, with the breakfast tray. He humphed as the kippers met his gaze.

'Right again, Holmes,' he said.

The taller man allowed a smile to flit across his lips.

'Good morning, gentlemen,' said the housekeeper.

'Any post, Mrs Hudson?' Holmes asked.

'Nothing today, sir.'

Holmes clicked his tongue and flicked his napkin into position.

'Surely Miss Adler would not have had time to catch the post . . . ' his companion began and shrank into silence as Holmes's eyes slashed through him, cutting him to ribbons.

'Will you be mother, Watson?' he asked icily.

The Doctor dutifully poured the coffee and tackled his kipper with gusto. 'Anything in the paper this morning, Holmes?'

'The usual trivia, Watson. I must admit, *The Thunderer* isn't what it was.'

'I've never trusted them since they carried that article on Lestrade's promotion to inspector.'

'Who?' Holmes paused before the porcelain hit his lips.

'Quite.'

'There is a little piece . . . oh, of no significance of course. And yet . . . '

'Ah?' The Doctor reached for his notebook.

'Finish your breakfast, my dear fellow. The game is not yet afoot, I fancy.'

'Tell me, Holmes,' Watson urged.

'Very well.' The taller man leaned back, running an elegant finger around the rim of his cup. 'Page eighteen, column three, sixteen . . . no, seventeen, lines down.'

Watson's jaw hung slack for a few seconds and then he ferreted in the paper. 'By Jove, Holmes, capital. How do you do it?'

'Come, Watson, would you have me betray all my secrets? What do you make of it?'

Watson buried himself in the article. Holmes poured more coffee, then, looking directly at the paper, said loudly, 'Doctor, you are moving your lips again.'

Watson dropped the paper. 'How did you know that? I was behind *The Times*, dammit!'

'You certainly were,' sighed Holmes, 'and you still are. The tiepin alone . . . Well, what of it?'

'A present,' Watson bridled. 'From a lady friend, if you must know.'

Holmes slammed down his cup. 'Not the tiepin, man. The article,' he roared.

'Ah, yes. The article. Some woman called Martha Tabram or Turner murdered.'

'What do you make of her?'

Watson laughed. 'Good God, Holmes, the whole thing is only half a dozen lines long. What am I to make of her? The poor soul was done to death.'

'Poor soul, Watson? So you *have* formed a judgement of her?'

'No, I . . . merely a figure of speech.'

'What of her profession?'

Watson checked the paper again. 'It doesn't say.'

'But it does, my dear fellow. Look again.'

He did. 'No, Holmes. I have to disagree with you.'

'That is your prerogative, Watson. It is also your tragedy. Let me help you. The deceased had two names.'

'So?'

'In your experience' – Holmes actually chuckled – 'what sort of person has two names?'

'A schizophrenic?' Watson guessed.

Holmes raised the eyebrow of derision.

'A criminal?'

'You're getting better, Doctor,' said Holmes. 'What sort of criminal?'

'Oh, really, Holmes— '

'She lived in Whitechapel, Watson.'

The Doctor sat with his mouth open again.

'According to Church of England estimates, there are eighty thousand prostitutes in the East End of London, most of them concentrated in Whitechapel.'

'Martha Tabram was a Lady of the Night?' Watson positively rubbed his hands together.

'Bravo, Watson. That would be my guess. How did she die?'

'Er . . . throat cut. God, how awful.'

Holmes placed a spidery finger to his thin, dark lips. 'Now,' he said, 'what sort of person cuts the throat of a prostitute?'

'A maniac,' was the best Watson could offer.

Holmes dismissed it: 'Glib nonsense, Watson. When it comes to murder, no one is a maniac. There are degrees of mania, levels of insanity. Some men you would call mad are in fact geniuses. I myself have walked that narrow ledge that separates genius from insanity, brilliance from bedlam . . . ' He was suddenly aware of his own rhetoric. 'I shall be away for a while, Watson,' he said.

'In Whitechapel?' Watson pressed forward, clutching the notebook convulsively.

Holmes looked at and through him. 'Do not press me, dear friend. This case interests me strangely. Perhaps, though, I will find out less as Sherlock Holmes and rather more as . . . '

'Yes? Yes?' Watson bubbled like a schoolboy with his first cigar. 'Which disguise is it to be?'

Holmes wagged a finger. 'Ah, no, Watson. That would be cheating. I shall be in touch, fear not.' He whipped the napkin from his lap, downed the last of his coffee and stood up. 'Have a nice day,' and he vanished into his room, humming manically.

Morley was dead. 'Nervous exhaustion,' said his friends. 'Drink,' said his enemies. 'Cirrhosis of the liver,' said the official findings. Whatever the truth, his caseload devolved on his brother officers at Scotland Yard. And all through the early summer, while the rain filled his basement, Assistant Commissioner Munro dithered first this way, then that. There was Frederick Abberline, the senior man, experienced, ruthless, capable. But something about the way his gardenia hung did not appeal. And then there were the unfortunate rumours surrounding Abberline and the fair sex. If he had the chance of sex, anywhere, anytime, then that was entirely fair. Then there was Frederick Wensley, gifted, dedicated, but he had this obsession with the City, talked to undesirables like Jews, Croats and constables. To get him to the Yard at all needed a team of drayhorses. There again, there was Tobias Gregson. He'd been a good copper once, but since they'd put him with the Special Irish Branch he and his reason had continually parted company. Rumour had it that his filing cabinet was devoted to one letter only: O. O for O'Brien, O'Shaughnessy, O'Banion, oh God. It was slander of course. The other drawer bulged with dossiers on men whose names ended in 'ski' or 'ovitch'. He and Wensley were not speaking – the Jew-lover and the Jew-hater. Rumour had it that 'Mr Vensel', as the Chosen Community knew him, was among Gregson's dossiers too. There was also Athelney Jones, newly taken aboard the River Police. 'A good all-rounder' was how Howard Vincent had described him, but the creator of the Criminal Investigation Department had a reputation for generosity. The roundest thing about Athelney Jones these days was his stomach. Strapped into his regulation patrol jacket, it plied the river from Chelsea to Wapping with Athelney Jones just behind it. He was altogether, Munro decided, too wet behind the ears. And in front of them, too, come to think of it.

And then, of course, there was Sholto Lestrade . . .

The inspector of that name peered over the rim of the chipped cup. The chipped face said it all: the skin of parchment, the nose of the ferret, the moustache of the walrus. Only the eyes were sad. Only the jaw was set. He had not taken off his Donegal and had thrown his bowler at the wall where the hat stand had been before the economies had taken their toll. The new Commissioner had much to answer for. Lestrade scrutinised the two men before him.

'Which of you is Derry?' he asked.

'Sir!' The taller constable stepped forward. 'Five-four-six-three-two, Derry, William, sir!'

Lestrade steadied his cup and his head and whispered, 'Tell me, Constable, have you ever been in the army?'

'Three years, sir. King's Own Yorkshire Light Infantry, sir.'

Lestrade shuddered as the boot thudded down again. 'Yes,' he said, wiping his face as though to obliterate it. 'Not light enough, apparently. How long on the Force?'

'Six years, sir.'

'With Mr Morley?'

'Two months, sir.'

'All right, Constable. Er . . . stand easy or something, would you?'

Lestrade noticed the feet slide outward, but the shoulders and the ramrod back moved not a jot. He looked at the other man.

'Don't tell me *you're* an army man, Toms?'

The Constable looked at the Inspector with some distaste. 'No, sir!' The boot came down on the uncomplaining floor. 'Royal Marines, sir. Four months.'

'Four months?' Lestrade raised an inspectorial eyebrow.

The Royal Marine crumbled a little. 'I couldn't stand the basic training, sir' and he ignored the snort of contempt from his colleague.

'Edward, is it?' Lestrade asked.

'Yes, sir,' – a pause – 'Edward Marjoram.'

Another snort.

'Do you have a cold, Constable?' Lestrade asked him.

'No, sir!' Derry snapped to attention again, eyes staring straight ahead.

'How long with Inspector Morley, Toms?' Lestrade asked.

'Nearly a year, sir.'

'Good. You may be of some help. Gentlemen, be seated.'

Derry looked startled. 'Sir?' The old habits died hard.

'That wooden thing behind you,' Lestrade explained; 'you probably don't have them in the army. We put our arses on them. Quaint, isn't it?'

It was Toms' turn to snort.

'I picked two short straws this morning,' Lestrade told them. 'I have been given the late Mr Morley's cases and the late Mr Morley's men. The only thing that's familiar to me is this office. Tell me, Derry, did they drink tea in the Yorkshire Light Infantry?'

'Oh, yes, sir.' The Constable was faintly embarrassed to have to admit it. His back was not touching the chair. Lestrade couldn't help thinking he looked wrong out of uniform.

'Then make me a cup. If Toms here didn't finish his basic training he won't know how. Oh, and have a small one yourselves.'

'Yes, sir.' Derry jerked upright. 'Thank you, sir!' and he saluted briskly.

'Remind me to have a word with you about that, Constable,' Lestrade said.

'Yes, sir. Very good, sir,' and he vanished into the latrine that doubled as a kitchen in the less-than-Great Scotland Yard.

'You were on Mr Morley's current case – that of Mr Edmund Gurney?' Lestrade asked Toms. The Constable nodded, swallowing hard.

'I've been through the notes. Three shoe-boxes. Quite a load. Let's have your version.'

'Sir?'

Lestrade lolled back in the chair and sighed. 'All right, Constable, while the Sergeant-Major there is being mother, you run along and get your notebook, there's a good Marine,' and as Toms made his exit Lestrade whispered, 'Goodbye, sailor.'

Dead cases irked Lestrade. There were problems enough when the corpse was fresh, when the cell door was open wide, when the forged ink was still wet. But after seven weeks the problems multiplied faster than Lestrade had been forced to in the dark days of his childhood at Mr Poulson's Academy for Nearly Respectable Gentlefolk. Accordingly, he took his battered Gladstone, his regulation long johns, should the weather turn, and braved the rigours of travel by Southern Railway. And he went alone. The sight of the sea again might upset Constable Toms and he couldn't stand the compulsive heel-clicking of Derry. Messrs W. H. Smith let him down. He'd read *The Flashing Lieutenant* before, completely misunderstanding the title, and *The Water Babies* was not the stuff of which inspectors of the Yard were made. It was in fact the bowdlerised version, but the manufacturing process of the wood pulp was of no interest to Lestrade.

The end of the season was descending on the villas and hotels of Brighton. Lestrade alighted from 'The Belle' and set off in search of the Royal Albion Hotel. It didn't have quite the panache of the Grand or the Metropole, but it was pleasant enough and certainly well beyond the pocket of an inspector of Scotland Yard. The manager was a portly man in his late fifties, inclined to nervous disorders and dyspepsia.

'I thought all this was resolved,' he fussed, mopping his sweating brow and polishing the top of the reception desk. He swigged from a blue glass bottle. 'For my dyspepsia,' he said quickly. Lestrade had never thought Milk of Magnesia good for anything else.

'An unfortunate incident,' the manager went on, 'very unfortunate. We lost trade, you know . . . '

'Tsk, tsk,' Lestrade shook his head in sympathy. 'Tell me about Mr Gurney,' he said.

The manager gulped. 'He arrived on the Friday.'

'That would be June twenty-second?'

The manager nodded, then his face froze maniacally as Guests arrived. 'Ah, good morning, ladies. Out for a stroll this morning?'

The Old Dears twittered to him, then noticed that Lestrade had failed to tip his bowler and left, muttering.

'Please,' the manager was excruciated, 'come into the office, will you?'

'What did you make of him?' Lestrade threw himself into a chair.

'Who?'

'The late Edmund Gurney,' Lestrade reminded him.

'Well, I hardly saw him. My clerk checked him in.'

'Room sixty-four.'

'Yes. He said he didn't want a view. Just privacy.'

'What did you make of that?'

'Make of it?' The manager swabbed his face anew. 'Look, Superintendent . . . ' He glanced frantically left, right and behind.

'I'll do my best,' said Lestrade, 'but at the moment it's Inspector.'

'Quite, well, you see, in the hotel trade . . . Oh dear, this is very difficult for me . . . '

'Let me help you. In the hotel trade it is best not to ask too many questions, am I right?'

The manager nodded.

'Discretion is the better part of valet?'

Lestrade was doing well.

'And forty-three couples called Smith stayed here last month alone.'

'How did you know that?' The manager was aghast.

'Oh, it's a little trick they teach us in the Metropolitan Police, sir. It's called reading. Your register doesn't have the incision of *The Woman in White* but it passes the time.'

'I believe Mr Gurney came here to meet someone.'

'Ah.'

'Assignations are not uncommon, Inspector. We merely provide a service. Oh, nothing dishonourable, I assure you.'

'Of course not,' Lestrade concurred. 'Why do you think Gurney came to meet someone?'

'Apparently, he asked my clerk, Gable, if there was a message for him. Seemed rather put out that there wasn't.'

'Anything else?'

'The next morning my clerk saw him taking coffee and brandy in the lounge with a man. Rather . . . well . . . working class, I'm afraid.'

Lestrade looked horrified. 'That was your clerk, Gable?'

'No, that was my clerk, Kent.'

'I'd like to see these men.'

'I'm very much afraid you can't, Inspector. They are no longer with us. Kent has gone into the newspaper business. Gable has gone into the theatre.'

'An actor?'

'That's a matter of opinion,' scowled the manager.

'Who found the body?'

'Dora, the third-floor maid.'

'Left?'

'No, still with us. You don't have to talk to her, do you?'

Lestrade stood up. 'I'm afraid I do, sir. Shall we?'

'No, no.' The Manager was determined that the door should remain closed. 'Wait here. I'll bring her to you.'

Dora added nothing that the Inspector did not already know. She had gone to clean the room and make the bed on Saturday afternoon. The door had been locked from the inside and the key was still in place. Unable to unlock it, and unusual in a menial of a little under five feet, she had shoulder-charged the thing and smashed it off its hinges. Despite her later complaints that the management should buy better fittings, she said management docked her wages and allowed her no time off at all, nor lightened her duties, despite the mild fracture. They wouldn't have treated her like that, Dora confided to Lestrade, if she'd been a Gas Hoperative or a matchgirl at Bryant and May's. They didn't ought to be so hoffhand. And her hunattached and all. The ramblings went on, but when Lestrade brought her back to the contents of Room 64 that Saturday in June, Dora became doe-eyed and recounted it all as though in a trance.

'I can see 'im now, sir,' she whispered. Lestrade toyed with glancing behind him, but reason got the better of him. 'Lyin' on the bed, 'e were. Dead, 'e were on 'is left.'

'Clothed?' Lestrade shattered the moment.

' 'Ere, this is a respectable hestablishment,' – Dora was loyal in her way – ''E 'ad 'is nightshirt on. Quite 'andsome, 'e were, come to think of it.' She caught sight of Lestrade's raised eyebrow and returned to her narrative. 'In 'is 'and 'e 'eld a sponge bag.'

'Anything else?'

She frowned in concentration. 'Yes,' she nodded, ' 'is nose.'

It was Lestrade's turn to frown. He could remember no mention of mutilation in the coroner's report. 'Oh, I see. He was holding the bag over his nose?'

'That's what I said,' Dora replied. 'There was this bottle by the bed.'

'Did you notice a smell in the room?'

'Well, I 'adn't 'ad a chance to empty the chamber pot.'

'No, something else.'

'They told me it was chlorophell 'e done it wiv. I din't smell nuffink, though.'

'Did Mr Gurney talk to you?' Lestrade asked.

'I told yer, Mister. 'E were dead.'

Lestrade flicked his moustache in lieu of a smile. 'I meant before that. On the previous day, for instance.'

' 'E just said 'ello. Proper gentleman, 'e were. Nice, like.'

'He didn't mention meeting anyone in Brighton?'

'Na.' Dora shook her head.

'Dora,' Lestrade leaned forward, 'how long have you been a chambermaid?'

'Nigh on ten years, sir. Since I were a gel.'

'You're used to beds, then?'

Dora pulled back in fear. ' 'Ere, I've 'eard 'bout you gennelmen from Lunnon. I'm a good gel, I am.'

'Of course you are, Dora.' Lestrade leaned back to reassure her by his distance. 'But could you tell, with your ten years' experience, whether Mr Gurney had been sleeping alone in his bed?'

Dora stood up, ready to make for the door. 'I told you,' she shouted, 'this is a respectable hestablishment— '

'It certainly is!' The manager hurtled from nowhere into the room and cuffed Dora heartily round the ear, 'but it won't be much longer if you raise your voice like that again. And you'll be out on the streets, my girl!'

Lestrade waited until the overwrought proprietor left, almost bowing in abject apology to Lestrade.

'Now, Dora,' Lestrade looked down at her, 'do you think Mr Gurney slept alone the last night of his life?'

She forced back her tears and sniffed. 'Yessir,' she said, 'I do.'

'Thank you,' said Lestrade.

The Inspector's next port of call was to the dingy offices of *The Brighton Gazette*, in search of one Douglas Blackburn, local hack.

'If I can help, Inspector, I surely will. I fancy your calling and mine result in the same worn leather, the same fruitless search.'

'Perhaps, Mr Blackburn,' answered Lestrade, not usually given to loathing people on sight, 'but I work for a living. How well did you know Edmund Gurney?'

'G. A. Smith and I carried out some experiments with him, whenever he was in Brighton.'

'Experiments?'

Blackburn looked surprised. 'Oh, come, Mr Lestrade.' The loathing was clearly mutual. 'You must be aware of Mr Gurney's business.'

'I'd like to hear it from you,' he answered.

'But I gave all this information at the inquest,' the news-hound protested.

'I know,' Lestrade told him, 'and now I'd like you to give it to me.'

'Very well,' Blackburn sighed. 'Gurney was a ghost-hunter, Inspector. A founder of the Society for Psychical Research. He roamed the country collecting material for books, treatises, et cetera.'

'About ghosts?'

'About the existence of the paranormal, Mr Lestrade.' Blackburn had already dismissed his inquisitor as an idiot. 'You've read *Phantasms of the Living*.'

It was a statement, not a question, and Lestrade ignored it. 'And what was your part in all this?'

'As a local journalist, I have various contacts. I am also, though perhaps I shouldn't say so, known for my integrity.'

Lestrade ignored that too. 'And Mr . . . Smith?'

'Likewise. He was for some months Mr Gurney's private secretary. They were very close.'

'Would you say Mr Smith has the appearance of a working man?' Lestrade asked.

Blackburn chuckled. 'Why, Mr Lestrade, I do believe you are a snob. If you're trying to tie either Mr Smith or myself to Gurney's death— '

'Should I be?' Lestrade interrupted. 'The jury decided that he was "accidentally suffocated by an overdose of chloroform taken probably for the relief of pain", and I quote.'

'I know you do,' said Blackburn archly. 'I wrote the same words in this very newspaper. An Inspector of Scotland Yard does not trouble himself by treading the footprints of men who have died by accident. You know something.'

'Quite a bit, Mr Blackburn. What I do not know is why I can eliminate you and Mr Smith from my enquiries. You were about to tell me.'

'Indeed,' Blackburn subsided a little. 'Smith was on his honeymoon the day Gurney died, in Ramsgate – yes, not my idea of nuptial bliss either. And I was in Brighton Infirmary having a corn removed. You will find the records speak for themselves.'

'I'm sure they do, Mr Blackburn,' Lestrade said. 'Can you think of a reason why Mr Gurney should want to take his own life?'

Blackburn shrugged. 'He was a moody man, Inspector, much given to self-doubt. A sensitive type, if you'll pardon the pun.'

As Lestrade was unaware of it he had no option but to pardon it. He was rising to go, when Blackburn stopped him.

'There is one thing,' he said, a different tone in his voice, 'something I found after the inquest on poor Edmund.'

'Oh?' Lestrade was all ears.

'Have a look at this.' The journalist handed the policeman a printed sheet. 'It's the Fashionable Visitor's List for the fourteenth of June.'

'So?'

'About half-way down.' Blackburn tapped the paper. 'Fifty-six Middle Street.'

Lestrade read the name. 'Mr Guerney, fifty-six Middle Street,' he repeated, 'A lodging house?'

Blackburn nodded.

'Have you been there?'

Blackburn shook his head.

'So if this Mr Guerney is our Mr Gurney . . . ' Lestrade was thinking aloud.

'Then he had been in Brighton for over a week before he died.'

'Is that unusual?'

'Not particularly. He was interested in a haunted house in Brighton. All I know is that he didn't contact me or George Smith.' Blackburn paused. 'I wish he had.'

The landlady at 56 Middle Street remembered Mr Gurney well. He was tall, at least five foot four, with sandy hair which may have been brown. His beard was immaculately groomed, to the point perhaps of not being there at all. His eyes? Well, one was grey, certainly. The other she could not swear to. No, she had not seen him before. Or had she? No, that was the other gentleman. The one with the strong accent. Scottish. County Clare if she knew her accents. Mr Gurney's entry in the ledger was nearly as unhelpful. No Christian name, no address other than 'London'. It was possible that he had received visitors while there, but then again . . . Lestrade left before he was tempted to reach for a blunt instrument with which to batter the woman to death.

Edmund Gurney's nearest and dearest could shed no further light. His wife and daughter affirmed that he was a warm, tender, loving husband and father. His brother, vicar of the very church in Pimlico where young Lestrade had sung in the choir before they discovered he had no voice at all, affirmed that the deceased was a martyr to neuralgia and often went for nights without sleep. So familiar did all this sound that Lestrade momentarily wondered to himself whether Gurney had not at one time been a policeman. The vicar admitted in a grave voice that his brother had been known to use narcotics, chloroform among them, to ameliorate his condition. Lestrade had no knowledge of anyone called Amelia and let the matter drop.

Mrs Henry Sidgwick was not in the end of much more use. Her husband, on whom Lestrade had called on his return to London, was lecturing in America and was therefore unavailable for comment. At first, Lestrade had hoped Mrs Sidgwick might be useful. She and her husband had founded the Society for Psychical Research along with Gurney some years before. She had the hard, murderous features of Kate Webster, who had tried to sell her mistress in little packets of lard a few years ago, but, unlike the aforementioned Kate, she had a sharp, observant mind.

'It was murder, Inspector,' she told him flatly.

'Oh?' Lestrade was surprised at her candour. Her wall-paper had taken him aback too.

'And the guilty parties are drudges named Innes and Pierce.'

Lestrade racked what passed for a brain in the tired cranium. Neither of those names leapt out at him from the shoe-boxes at the Yard. He had run his tape-measure up the inside legs of none by those names. Unless, of course, they were aliases.

'You seem very sure of all this, Mrs Sidgwick. May I ask why?'

'You've read *Phantasms of the Living*.' It was a statement

again. Lestrade had been here before. 'But did you read the critique of that immortal work by Innes and Pierce? They crucified poor Edmund, Inspector, crucified him. "Lord, what fools these mortals be".' She drew herself up to her full height. 'What wretched beings these reviewers are. Lacking the intellect to write themselves, they must attack and ridicule those who do. And we pay them to do it! There is no justice, Inspector, saving your presence.'

Lestrade smiled. 'So you think Edmund Gurney was so devastated by the attacks of his critics that he took his own life?'

Mrs Sidgwick nodded. 'Culpable homicide,' she said.

Lestrade reached for his hat.

'Of course,' she stood up and hurried round the room, drawing the heavy velvet curtains, 'we could ask him.'

'Who, madam?' Lestrade wondered if someone had come in.

'Edmund, of course,' she said, turning up the oil-lamp. 'I have been waiting for him to come through for some time. Unfortunately his wires keep crossing with the Prince Consort's.' She caught his glance. 'You are a sceptic, Mr Lestrade.'

'No, Mrs Sidgwick. I am a policeman. Good day.'

And there it had to rest. There was one more person to see, but that would involve Lestrade in more expense and more time. He must go north, tired of southern comfort, and penetrate the leafy glades of Northamptonshire, if glades there were and if those glades still had leaves, after the storms of the dismal summer of 1888. Two things kept him moving. One, he suspected, was the rather dubious cottage pie they served at The Stunned Old Duke of York. The other was the pencilled word in the bottom margin of Morley's notes on Gurney. A word written in Morley's own spidery hand. A word which echoed Mrs Sidgwick's first sentiments and the unspoken fears of Douglas Blackburn. It was the word 'murder'.

Mary Ann

Rhadegund Hall is approached by the Great North Road, left a bit, up a bit and you're there. So was Inspector Lestrade that Wednesday in August, a little before luncheon. The building itself, set in magisterial grounds, was new. An imposing, red-brick façade, fronted by elaborate wrought-iron gates. To the west stood the Gothic block of the chapel, dedicated to St Rhadegund, and to the east the equally imposing house of the Headmaster.

Lestrade crossed the lawns above the First Eleven Square, looking for signs of life. There were none, save the lowly chanting of a first declension from somewhere in the building's bowels. He recognised the sound from his own days at Mr Poulson's Academy at Blackheath. Had it been the second declension wafting on the breeze that morning at Rhadegund, Lestrade would not have recognised it. He had not got that far. Still, he reasoned, a lack of classics had proved no obstacle. Here he was on this bright, sunny morning, thirty-four years old and an Inspector of the Criminal Investigation Department at Scotland Yard. Not bad for a beginner.

He found a door and walked through it, remembering, as he usually did, to open it first. The darkness hit him like a wall and he groped his way forward through what was clearly a corridor, lined, as his eyes acclimatised, with the heavy pipes that were the lifeblood of the Rhadegund heating system, and with photographs of darkly handsome young men in caps and long shorts, posing heroically before what appeared to be the main doors of the school. He saw a light at the end of the tunnel and followed it until he found the door. Dark green lockers rose up sheer on each side of it, not unlike those at the Yard where he habitually hung his Donegal in wet weather, and where, in the unhealthy basement, the sergeants stored their tripe sandwiches and naughty French postcards.

'Yes,' a muffled voice responded to his knock. The glass was bubbled so that the occupant of the room appeared at first to have a few hundred heads. Lestrade was quite relieved to find he had only one.

'Cap size?' The occupant did not look up from an enormous ledger on the desk.

'Er . . . seven, I think,' Lestrade answered.

'Don't suppose you know your inside leg measurement?' the occupant grunted.

'No, I don't,' Lestrade said, 'and I don't think I'd tell you even if I did.'

'Now look here, young . . . ' The occupant looked up.

'Lestrade,' said Lestrade. 'Inspector Lestrade.'

'Is this some sort of joke?' the occupant asked with an even sourer look on his face than usual.

'If it is, I suppose it's on me,' said Lestrade. 'I'm looking for the Reverend Algernon Spooner.'

'The Chaplain?'

Lestrade nodded. The occupant relaxed his grim jaws. 'I'm sorry,' he said. 'I thought you were a new boy come for a fitting.'

Lestrade looked uncomprehending, never a rare situation.

'Oh, forgive me.' The occupant sensed the Inspector's bewilderment. 'I am the Bursar, Charles Mercer. My job is to kit out new boys and to replace items of uniform as necessary.'

Mercer the Bursar? Lestrade mused. It all seemed very unlikely. The Bursar rang a bell at his elbow and a schoolboy appeared through a panel in the wall, bent almost double under other huge ledgers. He was of a decidedly shadowy complexion.

'Ah, Singh Minor, this gentleman is a policeman. He wishes to see the Chaplain. Be a good chap and take him to the chapel, will you?'

'Yes, sir,' chirped the lad. 'This way, sir.'

Lestrade thanked Mercer and followed the boy through a labyrinth of passageways until they entered a quadrangle.

'Excuse me, sir,' said the boy. 'Are you really a Miltonian?'

Lestrade tried not to show his surprise that an Indian public schoolboy should be familiar with London thieves' cant. ' "Pig" would be nearer the mark,' he said. 'Why, are you a lag?'

'No,' the boy laughed. 'A Sikh, originally, but I'm not proud.'

The conversation was rapidly parting company with Lestrade and he was glad when Singh knocked on the vestry door.

'So you've got old Spooner at last, have you?' the boy asked. 'What is it? Kinchin-lay? Griddling? No, don't tell me – prating. It has to be.'

'Does your headmaster know about you?'

'Nails? No fear,' grinned the boy.

There was an intonation from within and Singh opened the door. 'A gentleman to see you, Mr Spooner,' he said with the diction and decorum of an angel. He winked at Lestrade. 'It's all right,' he said, 'he doesn't voker Romeny.'

'Well, that's a relief,' sighed Lestrade.

The Reverend Spooner was a largish man with a sharp nose and rimless spectacles. His bull neck ought to have belonged to another man. Perhaps Singh was right. He'd half-inched it from somebody else.

'Can I help?' The Reverend shook Lestrade's hand and offered him a pew.

'My name is Inspector Lestrade. I am making enquiries into the death of Mr Edmund Gurney at Brighton some weeks ago. I believe you were a close friend.'

The Chaplain suddenly jerked sideways as though from

a sharp blow and yanked open the door. The stunted nut-brown figure of young Singh collapsed onto the carpet.

'What don't good Christians do?' Spooner bellowed through his nose.

'Listen at keyholes, sir.' Singh scrambled upright.

'Quite right. Are you working for Mr Mercer at the moment?'

'Yes, sir.'

'Well, when you've finished, come back here. I have some crass bandlesticks for you to polish.'

Lestrade's ears played him false for a moment, but the boy said, 'Very good, sir,' and shambled off sheepishly.

'Now,' the Chaplain turned to Lestrade, 'where were we? Ah, yes, Edmund. A tragic loss, Inspector. Tragic.'

'When did you last see Mr Gurney, Mr Spooner?'

The Chaplain placed an ecclesiastical finger on his chin. 'Ah, let me see. Not for some time, I fear. Not certainly since the spring.'

'How did he seem when you saw him last?'

'Seem? Well, Edmund was always rather a sortured toul, Inspector.'

Lestrade blinked.

'I don't think Edmund was ever really happy. All that Other World nonsense, you see.'

'You didn't approve of Mr Gurney's dabblings in spiritualism, then?'

Spooner grew less ecumenical. 'Nankly, fro,' he said. 'Oh, I know there are those who subscribe to Christian spiritualism, but not for me. Better the naight and strarrow.'

Lestrade shifted uneasily in his chair and introduced a surreptitious finger into his ear, twisting his head slightly to catch whatever drift he could from the Chaplain.

'Tell me,' the Chaplain intoned, 'is there anything . . . suspicious . . . about Edmund's death?'

'Why do you ask?'

Spooner smiled. 'Come now, Inspector. I may be the cousin of a dear old queen. I may even be the Chaplain of a school. But I am *not* a fool. Senior police officers do not make enquiries into suicides. Do they?'

'I must— ' but Lestrade never finished his sentence because a scream shattered the silence of the morning vestry.

'What's that?' Lestrade was on his feet.

'It might be Matron,' Spooner suggested. 'What day is it?'

'Wednesday,' Lestrade reached the door first.

'No. It's Carman's day off.'

'Carman?'

'An amorous groundsman we have here. Too many rhododendron bushes, you see.'

Lestrade wasn't sure he did.

'This way.' Spooner set off at a fox-trot along the corridor, out into the quad, with Lestrade at his heels.

'Mr Spooner, Mr Spooner!' A little woman in white stood at the top of a flight of stone steps, jumping up and down.

'What is it, Mrs Shuttlecomb, the rats again?'

She flapped wildly, waving her apron at the Chaplain, screaming hysterically. Spooner reached her in one bound and slapped her heartily around the face. 'You're screaming hysterically,' he told her.

'I know, sir,' she continued as before, pointing vaguely behind her. Spooner shook her by the shoulders. No effect. He hit her again. This time she went down heavily and lay still.

'That looked suspiciously like grievous bodily harm.' Lestrade gave him his professional opinion.

'Muscular Christianity,' Spooner corrected him, and hurtled through the door.

Lestrade hurtled after him into what was obviously a laundry. The air was damp and filled with bleach. The floor was wet, a fact the Reverend Spooner had doubtless learned to live with. Not so Lestrade.

'Watch out for the— ' The Chaplain stopped in midsentence as the Inspector slid the length of the room, pirouetting acrobatically into a row of sheets. Alas, the sheets were merely a blind, disguising as they did the far wall.

' —soap,' Spooner concluded.

Lestrade dragged himself up the brickwork, moving like a creation of Mary Shelley's, as though with a bolt through his neck.

'Over here!' the Chaplain called. Lestrade edged towards the Chaplain, his head on one side like a badly stuffed budgerigar. 'Lood Gord,' he heard Spooner mutter.

Floating in the cold water of a large stone bath was the body of a girl, her dress and petticoats spread wide on the water, but heavy with suds.

'We must get her out.' Spooner plunged his hands into the water.

'No!' Lestrade wrenched him back and his neck clicked, causing him to cry in pain. 'There's no point. Please don't touch anything.' He circled the bath a few times, noting the tell-tale signs. The girl was about seventeen, he guessed, not unattractive. There was the inevitable froth around nose and mouth, although in the suds it was difficult to be sure.

'Who was she?' he asked.

'Maggie Hollis. She lives in the village.'

'Any reason why she should be here?'

'She works – oh, God – worked here. With the lady I had occasion to correct outside. Mrs Shuttlecomb, the wretched old besom. Was it an accident?'

Lestrade looked at Spooner, then at Maggie. Something in the suds caught his eye and he pulled up his cuff and thrust his hand into the water, ice cold. He raised the dead girl's left hand. The fingers were wrinkled. It didn't help – she was a washerwoman anyway. He looked at the moon face, the pale skin. His mother had been a laundress. But it was the right hand that held his attention then. He lifted that too. It was clenched tight, like a fist.

'I said— '

'I know what you said, Mr Spooner,' said Lestrade. 'No, I don't think it was an accident.' He pointed to the fist; 'what the coroner calls a cadaveric spasm,' he explained.

'What does that mean?'

'It means that the girl grabbed something as she died.'

'I don't follow.'

Lestrade began to prise open the fingers. 'If it's a bar of soap or a bag of blue, it could still be an accident, but if it's anything else . . . '

As the fingers snapped back, Lestrade saw what Maggie Hollis was gripping in her iron fist. It was a small, black cylinder, about two inches long, made of wood and bone.

'What do you make of this?'

Spooner looked at the object and shook his head. 'I've no idea,' he said.

'You'd better get some help,' Lestrade told him. 'Where's Matron?'

'On reflection, she's not due until tomorrow. You see, Inspector, we aren't actually open yet. The Tichaelmas Merm doesn't start until Monday.'

'I thought I heard a Latin lesson . . . '

'Ah, yes, the boarders. Or at least some of them. Their parents are in foreign parts, hill stations in India, mostly. You met Cherak Singh Minor. He and his brother are typical. I can't say I'm altogether happy with their presence.' He closed confidentially to Lestrade. 'Some of them are barely civilised, Lestrade. No conception of the Thirty-nine Articles.'

'Tut, tut,' Lestrade shook his head.

'But Dr Nails sees it otherwise, of course. Our Christian Duty et cetera, et cetera.'

'Dr Nails?'

'The Headmaster. He's been in the Himalayas himself all summer. Following in Whymper's footsteps.'

'Not all of them, I hope,' Lestrade said. 'Mr Spooner, do you have a key to this room?'

'No, but Mrs Shuttlecomb will have.' The Chaplain marched to the door and rummaged in the clothing of the prostrate laundress. 'Thought so.' He held it up triumphantly. Lestrade edged his way to the door, a good deal more gingerly than when he had come in, and locked it behind him, placing the key in his pocket.

'Do you know who else has a key?'

Spooner thought for a moment. 'Probably Adelstrop.'

'Adelstrop?'

'Head groundsman. Berfect plighter, if you ask me. Look, Lestrade, are you telling me,' Spooner bent to Lestrade's ear, a rakish angle since it nearly touched his shoulder, 'are you telling me poor Hollis was murdered?'

Lestrade nodded, rather with a gesture of the village idiot.

Spooner straightened. 'Lood Gord,' at least interjections were consistent, 'I'd better get the police. Oh . . . '

He stepped over the recumbent Mrs Shuttlecomb.

'Leave that to me,' Lestrade stopped him, 'and unless you want total panic on your hands you won't breathe a word about this to anyone, not for the moment.'

'Right.' Spooner marched down the steps.

'Haven't you forgotten something?' Lestrade asked.

Spooner turned. 'Um . . . oh, right, Inspector,' and turned to go.

'No, I mean Mrs Shuttlecomb.' He pointed to the lying laundress.

'Ah, yes, of course. I'll take her to the san. Best place, I think.'

He stooped and hauled the round little woman onto his shoulder, before taking the steps again.

'Of course.' Lestrade came down sideways. 'Maggie Hollis looks a solid wench. Whoever killed her would need to be pretty strong.'

'Yes . . . ' Spooner beamed. 'Oh, I see.' He regained his sangfroid. 'No, no, this is cleric's lift, Inspector. All theologians learn it to escape from the flames should their colleges be engulfed. It's not a matter of strength, but how one uses it.'

'Quite so,' Lestrade agreed.

*

The Inspector was soundly asleep in his bed. Constable Neil of J Division was minding his own business in the vicinity of the Minories. It was a mild night, the last one of August, promising an Indian summer and Neil was hoping for a few minutes' snooze before he called into the nearest fixed point and had his early morning cuppa. His corns threatened to get the better of him again. Still, he'd better make one last sweep before hanging up his truncheon and he turned the usual corners until he stumbled over something in a corner of the yard at Buck's Row. He cursed as his knees hit the cobbles and he scrambled up to look closer at the bundle of rags he had fallen over. He jerked back, catching his breath as he did so, and fumbled for his whistle. Where the hell were the reliefs? Never one around when you want one. The shrill jarring of the Metropolitan Pattern whistle, 1879 Patent, brought two other coppers running.

'Bill?' Neil squinted in the dark to catch the silver numbers on the collar – 96J.

'Jack?' Constable Thain called back.

'Who's that with you?'

'George Mizen, H Division. Who's that with you?'

'It's a corpse,' he whispered.

Mizen, the older man, checked his watch. It was a quarter to four. Thain took one look at Neil's bundle and spun away, vomiting in a corner. Neil, of sterner stuff, knelt down and pulled back the shabby brown Ulster with its brass buttons.

'Thain,' Mizen snapped, 'stop that and get a doctor. Llewellyn's the nearest one. Step on it.'

Thain veered away and the others heard his boots clattering on the cobbles.

'She's still warm,' Neil whispered.

'Right, lad. You wait 'ere and don't touch nothin'. I'm goin' to 'ave a look round.'

Dr Llewellyn hurried through the still, starry night. Carters were tumbling from doorways, tugging on flat caps and tying scarves. The City crawled into life. He would have arrived sooner but he'd got himself hopelessly tied up in his pyjama strings. He fumbled in the yard, desperately trying to shake the sleep from his eyes. 'Hold that damned thing steady!' he snarled at Thain whose lantern, like his stomach, was all over the place. So, it transpired, was the stomach on the ground. It had belonged to a middle-aged woman with dark, greying hair plastered across her neck. Her throat had been cut, he guessed in two parallel sweeps, probably from left to right. Even a cursory lifting of the head proved that windpipe, gullet and spinal cord had all been severed.

'Right.' He took the rather superfluous stethoscope from his ears. 'Can't do anything for her here. Get her to the mortuary, Constable. Constable?'

But Thain was lying beside the dead woman. It was left to Mizen and Neil to carry them both away.

Inspector Frederick George Abberline rolled over in bed. Slowly, the distant woodpecker hammering somewhere in the distant forests of his dreams sharpened and hardened to become the doorknocker downstairs. He sat bolt upright, causing the woman beside him to wake with a start.

'Sorry, my love,' he patted her and kissed her cheek, 'that sounds like duty calling.'

'What time is it?' she slurred.

He floundered about for his hunter. 'Good God, it's nearly half-past eight.'

He leapt out of bed, hauling on his red combinations and pausing at the mirror only to slick down his hair before throwing open the sash of the window.

'All right, Constable. No need to wake the dead. What's the matter?'

The constable in the street below saluted and stepped back. 'Beggin' your pardon, sir,' he said 'but there's been another one.'

Abberline straightened too suddenly and the sash parted his hair for him. 'Where?' he grimaced.

'Buck's Row, sir.'

'Buck's Row? That's Whitechapel.'

'Yessir.'

'Well, why the hell . . . oh, all right. Wait a minute. I'll be down. Have you got a wagon?'

'Yes, sir. Oh, and one more thing, sir.'

'Yes, Constable?'

'A message from Mrs Abberline, sir, asking when you'll be home.'

There was a shrill laugh from the bed. Abberline spun round with his finger to his lips and then back to the constable. 'Get me to the station and then tell Mrs Abberline that all surveillances take time. The criminal mind, tell her, cannot be rushed. And, dear though she is to me . . .'

More giggles from the bed.

' . . . my mind is and must be on higher things.' He slammed the sash down just in time so that the constable did not hear the 'Oh, Fred, you wicked, wicked man.'

'Spratling, isn't it?' Abberline snapped. The inspector in the patrol jacket stood to attention.

'It is, Mr Abberline.'

'All right.' Abberline threw the cold water over his face. 'What have your boys dug up?'

'It's another one,' he said.

Abberline had been here before. 'Oh?' he played dumb, a rôle he never found difficult.

'Like that Martha Tabram. Or similar, anyway.'

'Who is it this time?'

'One Mary Ann Nicholls,' Spratling consulted his black book, 'wife of one William Nicholls of thirty-seven Coburg Street, a printer of Messrs Perkins, Bacon and— '

'Yes, yes, all right. What happened?'

'Her throat was cut, left to right. Almost cut her head off, he did— '

'Who? The husband?'

Spratling shrugged. 'Person or persons unknown.'

Abberline nodded, wrestling with his tie. 'It'll be the husband.'

'She was disembowelled.'

Abberline looked up. This was a bit strong, even for Whitechapel.

'They didn't get him, then?' he said.

'I'm not sure it is the husband, sir. He seems to have a pretty tight story as to his whereabouts.'

'Of course he has.' Abberline began cleaning his nails with his letter-opener. 'They all do.'

'The doctor thinks she was cut about down . . . there . . . before her throat was cut.' He read from his own notes. 'The abdomen had been cut open from centre of bottom of ribs on right side— '

'Yes, all right, Spratling, thank you,' Abberline raised a hand, 'I haven't had my breakfast yet. Suspects apart from her husband?'

'Well, it's difficult,' the Inspector admitted. 'Nicholls was a prostitute.'

'Ah,' said Abberline, as though that said it all. 'Doing business in the street, was she?'

'Could be,' Spratling said. 'She'd been separated from the old man and was living at a lodging house in Flower and Dean Street. She couldn't afford the fourpence for her bed, apparently, but was going out to earn it.'

'Well,' Abberline put on his bowler again, 'I'll look into it, Inspector.'

'Sir, I believe we've got a maniac on our hands, sir.'

Abberline seared him with a glance. 'All right, I'll put one of our junior men on it. But now it's time for breakfast.'

In his outer office Abberline accosted the desk man. 'Sergeant, where's Lestrade?'

The Sergeant checked the register. 'Last seen 'eadin' in the general direction of Northampton, sir.'

'Northampton?' Abberline looked perplexed. 'What the

devil is he doing there? Oh well, I'll be in the Clarence if anything breaks, Sergeant. Apart from wind, of course,' and he left the building.

Dr Theophilus Nails was a martinet of the old school – the school in this case being St Rhadegund's. He was a burly man the wrong side of sixty, but that had not stopped him at all. In fact, it hadn't even slowed him down. When Lestrade entered the great man's study that afternoon early in September, he found the Headmaster still swathed in ropes and crampons.

'Ah,' Nails's voice could shatter glass. 'You must be Lestrade. Shocking, this business, what? What progress?'

'Well, sir, I— '

'Oh, forgive me. Seat. Brandy. In that order, what?'

Lestrade found himself complying with both orders. Like Wellington and his infantry, he didn't know what effect Nails had on his boys, but he certainly terrified him.

'I was hoping you could shed some light, sir.'

'I?' Nails paused in mid-swig, then downed it and poured again. 'I have only this morning arrived home after a month in the Himalayas. You climb?'

Lestrade was about to protest that he didn't, when he realised Nails's meaning and said, 'No.'

'Pity. Ought to be part of basic training for you chappies. I wish we had some cliff faces near here. I'd soon put the boys through it. Now, where were we? Ah yes, this wretched washerwoman.'

'Miss Hollis,' Lestrade informed him.

'Yes, quite. I didn't know her personally, of course. My chaplain tells me she was murdered. Can that be true?'

'I fear so,' said Lestrade.

The Headmaster tapped his desk top with an ice pick. 'How very, very awkward,' he said.

'Sir?'

'Well, dammit, Lestrade. Term starts in two days. There'll be a devil of a stink.'

'The boys?'

'The murder, man!' Nails frowned at the Donegalled figure in front of him. He was clearly an imbecile, what with his head on one side and all.

'May I ask, sir, why you ordered the local constabulary off the premises?'

'Certainly you may ask,' Nails told him. 'I can't have bobbies with their great feet trampling all over the First Eleven Square, Lestrade. This is a school. St Rhadegund's School. What would the governors say? The parents? I am a father to these boys, Lestrade. I am in *loco parentis*.'

Lestrade didn't doubt for a moment that the redoubtable Dr Nails was a father figure, but he really didn't see how trains fitted into the picture.

'The Chief Constable's son is on our books,' Nails explained, then rolled his eyes heavenwards, 'albeit in the Remove; I merely sent a message to Arnold and told him what I thought of his constabulary. He understood of course and agreed with me, but he pointed out how difficult it was to get recruits these days who could master gerundives.'

Lestrade nodded. He'd noticed this for years.

'How did this wretched girl die?'

'She was drowned, sir. In your laundry.'

'My laundry? Oh, no, Inspector, I never wash dirty linen in public. Who could have done it?'

'That is what I am endeavouring to find out,' Lestrade answered. 'Maggie Hollis died, I believe, late on Tuesday night. The coroner's report might help there, though we'll have to wait for that.'

'Oh, I'll get that for you. Old Risdon's grandson is on our books.'

'The Remove?' Lestrade asked.

'No, the Lower Fourths, but I fear that is his ultimate destination, yes.'

'I have interviewed everyone who was on the premises that night.'

'Even the boys?' Nails looked horrified.

'No, sir, Mr Spooner advised me I should wait until you returned.'

'Quite right. Oh, my boys may be young tearaways, Inspector, scallywags even. There may even be a bounder or two among 'em. But no really bad hats, I assure you.'

'Even so, sir. I must have your permission to interview them.'

'Must you? Oh well, I suppose, if you must. But I reserve the right to be present, Inspector.'

'As you wish.'

'Could none of the staff shed any light? That wretched woman Mrs Shuttlecomb for instance?'

'I'm afraid Mrs Shuttlecomb is in a coma, sir.'

'Good Lord, not the gin, was it?'

'No, the Chaplain.'

'Ah.'

'If I weren't so busy, I'd press charges.'

Nails waved it aside. 'Done us all a favour,' he assured him. 'Utterly wretched woman.'

'Are there only two keys to the laundry?'

'I believe so. Better ask Adelstrop.'

'Who?'

'You remember Adelstrop,' the Headmaster assured him.

'Yes, of course. He did his rounds at about ten-thirty and noticed nothing untoward.'

'Good, good,' Nails nodded. 'That's what I like, a tight ship.'

'Personally, I should have been happier had he witnessed a large man running from the laundry,' Lestrade told him.

'Ah,' beamed Nails, 'you've got someone in mind to pin this on.' A positive light gleamed in his eyes. 'Not Charles Bradlaugh, is it?'

'Who?'

'That upstart who has the temerity to represent this wonderful county of ours in Westminster. The man isn't only a profligate and debauchee, he's also an atheist.'

'I take it his son isn't on your books,' Lestrade asked.

'Certainly not. Not even in the Remove. I'd hang myself first.'

'No, Dr Nails, I have no one in mind. I merely meant that a young girl was done to death in a building in a school containing thirty-six assorted staff and, on the night in question, twenty boys. And no one heard a thing.'

'That's the nature of the beast, Inspector. No one saw the thuggees at work either.'

'That's a little out of my beat, sir,' Lestrade said. 'Do you happen to recognise this?' He handed Nails the little black cylinder he had found in the cadaverous hand of Maggie Hollis.

'Yes, I do. It's an amulet,' the Headmaster told him. He dropped it hard on the desk and the end fell off.

Lestrade started and cried out.

'It's all right, Inspector, it's supposed to do that. Look,' he pulled out a rolled piece of parchment, 'it's an extract from the Dharam Ganth. Very common where I've just come from.'

'Would you say they're common in Northamptonshire, sir?'

'Good Lord, no. Where did you get this?'

'It was clutched in the dead girl's hand,' Lestrade told him, 'and it's my guess she snatched it from her murderer at the moment of her death.'

'Good Heavens!'

The conversation ended abruptly as the Bursar knocked on the door and entered the room.

'Yes, Bursar?' Nails looked up.

'Excuse me, Headmaster. A telegram for the Inspector.'

Lestrade opened it. *Great Scotland Yard. Stop. Another Whitechapel Number. Stop. Get here. Stop. This must stop. Stop. Abberline.* Wearily, the Inspector shambled to his feet.

'Gentlemen, I'm afraid I shall have to leave you for a while. Dr Nails, may I question those twenty boys when I return?'

'Be my guest, Lestrade,' beamed Nails, and the Bursar saw him out.

'Mercer,' he scowled when Lestrade had gone, 'get the Chief Constable for me, will you? We can't have people like that trampling all over St Rhadegund's. Can't even hold his head up straight. And I don't believe he has any grasp of the classics at all.'

They shook their heads at the declining standards.

Leather Apron

'What have we got, George?'

The Sergeant finished stirring his tea with his pencil stump. 'From the wall, guv'nor?' he asked.

'That's why we put it up there,' Lestrade said. 'So much easier than shoe-boxes.' He reached for the Sergeant's pencil stub, sucked it thoughtfully and committed it to the deep, stirring wistfully.

'Looks like two of 'em,' George said.

'Go on, then.' Lestrade lolled back in his chair and closed his eyes. 'Pretend I've just come in and know absolutely nothing.' That wasn't far from the truth. 'Assistant Commissioner Rodney is having one of his accursed monthly meetings tomorrow and I'm having one of my headaches.'

'Right, sir.' Sergeant George read the yellowed pages pinned to the board. 'Martha Tabram, aged thirty-five, found in the early hours of the seventh August on a staircase in George Yard Buildings off Commercial Street.'

'Cause of death?'

'Stabbing, sir. Thirty-nine holes to throat and stomach.'

'Weapon?'

'Something sharp, sir.'

'You didn't do it, then, George,' Lestrade sighed.

'No, sir, I was on duty at . . . oh, I see, sir.' The Sergeant saw Lestrade's eyes flicker for a second in disbelief. 'It was possibly a bayonet, sir. And the deceased had been seen a few hours before her death in the company of another prostitute and two soldiers.'

'And?'

'No.' George scanned the wall carefully. 'Just that, sir.'

'No.' Lestrade kicked his feet off the desk. 'I mean and what happened?'

'Mr Abberline pulled 'em in, sir. The other woman couldn't identify anybody. Said they all looked the same in uniform. According to the company commander, they were the only ones on leave that day he couldn't account for. But without a positive identification . . . '

'Nothing else?'

'No, sir. Shoe-box marked "pending".'

Yes, thought Lestrade, there were a lot of those. 'What about the latest one?'

'Mary Ann Nicholls, aged forty-two. Also a prostitute, found in Buck's Row. Skirt above her knees, if you get my drift. Found about three-thirty, Friday thirty-first ult. Two cuts to the throat, from left to right. The second one nearly eight inches long, almost depac, detap . . . cut her head off, sir. Most of front teeth missing. Abdomen slashed, intestines chucked about.'

'Where did the post mortem take place?'

'Er . . . Montague Street workhouse, guv'nor.'

'Wasn't there another one?' Lestrade was talking to himself really

'Not in Montague Street, sir,' Sergeant George was an old Q Division hand. He'd been born in those tawdry gutters. All in all, he hadn't progressed very far.

'No, I mean killing,' Lestrade explained. 'April, wasn't it? Get me that shoe-box. No, left, *left*, Sergeant. Yes, that's it.'

'Name, sir?' George thumbed through the sheafs of paper.

'Smith,' Lestrade said apologetically.

George's shoulders fell. 'There are another sixteen of these, sir, crawling with Smiths.'

'No, it's in that one, George. Emma, er . . . George Street, Spitalfields.'

'Blimey, guv.' George was impressed. 'You're dead right,'

an unfortunate turn of phrase perhaps, 'number eighteen. Found in the early hours at Osborn Street, still alive. Said four men had grabbed her. Face slashed and a blunt object shoved up . . . ' His voice tailed away.

Lestrade looked up. 'All right, Sergeant. I get the picture. Don't make funny reading, the shoe-boxes, do they? Could she identify her attackers?'

George shrugged. 'Don't say. She died the next day of peti . . . perinon . . . stomach trouble.'

Lestrade leaned forward. 'Your verdict, then, Sergeant?'

'I leave that to the jury, sir,' George beamed.

'Yes, I'll do the wit,' Lestrade said. 'What's our common theme, our link?'

George thought long and hard, gazing torturedly between wall and shoe-box and back again.

'Mr Abberline thinks it's because they were whores, sir, though I must admit he didn't include this Emma Smith.'

'No,' Lestrade shook his head. 'I'm not sure we should either. Every other woman in Whitechapel and Spitalfields walks the night, Sergeant. That's a pointless road to walk down. Look again at Smith and Tabram.'

George did. Nothing.

'Where they were found,' Lestrade said slowly, 'or where they lived.'

The Sergeant stiffened and swallowed hard.

'Exactly,' Lestrade nodded. 'Emma Smith lived in George Street. Martha Tabram was found cut about in George Yard. If I can find that name in connection with Mary Nicholls, I've got enough coincidence to hang you, George George.'

George stepped back as though he had trodden in a cowpat. Then he saw the wry smile creep over the yellowed face of the Inspector. 'Get on, sir, you're pulling my leg!' he grinned.

'I wouldn't even touch your leg without surgical forceps, Sergeant. But you're absolutely right. I must get on.'

Military knuckles crashed heavily on Lestrade's door and Constable Derry appeared, saluting smartly so that his hand quivered against his temple.

'Inspector Spratling to see you, sir.'

'Thank you, Constable. Show him in.'

'Very good, sir!' The steel-shod boot came down.

'Remind me to have a word with him about that, George, will you? Cut along to Mr Abberline and tell him . . . tell him we're making satisfactory progress.'

'Are we, sir?' George thought he might have missed a chunk of the recent conversation.

'No,' said Lestrade blankly, 'but we don't need to tell Mr Abberline that, do we?'

'Quite right, guv'nor.' George paused to let Spratling in, then closed the door behind him.

'Morning, Sholto.' Spratling took the offered chair. 'Wasn't that George George?'

'It was, Jack. Do you know him?'

'From when I was in Q Division,' Spratling said. 'Just like his parents. No imagination.'

It took one to know one, Lestrade surmised. 'Got anything for me on this Mary Nicholls?' Lestrade asked.

'So the Yard *is* in on it?'

'Does that bother you, Jack?'

'Not unduly, Sholto. I was told to report the situation to Abberline. To be honest, I'm not exactly cock-a-hoop about it.'

'You haven't got to work with him,' Lestrade reminded him.

'That's true. So you're the "junior man", are you?'

'What?' Lestrade bridled. He'd been eleven years on the Force and four before that with the City. All right, so his head was a little on one side at the moment, but the police surgeon had said it would pass. There was no call for Jack Spratling to be rude.

'That's how Abberline described you. "I'll put one of our junior men on it", he said. As I live and breathe.'

'Well, I'm not sure Mr Abberline will be doing either of those things for long. Now that Munro's resigned, I wonder who'll be next?'

'Who's taking over from him?'

'The word is it's Assistant Commissioner Rodney . . . '

Spratling gazed heavenward. 'Well, that sets us back about six months!'

'Right. Now, the Nicholls case.'

'You've read the boxes?'

Lestrade had.

'Then you know as much as I do. Except . . . '

'Yes?'

'Well, I don't know if it's important . . . '

'Come on, Jack. Out with it. We're not going to catch this bastard if we don't co-operate.'

Spratling chuckled. Lestrade was aware of the piety of hope behind his last remark too.

'Well, one of my blokes reported seeing a tall old woman – a washerwoman, he thought – hanging around Buck's Row for three nights in succession after the murder.'

'Was she a regular, this washerwoman?'

'No. He'd never seen her before. And there was something else . . . '

'Oh?'

'Her hands. He was moving her on, giving her a playful tap with his truncheon, when he happened to touch her hand. It was smooth as glass. What do you make of that?'

'She had a glass hand?'

'Come off it, Sholto. Wasn't your old mum a washerwoman?'

Lestrade nodded. 'Yes,' he smiled fondly. 'Hands like sandpaper.'

'Well then?'

Lestrade leaned back in his chair. 'I've had a lot of washerwomen recently,' he said.

'Oh yes,' Spratling nudged him, 'you single blokes are all right. If Mrs Spratling thought I'd . . . '

'How is Ermintrude?' Lestrade beamed.

'Don't ask,' Spratling groaned. 'I was a happy man when I married her. Take my advice, Sholto. You stay single.'

'I'll try, Jack,' Lestrade laughed. 'I'll try.'

They found Annie Chapman around dawn that Saturday. It was September and a light drizzle was drifting over the river, curling up over the Isle of Dogs and west into wakeful Whitechapel. She was staring at the lowering sky, oblivious to the rain and the dogs that snuffled round her. This time they called in Lestrade and he fought his way through the police-ringed throng that filled one end of Hanbury Street. Inspector Abberline would have gone, but he was on another of those curious and secret surveillances that seemed to dog the man's life at the moment. He'd stagger into the Yard about nineish and explain his gait by the number of stairs he'd had to climb. Inspector Fred Wensley wondered why Abberline was maintaining a surveillance from the top of Wren's monument.

And it was Fred Wensley who was waiting in the back yard of Number 29, crouching beside what was left of another middle-aged woman.

'Fred,' said Lestrade as the constables let him through, 'what have you got?'

'Annie Chapman,' said Wensley in his soft, Dorset accent, 'also called Dark Annie.'

'Prostitute,' the Inspectors chorused.

Lestrade looked at the corpse. She lay next to the stone steps he had just descended. Her tongue protruded blackly from her mouth and her throat was dark with dried blood.

'Had your breakfast?' Wensley asked by way of warning.

Lestrade followed his gaze to the woman's stomach. Part of it was draped over her shoulder.

Lestrade looked up at the eager faces pressed through the railings above him. 'Constable!' he bellowed, trying to re-assert reality through the sound of his own voice. 'Get those people away from there.'

'She died over there,' said Wensley. 'Look at the blood on the wall.'

Lestrade did. 'Anything else?'

'My boys found this.' Wensley handed Lestrade a piece of paper. It contained two blue pills.

'Your guess?'

'Could be for liver,' shrugged Wensley. 'Lots of carters live around here.'

'Could have been dropped by the Archbishop of Canterbury three years ago.' Lestrade dismissed it.

'Mr Wensley, sir,' a constable came at the double, 'something else, sir, in the corner of the yard.'

'Give it to Mr Lestrade, Constable.' Fred Wensley knew when he was outranked.

Lestrade looked at the piece of paper the man had found. It was part of an envelope and bore the faded post date 28 August, 1888. Eleven days old. This at least was a warmer clue. He turned it over to reveal an embossed crest – the cross of St George and the star and garter with a single plume curling over it.

'What do you make of this, Fred?'

'Well, I voker Romeny, Yiddish, Hebrew and West Country, but Latin was never my strong suit, Sholto. You're a man of letters.'

'May I help?' a voice rang out from the railings above.

The knot of policemen around Dark Annie looked up to see a rather gaunt, elderly man struggling passively with one of the constables.

'Who are you?' Lestrade asked.

The old man removed his hat, despite the rain. 'Allow me to introduthe mythelf,' he lisped. 'I am Profethor Therrinford of the Univerthity of London.'

'Professor?' Wensley repeated.

'Of languageth,' the gent affirmed.

A nod from Lestrade and the constables unlatched the door and let the man through. He balanced the pince-nez on the end of his long, elegant nose. 'Mmm,' he said, 'not

Latin, my dear thir. French. Medieval French.'

'What does it mean?' Wensley asked.

'You mean you haven't theen it before?' The professor was incredulous.

'Well, I have, of course.' Wensley didn't bridle often, but when he did he didn't care who knew it. 'I just can't translate it.'

'*Honi thoit qui mal y penthe*,' Sherrinford read. 'Roughly, "evil to him who evil thinkth".'

'That's rather apt,' Wensley said to Lestrade.

'Isn't it?' Lestrade fixed his gaze on the professor. 'And how handy, Mr Holmes, you happened along.'

The professor looked up, snatching off his pince-nez and shuffling uneasily. 'I beg your pardon,' he said.

'You are Mr Sherlock Holmes,' Lestrade repeated, 'of two hundred and twenty-one B Baker Street . . . unleth I mith my gueth?'

Holmes hurled the Homburg to the cobbles. 'Damn you, Lestrade,' he growled.

'And thank you, Mr Holmes,' Lestrade bowed stiffly. 'And if I catch you impersonating professors of the University again, I'll put you away.'

But Holmes had already bounded up the steps.

'What was all that?' Wensley asked him.

'An old adversary,' Lestrade chuckled. 'Better get Dark Annie to the mortuary. And Fred . . . '

'Sholto?'

'Have a good look at her before you let a coroner near her, won't you?'

When Inspector Lestrade turned his back on Hanbury Street with its gaunt, derelict lodging houses and filthy tenements, he did three things. First, he hailed a passing constable, dripping miserably towards the end of his beat, tore off a sheet of the man's notepad and wrote wetly on his obliging back. An urgent message to Inspector Spratling of J Division. Second, he hailed a cab to the premises of

Messrs Stillwell & Co., Cap and Accoutrement Makers to the Army. He found their doors bolted and barred but it was astonishing what a boot through plate glass could do in waking up a sleeping nightwatchman. Third, he lacerated his leg rather badly and so it was not until nearly lunchtime when he limped out of Charing Cross Infirmary that he received the piece of news he had been hoping for – the reply from Spratling. He screwed up the paper and shouted in delight, causing passers-by on the Strand to hurry on, lest he be an escapee or a Fabian Socialist. He hailed another constable, who was just about to move on this odd, drenched, limping man with his head on the skew, and told him to take a message to the Yard. He himself sped west, to the great land where young men went at the behest of short-sighted American newspaper proprietors; where a man did what a man had to do, once the place had been made safe for women and children. And by four o'clock he had got to Hounslow.

The barracks at Hounslow were typical of army barracks anywhere (except India, but Lestrade had never been there). As he crossed the windswept square, hobbling a little and veering to the right, the mingling smells of pipe-clay and ammonia hit him with the cross-winds from the cavalry quarters. Stables below, men above, for the use of. He was grateful to turn the corner into the less-noisome quarters of the Royal Sussex Regiment. Asking his way of the sentry parading in full pack, he limped gamely up the stone steps to an oak-panelled door.

'Enter!' a voice barked.

Lestrade did so and found himself with a sergeant-major of Constable Derry's stamp, only louder.

'Inspector Lestrade, Scotland Yard, to see the Colonel.'

'Not in, sir!' bawled the Sergeant-Major with the force of a howitzer.

'Major?'

'Not in, sir!'

Lestrade began to wonder if the Sergeant-Major was capable of any other sort of response. He was also beginning to doubt his own acquaintance with army ranks. What was next?

'Captain?' a quieter voice asked.

'That's right,' said Lestrade aloud.

'Wedgwood,' the Captain introduced himself. 'I'm the Adjutant. Can I help?'

'I hope so, sir.' Lestrade took the chair.

'Sar'nt-Major.' The Captain unhooked his forage cap so that the strap didn't affect his immaculate whiskers and threw it at the wall. It bounced off and landed on the floor.

'Army cuts,' he explained to Lestrade to cover the gesture. 'There used to be a hat-rack there before the dear old Duke of Cambridge took up accountancy.'

'Yes, sir,' smiled Lestrade. 'I know the feeling. We have a Commissioner with much the same ideas.'

'Oh, yes, how is Charlie Warren?'

Lestrade had never met the man and was certainly not on Christian name terms with him.

'Sir?' the Sergeant-Major bawled.

'What is it, Sar'nt-Major?' The Captain looked perplexed.

The Sergeant-Major did too. 'Excuse me, sir, I thought you spoke to me, sir.'

'Really?' Wedgwood offered Lestrade a cigar. 'Ah yes. Will you take tea, Inspector?'

'Thank you.'

'Sugar, sir?' the Sergeant-Major bellowed.

'Yes, please,' said Lestrade, lowering his ear even closer to his shoulder to avoid the blast.

'Milk, sir?'

Lestrade nodded, wincing now, and sighing gratefully when the man left.

'He is a little overbearing, isn't he? He was with Napier at Magdala. Had to shout a little over the cannonade. His vocal cords never got back to normal. Funny thing, war.'

'Do you recognise this, sir?' Lestrade handed Wedgwood the torn envelope.

'It's part of an envelope,' said the Adjutant after due consideration. What marvellous officer material was coming through these days, Lestrade mused.

'The crest, sir?'

'Oh, yes, it's one of ours, all right. I've a whole stack of them here. Why, is it important?'

'It could be. Can you explain how it came to be found in Whitechapel?'

'Whitechapel? That's odd.'

'Is it?'

'Yes. You're the second chappie to enquire about Whitechapel today.'

Lestrade became uneasy. 'Really?'

'Yes, the other was a professor from Sandhurst. He was doing research into the old Thirty-fifth. Seemed convinced there was some link between us and the East End. I told him we recruited almost entirely in Sussex . . . '

'Did you catch this professor's name?'

'I believe it was . . . Sherrinforth, or something like that.'

'A tall man? Large forehead? Long nose?'

'No. But I must confess I didn't remember him from my Sandhurst days. He seemed rather vague. But then, these military history chappies. Vague as a Generals' Mess. Why the interest?'

'This envelope was found near the body of a woman in the early hours of this morning, sir.'

'Good God.' The Adjutant was appalled. 'I am appalled, Inspector. Are you implying that a man of the Royal Sussex Regiment is responsible for this murder?'

'Murder, sir? Did I mention murder?'

'Well, I naturally assumed . . . '

'Are any of your men on leave, sir? And do they live in the East End?'

The Adjutant wearily reached for a ledger, not taking his eyes off Lestrade. 'I remember a few months ago a couple of our chaps were hauled in by you people. What do you call it? An indemnity parade?'

'Something like that,' said Lestrade. 'Do these men happen to be on leave now?'

The Adjutant checked the list and shook his head. 'No, Inspector, they are both here. In fact you should have passed one of them on your way in.'

'Would it be likely that a private soldier would use this stationery, Captain?' Lestrade asked.

Wedgwood thought for a moment. 'I doubt it, Inspector. Most of our chaps are literate, but they don't go in for writing letters, not even on campaign. I remember in the Sudan— '

'I'm sure you do,' Lestrade broke in, 'but my business is rather urgent, sir. I am forced to conclude, then, that this envelope was dropped by an officer of the Regiment.'

'Unthinkable!' Wedgwood was capable of roaring as loudly as his Sergeant-Major.

'Do you have a list of their home addresses?'

'No,' Wedgwood replied, 'and even if I had, two things would pertain. One, none of them would live in Whitechapel. And two, I wouldn't give them to you. Good afternoon.'

Lestrade left without his tea. For the moment there was no more to be said.

It was a jovial Inspector Abberline who met Lestrade that Monday morning. True, Mrs Abberline was away visiting relatives and was not expected back for a week, but it was Abberline's professional life, not his habits, that caused the gardenia in his lapel to bloom anew and for his grin to be cheesier than usual. An old copper had told Lestrade long ago to beware of smiling inspectors. It always meant one of two things. Either their wives were away or they'd got their man.

'Mrs Abberline away?' Lestrade asked, as he pushed Constable Toms off his chair.

'No, Lestrade,' Abberline grinned. 'I've got my man.'

'What for?'

'Don't be fly with me, Lestrade. I remember when you were a constable, wetter behind the ears than anything you've got here.' He shot a cruel glance at Toms. 'I've got the Whitechapel murderer.'

'Oh?'

'Oh, yes.' Abberline sat down uninvited, sniffing his gardenia ostentatiously. 'Ought to be a Chief in this for me, I shouldn't wonder.'

'May I ask who?'

'Better than that. You can look at him. For the usual consideration I'll let you poke him with a sharp stick. One John Pizer. It'll be in the papers tomorrow.'

'Cough, did he?'

'A few times, yes,' confessed Abberline, 'but I didn't hit him that hard. It was the leather apron that clinched it.'

'Leather apron?'

'If you'd waited around yesterday, Lestrade, instead of haring off to Hounslow, wasting the Army's time and chasing your own tail, you'd have discovered that a leather apron was found wringing wet near a standpipe not fifty yards from Hanbury Street. It was John Pizer's. Never mind, Lestrade, better luck next time,' and he swept out, wiping his fingers on the back of the chair as he did so, checking for dust.

'Toms!' snarled Lestrade. It was half-past eight on a Monday morning. The week had not begun well.

'Sir!' the Constable straightened in an ex-Marine sort of way.

'Where've they got this Pizer?'

'Leman Street, sir.'

'Fred Wensley's patch? Good. Where's Sergeant George?'

Toms consulted the roster. 'Rest day, sir.'

'Nonsense.' Lestrade snatched up the bowler. The Donegal hadn't left his back. 'Sergeants don't have rest days. Get him. I want him at Leman Street within the hour.'

'Very good, sir.'

*

Fred Wensley was tucking into his bagels when Lestrade arrived.

'You've got a prisoner here, Inspector,' Lestrade said, 'I'd like to see him.'

'We're very formal this morning, Sholto,' mumbled Wensley. 'Had a visit from the Commissioner, have we?'

'Thank you, Fred. Tell me about this Pizer.'

'I brought him in this morning.'

'*You* brought him in?'

'All right.' Wensley was patience itself, he'd known Lestrade for years. Not like him to be ruffled. 'Constables Niven, Beckett and Allen and myself. Can't be too careful. We're not too popular since Bloody Sunday, you know.'

'Abberline told me he'd got him.'

Wensley laughed. 'Figure of speech, Sholto,' he said. 'But that's our Inspector Abberline all over, isn't it? If there's any credit due, he'll take it.'

'So,' Lestrade was calmer, 'is Pizer our man?'

Wensley shrugged before tackling another bagel. 'I don't know. It stacks up against him pretty bad. Here's the apron.'

He reached over to a drawer and emptied its contents onto his desk. 'And we found these knives at Pizer's place.'

'Which is where?'

'Mulberry Street, Number twenty-two.'

'So he knows the area,' Lestrade mused.

'Like the back of his hand.'

'What does he do, apart from murdering prostitutes, I mean?'

'He's a cobbler. Hence "Leather Apron". It's a sort of nickname.'

'And they're his?' Lestrade pointed to the desk top.

'He admits he owns the knives. Claims he trims leather with them.'

'And the apron?'

Wensley shook his head.

'And that's all Abberline's got?' Lestrade sat back in disbelief.

'Two other things,' Wensley said: 'Pizer wears a deerstalker and a man wearing a deerstalker was seen talking to Annie Chapman on the night she died.'

'A deerstalker?' That was beginning to sound alarm bells in Lestrade's head. 'Do we have a description?'

'Tweed cloth, brown flaps— '

'Not the cap,' Lestrade cut in, 'the man talking to Chapman.'

'Ah, I see.' Wensley dug under his bagels in the shoebox and produced a wad of depositions. 'Er . . . let's see. Fortyish, foreign-looking, shabby . . . '

'Well, that could be you or me, Fred,' Lestrade commented.

' . . . haggling with Chapman over a price for her services . . . '

'Could still be you,' Lestrade commented.

'Thanks, Sholto, I love you too.'

'What's the other thing Abberline's got?' Lestrade asked, 'apart from the brass neck to call himself a policeman at all?'

'Pizer's been in hiding. We had to break down the door at Mulberry Street. The mob were after him.'

'The mob?'

'Mr Abberline in his wisdom let it be known that we'd found a leather apron near the body of Chapman and that this apron definitely belonged to the murderer.'

'I see. So the locals were out for blood?'

'I know those streets, Sholto,' Wensley was serious; 'it's bad enough for the Jews anyway, but something like this . . . . If Abberline's wrong about Pizer, I can't answer for what happens in Whitechapel. It's not going to be pretty.'

'It never was, Fred. Did you get any joy from the lodgers at Hanbury Street?'

Wensley shook his head. 'One of life's little coincidences, Sholto,' he said. 'Seventeen people, all blind, deaf and dumb, living in the same lodging house.'

'Can I talk to Pizer?'

Wensley nodded. 'He's an animal, Sholto. Watch yourself.'

The animal was squarely built, rather shambling, with the short-cropped hair of the labouring classes. They had put him in a grey fustian suit and had handcuffed him to the iron bedstead.

'Constable, get these off.'

'Mr Abberline's orders, sir,' the uniformed man protested.

'Now, Constable,' Lestrade said quietly. There was something in his tone that made the man comply.

Pizer sat on the crawling mattress, rubbing his chafed wrists.

'Are you ready then, Pizer?' Lestrade asked.

No response, just small, shifty eyes staring at the floor.

'Constable,' Lestrade stopped the man as he hesitated in the doorway, 'you can bring the rope now.'

'Rope?' Pizer and the constable chorused.

'Certainly,' said Lestrade in mild surprise, 'no point in bothering Mr Berry. We'll do it now.' He nodded to the bewildered constable, who shuffled uneasily outside.

'Do what?' Pizer asked in his thick, guttural accent.

Lestrade looked up at the ceiling. 'Hmmm.' He seemed distant. 'Oh, hang you, my dear fellow. That beam should take the strain, I think.'

'You can't do that!' Pizer snarled, standing up now.

'Why not?' Lestrade continued the game. 'Ah, you mean the trial?'

Pizer nodded, his little eyes almost normal size in his terror.

'Where were you born, Pizer?' Lestrade asked.

'Poland,' the man answered.

'And doubtless you've heard stories of our legendary British justice? How a man is innocent until he's proven guilty?'

Pizer nodded, swallowing hard.

Lestrade chuckled. 'Tell me,' he said, 'have you heard the one about Goldilocks and the Three Bears? No, where we are sure a man is guilty of a crime, we hang him straight away. No fuss.'

'That man,' Pizer pointed hysterically to the door, 'that Mr Venzel. He say I have trial first.'

Lestrade looked confused. 'Mr Venzel? Oh, Inspector Wensley? Yes, well, he's rather new. Doesn't really understand. Oh dear, we haven't got a rabbi. Would an Anglican chaplain do? Only I'm due at the pub later.'

Pizer stood quivering for a moment, then launched himself at Lestrade, bellowing in fear and rage. The Inspector sidestepped neatly, considering his neck and his leg, and brought his knee up in Pizer's groin. The Pole lay axed on the floor, gurgling quietly.

The crash of furniture brought the constable scurrying back. 'Are you all right, sir?' he asked. 'I couldn't find any rope.'

Lestrade looked up at him with the eyes of a basilisk. 'Bugger off, there's a good constable. Tell Mr Wensley I could do with a cup of tea.'

The constable saluted in a flurry of confusion and bounded up the stairs. Lestrade sat on the chest of the groaning Pole and jerked up his head. 'Now, let's cut the nonsense, shall we?' he hissed. 'Where were you on Friday night and Saturday morning? Think!' he bounced the man's head on the flagstones a few times, 'or you'll wish I'd let the mob have you.'

'Home. At Mulberry Street,' Pizer moaned. 'My mother – she there. My brother – he there.'

'Why didn't you tell Mr Venzel that?'

'He no— ' Pizer began.

'I know,' Lestrade broke in, 'he no threaten to hang you, eh?'

Pizer nodded as best he could with Lestrade holding on to his hair.

'All right, think back,' Lestrade's iron knuckles in his skull were strong persuaders, 'the last day of August, It was a Friday. Where were you – evening; small hours of Saturday?'

'Er . . . '

Again the skull went down with sickening force on the cold stone. 'Think!' screamed Lestrade.

'Holloway Road,' Pizer screamed back. 'I in lodging house. People there – they know me. They know me.'

Lestrade let the head fall back and stepped off his man. He let him get up and Pizer rolled onto the bed to join the rest of the crawling company.

'You knew Annie Chapman?' he asked.

Pizer nodded. 'Yes,' he said. 'We sometimes at same lodging house.'

'Have you been with her?' Lestrade asked.

The Pole looked even more stupid.

'Slept with her, man. I don't know the Polish for it.'

'Ya,' Pizer nodded. 'I get into fight with Sievey.'

'Who's Sievey?'

'He make sieve. He her husband.'

'Did she live with her husband?' Lestrade asked.

'No, Not now. He beat her.'

Lestrade stood up and kicked with his good foot for someone to open the door. 'Well, nobody else will do that now,' he said quietly. The bewildered constable arrived again. 'Thank you for your help, Mr Pizer,' Lestrade smiled.

'You not goin' to kill me?' The Pole stood up again.

'You may not know it, Mr Pizer,' he said, 'but I just saved your life.'

At the top of the stairs, Sergeant George was waiting. His face registered all the feelings of a man who had lost his rest day.

'Ah, George, there you are. Good man. Get over to twenty-two Mulberry Street. Better take a constable with you – not this one; he doesn't know what day it is. What's your name, Constable?' Lestrade rounded on the man.

'Dew, sir. Walter Dew.'

'Right, I'll be sure not to ask for you next time. George, you're looking for the brother and mother of John Pizer.'

'He's a cobbler,' ventured Dew.

'It's all cobblers,' grunted Lestrade. 'Find out where this Pizer was on Friday night, will you? And then get to Holloway Road. One of the lodging houses there. See if any of 'em had Pizer staying there the night Mary Nicholls died. Got it?'

'I probably will have before this is over, guv'nor,' George muttered.

Lestrade slapped his back. 'That's what I like, Sergeant, dedication *and* enthusiasm. It's a winning combination.'

Inspector and sergeant went their different ways. At the outer desk, Fred Wensley confronted Lestrade. 'Sholto.' He introduced a shabbily dressed young man beside him. 'This is Mr Richardson,' he said. 'He says if we're finished with his mother's leather apron which she had washed and left on the fence of Number twenty-four Hanbury Street, could he have it back?'

Lestrade wandered quietly away.

Long Liz

Charles Bradlaugh stood before the Gothic hearth in his country home. He turned at the click of the door behind him.

'Inspector Lestrade to see you, sir,' the maid bobbed.

'Thank you, Hetty.' Bradlaugh crossed the Persian carpet and took the policeman's hand. 'Good of you to come.'

'My pleasure,' said Lestrade. 'I kept bumping into brick walls in London.'

'Is that why . . . ?' Bradlaugh tilted his head so that it was at the same angle as Lestrade's.

'Oh, the neck? No.' Lestrade did his best to smile. 'I was speaking metaphysically.'

Bradlaugh flashed him an old Free thinker's look and poured them brandies.

'I know you're on duty, Inspector.'

'I know you know, sir,' said Lestrade, raising the glass.

'Here's iron in your necessaries!' Bradlaugh raised his.

'Sir?'

'An old toast, Lestrade, from my days in the Dragoon Guards. Have a seat.'

Lestrade picked the mastiff's chair. Luckily for them both, the great brindled beast was not in residence, but his weight over the years had caused the springs to go and Lestrade found his hams disappearing into the bowels of the upholstery and his knees meeting with a sickening crack. He wrestled manfully with the glass, trying to appear natural with his arms resting on those of the chair on a par with his parting and his feet swinging inches off the rug.

'That's it,' said Bradlaugh. 'Relax. What do you know of Rhadegund Hall?'

'It's a school, sir. A boarding establishment for the sons of gentlefolk.'

'Yes, well they're about as gentle as a shoal of piranhas, Lestrade.'

The Inspector wasn't surprised. He'd never liked dogs.

'You were there a month ago?'

'Yes.'

'Investigating the death of a servant girl?'

'Correct.'

'What progress did you make?'

Lestrade looked at the large, silver-haired man before him. He wasn't comfortable in his presence. Free thinking and the law did not go hand in hand.

'Forgive me, Mr Bradlaugh, I realise you are the Member of Parliament for this county— '

'Oh, come, Lestrade,' it was as though Bradlaugh had read his mind, 'I am also Charles Bradlaugh the iconoclast . . . '

Lestrade hadn't known he was a sculptor.

'Charles Bradlaugh, founder of *The National Reformer*, Charles Bradlaugh, the co-writer with dear Mrs Besant of the so-called obscene work on the control of conception. Charles Bradlaugh, who refused to take the oath in the Commons.'

At best, thought Lestrade, a man of many parts. At worst, a schizophrenic.

'I realise that Free thinking and the Law do not go together, Inspector . . . '

Lestrade gripped his brandy balloon more firmly.

' . . . but this is not a matter of politics. It is a matter of plain duty. The girl was murdered.'

'Forgive me, sir,' Lestrade said, 'but what is your interest in the matter?'

'As a fellow human being, I am of course appalled. On a more personal level, the gardener here was the girl's godfather. You should talk to him before you go. You can't miss him; talks as though his cheeks were padded with cotton wool. He's a good soul, Lestrade. Salt of the earth. He's not happy.'

'I understood I'd been taken off the case, Mr Bradlaugh,' Lestrade said. 'That the local police were handling it. It was only the merest chance I happened to be there in the first place.'

'That *is* politics, Lestrade. If I'm any judge . . . '

Was he on the bench as well? Lestrade wondered.

' . . . that old deviant Nails is behind this.'

'The murder, you mean?' Lestrade's ears pricked up.

'Perhaps. But I actually meant he was instrumental in getting you off the case. To protect his precious school.'

'I gather you do not approve of St Rhadegund's, Mr Bradlaugh.'

'I've never forgiven the Clarendon Commission, Lestrade, any more, I suppose, than you have.'

'Well, I— '

'Quite. Perpetuating the snobbery and violence of the shirking classes. There are times when I feel quite Socialist . . . '

'Surely not,' Lestrade thought it best to say.

'On behalf of old Diggles, my groundsman, Lestrade, I'd like you to go back to Rhadegund Hall. I don't know what Nails is up to, but it's no good if I know my onions.'

A market gardener too, mused Lestrade.

'Here,' Bradlaugh gave Lestrade an envelope, 'this will get the Chief Constable of the county off your neck . . . er, I mean . . . tell me, I hate to pry, but is that congenital?' He pointed to Lestrade's neck.

The Inspector was a little alarmed. 'I hope not,' he had to be hauled to his feet, 'the tailor who made it for me swore it was velvet.'

Diggles was locked in mortal combat with the compost heap when Lestrade found him. And the heap looked within sight of victory.

'I am Inspector Lestrade of Scotland Yard,' he introduced himself.

'Fred Diggles,' slurred the old man, tugging his cap.

'I am investigating the death of your goddaughter, Maggie Hollis.'

'God bless you, sir.' The old man's eyes filled with tears and the compost began to steam from his moleskin trousers.

'Is there anything you can tell me?' Lestrade asked.

Diggles closed to the Yard man, but Lestrade was faster and kept his distance.

'She were 'eving a babby,' he grimaced.

'Were she? Was she?' Lestrade corrected himself. He had not seen a coroner's report. Assistant Commissioner Rodney had given him his marching orders before it was ready. 'Who was the father?'

Old Diggles shook his head. 'I dunno,' he said sagely, 'but it weren't a local lad.'

'How do you know that?' Lestrade asked, backing to avoid the full force of spray from Diggles's impediment.

' 'Ad airs, my Maggie did. Airs and graces. Stuck up, she were. Comes of workin' up at that school. She wouldn't mix with local lads. Not good enough for 'er, she always said. You take my advice,' he prodded Lestrade's Donegal with a dibber, 'you'll talk to one of them 'igh and mighty fellas up there.'

'The boys, you mean?'

Old Diggles nodded. 'It's in the blood, y'see. They been givin' their nannies and tweenies one since they wuz this 'igh. One of them will 'ave done for our Maggie. Only that there 'eadmaster don't want it known, see. He want it 'ushed up, 'e do. Doctor!' Diggles spat contemptuously. 'He couldn't cure a ham, 'e couldn't.'

'Thank you, Mr Diggles.' Lestrade retreated before the compost got to him irrevocably. 'I'll be in touch.'

The Chief Constable of Northamptonshire could not see Lestrade personally. He was with the otter hounds at the time and then there was the Autumn Yeomanry Camp and he had his troop to attend to. He did, however, accede to Mr Bradlaugh's request to allow Lestrade back on the case. He really had little choice. Unbeknown to Lestrade, Bradlaugh's envelope contained a few other items: a lock of hair, a piece of lace from French drawers and a rather purple love letter, all belonging to Lady Conyngham, a very dear friend of the Chief Constable's wife and, evidently, an even dearer friend of the Chief Constable. So the Northamptonshire Constabulary, in the person of Inspector Pearcey, bowed out to the Metropolitan Constabulary, in the person of Inspector Lestrade. The bowing out was none too graceful, however.

'Well?' Pearcey was a bovine man, straight from Miss Abercromby's School of Charm and Deportment, recently opened in the Elephant and Castle.

'Well, what have you got for me?' Lestrade tried patience as his first tack.

'Utter contempt,' Pearcey answered.

Lestrade smiled. 'Well, now we've got the niceties over, Inspector, perhaps we can get down to business?'

'You expect my co-operation?' Pearcey rammed a pound of orange snuff vaguely in the direction of his face.

'That would be too much. Are you a sportsman, Mr Pearcey?'

'Well, I have a flutter now and again . . . ' Pearcey admitted.

'I was thinking of running,' Lestrade said.

'I should.' Pearcey's great sides wobbled with his apparent wit – girth shaken by mirth.

'You know – a relay race,' Lestrade went on, 'when one runner hands his baton to another? That's all I want you to do. Pass the baton to me. I'm not expecting you to run with me as well. Frankly, I haven't got the time.'

'What do you mean?' Pearcey straightened in his desk, suddenly aware that he was losing this one, and his constables were sniggering at him.

'You've had a dead girl on your slab for the best part of three weeks. Now, for the last time, what progress have you made?'

Pearcey's head sank sulkily into his shoulders. He set his jaw and flicked open the relevant ledger.

'Margaret Hollis,' he read, 'age seventeen years. Cause of death, drowning.'

'Marks on the body?' Lestrade interrupted.

'Bruising to wrists and arms,' Pearcey told him.

'So she was held down. Go on.'

'Nearly three months pregnant.'

'Any signs of sexual assault?'

'From three months ago? Come off it, Lestrade!'

'I was referring to the time of death.'

Pearcey scanned the reports. 'Nothing,' he said.

'Who have you interviewed?'

'Family. Mother, three brothers. Children all younger. Father deceased.'

'When?'

'Er . . . six years ago. Threshing accident.'

'Did you get anywhere with the girl's lover?'

Pearcey shook his head. 'Could be anybody, either in the village or— '

' —or the school,' Lestrade finished the sentence for him.

'No.' Pearcey was adamant. 'Couldn't be the school.'

'Why not?'

'Look, Lestrade, I've got strict orders from upstairs. *All the way* upstairs. Leave the school alone.'

Lestrade leaned towards him. 'Well, Pearcey, I have no such orders. Don't you think it odd that a girl should be murdered in a school laundry, that there should be no sign of forced entry to the laundry and that you go nowhere near the place?'

'Like I said, I've got my orders.'

Lestrade stood up. 'Right. If I were you, Pearcey, I'd conduct a discreet but careful enquiry into why "upstairs" doesn't want you messing around St Rhadegund's. It might pay some dividends. And then', he tapped the Inspector on the shoulder, 'I'd get rid of that chip if I were you.'

By the time Lestrade arrived at Rhadegund Hall it was already dusk. The air was clear and the wind sharp, gusting with icy barbs around cloister and Donegal. A little begowned figure stood in the leeward angle of the Fives Court, flitting nervously like a confused bat, watching the hansom as it rattled round the drive and into the outer quadrangle. The bat swooped and darted through the limes and privet hedges and hailed the Inspector.

'Mr Lestrade?'

'Yes.'

'Saunders-Foote. With a hyphen. Classics.'

'Mr Foote-Classics.' Lestrade shook his hand, fumbling in his pocket with the other one. 'Oh dear, I appear to have no change.'

'Oh, allow me.' The classics master handed a clutch of coins to the cabbie who solemnly bit them one by one before reining up and driving away. After all, the man was a teacher. You couldn't be too careful.

'I'm so glad you've come,' said Saunders-Foote.

'I wasn't aware anyone knew I was coming.'

'Your fame, sir, goes before you.' He held Lestrade's arm and the stars and gaslight from the windows shone in his spectacles. 'There's been another one, you know.'

'Another?' Lestrade stiffened even more in the chill blast and he felt his neck lock even tighter.

'Poor Denton. This way.' Lestrade shuffled through the gathered gloom in the classics master's wake, both of them flapping, with gown and Donegal, like old sheets in a drying yard. They passed the hallowed First Eleven Square, Saunders-Foote glancing nervously up to the leaded windows above, past which dimly lit figures moved as in a dream. There was a whistling hiss punctuated by a scream, then a moan. Lestrade's step faltered. He knew the sound of Actual Bodily Harm when he heard it.

'I beg of you,' gabbled Saunders-Foote, 'do not look that way. It's the Headmaster's study and it's . . . ' he gulped, 'the flogging hour.'

'Do you not approve of flogging, Mr Foote-Classics?' Lestrade asked, peering ahead to where the dark line of trees heralded the edge of the jungle around this oasis of civilisation.

Saunders-Foote shuddered. 'Barbaric,' he said. 'Rivalling the excesses of Caligula at his worst.'

Lestrade supposed Caligula to have been the old man's own headmaster many years ago.

'Did you know they've abolished flogging in the Army, Mr Lestrade?'

Lestrade did know that.

'Yet in the great English public schools it goes on unabated. And there's worse . . . '

'Worse, Mr Foote-Classics?' Lestrade would have probed deeper, but suddenly felt a sickening crack around the head and went down heavily.

'Oh dear.' Saunders-Foote grovelled in the grass trying to find Lestrade. 'I'm afraid you've walked into one of our rugby posts, Mr Lestrade. I keep asking Carman to paint them white. Of course, he's always . . . '

'In the rhododendron bushes,' groaned Lestrade. 'Yes, I remember.' He was euphoric for a moment when he realised his head no longer leaned to the right. Now it positively lunged to the left. Such was life.

'Are you all right?' Saunders-Foote asked, dusting the man down.

'I'll see Matron later,' Lestrade comforted him, dabbing at the bloodied temple.

'Oh, I fear she'll be no use,' Saunders-Foote fretted. 'I am quite sure Denton is dead. This way.'

Lestrade was warier now. At least there weren't likely to be any rugby posts in the woods. Conversely of course, the odds against trees were rather diminished. Even a city dweller like Lestrade knew what they had in common

– their hardness and their tendency not to move out of the way.

'Down here.' The little classics master's even littler legs scrambled down a series of banks and ravines. From below, Lestrade heard the rush and roar of a stream, swollen after the recent rains and crashing tempestuously over shiny green rocks. It was several bramble slashes later that Lestrade knelt in the soggy bracken, a veritable wreck of a man, knowing all over again why he hated the countryside.

'There!' Saunders-Foote pointed a quaking finger and turned away, sobbing hysterically.

Lestrade peered through the black tangle of trees, praying for a bull's-eye. He patted the pulsating pedant kneeling by his side and stumbled forward. Just in time he clutched clumps of grass, overhanging roots and branches and a lot of thin air and prevented himself from slithering into the seething foam below. Hooked grotesquely on an uprooted tree lay the body of a man, the water hissing and swirling around his waist. Like Lestrade's, his head lay to the left, his eyes shut tight, a pair of shattered spectacles hooked on a chain around his neck. Even in the near darkness Lestrade could see he was a young man, perhaps mid-twenties and limply good looking in an odd sort of way. He crawled back up to Saunders-Foote.

'Who is he?' he asked.

'Is?' Saunders-Foote exploded. 'You mean he's alive?'

'No, I'm afraid not,' Lestrade had to tell him.

The older man sank back, sobbing, above the roar and gurgle of the stream. 'Anthony Denton, poor boy. Such a fine spirit. Such a noble Denton.'

'Yes, yes.' Lestrade could do without the eulogy. 'Is he a master?'

Saunders-Foote nodded. 'Classics, like myself.'

Lestrade was confused. 'He was related to you?'

Even in his grief, Saunders-Foote sensed the idiocy. 'No, I mean he taught the classics – you know, Latin and Greek. Homer, Aristotle, Plato, Livy.'

'Of course.' Lestrade could not remember any of those in the Penny Dreadfuls. Still, education was so progressive these days. And he did know Plato was a planet. 'How long had he been with you?'

'About an hour. We usually walked above the river after luncheon.'

'No, I mean at the school. How long had he been at Saint Rhadegund's?'

'Oh, this was his first term. I had become . . . ' he sobbed convulsively ' . . . very attached.'

Lestrade lifted the little man up. 'Come on,' he said. 'We can't do much here until first light. Let's get back to the school. I'd like Matron to patch me up and Dr Nails— '

'No, no, you can't tell Nails.' Saunders-Foote snatched at Lestrade's sleeve.

'Why not?' The Inspector asked him.

'Well, I . . . that is, the reputation of the school— '

'A man is dead, Mr Foote-Classics.'

'But it was an accident, Mr Lestrade. Surely . . . '

'Was it, Mr Foote-Classics? Then why, when you met me at the hansom, did you say, "There's been another"?'

'Er . . . well, death. Deaths. First that poor girl's drowning accident and now— '

'Now this young man's accidentally breaking his neck with his own spectacle chain.' Lestrade clicked his tongue. 'Isn't coincidence an amazing thing, Mr Foote-Classics?'

In the bad light of the evening, with the gas lamps turned low in accordance with the Bursar's edict to conserve money, Lestrade could understand why Mr Carman, the under groundsman should pursue Matron. She was what in some circles passed for a comely lass, though admittedly they were not the circles in which Lestrade moved. And he was looking at her from a rakish angle. She had the forearms of a plate-layer, however, and the Inspector felt decidedly worse after her ministrations than before. She worked quickly and loudly, liberally applying astringents to his cuts and bruises. Her incessant chatter was preferable to, and probably designed to disguise, the sound of retching from an adjacent room.

'It's Spencer Minor,' she explained. 'Yesterday's mince making a reappearance, I shouldn't wonder. Tell me, Mr Lestrade, do you like Kettering?'

Lestrade was about to reply that he'd never kettered in his life when the door crashed back to reveal the terrible Theophilus Nails, still in gown and mortarboard. Steam seemed to be escaping from his ears as he surveyed the scene.

'So, it's true!' he bellowed. 'Matron, get out . . . '

In mid-dab, the muscular nightingale departed.

' . . . And whoever it is in there,' Nails roared through the partition, 'stop vomiting this instant!'

Spencer Minor obliged and Nails turned on his man with all the agility of an expert mountaineer and martinet. For a moment, he thought he remembered Lestrade's head leaning the other way, but the light or his memory must have been false to him. 'I thought we'd parted company, Mr Lestrade,' he bellowed. The word 'whisper' was not in his vocabulary.

'So did I, sir,' Lestrade felt himself again under the gaze of old Mr Poulson. No wonder Nails's staff went in fear of him. 'But I was recalled.'

'Recalled? By whom?'

'At the request of Mr Bradlaugh, MP for— '

'Bradlaugh?' Nails produced a thin, evil cane from nowhere and proceeded to attack Matron's medicine bottles. 'I thought I made my views on that fellow clear to you.'

'This *is* his county, sir,' Lestrade reminded him.

'*His* county, Lestrade? Have you policemen no concept of the electoral procedure of this nation? Thanks to that unprincipled maniac, Gladstone, even sections of the working classes now have the vote and men like Bradlaugh are at the behest – the behest, mind you – of all of them. Besides, the fellow refused to take the oath. I cannot abide agnosticism. It is worse than self-abuse.'

'Quite so, sir, but I have a job to complete.'

'I shall contact the Chief Constable . . . ' Nails fumed, wildly looking around for something else to hit.

'It was the Chief Constable who authorised my return, Dr Nails. I fear that door is closed.'

'All over this wretched girl . . . '

'And a wretched classics master,' Lestrade told him.

'What?'

Lestrade remembered the presence of Spencer Minor and motioned the Headmaster into the corridor. 'One of your staff is dead, sir. Mr Denton.'

'Young Denton? Good God, man, he was only twenty-two. Heart, was it?'

'Until daylight, sir, I am unable to say, But I have reason to believe he was murdered.'

The Headmaster snatched Lestrade's lapels. 'Murdered? This is a public school. It is eighteen eighty-eight. These things don't happen. What if Oundle find out?'

'May we go to your study, Dr Nails? This corridor is hardly the place— '

'I want this stopped, Lestrade. I want it stopped now. If it's a matter of money, I can see the Bursar . . . '

Lestrade shook his head. 'Your study, sir?' he reminded him and followed the man through the bowels of the building, up the worn stone steps, past snoring dormitories to the great studded door. Sewing by the firelight sat a demure little woman, barely the height of the Queen, God Bless Her.

'Oh, Lestrade. My wife, Gwendoline. Gwendoline, Lestrade.'

She held out her hand. 'Mr Lestrade,' she smiled sweetly. 'How charming. Now, don't tell me, Theophilus . . . ' She scrutinised Lestrade carefully. 'Logic,' she beamed triumphantly.

'I beg your pardon, madam?' Lestrade hadn't the faintest idea what she was talking about.

'You must be Theophilus's new logic master – old Butler's replacement?'

'Believe me,' said Nails harshly, 'this man's connection with logic is slight indeed.'

'Oh.' Mrs Nails looked surprised, her instincts were usually sound in these matters. 'My instincts are usually sound in these matters.' She clapped her hands in delight. 'If it isn't logic, it must be science . . . '

'Oh, really, Gwendoline.' Nails hurled his mortarboard onto the desk. 'Lestrade isn't a master at all. He's a policeman.'

'Really?' Mrs Nails's eyes widened. 'How very exciting.' Then her face darkened. 'Don't tell me old Bowsett has been complaining about the boys again?'

'Bowsett?' Lestrade repeated.

'He's a local farmer.' Nails unhooked his gown and lit a monstrous pipe. He noticed Gwendoline's disapproving gesture and went ahead anyway. 'Over Blatherwyck way. Some of my chaps have a nasty habit of bathing naked in his pond and scrumping his apples.'

Lestrade clicked his tongue.

'Nothing wrong with that, Lestrade. I used to do the same thing myself under Arnold at Rugby. Healthy, competitive spirit. The day a chap can't pinch the odd apple while in the altogether, England will go to the wall, believe me.'

'Remember Adam and Eve, dearest,' Gwendoline reminded him.

'Don't preach theology to me, woman. I've got a degree in the subject. Now you're here, Lestrade, you'd better sit down. What of Denton?'

Lestrade flashed a glance at Mrs Nails.

'Speak, Lestrade. Anything which concerns this school concerns me. My wife is soul of my soul, heart of my heart and so on and so forth. Anyway, she makes the sandwiches for the boys' tea. Speak.'

'Very well.' Lestrade eased himself into the settee whose petit-point Mrs Nails had embroidered herself. 'When I arrived here earlier this evening I was met by Mr Foote-Classics— '

'Who?'

'Mr Saunders Foote-Classics.'

'Oh.' Nails looked a little blank. 'Go on.'

'He took me to the woods out there and to a steep ravine.' He patted his bandaged head by way of explanation. 'There I found the body of Anthony Denton. It was difficult light and the body had been in the water, half-submerged . . .'

Gwendoline fanned herself rapidly for a moment until the Headmaster snapped, 'Come off it, Gwendoline. Your father was a butcher. You must have seen more entrails than Lestrade here has solved cases. Mind you . . . '

'I believe he had been strangled, sir,' Lestrade told them.

'Strangled?' It was probably the first time in his life that the Headmaster's voice had dropped below a thunderclap.

'With his own spectacles chain.'

'Good Lord,' muttered Nails.

'What can you tell me about the deceased, sir?' Lestrade asked him.

'Denton? Well, not a lot, really. He'd only been with us a few weeks. This was his first term.'

'And where before that?'

'Oxford,' said Nails. 'All Souls.'

'Did you make the appointment?'

'Of course.' Nails was outraged that Lestrade might have thought otherwise. 'I never listen to the Governors in these matters. That ghastly Cardigan woman . . . '

Even he shuddered at the thought of it and Mrs Nails patted his brow with a chorus of heart-felt 'There, there's.

'He came of a good family. Impeccable degree, of course. Studied under Golightly.'

'Golightly?'

'One of the greatest scholars of this – or any other – age, Lestrade,' Nails sighed, contempt for the illiterate man seeping from every pore.

'And Denton would have left Oxford . . . ?'

'A few months ago. He came here from Kent – Maidstone, I believe.'

'Did he form any attachments here?' Lestrade asked.

'Attachments?' Nails frowned.

'Yes, was he particularly friendly with anyone?'

'I daresay old Saunders-Foote would have taken him under his wing. Getting a little unsavoury, is Saunders-Foote. He didn't go on his Grand Tour until he was sixty-one, Lestrade, and rumour has it he fell among gondoliers. Never been the same since. I find myself caring for the man less and less. Not sure his influence on the boys is as wholesome as it might be. I feel perhaps he should have retired at eighty . . . '

'Anyone else?'

'I really don't know. I have a large, thriving school to run, Lestrade. I cannot be held responsible for . . . One moment. You say Saunders-Foote met you with the news of Denton's demise?'

Lestrade nodded.

'How did he know about it?'

'He was in the habit of taking lunchtime strolls with Denton. They walked to the river . . . '

'Really?' Nails's eyebrow all but disappeared under his hairline. It had some way to go.

'Apparently, Mr Denton paused to relieve himself . . . '

'Really?' The Headmaster's other eyebrow joined the first.

' . . . while Mr . . . er . . . Saunders-Foote,' at last the glimmer of realisation, 'wandered on.'

'Thank God,' Nails muttered. 'What then?'

'Well, Mr Saunders-Foote realised that Denton was a very long time. He went back to look for him. I understand he heard a bell tolling.'

'Yes. That would be Ruffage. The commencement of afternoon lessons.'

'You call the afternoon lessons Ruffage?' Lestrade didn't like to miss a point and every school had its quirky traditions.

'No, no. Ruffage is my Captain of School, Lestrade. Capital fellow. One of his myriad duties is to ring the afternoon bell. Ruffages have been ringing that bell for generations.'

'Yes, well, there was no sign of Denton. Saunders-Foote searched for a while . . . '

'Missing his lesson with the Upper Thirds,' Nails observed. 'Why on earth didn't he report it?'

'I was wondering that. He eventually found him some hundreds of yards downstream. Tell me, is the current always that strong?'

'Yes, it's always dangerous at this time of the year. Saunders-Foote should have known that, even if Denton didn't. It's a tributary of the Welland, doesn't level out until Deene. Rhadegund Hall is built on the one craggy outcrop in Northamptonshire. And I do love high places, Lestrade. Pity,' Nails sighed lovingly, 'they didn't give me Harrow-on-the-Hill.'

'Dr Nails,' said Lestrade, 'when I was here last I was not able to talk to your boys. May I do so now?'

Nails looked at him. 'Very well,' he said, 'though I must again insist on being present. And you'll have an additional problem, Lestrade.'

'Oh?'

'When that washerwoman died there were thirty boys in attendance. Now, in full term, there are nearly four hundred. And Lestrade . . . '

'Sir?'

'On no account must this – any of it – be allowed to leak. The Chief Constable was the very soul of discretion. One death here might be regarded as carelessness. Two could close the place. This is St Rhadegund's. Are you with me?'

'All the way, Dr Nails,' said Lestrade.

Dr John Watson had not seen his friend and confidante Sherlock Holmes for nearly a month. The Great Detective had gone underground, via Baker Street and then east in the direction of Aldgate. In that time, Holmes had impersonated a number of costers and petty-thieves, a Sandhurst professor, a London University professor and was now swinging his way down the Minories in all the tawdry finery of an East End slut. Watson was going his way too, not in the sense of female impersonation, but coming back from the surgery of his old colleague, Lionel Druitt.

'Are you feeling good-natured, dearie?' Holmes croaked, flashing the teeth with the 'gaps' created by black gum.

Watson bridled. It was not the first time he had been importuned, neither probably would it be the last. It was, after all, a natural hazard east and indeed west of the Temple.

'How dare you, madam!' He coloured crimson and tipped his bowler.

'Oh, go on, ducks. Only cost you fourpence,' and Holmes threw his dingy petticoat over his head.

For a moment, Watson found himself looking, but only in a professional capacity of course, and he tapped the doxy firmly with his cane.

'My good woman, stop pestering me at once or I shall call a policeman.'

'I've just 'ad two of 'em over there,' cackled Holmes, then, to save the good Doctor's blood pressure, dropped into his suave, normal tones, 'steady, my dear fellow.'

Watson visibly jumped. 'Holmes!'

The Great Impersonator stamped heavily on the Doctor's spats and the medical man howled in pain and shock so as not to draw attention to himself.

'Good God, Holmes. For a moment there . . . '

'No, no,' Holmes chuckled, 'you probably haven't the change.'

Watson coloured again. 'How goes it?'

'Slowly, Watson, but I am making progress. Here,' he stuffed a piece of paper into the Doctor's pocket, 'that's the address of one George Lusk of Whitechapel. I cannot reach him either as myself or . . . otherwise. You're a Poor doctor— '

'Steady on, Holmes.' Watson was easily affronted.

'I mean, old friend,' Holmes hissed murderously, 'you are a Poor *Law* doctor, carrying out your treatment at reduced rates . . . '

'For nothing, Holmes,' the humanitarian medico reminded him.

'Quite. So you have every right to be in the vicinity.'

'So who is this Lusk?'

'He is in the process of forming a vigilante committee to protect the citizens of Whitechapel from the beast who walks among us. As such, he could be important to my plan.'

'Which is?' Watson lifted his coat to search for his notebook.

'Ooh,' Holmes reverted to his harlot as a potential eavesdropper passed by, 'you are a one!'

'Perverted beast!' roared the passer-by, eavesdropping as she went.

'Madam, I appeal to you . . . ' Watson could not allow his honour to be so impugned.

'Oh no you don't,' the lady assured him and hurried on her way, regretting her lack of chaperon.

Holmes tapped the side of his nose. 'Not now, Watson. You shall be privy to my plan in due course. Who's on the Whitechapel case? I haven't seen a paper for days.'

'Well, the City Force are doing the usual pas-de-deux,' Watson chuckled, 'round in circles. The Yard have put Abberline on it.'

'Where's Lestrade?'

'No mention in any of the dailies,' Watson shrugged.

'Thank God,' Holmes muttered. 'Right, Watson. Go to Lusk and find out all you can. I'll be in touch. Thank you, dearie,' he suddenly shrieked. 'Mind 'ow you go.'

'Holmes,' Watson followed the swaying figure for a while, whispering, 'was it true about those two policemen?'

* * *

Lestrade sent George George to Maidstone. Kent wasn't the Inspector's favourite county and he felt the Sergeant should have the dubious pleasure of pirouetting through the less-than-salubrious streets of the town that housed England's largest cavalry depot. It was doubly unfortunate for George that the deceased Denton's grandfather, his only living relative, was not particularly helpful on his grandson's death, nor concerned about it. He was, however, an antiquarian and amateur archaeologist and by the time he caught the London train George was intimately acquainted with the Shire Moote, the paper-making mills at Tovil, and knew every member of the Woodville and Wyatt families who had made the town great since Domesday. Of the demised Denton he could glean little. He had been a solitary boy, a martyr to his sniff and had been rather short-sighted. The old man had not seen him for well over a year. When George told him the boy was dead, he assumed it was a bronchial spasm and turned unflinchingly to the great tome he was penning: 'Maidstone and its Importance in Western Civilisation as Evinced in the Life of William Hazlitt, Essayist, Born in Maidstone 1778. Left Maidstone 1780.' George treated himself to a hipflask on his way to the station. He thought he'd earned its contents.

All in all, Lestrade didn't fare much better in Oxford. He passed the Radcliffe Camera but it was a dull day and he hadn't time for photographs. The Warden of All Souls was a kindly soul himself, shocked to hear of the departure of Denton from this vale of tears.

'We get very fond of our undergraduates, Mr Lestrade,' he said, blowing his nose with the delicacy of a walrus. 'There are only four of them, you see.'

'Can't get the students, Professor?' Lestrade asked him.

'No, no, we have students aplenty. For in truth when does a man stop being a student? When does he ever really know himself?'

'Quite,' was the most erudite answer Lestrade could give.

'But all but four of our students are Fellows.'

'You take women?' Lestrade was surprised, but perhaps under his gown even the Warden sported a pair of blue stockings.

The Warden turned a little pale and had to steady himself by an ogee arch for a minute. 'No, they are graduates,' he explained when his colour had come back, 'Fellows of the College.'

'I see. How well did you know Anthony Denton?'

'As well as any academic ship that passes in the night of ignorance, riding the seas of scepticism.'

'You know he'd been appointed a master at St Rhadegund's?'

'Yes. Tell me, Inspector, did you know St Rhadegund's husband was a murderer?'

'No, I didn't,' Lestrade said, crossing the quad. 'Do you think there's a connection?'

The Warden chuckled. 'I hardly think so. St Rhadegund did die rather a long time ago – nearly thirteen hundred years to be exact.'

'Ah, we're getting there,' Lestrade beamed, attempting to lighten the moment.

The Warden ignored him, standing still in awe of the huge grey façade that reared up before him. 'I never cease to be impressed.' He clasped his hands. 'Founded in fourteen thirty-eight by Henry Chichele.'

'Bless you,' offered Lestrade, and instantly regretted it.

'Yes,' the Warden went on unchecked, 'in memory of Agincourt, Deo gratias.'

The conversation was deepening rapidly. Lestrade sensed the current carrying him away.

'The College of the Souls of all the Faithful Departed,' the Warden was in full flood, 'including my Bible clerk, Anthony Denton.' He turned from the sweep of the Gothic magnificence to the shabby little man in the Donegal. 'I can't help you, Inspector. I wish I could. The Anthony Denton I knew had no enemies and probably very few friends. This is all too shocking. Too shocking. You must see these things all the time. We don't. Ours is a cosy, sheltered world. Unreal in a way, but we cannot change it.' He sighed and clasped his hands again, smiling at the stone monument to Henry Chichele. 'Nor should we.'

Lestrade left him to his academic seclusion and vanished through a medieval archway into Catte Street, pausing only to have his shin lacerated by the college cat. Clearly it was a custom initiated by Henry Chichele.

Midnight found the policemen together, the Inspector and his sergeant, sagging under the oil-lamps as the cocoa steamed and Lestrade wreathed himself in smoke. The clock on the wall clanked the hour of twelve and the Inspector told himself again he must get a new striker for it. In distant corridors the clash of steel on stone could be heard as Sergeant Derry marched off duty. Lestrade stood up, twisting his head in the hope he would hear the click that told him his spine had reunited, but there was nothing.

'You're asleep, George.' He looked down at the wreck in the corner.

'Sorry, guv'nor. You're right.'

'All right. One more time and we can all go home. What do the laws of coincidence say?'

George forced his eyelids to stay somewhere near his eyebrows. 'The laws of coincidence do not stretch to two accidental deaths in one place within a month of each other.'

'Especially?'

'Especially if that place is a school.'

'Murder one we know about. Murder two?'

'Deceased is a young man, one Anthony Denton. Twenty-two, a new teacher. Been at the school for a few weeks. One grandfather. Doesn't care whether he's dead or alive.'

'Cause of death?'

'Er . . . strangulation.'

'Yes,' Lestrade stopped him, 'done with the chain around his spectacles, but . . . '

'But?' George, even in his less-than-immaculate state of wakefulness, knew when his guv'nor's nose was twitching.

'But there's something about that. The neck was broken.'

'By a spectacle chain? Why didn't *it* break? It doesn't make sense.'

'That's what I like about you, George,' Lestrade sighed. 'You have this knack of coming up with unanswerable questions. Of raising awkward issues. I wonder you're not Commissioner.'

'What do you make of it, then?' the Sergeant asked.

'Not a lot, at the moment,' Lestrade confessed. 'The coroner's report *might* help.'

George guffawed and Lestrade shrugged. 'Well, it's late,' he said, 'but this much we know. Whoever killed Denton was waiting for him in those woods.'

'A passing maniac?' George suggested. 'What about gypsies? Was he robbed?'

'That's three questions for the price of one,' Lestrade said, looking at his reflection in the window and searching vaguely for his collar studs. 'Maniac, possibly. You and I know the Northamptonshire countryside is teeming with them, all set to leap on peeing classics masters and throttle them before flinging them in a river. All this in broad daylight and totally unobserved. Gypsies? Getting warmer? Colder? I don't know. The only reason they'll kill is for gain, but no, as far as we know, Denton wasn't robbed. When we fished his body out in the morning his wallet was still in place, and his watch. He had four and threepence-halfpenny on him.'

'Oh?'

'His yearly salary,' Lestrade said.

'What do you reckon to this old codger, then?' George asked.

'Saunders-Foote?' Lestrade asked. 'I'm not sure.'

'Could he have done it?'

Lestrade had pondered this one himself, several times. Saunders-Foote would not have been the first murderer to draw attention to his crime. It was the lurid compulsion of the killer to boast, to taunt his would-be executioner by leading him into the very pit itself and to fling his expertise in his face – for some men, it was the very thrill of it, the whole point of the exercise. And it had taken him some hours to report the incident.

'He's old,' Lestrade was talking to himself really, 'quite frail. Denton was a young man, strong . . . '

'But from behind? Sudden. And with a bit of luck?' George was an old hand at probing every avenue with his guv'nor.

'All right. What's his motive?'

George thought. He was better at that than most policemen.

'Is he a Mary-Ann, this Saunders-Foote?'

Lestrade shrugged. 'Perhaps. Go on.'

'What if he makes advances to Denton? Takes him into the woods for a few surprises?'

'And?'

'Denton is as other men. Saunders-Foote has made a mistake, but Denton gets annoyed, threatens to tell the guv'nor.'

'Nails?'

'Yes. He wouldn't like that, would he? *His* school and all?'

Lestrade chewed the ends of his moustache. 'It's thin, George,' he said. 'Where's your proof?'

'Ah,' said George, 'that little knack you say I've got, sir? Well, you've got it too.'

'What about coincidence, George?' Lestrade stubbed out the last of his cigar in the last of his cocoa. 'What's the link between these two?'

'Ah,' mused George again. 'The missing link.'

Lestrade turned. 'I didn't see the Commissioner come in,' he said.

'Was he . . . was he her lover?' George had suddenly woken up. 'The dead girl – Maggie Hollis – was pregnant.

What if Denton was the father? He killed her to avoid the scandal . . . '

'And then kills himself with remorse?' beamed Lestrade. 'Most determined case of suicide I ever saw.'

'All right, sir,' grinned George. 'It's been a long day.'

'It has that, George. Let's go home.'

The Yard men stumbled out into a drizzly night, buttoning up against the cold.

A mile or more from them Elizabeth Stride – Long Liz – shivered against a wall in Whitechapel. A knife flashed in the darkness.

The Double Event

A diminutive Cockney was waiting for Lestrade as he staggered out of the hansom the next morning.

'Are you the copper what's in charge of the case?' he asked, jabbing him in the waistcoat with a finger less than respectful.

'Not exactly,' said Lestrade. 'Who are you?'

'George Lusk, Builder. My card.' The little man produced the grubby object from his pocket.

'Thank you, Mr Lusk. If I ever need a portico or an annexe, I shall make a point of calling on you.'

'I've been called on already,' said Lusk, following Lestrade through the alleyways as policemen on corners snapped to attention. 'A Dr Watson has been to see me.'

'Watson?' Lestrade stopped in his tracks. 'What did he want?'

'I couldn't make it out. 'E arsked if I'd seen a tall prostitute in a red dress, rather mannish lookin', by all accounts.'

Lestrade mused. 'I wonder what Watson wants with a prostitute?'

Lust guffawed. 'Well, if you don't know, mate, there's no point in me tellin' yer.'

'But a mannish-looking one?' Lestrade was talking to himself.

'Maybe the Doctor's a bit that way,' Lusk suggested, inclining his neck. Then he realised that that was the inclination of Lestrade's neck too and kept his back to the wall. 'Of course,' he suddenly said, 'there is another possibility.'

'Oh?' Lestrade was mentally elsewhere, looking for signs of a detective. He'd come to the wrong city.

'Who is this Watson? You sound as if you know him.'

'After a fashion,' Lestrade admitted.

'Well, then, wassis game?'

'Medicine,' replied Lestrade.

'Yeah, but 'e kept on about 'ow there was 'elp at 'and. The greatest detective in London, 'e said. Who did 'e mean?'

'Me.' A voice down the alley made them both turn as Chief Inspector Abberline appeared. 'What are you doing here, Lestrade, and who's this?'

'Passing,' said Lestrade 'and this is Mr Lusk, Builder.'

'Builder?' Abberline repeated.

'I am wearing my huvver 'at vis morning, gentlemen.' Lusk stood to his full five foot one. 'Chairman of the Whitechapel Vigilante Committee.'

'Vigilante?' snapped Abberline. 'You've got a nerve, Lusk.'

'It's you wot's got the nerve. You coppers. There's annuver one of 'em over there – that's three.'

'Thank God for the Ragged Schools,' muttered Lestrade.

'I'll Ragged School you!' screeched Lusk. 'You coppers. If you done your job proper, she wouldn't be lyin' there.'

'And if we'd let you do yours,' Abberline rounded on him, 'you'd have hanged John Pizer and half the slaughtermen in Whitechapel.'

'We still might, don't you worry.' Lusk stared at his man's tiepin with menaces.

'What did you mean when you said there was another possibility?' Lestrade asked, by way of breaking up two sparring partners.

'What?' Lusk came down off his toe tips. 'Oh, that. Well it's obvious, innit? The reason your blokes and my blokes 'aven't caught the poxy bastard is that 'e dresses up as a woman. And 'aven't we bin lookin' for a man? And this bloke, this Watson, 'e's a doctor, inne? Well, there you are; stands to reason, don't it? 'E dresses up as a tart and 'acks 'em wiv 'is knife. 'Is *surgeon's* knife.'

All three men fell silent, then Abberline turned to Lestrade. 'I'm looking for Fred Wensley.'

'Aren't we all?' Lestrade and the Chief Inspector went their separate ways.

'Well, never mind about that!' Lusk screamed. 'We'll do it our bloody selves, my blokes an' me. We'll get this Wensley, 'ooever 'e is and that bloody doctor, walkin' around in women's clothin'. It ain't natural.'

In the City, all roads lead to Fred Wensley. George Lusk must have been one of the very few who hadn't heard of him. And so it was that Abberline and Lestrade, who had separated the best of enemies, met again moments later in Berners Street where the wind whipped Lestrade's Donegal and ruffled Abberline's astrakhan. In the middle of a knot of policemen stood their quarry, the Dorsetman Fred Wensley, who had made the City his home.

'What have we got, Fred?' Lestrade asked.

'Lestrade,' Abberline interrupted, 'may I remind you that *I* am in charge of this case. What have we got, Wensley?'

'We can't go on meeting like this, Sholto.' Wensley ignored his superior. 'Have a cashew nut. Oh, better not. Evidence.'

'Wensley!' Abberline snapped. It had not been his morning so far. Mrs Abberline was currently at home with an army of relations. He couldn't even get at the downstairs maid.

'Sorry, Mr Abberline,' Wensley smiled engagingly. 'I hope you haven't had a big breakfast.'

He clicked his fingers and a constable pulled back the tarpaulin sheet, Metropolitan Police, For the Use of, to reveal a middle-aged woman, lying on her left side, caked in mud, her left arm behind her back, her mouth slightly open and the knot of her check scarf carried by a knife's edge into the gash across her throat that had cut her windpipe.

'I've seen worse,' shrugged Abberline.

'Good,' said Wensley. 'I'll take you to Mitre Square in a minute to see another one.'

'Another?' Abberline and Lestrade chorused.

Wensley nodded. 'That makes two in one night. And four in all.'

'Does Lusk know about this?' Abberline asked.

'Who?'

'Chairman of the Vigilante Committee,' Lestrade told him. 'Apparently they don't have much faith in the officer in charge of the case.' All eyes turned to Abberline, who blustered.

'Who's this one?' He kicked the corpse with his boot.

The smile vanished from Wensley's face. These were his people, albeit his adopted people. He cared for them passionately.

'Fred,' said Lestrade, sensing the moment. 'Who was she?'

'Elizabeth Stride,' Wensley said, through clenched teeth, 'known as Long Liz. She was Swedish originally. A prostitute.'

'Who found her?' Abberline asked.

'We've got him at Leman Street,' Wensley told him. 'A hawker called Louis Diemschutz. He's clean.'

'As a sewer rat,' snorted Abberline. 'I want to work on him myself.'

'What else do we know about Long Liz?' Lestrade asked.

'She lived in various lodgings – Fashion Street, Flower and Dean, Dorset. We've got a sighting of her with a man about quarter to midnight last night.'

'Well?' Abberline snapped, anxious to bend the odd iron bar over the head of Louis Diemschutz.

'Middle aged, the informant said. Quietly spoken, decently dressed. He was wearing what may have been a sailor's cap. He kissed Liz and said – and I quote – "You'd say anything but your prayers".'

'Well, Lestrade. Ideas?' Abberline barked.

'*Could* be Doctor Watson,' mused Lestrade.

'Who?'

'Nothing. Ignore me. I haven't had my breakfast yet. Any other witnesses?'

'Constable Smith here.'

Wensley stepped back and allowed the solid, plodding constable to emerge from the group of capes and helmets at his back. Smith had been up all night. He was wet and hungry and tired.

'Is your name Smith?' Abberline asked him.

'It is, sir.'

'A likely story. What do you know about this?'

Smith hauled out the notebook. 'I saw the deceased at approximately half-past midnight. She was in conversation with a gentleman— '

'Smith,' snarled Abberline, 'I have a murderer to catch. I would like to do that before Hell freezes over, if it's all the same to you!'

'Yes, sir. Very good, sir. He was a toff, sir. Tall. Overcoat. Deerstalker, collar and tie.'

'*Could* be Sherlock Holmes,' mused Lestrade.

'Who?' Abberline rounded on him.

'As I said, sir, I haven't had breakfast.'

'Is that it?' Abberline shouted in Smith's ear.

'Er . . . yes, sir.'

'Pathetic.'

'What about the parcel, Constable,' Wensley reminded him.

'Oh, yes, sir. Thank you, sir. The gentleman had a parcel with him, sir.'

There was a silence.

'I see,' said Abberline. 'So we are to conclude that the murderer works for the Post Office, are we? Thank you, Constable. Wensley, you and Lestrade get over to that other murder. I've got my man. This Louis Diemschutz. Smith, come with me to Leman Street. I want you to positively identify him as the murderer. With total impartiality, of course.'

Lestrade and Wensley watched him go – the unspeakable pursuing the uncatchable.

'Cashews,' said Lestrade.

'Bless you,' commiserated Wensley.

'The evidence you offered me,' Lestrade reminded him.

'Oh, yes.' Wensley fumbled in his pocket for his nuts. 'Found in her left hand.'

'Any significance?'

Wensley shrugged. 'Perhaps the murderer gave them to her. Perhaps she bought them. Who knows? We'd better go.' He waved to the dripping policeman sitting on top of the cab and the hack clattered across the cobbles to them. 'Mitre Square, Constable. Double up.'

Constable Watkins smelled of rum. And even now, hours after the finding of Catherine Eddowes, he was pale and shaking.

'Like a pig in Smithfield,' he mumbled to Lestrade.

Wensley patted his sodden shoulder.

'What time did you find her, Constable?' Lestrade asked.

'Er . . . it would be about quarter to two, sir. I know because my ol' man's watch was playin' up and I'd taken it to be cleaned— '

'All right, Constable,' Wensley was sharper, 'we don't want your life story, lad.'

'No, sir.' Watkins looked crestfallen. 'Sorry, sir. I 'aven't been well. Not since . . . '

'Not since quarter to two, eh, lad?' Lestrade asked.

Watkins tried to smile.

'Your old man's watch?' Lestrade smiled for him. 'On the Force, was he?'

'Yes, sir,' Watkins brightened.

'So was mine,' said Lestrade. 'Now cut along and watch Mr Wensley's horse, there's a good lad.'

They watched him go and heard him mutter, 'Why, what's it going to do?' but chose to ignore it.

'You won't like this one, Sholto,' Wensley told him.

'Never thought I'd see you go soft on a rookie, though.'

Lestrade caught the smirk and shrugged. 'I was one myself once. Let's have a look at this Catherine Eddowes.'

She lay on her back in the rain-sodden mud in a corner of the Square, her right leg bent up, her skirts and petticoats disarranged. The same tell-tale gash across her throat, wide and dark. The dark, swollen face was slashed, but not at random. Her nose had gone, her right ear. Vertical nicks scarred her eyelids. Like Chapman and Nicholls she had been disembowelled, a series of jagged diagonal cuts from groin to chest. Her entrails lay over her right shoulder. Lestrade caught his breath. For a moment Wensley fancied he saw the man turn pale, but it must have been a trick of the light.

'I hope she was dead when he did that to her,' the Dorsetman said.

'If she was dead,' hissed Lestrade, 'there'd have been no need to bother. What's this?'

'Constable Long, sir.' An older man saluted at Lestrade's elbow. 'I found this, sir. It's covered in blood.'

Lestrade and Wensley looked at it – a tattered piece of cloth, once white, now bricky red.

'Where did you find it?' Lestrade asked.

'A stairway, sir, Wentworth Buildings, Goulston Street.'

'Fred?'

'Around the corner, in the direction of Spitalfields.'

'Beggin' yer pardon, sir,' Long said.

'Out with it, Constable,' Lestrade turned to him.

'It wasn't there earlier, sir. Not at twenty-parst two when I done me rounds. And there's somefink else . . . '

'Yes?'

'It's a message, sir, on the wall . . . '

'Show us,' said Lestrade, and they followed Long past the quivering form of Constable Watkins. But they were not fast enough. At the corner of Goulston Street, the shape that Fred Wensley for one dreaded to see loomed into view. The top hat, the astrakhan collar, the narrow eyes and pencil moustache said it all. Lestrade instinctively felt Wensley stiffen.

'God, no,' he heard the Dorsetman mutter.

'You're late, gentlemen,' the figure said. 'I have been here for ten minutes. Wensley, isn't it?'

'Yes, sir.' He all but saluted, unforgivable faux pas though it was for a plainclothesman.

'Who's this?'

'Inspector Lestrade, sir,' Wensley introduced him.

'Do you know who I am?' the taller man asked.

Lestrade stroked his chin thoughtfully. 'Charlie Peace?' he volunteered.

The top-hatted gentleman exploded. 'I am Sir Charles Warren, Commissioner of the Metropolitan Police, and I could have you for breakfast.'

'I'm a little peckish too, sir,' Lestrade told him. Seniority, especially ignorant, unpromoted seniority, was calculated to climb right up every orifice Lestrade possessed.

'Lestrade.' Warren closed on his man, dazzling him with the diamonds in his tiepin. 'Yes, I've heard of you.'

'I'm flattered,' bowed Lestrade.

'You needn't be,' Warren snapped. 'I don't like prima donnas, Lestrade.'

The Inspector was about to protest that he didn't care for Italians either when the Commissioner swept back into the shadows from whence he had emerged. 'Come with me, both of you.'

They followed him through the early Sunday morning, the rain drifting still across the City. 'There,' he pointed with his Major-General's finger at the crude chalk letters under the portico of the tenement block.

'Wensley, this is your patch. What do you make of that?'

The Dorsetman read it aloud. 'The Juwes are the men who will not be blamed for nothing.'

'Well?' Warren snapped.

'I don't know, sir.'

'Don't know? Don't know, Wensley? You do realise I have an audience with Her Majesty this afternoon? She will want answers, Wensley, answers. The press have already had a field day.' The Major-General knew all about Field Days.

'Lestrade?' Warren rounded on him.

'Constable.' Lestrade turned to Long, 'copy that down. Carefully, mind. Exactly as it is there. We'll get a photographer.'

'Constable!' roared Warren. 'Rub that out!'

'What?' Lestrade and Wensley chorused.

'Now, Constable. Or so help me I'll have you off the Force, no pension.'

Long sprang forward as though from a catapult and applied the hem of his cape. Lestrade grabbed his arm.

'Unhand him, Lestrade. That is an order. You are interfering with a policeman in pursuance of his duty.'

'So are you, sir,' Lestrade bounced back. 'That is vital evidence.'

'Have you heard of Bloody Sunday, Lestrade?' Warren stood nose to forehead with Lestrade. Wensley wondered how many years Lestrade would get for striking the Commissioner of the Metropolitan Police and for a moment he thought he saw Lestrade's knee poise itself under the Donegal to make contact with the Commissioner's groin.

'I was there,' growled Lestrade, 'right in the centre.'

'Right!' bawled Warren, as though on the parade ground. 'Then you'll know why that has to go. If this gets out, every Jew in the City will be a target. It'll be a bloodbath, Lestrade, and you'll be the cause of it.'

'Look at the spelling!' Lestrade shouted. 'What if it's not the Jews?'

'Not the Jews? Not the Jews, you cretin? Of course it's the Jews. I'm going to talk to Rodney about you, Lestrade. See how you look in a tall blue helmet. Haven't you got another case to go to?'

A silence fell on Goulston Street.

'Do I assume you are taking me off the case, sir?' Lestrade asked.

'You do,' grimaced Warren. 'Wensley, come with me. I want you to arrange for photographs of the dead woman's eyes.'

'Sir?' Wensley thought perhaps he'd misheard.

'Science, Wensley, science,' Warren explained as though to a child. 'By taking a photograph of the eyes we will see, stamped on the iris, an image of the last thing she saw while she lived. In a flash, as it were, the Whitechapel murderer.'

'With respect, sir . . . ' Lestrade was first to break the astonished silence.

'You don't know the meaning of the word, sir. Good morning. Have you finished, Constable?'

Long had. The chalked words had gone. And so had Lestrade, north on that wet Sunday, to Rhadegund Hall.

He read the words carved on the weathered seat: 'Who Spot the Verb and Stop the Ball Shall Say if England Stand or Fall'. He ran his finger over the elaborate carving and sat down heavily with his back against the wood. Northamptonshire was kinder than London; the evening more mellow than the dawn. An Indian summer – the kind of which Cherak Singh dreamed, no doubt – had settled on the russet woods where the owls hooted in the dark purple.

'Are you a god?' A voice jarred the stillness of the moment.

'I beg your pardon?' It was not a question Lestrade had been asked before. The regal young man before him pointed to the seat with a thin cane he was twirling in his fingers.

'Only gods are allowed to sit on the Altar. Aren't you a shade old?'

'And aren't you a shade young to be questioning your betters?' Mercer strode across the quad.

'Ah, Bursar. Do you know this fellow?' the young man

asked loftily, as though Lestrade left a smell under his nose.

'I do. Why aren't you in chapel, Hardman?'

The young man closed to him confidentially. 'Confidentially, Bursar, I've been chucked out of the choir. Dreadful, isn't it? I don't know what my old man the Field Marshal would say.'

'He'd probably have you shot, Hardman. Which is what I shall do if you don't cut along.'

'But this fellow . . . is he here on school business?'

'I am,' said Lestrade, sensing he had been talked through and over long enough.

'Oh,' said Hardman, with all the arrogance of a Field Marshal's son. 'In that case, I shan't detain you gentlemen any longer. Goodnight to you.'

They waited until he had disappeared into the dark of the buildings.

'What did he mean, was I a god?' Lestrade asked.

'A school prefect,' Mercer explained. 'Hardman is only a House prefect as yet – an inferior being here at Rhadegund. No doubt in the fullness of time he'll find his place here on the Altar.'

'You don't care for young Hardman, Mr Mercer?'

The Bursar frowned at the Inspector, pale in the twilight. 'No, I don't. Actually,' he led Lestrade along the edge of the First Eleven Square, 'I don't care for boys at all. Vicious, smelly, unpleasant creatures.'

'Weren't you one yourself?' Lestrade smiled.

Mercer looked at him with cold disdain. 'No,' he said. 'As for Hardman, he's a particularly nasty piece of work. Has quite a coterie in the Remove and the Lower Sixth.'

Well, Lestrade presumed he had to keep it somewhere.

'Any joy with poor old Denton's death?' Mercer asked.

'Very little, I'm afraid,' Lestrade confessed. He hadn't the heart to tell the dear old Bursar that he really didn't give a damn about the mystery at Rhadegund Hall, that he was still bristling from his clash that morning with that buffoon Warren. But what happened next shook him out of that. He collided with an upper-class urchin of uncertain age whose macassared head caught him neatly in the pit of the stomach as he rounded the laundry tower.

'Oh, well tackled, Channing-Lover,' applauded the Bursar. 'Unfortunately, Inspector Lestrade doesn't have the ball.'

Lestrade disentangled himself from the lad, surreptitiously checking his nether-wear to see whether Mercer was right.

'Sir! Sir!' gabbled the unlikely prop-forward. 'I must find a master, sir.'

'I'm sorry I am not quite "of the blood",' sighed Mercer, used to such slights over the years. 'Won't I do?'

Channing-Lover thought for a moment while Lestrade continued to pluck ivy from his clothing.

'It's Singh Major, sir. You'd better come quick. There's been a ghastly accident.'

Lestrade was unsure in his winded state with darkness descending whether Singh Major was a chap or a reference to the wailing of the choir which crept with the wind behind it around the corners of the quad. But Mercer followed Channing-Lover at a trot and Lestrade thought it best to follow him. They crossed the leaf-strewn quads without number, below the Headmaster's house, across the Butts and on to where the Welland had been dammed and tamed to form a boating lake for the chaps. At the water's edge, stagnant and alive with gnats, the running trio found an open boat drifting with the breeze and in it the naked corpse of an Indian boy.

'My God,' muttered Mercer. 'Channing-Lover, what have you done?'

'Me, sir?' In the heat of the moment, the boy's incipient manhood deserted him and he positively shrieked. 'I found him, sir! That is, Carstairs and I . . . '

'When?' Lestrade asked.

'About ten minutes ago, sir,' Channing-Lover was shaking a little now, what with the night air and the shock.

'Who is Carstairs?'

'House prefect,' Mercer told him. 'Channing-Lover is his fag.' He sensed Lestrade's bewilderment. 'That means he runs errands for him, cleans his study, and so on.'

'Thank you,' said Lestrade, 'I am familiar with the term. Where is Carstairs now?'

'I don't know,' Channing-Lover began to whimper. 'We each ran towards the school to get help.'

'And you found it first,' Mercer observed. 'What were you and Carstairs doing down here anyway?'

Silence but for the lapping of the water.

'Channing-Lover?' Mercer reminded the boy of his presence. But a greater Presence was approaching at the double, gown flying, mortarboard quivering.

'If I've been brought here on a fool's errand, Carstairs, I'll flay you alive . . . '

The unmistakable decibels of Dr Nails sent shivers over the surface of the lake.

'Lestrade, Mercer,' Nails took in the scene, 'Channing-Lover, you snivelling little prig. I thought you'd be at the bottom of this. Carstairs, you unnatural beast, what have you and Channing-Lover been up to? I thought we'd heard the last of all that after the Founder's Day incident of last year. Frankly, Carstairs, it's only because your father was a mountaineer I closed my eyes to that at all. The goat of course will never recover— '

'With respect, Headmaster . . . ' Lestrade cut in.

'Eh?' Nails turned on him with the speed of a scorpion. 'I don't believe you know the meaning of the word. What is it now? This isn't a police matter.'

'What's in the boat is,' Lestrade said quietly.

All eyes followed his finger to the body of Singh Major that lolled across the bow, his black hair dragging in the water like sargasso weed.

'Who's that?' Nails peered in the gloom. 'Some idiot playing the giddy goat?'

The thoughts of most present turned to Carstairs and Channing-Lover, unnaturally enough.

'It's Cherak Singh Major,' Carstairs volunteered. 'He's dead.'

'Dead?' Nails repeated.

'Look at this,' said Lestrade, leaning forward to steady the boat. 'His hand appears to be caught in his rowlocks.'

'Medically impossible, surely?' said Nails. They all looked at him.

'What do you make of it, Lestrade?' Mercer asked.

'Dr Nails, I would be grateful if these young men could be kept in quarantine, so to speak, until I have a chance to talk to them. I don't want this body disturbed and I don't want panic through the school. Carstairs, Channing-Lover, who else knows about this?'

'I'll ask the questions, Lestrade,' Nails insisted.

'Headmaster, may I remind you that three people have died at your school in mysterious circumstances in the last month. I have been placed in charge of this inquiry and I can do it far better with your help than with your obstruction.'

For the first time in his life, Nails was speechless, but it was with anger rather than realisation of his own deficiencies. Carstairs and Mercer smiled quietly to themselves, each of them glad in his own way for the cover of darkness. In any case, Channing-Lover was nearest and Nails slapped him loudly across the head. 'And don't slouch, boy. It shows a lack of intellect!' And he strode off towards the buildings.

'Mr Mercer, can I rely on you to send a telegram to Scotland Yard? I shall need officers to assist me.'

'Of course. What about Singh?'

'I'll rope him off. The night air won't help, but I'd rather study the body in its present position in daylight. Can we keep everybody on the premises tomorrow?'

'We can try,' shrugged Mercer, 'but Singh Minor is the problem.'

'Singh Minor?'

'Yes. You met him, I believe, when you first arrived. The boy in the boat is his elder brother.'

*

Carstairs and Channing-Lover were at first furtive, clandestine even. Years of sneaking behind the bicycle sheds, the laundry tower, the Butts and the boating lake had turned happy-go-lucky boys into neurotic, spotty youths, and years of self-induced blindness stretched ahead of them.

'Channing-Lover has already told me what happened,' Lestrade lied. 'All I need to know now is who actually hit Singh with the log.'

Carstairs sat upright. 'That little sneak!' he hissed. 'You realise the bounder is lying through his pretty little teeth, don't you?'

'It wasn't a log you hit him with?' Lestrade remained as obtuse as only he could.

'I didn't hit him with anything. Look, Sergeant . . . ' In his own limp-wristed way, Carstairs was as arrogant as Hardman.

'Inspector, sonny,' snapped Lestrade, 'and make no mistake: Mr Berry the hangman can accommodate the necks of public schoolboys as well as the next man.'

'I didn't kill him.' Carstairs' voice remained calm, but Lestrade knew a gibbering idiot when he saw one.

'Then what did you do?'

'I was merely walking with Channing-Lover by the lake . . . '

'Why?' asked Lestrade.

Carstairs stared at him. 'Were you never at public school, Inspector?' A more worldly man would have known the answer to that by the cut of his bowler.

'No,' Lestrade scowled. 'Get to the point.'

'We saw the boat moving towards us from the centre of the lake. At first we thought it was old Adelstrop— '

'Adelstrop?'

'Yes, he's the old duffer who tends to the boats. No one's allowed in them except in the summer term. They're usually locked in the boathouse by now.'

'Go on.'

'It was nearly dark. Channers noticed someone lying face down in the boat, his hand, as it were manacled to the side. He was naked. We thought . . . then we realised he was dead.'

'Did you know who it was?'

'Not at first. But there aren't many niggers at St Rhadegund's, Mr Lestrade. Only two in fact: Singhs Major and Minor.'

'How well did you know the elder Singh?' Lestrade asked.

'Scarcely at all,' said Carstairs. 'He wasn't my type.'

'Black?'

'Straight,' said Carstairs flatly. 'Rather fond of the ladies by all accounts.'

'Really?'

'Look, Inspector, I don't know what Channing-Lover has told you . . . '

'The same as you, Mr Carstairs,' Lestrade lolled back in his chair, 'which either means you've cooked up a tight story together, or . . . '

'Or?' Carstairs leaned forward.

' . . . or you've told me the truth. Can you think of any reason why anyone should kill Singh Major?'

Carstairs shook his head slowly. 'He seemed a nice chap. Unless . . . '

'Yes?'

'Well, Bracegirdle didn't care for him. Too many memories.'

'Who is Bracegirdle?'

'The Corps Commandant and games instructor. I'm surprised you haven't met him.'

'What do you mean, "memories"?'

'I really think you'd better ask him, Inspector.'

Lestrade looked at the youth before him, dark circles under the eyes, nails chewed to the quick, but managing still a certain hauteur in adversity. Such people, Lestrade had heard, were invaluable in a shipwreck. And probably an unnecessary hindrance in a murder inquiry. Swearing him to total silence on the affair, he let him go.

Channing-Lover was no use either. Having recovered his composure after the shock of discovering Singh, he was bland, inscrutable even. Only when Lestrade touched on his relationship with Carstairs and the reason for his peculiar mincing gait, did the coolness melt. Lestrade put it down to solitary vices in the dorm and sent Channing-Lover back to bed. His own bed.

Lestrade had promised that he would not interview any of Nails's boys without the Great Man being present; another reason why he had sworn Carstairs and Pollux to secrecy. So he decided to break the news to Singh Minor after he had checked the body in the lake. He collected Mercer and Nails a little before dawn and the Headmaster supervised with totally unhelpful 'Right a little's and 'Left a shade's, while policeman and Bursar hauled the stiffened corpse ashore.

'Rigor,' murmured Lestrade.

'Sikh,' Nails corrected him, 'though utterly Christianised, I assure you.'

'What do you make of this?' Lestrade pointed to the waterlogged hemp noose, biting deep into the deceased's neck.

Mercer bent closer, then his eyes widened. 'You had better ask the Headmaster,' he said.

'Eh?' Nails flustered. For all his murderous skill with a cane, he was not at home with cadavers.

'The rope,' said Lestrade.

'Good God!' Nails shrank back. 'That's . . . mountaineering rope,' he almost whispered. Aware that all three were staring at him, one albeit inadvertently, the Headmaster bridled. 'It's common enough,' he shrugged. 'Nothing special about it. You've done the Himalayas, Mercer. Tell him.'

'It's true enough,' the Bursar said. 'All sorts of ropes are used for scaling mountains, Inspector. It's just that this one is the most popular.'

'The sort we'd find in your study?' Lestrade stood up to face Nails.

'Now look here— ' the Head bellowed.

'Headmaster,' Mercer interrupted him, and pointed to a handful of boys, led by a master, jogging doggedly across the ploughed field of the hill.

'Damn, it's Bracegirdle. I'd forgotten his damned cross-country. I'd better divert them or they'll come this way. You'd better put Singh in the san, Mercer. I must write to his father, the Maharajah,' and he strode off.

'I didn't know you climbed mountains too,' Lestrade said to the Bursar. Mercer chuckled, a rare enough phenomenon in a man who kept accounts.

'I don't. Or at least, I haven't for years. It's all that kept me sane in the Civil Service.'

Lestrade could understand that. 'When we've taken Singh inside,' he said, 'where will I find Mr Bracegirdle?'

'The Major? He'll probably be in the gym after breakfast. I believe he has the Remove.'

Hardman paced the floor of his study. Draped on furniture around the room were his cronies and on the carpet before the fire the solitary figure of Singh Minor, feeling more solitary by the minute.

'The point is, nigger,' Hardman pirouetted to land in an armchair, 'your brother is dead.'

Singh hung his head. They had dragged him from his bed before breakfast and had broken the news to him without ceremony or compassion. Channing-Lover had talked, very rapidly in fact, with Hardman's boot pressing on his windpipe, and the whole sorry story had come out.

'Isn't it true that you fellows slum it in the East End during the vacs?' Hardman asked him.

Singh nodded.

'Why you do that one can't imagine, but I would suppose you mix with riff-raff like this Lestrade. What do you know of him?'

'He's a detective. From Scotland Yard.'

'And when he turns up, your brother dies. Coincidence, eh?'

'He has nothing to do with it.'

'Hasn't he?'

'This school's going to pot, Singh,' a crony piped out. 'First niggers, then coppers, then murder. We've got to do something, Hardman.'

'Quite, Dollery. All in the fullness of time.'

There was an abrupt knock at the door and Ruffage, Captain of the School, strode in. He was elegant, relaxed, sporting a monocle, though his eyesight was perfect.

'Ah, Ruffage,' Hardman crossed to him, 'you've heard about Singh Major?'

The whole school had.

'Niggers, coppers, murder,' jabbered Dollery. 'What's the school coming to?'

'Shut up, Dollery,' Ruffage said. 'Why did you want to see me, Hardman?'

'You're Captain of the School,' Hardman closed to him confidentially. 'You're closer to Nails than anyone. What's to be done?'

Ruffage turned to him. 'Get on with your lessons, Hardman. That's what your old man is paying for.'

There was a murmur of unease rippling the room. Ruffage sensed it and squared his shoulders. 'What do you suggest?' he asked them.

Hardman circled Singh a few times and clapped an uncharacteristic arm around his shoulder. 'Poor old Singh's brother has been murdered, Ruffage. Here, at Rhadegund's. The Sikh code of honour, not to mention Rhadegundian honour, demands a life for a life.'

'I'm a Christian,' mumbled Singh.

'All the better, old chap,' Hardman hissed through grated teeth. 'You will know that in the Good Book – ours, not yours – it says "an eye for an eye and a tooth for a tooth" . . . '

'Ah, but ecumenically— '

'Shut up, Dollery!' the room re-echoed.

'That's all very well,' Ruffage stood his ground, 'but even assuming for one moment I go along with your somewhat misplaced code of ethics, who had you in mind? Whose eye and tooth are you after?'

Hardman clapped Singh heartily and sighed. Then he broke away, staring out of the window to where Lestrade was crossing the quad below. 'What about that policeman chappie?' he asked quietly. The murmurs dropped to silence.

'That would be unlucky, Hardman,' Dollery said. The House prefect whirled on the lesser boy and snapped, 'Dollery, you are henceforth banned from this study. Any further disobedience will merit a flogging. Now get out.'

'Yes Hardman,' and the crestfallen crony left.

'Is it wise to follow this course, Hardman?' Ruffage asked him, pocketing the monocle.

Hardman leaned against the cold stone of the sill. 'I'm not talking about killing him, Ruffage. Just untidying him a little – if that were possible, given his appalling taste in clothes.'

'I don't see where it will lead you,' Ruffage persisted.

'It's a gesture,' said Hardman, 'to show we don't like outsiders sticking their oar in – begging your pardon of course, Singh Minor.'

'What if it lands you in jail?' Ruffage asked. 'This fellow's from the Yard.'

'My father the Field Marshal', Hardman could drop a name like anyone else, 'was in the same regiment as Charlie Warren, Commissioner of the Metropolitan Police. One word from me to him via him about him and Lestrade would be shovelling the horse dung in the Yard.'

Ruffage clicked open the door. 'Leave it at that, then,' he said. 'If you honestly believe we should take care of our own, talk to your father the Field Marshal. Break Lestrade. But, Hardman,' he paused, making sure he had their attention, 'leave it at that. If anything should happen to Lestrade, I shall take it personally,' and he saw himself out, careful to face front the whole time. One didn't turn one's back on Hardman.

An enormously fat boy was lumbering up to the vaulting horse as Lestrade found the gymnasium. Amid cackles and guffaws of delight, he landed squarely on it and the timbers cracked under his weight.

'Get out of it, Eaden, you pathetic misfit!' a field officer's voice barked.

Lestrade followed the sound to an upright, solidly built gentleman, marginally the wrong side of fifty, but trim and with biceps of iron.

'Major Bracegirdle?' the Inspector asked.

'That's me,' The moustaches bristled. 'Who's asking?'

'I am,' said Lestrade, a little non-plussed by the question.

Bracegirdle's moustaches drooped as they invariably did in the presence of true idiocy. Indeed, in his long career at St Rhadegund's, they had scarcely been upright. 'What I mean is,' – the Remove, five of whom were helping the hapless Eaden to his feet, had never seen him so patient – 'to whom am I speaking?'

'Ah, I see. Inspector Lestrade, Scotland Yard.'

Bracegirdle crushed his hand in greeting. 'Yes, of course. Saw you at the lake this morning, fishing Thing Major out of the boat.'

'You saw that?' Lestrade had hoped Nails's intervention would have prevented it.

'Of course. So did half the bloody third form. If Nails were fitter, of course, he'd have headed us off at the stile. Still, there it is. How can I help?'

'I've called at a bad time,' Lestrade observed as seven of the Remove bore Eaden past them like a Viking funeral procession.

'There's never a good time.' Bracegirdle stopped the cortège and tapped the pallid Eaden with a riding crop. 'You'll be all right, boy. Just a few stitches. Smarts, doesn't it? Ovett, take the others on a run, will you – eight times round the lake. Last one back's a cissy.'

Lestrade followed Bracegirdle into the darkness of his locker room. The walls were hung with trophies of the field, hunting and sporting. Various webbing pouches and strappings were piled loosely in a corner and Lestrade was invited to sit on them.

'I understand you didn't care for Singh Major?' the Inspector fished.

Bracegirdle began hanging up boxing gloves and throwing iron bars around. 'Hated him,' he confessed, 'and his insufferable little brother.'

'Is it usual for masters to hate their charges, Major?' Lestrade asked.

'Don't talk to me about charges,' Bracegirdle replied. 'My father, God rest him, was at Chilianwala. There was a charge! Some Sikh bastard shot him in the back.'

'I'm sorry,' said Lestrade. He had had a father too, though there were those at the Yard who doubted it. 'Still, live and let live, eh?'

'Let live? Did the Nana Sahib let the women and children live at Cawnpore? No, he did not, sir! I was there. With Havelock at the relief,' he bent one of the bars in remembrance of it, 'I saw with my own eyes what those little brown bastards did to our women and children. I was up to my spurs in blood, Lestrade, as I stand here. I shall never forget it as long as I live. Savages!' He spat onto the pile of fencing jackets beside Lestrade. 'They'll never be civilised, Lestrade. Not like us.'

'What did you do?' the Inspector asked.

'What any decent Englishman would do.' Bracegirdle stood to his full height. 'I went out and tied the nearest damned nigger I could find to the mouth of a cannon and blew him to pieces!'

Lestrade smiled weakly. It was a silly question really.

'Then, two years ago, Nails allowed the little bastards here at Rhadegund Hall. It defies belief.'

'Perhaps he needs the money,' Lestrade suggested.

Bracegirdle paused. 'Not that much, Lestrade. No one needs money that much.'

'I want to ask you a direct question, Major,' the Inspector said. 'I'd like an honest answer to it.'

'Fire away!'

Lestrade stood up. 'Did you kill Singh Major?'

'No, sir.'

'Did you kill Anthony Denton?'

'No, sir.'

'Did you kill Margaret Hollis?'

'No, sir.'

They were emphatic, old soldier's answers, firm-lipped, iron jawed, clear eyed. If Lestrade was any judge of men at all after his fifteen years on the Force, the man was telling the truth.

'Very well,' he said and rummaged in his pocket. 'What do you make of this?'

He held up the amulet which he had found in Maggie Hollis's hand. Bracegirdle looked closely. 'It's an amulet,' he said, 'with some gibberish written inside it. Was it Singh's?'

'I'm beginning to wonder. Do you know where I might find his brother?'

'From Hell . . . '

Bracegirdle did not know where Singh Minor was. Neither did anybody else. He had been there at breakfast before news of Singh Major broke. No one in his House had seen him, least of all Hardman, the House prefect. Yet Dr Nails had forbidden anyone to leave the grounds. Singh's bed had been made. He ought to have been in mathematics, but Lestrade could understand him wanting to miss that. Besides, he had an appointment with Singh Major.

Matron and the Bursar had laid out the young man in the san. Since Spencer Minor had wisely given the mince a wide berth, Singh was its only occupant. Lestrade thrust his hands in his pockets, circled the naked corpse once, then again. A young man, seventeen or eighteen years of age, handsome in a dark sort of way. No marks on the body, except the bruising around the noose at his throat, the mountaineer's noose. What would Mr Berry make of that? There would be a post mortem of course in a day or two and he would know if Singh had died in the water or in the boat. If he was drowned, why the noose? And if he was hanged, why the boat? And why was he naked? And where were his clothes? And what was his connection with Maggie Hollis, the pregnant laundress? And with Anthony Denton, the young classics master? And why couldn't Lestrade answer any of these questions? A knock at the door produced Matron who in turn produced a welcome face, even if it did belong to Sergeant George.

'Got your telegram, guv'nor,' he grinned. 'Blimey.' He

surveyed what remained of Cherak Singh. 'What's his problem?'

'Whatever it is,' sighed Lestrade, 'it's ours, too. Let's get down to the village. I'll let you buy me a drink.'

Snug in the settle of The Nag's Head Lestrade placed his feet on the firedogs and soaked up the atmosphere of pipe smoke and beer.

'I smuggled this out.' George returned with the pints and unfolded a letter for Lestrade's perusal. The Inspector read it between sips.

'*Dear Boss* . . . who's that?'

'It was addressed to the Central News Office in Fleet Street.'

Lestrade read on: '*I keep on hearing the police have caught me but they wont fix me just yet.*' This writing's grim, George; not yours, is it? *That joke about Leather Apron gave me real fits* . . . so he reads the papers.'

'There's plenty to read. I tell you, sir, there's panic in London. I've never seen anything like it in twelve years on the Force.'

'*I am down on whores* . . . ' Lestrade read on, lowering his voice as he realised an eerie silence had descended on the snug. Even the clock seemed to have stopped ' . . . *and I shant quit ripping them till I do get buckled* . . . Down on whores, George.'

'Yes, sir.'

'What does that mean to you?'

'He doesn't like prostitutes, sir,' was the best the Sergeant could do at short notice.

'Thank you, George,' said Lestrade. 'Remind me to mention you in despatches. *Think*, man.'

'Somebody with a grudge against them, sir.' George was warming up as the beer began to reach various parts Lestrade could not.

'Gladstone?' Lestrade suggested.

'A religious maniac, surely,' George countered.

'Gladstone,' repeated Lestrade, who returned to the letter. '*Grand work the last job was. I gave the lady no time to squeal* . . . who does he mean? When was this posted?' There was no envelope.

'The twenty-fifth ult., sir. That would make it . . . Annie Chapman.'

'*I love my work and want to start again*,' he paused, '*You will soon hear from me with my funny little games.*' He dropped the crumpled paper on the table. 'It's a game to him, George. He's taunting us.'

'Read on, guv'nor. It gets better.'

'*I saved some of the . . . proper red stuff in a ginger beer bottle over the last job to write with but it went thick like glue and I cant use it* . . . ' Lestrade looked at George. The Sergeant shrugged.

'*Red ink is fit enough I hope ha ha. The next job I do I shall clip the ladys ears off and send to the police officers just for jolly wouldnt you* . . . ' Lestrade looked at George again.

'No ears arrived yet, sir. Mind you, I wouldn't like to enquire too closely as to what was in Constable Derry's sandwiches yesterday.'

'*Keep this letter back till I do a bit more work then give it straight out. My knifes nice and sharp I want to get to work right away if I get a chance. Good luck. Yours truly . . . Jack the Ripper.*'

'Yes,' George leaned forward, 'and all this time we've been calling him the Whitechapel murderer.'

But the letter had a postscript. '*Dont mind me giving the trade name wasnt good enough to post this before I got all the red ink off my hands curse it. No luck yet. They say Im a doctor now ha ha.*' Lestrade sat back. 'Why did you bring this?' he asked. 'I've been taken off that case, remember. By the Commissioner, no less.'

'Ah,' George beamed, with the air of a man who keeps his ear to the grindstone, 'but he may not be Commissioner much longer.'

'Oh?' As countless people had realised, Lestrade was all ears.

'They're all after his blood. Except the Ripper, apparently. Every morning paper in the City is demanding Charles Warren's resignation. They say there's a cover-up going on.'

'Do they?' Lestrade had been away from the hub of things for two days. Already he was hopelessly out of touch.

'He's seeing the Queen this very day.'

'I wonder which of them will go?' Lestrade mused.

'Inspector Wensley urged me to bring this, sir,' George told him.

'You were taking a chance, though. This is evidence.'

'Well, we've all got to go sometime.' George was fairly philosophical for a sergeant. 'I think Mr Wensley would appreciate some help, sir.'

'What's Abberline doing? No, don't tell me.' Lestrade perused the letter again. 'First, he made an official complaint to the press for publishing that nonsense about Leather Apron.'

George nodded.

'Then he paid a call at Leman Street Station where the incident happened and shouted at everybody in sight.'

He nodded again.

'Then he investigated proprietors and retailers of ginger beer.'

Another nod.

'Followed by proprietors and retailers of red ink.'

'Spot on!' said George in admiration. 'How did you know that, guv'nor?'

'Oh, just wild guesses,' smiled Lestrade. 'When's he starting on the hospitals and Harley Street?'

'Sir?'

Lestrade quoted again. '*They say Im a doctor now ha ha.*'

'I'm not sure he's had time, sir.'

'Tut, tut. Has Fred Wensley seen this?'

'Yes,' said George.

'What does he think? Is it genuine?'

'He thinks it is, sir.'

Lestrade stood up and walked into a pool of sunshine on the uneven flagstones of the floor. 'That's good enough for me. When are Derry and Toms due?'

'Tomorrow, sir. First train.'

'All right, George. You scratch my back, I'll scratch Fred Wensley's. There are nearly four hundred boys up the road and I want depositions from them all. Derry and Toms can help.'

'Are you sure about that, sir?'

'I like to see wit in a man,' said Lestrade, stonily. 'You'll certainly need it around here. Every word you write, every question you ask will be watched over by the Headmaster, Dr Nails.'

'A doctor, eh?' George was elsewhere.

'Of theology, George,' said Lestrade. 'Don't mix your cases.'

'With respect, guv'nor, isn't that what you're doing?'

'Some have cases thrust upon them,' said Lestrade as he drained his tankard. 'Your shout, I think.'

'Where will you be, sir?'

'Sitting here waiting for it.'

'No, I mean while I'm taking statements.'

'I'd better go and hold Wensley's hand. And George . . . '

'Sir?'

'We may not have Jack the Ripper at Rhadegund Hall, but something is worrying the sheep. Keep your eyes open.' He turned in search of the latrine and collided with a warming pan.

The little old lady sat dozing by the fire in the drawing room. The tall gentleman with the plumed hat cleared his throat forcefully, causing the little old lady to sit bolt upright so that the dog on her lap shook and growled.

'Do you have the ague, Sir Charles?' she asked through pursed lips.

'No, ma'am,' he answered, clicking his boots again, 'I was merely wondering . . . '

'If we were awake? Of course we were. Tell me, these dreadful murders in Whitechapel. Who is behind it?'

'We have our suspects, ma'am. Personally, I favour the Jews.'

'Do you?' the old lady said with some distaste and struggled to her feet so that the dog pounced on Sir Charles's sash ends and proceeded to tear them to shreds.

'Is he worrying you?' she asked.

'Not unduly, ma'am,' the Commissioner of the Metropolitan Police answered, praying the little cur would not cock its leg all over his patent leather, 'but I feel he is disturbing my tassels a little.'

'We must improve the lighting in those mean streets,' she went on, running her chubby little fingers over the marble nose of the Teutonic Hero whose busts adorned every corner. 'We will talk to Mr Matthews. We are not sufficiently gas-and-watered. As for you,' the lugubrious eyes took on a brittle grey in the morning light, the old sparkle still there, glancing from the chandeliers, the mirrors and back again, 'you must improve our detective force. Who is in charge?'

'Chief Inspector Abberline, ma'am.'

'Abberline? Never heard of him.' She paced the floor, resting now and again, leaning on various busts as she went. Charles Warren was aware of various Indian figures hovering in ante rooms. It unnerved him more than the vicious little lap dog chewing holes in his coat tails, snarling and yapping. 'Dear Lord Beaconsfield once told me of a young policeman he had met. Apparently, he was singularly impressed by him. His name was . . . Depraved . . . was that it? No. Deranged? No.'

'Lestrade, ma'am?' Warren was even more unnerved by this time.

'No, I don't believe it was that. However, if it were, is this man still on the Force?'

'Yes, ma'am, but on another case, I fear.'

'Bring him back, Sir Charles. We insist upon it. Lord Beaconsfield was certain this young man would go far.'

'Well, Northamptonshire, anyway,' Warren muttered.

The old lady spun round with an agility rare in one so age crazed. 'Put this Lestrade in charge. Before heads start to roll.'

A clock, in the likeness of the late Prince Albert, chimed the hour. 'Ah, Karim,' she called shrilly and one of the Indian shadows appeared, bowing low, 'is Lord Salisbury without?'

'Yes, madam,' bowed Karim.

'Admit him. And Sir Charles . . . '

'Your Majesty?'

'Is there something the matter with your leg?'

'No, ma'am, merely that your spaniel— '

'Shiztu!' the Queen corrected him.

'Bless you, ma'am,' and the Commissioner left, bowing thrice.

The Inspectors faced each other over mugs of tea. It was something of a red-letter day, not merely because of those purporting to be from the Whitechapel murderer, but because Fred Wensley had come to the Yard without the aid of the wild horses.

'So tell me again,' said Lestrade, unable in his heart of hearts to bear the silence, now that George, Derry and Toms were away at Rhadegund Hall.

'His name's Honeybun. Isaiah Honeybun.'

'God!'

'Perhaps. Or at least His right-hand man. He asked me if I felt I had a vocation.'

'And did you?'

'Not for months. You know how it is. Rest days are a thing of the past.'

Lestrade nodded in agreement. 'And Abberline sent him?'

'No, no. From what I gathered from the Chief Inspector's demeanour at Leman Street yesterday, an invitation from on High is the last thing he wanted. The word is that it was Warren's idea.'

'Oh, well . . . ' Lestrade shrugged, pushing the empty mug away from him, 'that says it all. Where's he come from?'

'Three years in the Post Office. Before that, Cheltenham, man and boy,' Wensley told him.

'Not exactly a walk on the wild side,' mused Lestrade. 'What does he make of this lot, this visiting angel?'

A sharp rap at the door punctuated his question, and a tall, rather sallow man with a clipped moustache and firm jaw strode into the room.

'Would you be Chief Inspector Abberline?' he asked.

'Not for ready money,' Lestrade answered. 'I'm Lestrade. Who are you.'

'Isaiah Honeybun.' He extended a hand. 'Your brother in Christ.'

'Ah, quite.' Lestrade felt his fingers give a little under the muscular grip. 'Late of Cheltenham, I understand.'

'And the Post Office,' Honeybun reminded him.

'Get many mutilations in the Post Office?' Lestrade asked.

Honeybun looked confused.

'What about Cheltenham?' Wensley asked.

'There are sinners everywhere, Inspector,' Honeybun reminded him.

'How true.' Lestrade's face had not yet lost the grin it had taken on at Honeybun's entrance. 'Tea?'

'Thank you, I don't. It leads to indigestion and dims the brain.'

'Of course.' Lestrade flashed a desperate glance at Wensley who suddenly found the rococo ceiling fascinating.

'You do sit down?' Lestrade needed to be reassured.

'Not for long,' said Honeybun. 'If the Almighty had intended us to sit he would not have given us legs. Idle posteriors make idle people.'

'They do indeed. Do you know, Fred, that could have been me talking?'

'Could it, Sholto?' Wensley began to cough uncontrollably and started stuffing his handkerchief in his mouth.

'Are you familiar with the Whitechapel case, Inspector?' Lestrade asked him.

'Please – call me Isaiah. I have perused the shoe-boxes,' Honeybun told him. 'Nasty business, very nasty.'

'The worst I've seen,' Wensley confided.

'I was referring to the shoe-boxes,' said Honeybun. 'Would you like my candid opinion?'

'Of the shoe-boxes?' asked Lestrade.

'The murders,' Honeybun explained.

The Yard men sat and waited. Honeybun reached in his pocket and fished out a Bible. He placed it on the desk and placed a hand on it. ' "Now the serpent",' he said, ' "was more subtil than any beast of the field",' and sat back.

The Yard men looked at each other.

'Isaiah . . . ' Lestrade was first to break the silence.

'Genesis,' Honeybun corrected him.

The Yard men looked at each other again.

' "He did grind in the prison house",' said Honeybun.

'You've got somebody in mind?' Wensley asked, still prepared to be enthusiastic. 'A turnkey? I don't remember reading that in the shoe-boxes.'

' "Where thou lodgest, I will lodge",' countered Honeybun.

'Yes, my sergeant thinks we are looking for a lodger,' said Lestrade, trying valiantly to follow the man from Cheltenham.

' "Elijah passed by him, and cast his mantle upon him",' Honeybun was in his element.

Wensley glanced at Lestrade. 'This Elijah is an accomplice?'

'Gentlemen!' Honeybun smiled, holding up the Book. 'It is all in here. All the answers we will ever need.'

'Yes, but— ' Lestrade began.

' "Who will find a virtuous woman"?' asked Honeybun.

'I've been trying for years,' muttered Wensley.

'Our man, gentlemen,' Honeybun leaned forward as though

the new hat rack had ears, 'is a Policeman. Possibly over-zealous, but a policeman nonetheless.'

'He's killed all four?' Lestrade asked.

' "One event happeneth to them all",' Honeybun answered him.

'How can we catch him?' Wensley asked.

' "As a dog returneth to his vomit, so a fool returneth to his folly".'

'Honeybun!' Lestrade roared, slamming his fist down so that Inspectors and mugs jumped in all directions. 'Do you think you could give us a straight answer *without* quoting the scriptures?'

Honeybun looked shocked. The thought had never occurred to him. 'Very well,' he said at last, while Wensley sponged his waistcoat. 'For the past day, gentlemen, I have been patrolling Whitechapel. I have seen them, gentlemen, the People of the Abyss. Little boys barely up to lectern height who steal for a living. Little girls who sell their bodies. Women who are the very dregs of society. Scum. Filth.'

'They're my people,' Wensley said quietly. 'Oh, they're poor, all right. Some of them are bent. Perhaps one of them is the Whitechapel murderer.' He leaned forward to Honeybun, his face ashy grey. Lestrade knew the signs of old. 'But they're not scum, Mr Honeybun. Neither are they filth.'

'I'm afraid I must beg leave to differ,' Honeybun persisted. 'God made them all in His Own Image, I will grant you. But they have turned their backs on Him, Mr Wensley. They have cursed God and they shall die.'

'So you think it's one of our own?' Lestrade asked. The thought, he had to admit, had occurred to him before, and it made him uneasy.

'It's part of our duty, Mr Lestrade. God is working through us to cleanse the world of its excrement. We are His instruments.'

Wensley's fist clenched tight with realisation of what the maniac from Cheltenham was talking about. Lestrade patted his hand, smiling sweetly. 'Do you have anybody in mind?' he asked.

'Not as yet,' said Honeybun, 'but God is with me. Oh,' he scooped out his half-hunter, 'is that the time? I must away to Saint Botolph's. Bellringing. Goodnight, gentlemen. The Lord Make His Face To Shine Upon You,' and he left.

The silence was audible, or it would have been had not Honeybun's vocal cords rendered it otherwise with a rousing 'Onward Christian Soldiers' as he made for the stairs.

'Sholto,' Wensley looked at Lestrade, 'is it me or was that man mad?'

'It's you, Fred. Here.' Lestrade rummaged behind the *Depositions For The Year 1887, Volume XXI* and poured half the contents of a hip flask into Wensley's mug. 'This might dim your brain, but it won't give you indigestion.'

Wensley swigged gratefully. 'But he really means it, Sholto. He sees himself as some sort of avenging angel . . . You don't think it's him, do you?'

Lestrade should have laughed, but he didn't. 'What do you suggest, Fred? We put a man on Inspector Honeybun? And shouldn't we then put a man on that man, just in case? Where would it end? I'd be surveilling myself!'

'Ah, yes,' chuckled Wensley grimly. '*Quis custodiet ipsos custodes*?' He had been to a good school.

'That's easy for you to say.' Lestrade lit them both a cigar. 'Come on, then, let's have it. How's he doing it, this lodging policeman? This Jew who wears a leather apron and drinks ginger beer and writes badly in red ink? How does he kill these women?'

'My guess would be from behind.' Wensley watched the blue smoke rise.

'The coroner's report says from in front. Strangled first or suffocated, and that the murderer has medical knowledge.'

'Well, you've seen more Sights than I have, Sholto,' admitted Wensley, 'but where are the signs of a struggle?

These ladies may have had some gin inside them. It was dark. But even so they'd been around. They could take care of themselves. Not one of them would have taken it lying down.'

'Up against a wall, then?' Lestrade asked.

'For my money,' nodded Wensley.

'I'll forget you said that,' Lestrade beamed.

'Turn round, Sholto.' Wensley clamped his cigar firmly between his teeth and placed his knee in his fellow inspector's back, catching him around the jaw with his left hand and jerking him back.

'Like so,' he said. 'My fingers would leave bruises exactly where we found them on Chapman, Nicholls, Stride and Eddowes, and their throats would have been open to the knife.' He drew his finger across Lestrade's epiglottis.

'Right handed, then?' Lestrade gulped. 'Are you going to put me down?'

'Oh, sorry, Sholto.' Wensley relaxed his grip. 'Got a bit carried away there. Didn't nick you, did I?' He inspected his fingernails.

'I haven't done anything yet,' said Lestrade, 'which reminds me. I've got a visit to make. Fancy a trip upstairs?'

'Special Branch? No thanks. I'd rather go bellringing.'

They had given the Special Irish Branch the whole of the top storey. A little extravagant, perhaps, for seventeen coppers, but with Fenians you couldn't be too careful. Inspector Tobias Gregson did not want another Phoenix Park Murder on his hands and rumour had it that the loft at Scotland Yard was full of pigeons trained to fly swift and true between Gregson and Liverpool and Gregson and Haverfordwest, watching the mail packets from the Emerald Isle and depositing droppings on likely agitators so that they were marked men.

Not a pigeon could be heard, however, as Lestrade entered the loft on that Wednesday morning. Only the erratic click of Gregson's Remington.

'Well, well, Lestrade. We are honoured. Are you lost?'

'No, no,' came the reply, 'just passing through.'

Gregson was a large, square man with greying hair and deep-set eyes that spoke of single-mindedness bordering on obsession. 'You're snooping!' Gregson spat accusingly. A clutch of constables looked up.

'No, no,' Lestrade remained rise-resistant. 'I always walk that way.'

'I hear you're back on the Whitechapel case. Like a bloody yo-yo, eh?'

'Just one of life's little ups and downs.'

'You know it's the Jews, don't you?' Gregson swung away from his desk, pocketing his Waverley.

'Abberline thinks it is, yes.' Lestrade began to bend his already bent neck around various doors.

'I've been working with Athelney Jones,' beamed Gregson.

'Each to his own,' smiled Lestrade.

'We've narrowed it down. Possibility of three foreign ships in the Royal Albert on the nights in question. Each of them with largely Jewish crews.'

'I thought we'd cleared up Leather Apron.' Lestrade paused in his search.

'Ah, that was a false clue, Lestrade. Your old friend Wensley fell for that one, didn't he?'

'So did Abberline.'

'Yes, well, he'd fall for anything, wouldn't he? You and I are men of the world.'

'How many people has Abberline arested so far?' Lestrade asked.

'Up to last Saturday, thirty-eight.'

'Didn't he do well?' Lestrade asked.

'What do you think of this doctor theory?'

'Tobias, I'd love to talk nonsense with you all morning, but unfortunately I have a murderer to catch.' He found the right door and waved goodbye to the Special Branch man. Quietly fuming as he was, under the shock of hair, Gregson kicked a constable and got back to his work.

'Ah, Inspector,' the little man in the corner of the room adjusted the thick-lensed spectacles above his hair-line and stirred his cocoa purposefully with his pencil, 'I think I've got something.'

Lestrade didn't venture too close in case he caught it.

'Do have a seat. This letter of yours— '

'I didn't write it,' Lestrade was quick to assure him.

The boffin's spectacles plummeted down to the bridge of his nose. 'Indeed not,' he said, eyeing Lestrade curiously, 'it was written by a child.'

'A child?' Lestrade wasn't sure he had heard right.

'Various things affect our handwriting, Lestrade, and it's all there in graphology – *graphein*, 'to write'; *logos*, 'discourse'. The state of health of the writer, the emotions, the inner self. Or, of course, external circumstances. When Lord Nelson lost his right arm, for instance— '

'I assume this letter was not written by Lord Nelson?' Lestrade may not have been an expert, but he was no fool.

'Indeed not,' smiled the boffin, 'unless our postal service is rather worse than I feared,' and he emitted a series of donkey-like brays which Lestrade could only assume was laughter.

'You are familiar with M. Michon's definitive *Système de Graphologie*?'

'No.'

'Or the work of Michon's pupil, Crépieux-Jamin?'

'No.'

The boffin sighed. What sort of inspectors were they appointing these days?

'Let's get to business.' The boffin and Lestrade closed over the papers on the desk, the oil-lamp glaring fiercely in the darkened corner. 'No punctuation, do you see?'

'I do,' Lestrade admitted. 'What does that tell us?'

'That the writer is only semi-literate. Or is he?'

'I thought I was asking the questions.'

'A semi-literate would never spell "knife" with a k. And

this quaint phraseology – "real fits", "till I do get buckled", "just for jolly" – it's stage Cockney, Lestrade. Artificial. Nobody in the East End really talks – or writes – like that.'

'So what is your conclusion?'

The boffin shuffled the papers, turned them this way and that. Then he sat back and looked Lestrade in the eye. 'They were written by a male, between the ages of thirteen and twenty-one, of above-average intelligence. He's right handed but has tried to disguise his letters, possibly by taping his fingers together.'

'I see. Well, that's very interesting,' mused Lestrade, drawing back into the shadows. 'That certainly narrows the field down to a few million people.'

'Indeed not,' asserted the boffin, somewhat hurt. 'Your young man is almost certainly attending – or has attended – an English public school and is a Rajput, Jat or just possibly . . . '

But Lestrade had gone, bounding down the rickety stairs past the bewildered Tobias Gregson as fast as his neck could carry him.

' . . . a Sikh!' He finished the sentence for the boffin as he bounded into the lift. The mad jigsaw was beginning to fit.

The three policemen sat in the library, almost certainly the first time in their varied lives that they had been near so many books. Lestrade entered quietly, not wishing to wake them. It was well past midnight and the oil-lamps burned dimly at George's table. Lestrade picked up his reading matter. Depositions. Scores of them by the look of it. The Sergeant had been busy. Snoring next to him, though still acutely at attention in the upright chair, Constable Derry had been dipping into Plutarch's *Lives*. Even in translation he had not got beyond the first page. Constable Toms lounged in a more relaxed manner, his head beside a stone gargoyle that had caught many a schoolboy a nasty one as he rushed, at the sound of the great Rhadegund bell, for the door. Lestrade edged the last volume of Gibbon's *Decline and Fall* from the man's nerveless fingers, only to reveal a rather lurid penny dreadful and American to boot. The author's name was bizarre enough – Ned Buntline – but the title *Wyatt Earp, Frontier Marshal* was totally ludicrous. Lestrade cleared his throat and read aloud, ' "Make your play, Earp"!'

Three policemen leapt to their feet, truncheons akimbo as Lestrade raised an indulgent eyebrow and read on, ' "Earp's Peacemaker roared into life as three-fingered Jake grabbed his Thumb-breaker" . . . I should have thought *Decline and Fall* was more your cup of poison, Toms.'

'Yes, sir, sorry, sir,' the shaken Constable looked pale.

Lestrade threw the Buntline Special onto the table, followed rapidly by the Donegal and bowler.

'Where is Singh Minor?' he asked them.

Derry riffled through his notes, lurking as they had been under Plutarch. 'I didn't talk to him, sir,' he said.

'Toms?'

'No, sir.'

'How many boys have you talked to, George?' Lestrade asked.

'*All* of them' the Sergeant yawned. 'That's why we were less-than wakeful just now, sir. It's been a long few days.'

'Indeed it has.' Lestrade pulled up a chair for himself. 'Was Dr Nails present throughout?'

'Throughout,' grunted George. 'Or another old master, Gainsborough.'

'I had the Chaplain,' said Derry. 'Is he all right, that bloke?'

'Perfectly,' smiled Lestrade. 'It's just that his cousin is Chaplain to the Archbishop of Canterbury, that's all.'

'I had the Bursar,' Toms told him. 'Talk about mean. I had to interview the boys by candlelight after dark. He'd have a fit if he saw us using oil-lamps.'

'And what of Cherak Singh?' Lestrade asked George.

'That's the damnedest thing, guv'nor,' the Sergeant said. 'He's gone to ground. Vanished.'

'Has he now? You've looked?'

'Haven't had time, sir. We've been working round the clock . . . '

'Yes, all right.' Lestrade recognised the onset of a complaint when he heard it. He'd suffered from a few himself, in his time.

'The boys carried out a full search.'

'Did they?' Lestrade looked up. 'On whose instructions?'

'Dr Bloody Nails. That bloke's the end, he really is.'

'Who organised it?' Lestrade asked.

'Mercer the Bursar.'

'And no luck?'

The three policemen shook their heads.

'Why the interest in Singh, sir?' Toms asked. 'Is he involved in this case, do you think?'

'In this case?' Lestrade pulled out a cigar. 'I don't know, but I think he's involved in my case.'

'*Your* case, guv'nor?' queried George.

'All right.' Lestrade misunderstood the inflection. 'Abberline's case. The Whitechapel murders.'

'Whitechapel?' the three policemen chorused.

'Seems to be an echo in here.' Lestrade threw glances around the panelled walls from which long-dead headmasters glanced back.

'How?' George asked.

'When I first came to this school,' Lestrade blew smoke rings to the ceiling, 'Singh Minor was the first lad I met. His East End patter was astonishing. Spoke it like a native, he did.'

'How come?'

'That's what I'd like to find out. There's a connection with Whitechapel, there's got to be.'

'Well, it's odd, I'll grant you,' George ruminated, 'but it's pretty flimsy, sir.'

'It would be, George, were it not for the fact that I

think Singh Minor – or perhaps Singh Major – wrote the letter you smuggled out for me.'

'What? The one signed "Jack the Ripper"?'

Lestrade nodded.

'Do you mean the little nigger minstrel is the Whitechapel murderer?' Derry asked, feeling the hairs on the nape of his military neck crawling.

'I mean nothing of the sort, Constable,' said Lestrade. 'But that lad knows more than he's letting on. Mind you, he's not exactly letting on anything at the moment, is he?'

'Dollery!' Toms suddenly shouted.

'Stub your toe?' Lestrade asked.

'Sergeant, let me see the depositions. Number one-o-six if I remember right.'

Lestrade and George exchanged glances. Neither of them for a moment intended to let Toms know they were impressed. The Constable riffled through the pages. 'Here,' he said after a moment's riffling, 'Dollery, T.U.R.D.'

'What?' Lestrade asked.

'His initials, sir. Thomas Ulric Rufus Dollery.'

'Dollery Dollery?' George grunted in disbelief.

'That's the public schools for you,' sighed Lestrade, never quite able to shake off the stigma of Mr Poulson's Academy, Blackheath. 'Almost as bad as George George. What about him?'

'He was decidedly nervous, sir,' explained Toms. 'Chewed his nails a lot.'

'Ah,' murmured George. 'Perhaps he's been lighting up behind the temporary buildings.'

'Or meeting Matron in the shrubbery,' Derry suggested.

Lestrade read Dollery's statement. He looked up at Toms. 'He carried a rabbit's foot?' The Inspector's eyes narrowed.

'And held it in front of him throughout our little chat, sir,' said Toms. 'Sort of stroking it, he was.'

'What did the Bursar make of it?'

'He didn't comment at the time, but when I asked him

afterwards he said Dollery was a rum type, given to solitary vices.'

'Ah,' nodded Lestrade, 'and when you asked about the Singhs?'

'He became very agitated, sir, twisting the foot around his fingers like his life depended on it.'

'All right, Toms – and good work to remember, by the way – I'll talk to young Dollery in the morning. Gentlemen,' he stood up, 'it's been a long day and tomorrow will be worse. I want every inch of these grounds combed for Cherak Singh. We meet at dawn,' he made for the door, 'and Toms . . . '

'Sir?' The Constable was on his feet.

Lestrade drawled in what he imagined to be an American accent, 'Better pack your thumb-breaker.'

The guffaws died in the darkness.

It was a little before three that Lestrade heard it. At first it was part of his dream. He was back at Poulson's Academy again and the Great Man was bending over him shouting, 'Remember, boy, when you stand for the Queen, put your hands down your trousers!' The clanging in his head was the dinner gong, the nourishing oxtail broth that old Mrs Poulson daily served and reserved. True, it may have seen a few tails in its time – and could no doubt tell a few as well – but it had been no nearer to an ox than the floor of a cowshed. But the smell in Lestrade's nostrils was not the broth. It was more acrid. Penetrating. The spotted dick? No, it was smoke. And as he sat bolt upright the clanging in his head became the Rhadegund bell, Ruffage whirling the great rope for all he was worth. There was a crackling and a fierce glow outside his attic window and a frantic knocking at his door.

'Mr Lestrade, sir, the library's on fire.'

The Inspector hauled his Donegal over his nightshirt and yanked open the door. A dishevelled George stood there, quaking.

'Come on, man.' Lestrade rushed past him. 'Get Derry and Toms. It'll be all hands to the pumps.'

He reached the top of the stairs and somersaulted gracefully down them, bouncing off each landing with an agility rare in a man whose neck was already several degrees to larboard.

'Are you all right, sir?' George reached the bottom more slowly, having come down in the conventional manner.

'Of course,' snorted Lestrade, his pride among the things that were dented. 'Have you never seen the Yard Fire Roll?' he bluffed. 'Remind me to show it to you sometime.'

They raced across the quadrangle, already scurrying with boys of all ages in flapping nightshirts and caps. Flames shot skyward from the Victorian Gothic shell of the library, spitting and cracking in their greed for the fan-vaulted timbers and the stars. Over the panic and the noise one voice was louder, calmer. Dr Nails, haughty in scarlet bed-cap and matching slippers strode among the boys like a Colossus.

'You, boy, stop snivelling. We only allow men at Rhadegund. Remind me to expel you tomorrow. Ruffage, form a chain, man. Good, good. Rally on me, Rhadegundians. Rally! Rally!'

Lestrade collided briefly with Bracegirdle and heard the games master mutter, 'Listen to him! Thinks he's umpiring a tennis match!'

As Derry and Toms snatched buckets and passed them hand over hand along Ruffage's thin white line, the Chaplain emerged on a parapet overhead, bawling incantations at the conflagration.

'That's what you call a hellfire sermon,' George muttered to Lestrade.

'Ah, Lestrade.' The Headmaster had caught them with their trousers off. 'Glad you chaps are lending a hand, but we can manage. Saunders-Foote!' He hauled the little Latin master to a standstill before him. 'Who have you sent for the Brigade?'

'Er . . . Adelstrop,' Saunders-Foote dithered.

'Adelstrop! You blithering idiot!' Lestrade thought Nails was going to fell the man on the spot. 'He's got a wooden leg. Rome could burn down before he reached anybody. Where's young Snitterfield? A music master should be able to handle a gig.'

'Don't bother, Head,' Bracegirdle reached him at this point, 'the library will have gone by the time he hitches the horse. I'll run.'

'Splendid, Major, splendid. Take young Ovett with you.'

'He's got one of his off days, Head,' Bracegirdle told him, and made for the drive, the Bursar running with him part of the way, carrying his coat.

While the human chain fought doggedly into the dawn, exhorted every second by the Headmaster, and Matron and her staff helped the walking wounded to the san, overcome by exhaustion and smoke, the flames died back. In the light of day it was like a battlefield. Water, buckets and boys lay everywhere. Nails and Lestrade, like a General and his Chief of Staff, walked in the charred timbers that had once been Rhadegund's great library.

'Damnedest thing,' Nails muttered, strangely muted now he was so hoarse from a night of shouting. 'The Brigade not coming. I'll play merry Hell with Bracegirdle when I see him.'

'Oh my God!' Lestrade stumbled over something, hardly a rare occurrence.

'What's the matter?' Nails asked.

Lestrade squatted over the coals. 'It's a body,' he said.

'A body in the library?' Nails was incredulous. 'Whose?'

Lestrade prodded the blackened corpse with his Apache knife, turning the charcoaled limbs this way and that. 'It's a boy,' he said, and then crouched lower, sifting the area under what had been the trunk. He fished out a little black metal container, curiously wrought. He tried the top. It would not unscrew, fused as it had been in the heat. But he knew what it was. He had seen a similar one, not long ago, in the drowned hand of Maggie Hollis, the laundress.

'Fire and Water,' he mused aloud.

'Eh?'

'Nothing, Headmaster. Merely the elements of a classic mystery.'

'Who was the boy, do you know? We must hold a roll call at once.'

'Yes, do,' Lestrade stood up. 'If you're a betting man, Dr Nails . . . '

The Headmaster looked horrified.

' . . . you'll put your money on Cherak Singh Minor.'

Barnaby and Burgho

Constable Toms had succumbed to the smoke as he fought the blaze in the library. He was resting now in the san, acutely embarrassed at being in the same dormitory as so many toffee-nosed children. It was no consolation to them or him that Mr Saunders-Foote, the classics master, was in there too. In Matron's opinion he was suffering from nervous exhaustion. The death of Denton had hit him hard and the fire was the last straw. He lay shivering and mumbling in a bed behind a screen partition erected by Matron and her ladies.

'How is my constable?' Lestrade asked the Nightingale of St Rhadegund's.

'He'll be all right,' she said. 'Is that neck of yours still giving you trouble?'

'No,' said Lestrade, to whom the slanted view had become yet another of life's little hazards, 'it only hurts when I stand like this.'

He did so and winced. Matron sat him down and began to apply supple fingers to his back. The Inspector felt his spine tingle. 'Have a care, Matron,' he said, nodding in the direction of the beds. 'We're in mixed company.'

'Oh.' She cuffed him playfully around the head with a towel. 'Sit back, Mr Lestrade and think of England.'

He did so, but it was a dark corner of England that crept into his mind.

'May I ask you something?' she said suddenly.

He raised a hand in acquiescence.

'Is this fire connected with the . . . deaths?'

Lestrade felt his neck tensing again despite the warmth of the nurse's fingers. 'Let's say the game of hide and Sikh is over,' he said.

'Is that what it is, Inspector?' She stared at the back of his head. 'A game?'

'Lestrade!' The bedpans jumped and rattled as Dr Nails crashed into the san.

'Stand by your beds,' shouted a lad nearest the door and pyjamaed boys tumbled to attention.

'You're not on the parade-ground now, Montgomery. There's a time and place. Matron, put the Inspector down. I need him,' and he swept back through the door.

'The Headmaster's Voice,' wailed Saunders-Foote behind his curtain and lapsed into delirium again.

'Tell me, Matron.' Lestrade was fastening his studs. 'Have you found his bottle yet?'

Matron looked shocked. 'Mr Saunders-Foote?' she gasped. 'Never!'

'I fear so,' said Lestrade. 'Try his gown. Inside pocket. Left side.'

Matron vanished behind the screen in a flurry of disbelief, anxious to prove the Inspector wrong. She returned with a bottle, empty.

'How did you know?' she asked, suddenly aware of the boys and consigning it to the bin.

'Ah, years of experience,' smiled Lestrade. He glanced at the label. 'Teacher's, I see.'

Matron hurried to him, pressing his arm. 'Come back tonight . . . if you can. Turn left at the top of the stairs.'

'Lestrade!' Nails was not a man to be kept waiting.

The Inspector looked deep into the clear blue eyes of the angel of the san. 'Left at the top of the stairs,' he repeated and followed his calling.

Carman, the under groundsman, sat perched on the Rhadegund trap. Top-hatted within it was a pompous, fierce-eyed individual who reminded Lestrade of Lord

Shaftesbury. Nails was perfunctory in his introductions, as they climbed aboard. 'Lestrade, Gainsborough, my Second Master. Gainsborough, Lestrade.'

The Second Master grunted and Carman applied his whip, the Rhadegund trap spinning out across the gravel drive in the leaden morning towards the line of elms which marked the road.

'May I ask where we are going?' Lestrade buttoned his Donegal against the inclemency of the October weather.

Nails turned to Gainsborough, then to Carman. 'There's a shilling in it if your customary deafness should return,' he said to the driver.

'Eh, sir?' Carman replied, his whip hand snaking backwards to accept the proffered coin.

'Right. Bracegirdle's dead,' said Nails.

'Bracegirdle?' Lestrade repeated.

'Corps Commandant and physical training wallah,' Gainsborough explained.

'Yes, I know,' said Lestrade. 'How did he die?'

'Good God, man,' thundered Nails, 'I don't keep a dog and bark myself. You're the professional, dammit. You tell me.'

'Where is the body?'

'Whoa!' Carman hauled at the reins and the Rhadegund hack skidded to a halt.

'Over there,' Gainsborough pointed.

The three men alighted and waded through the gusting leaves to a clearing above the stream. Major Bracegirdle lay on his back, staring sightlessly at the sky. An ornate officer's sword jutted from his chest.

'My God,' muttered Nails. 'How many more of them?'

'Who found him?' Lestrade asked.

'I did,' said Gainsborough, 'on my morning constitutional.'

'Didn't I see you in the quad last night, coping with the fire?' Lestrade asked.

'I did my bit,' Gainsborough confessed. 'Why?'

'After a night like that, which you'll agree was a little out of the ordinary, you still took a walk?'

'Boys are creatures of habit, Lestrade,' Gainsborough told him. 'Most of them unpleasant. And so indeed are we. After all, what are we but overgrown boys?'

Nails and Lestrade looked at each other. Clearly, they neither of them fully accepted that premise.

'What time did you find the body?' Lestrade mechanically checked the ground around Bracegirdle. If there were tracks there once, they were gone now under the swirling leaves and the swirling winds.

'Oh, half-past eight or so, I was on my way back. Chapel isn't until nine-thirty on Fridays. All was well after the fire. I didn't think I'd be missed.'

Lestrade knelt beside the body. Stiff. Cold. A thin film of dew coated the bluish lips and matted the hair. The little moustache bristled no more.

'When did you see the Major last?' Lestrade glanced up at Nails.

'Same time as you did. When he offered to fetch the Fire Brigade. No wonder the blighters didn't turn up. I was all set to horse-whip the lot of them.'

'Mr Gainsborough?'

'I believe I saw him fighting the fire, like everybody else,' the Second Master replied. 'I must admit I wasn't paying much attention to him.'

'What is this?' Lestrade pointed to the murder weapon.

'It's the Rhadegund Sword of Honour,' said Nails, soberly. 'Awarded each year to the most promising cadet. If you look at the hilt it bears the Rhadegund crest . . . '

Lestrade held back the man's arm and gingerly lifted the blade from the deceased's ribcage. Brown blood had congealed a third of the way from the tip.

'What are these names on the blade?' He pointed to a series of engraved scrolls.

'The recipients of the sword,' explained Nails. 'That nearest the point is the most recent.'

Lestrade read the name. 'So the sword is currently carried by Master Ruffage? Isn't he your . . . ?'

'My Captain of School? Yes. Look, Lestrade, this is nonsense. I know Ruffage like my own right arm. Ruffages have been at Rhadegund for centuries.'

'And how did he get on with Major Bracegirdle?'

'That's an offensive question!' snapped Nails.

'Headmaster, we must face facts.' Gainsborough was calmer: 'As bearer of the sword, Ruffage was one of three people who had access to it. The others were Bracegirdle and . . . '

'And?' Lestrade rose slowly.

'And myself,' said Nails, thereby saving Gainsborough the embarrassment of implicating his headmaster. 'And, before you ask, I had nothing against Bracegirdle personally— '

'And impersonally?'

Nails seethed inwardly. 'I do not allow myself to become involved with anyone, staff or boys, in anything other than a professional capacity.'

Lestrade looked at the hard eyes, the antique whiskers. They gave nothing away.

'Then I must talk to young Ruffage,' he said. 'Carman!'

The man on the cab did not move, but remained staring fixedly ahead.

'Would you ask your man to take us back to the school,' Lestrade said to Nails. 'He is to bring my sergeant and constables out here and he is to offer them every assistance. I want to talk to Ruffage and a lad named Dollery, not necessarily in that order.'

'I see,' said Nails.

'And, Headmaster, I intend to see them alone.'

'Do you now?'

'Then I should like to see all your staff.'

'Collectively?' Nails was trying hard to keep his temper in check.

'No,' said Lestrade, making for the trap, 'together would be best.'

*

In the aftermath of the fire, the staff were anxious to continue as though nothing had happened. To that end, lessons were as normal, though Ruffage and Ovett had to take over Bracegirdle's Swedish Drill and so it was that while George, Derry and the still-coughing Toms carried the dead Major to the Rhadegund trap and laid him down under a pile of Matron's blankets, Lestrade used Gainsborough's study to interview Dollery, T.U.R.D.

'How well did you know Cherak Singh Major?' he asked the lumpish blond-haired boy, sitting on the edge of Gainsborough's chair in front of him.

'Not very,' he said. 'He wasn't in my House.'

'Presumably, neither was his brother?'

'No.' Dollery was clearly ill at ease.

'Atchhhhoooo!' Lestrade suddenly roared as the sneeze surged through him, rocking him momentarily on his heels. 'Excuse me,' he said. 'Must be winter coming.'

'Sorrow,' said Dollery, mournfully, shaking his head. 'Bless you.'

'Pardon?'

'It's Friday, you see. Sneeze on Friday, sneeze for sorrow.'

'Ah . . . tchhhoooo!' Lestrade exploded again.

'A wish,' said Dollery. 'Bless you.'

'Bless *you*,' said Lestrade. 'I see it's catching,' and he sneezed again.

'Bless you. Three times,' said Dollery. 'You will receive a letter.'

'Well, that's a fairly safe bet.'

'You sneeze to the left, sir,' Dollery moaned.

'No, not really, it's just that my neck . . . Why, what does that mean?'

'Bad luck.' Dollery whipped out his rabbit's foot, the one Constable Toms had mentioned.

'Do I take it you are superstitious, Mr Dollery?' Lestrade asked.

'Good Lord, no,' Dollery grinned. The effort positively

hurt him. He stroked his rabbit's foot. 'Just careful.'

Lestrade got up and walked round the room, watching the young man from the corner of his eye.

'Margaret Hollis was pregnant,' he said suddenly.

'Oh?' said Dollery. 'Why are you telling me that?'

'Was the child yours?'

Dollery turned crimson. 'Er . . . no . . . I don't know how . . . er . . . no.'

'Whose, then?'

'I don't know.'

Lestrade scanned Gainsborough's shelves. Not a *Police Gazette* in sight.

'Did Mr Denton teach you?'

'No.' Dollery was beginning to tremble.

'Saunders-Foote?'

'Yes. In the Lower Fifths.'

'Did he ever mention Denton to you? Talk about him?'

'No, sir, that would be . . . unprofessional for a master. They don't talk to us. Not in that way.'

'What way?' Lestrade was hounding his man, metaphorically driving him to the wall.

'Well, personally . . . Isn't that what you meant?' Dollery's lip was quivering. Lestrade snatched the rabbit's foot. Dollery lunged for it, crying out, but the Inspector was faster and he bounced the boy's head off Gainsborough's desk. The cry brought Gainsborough's head craning round the door.

'Yes?' hissed Lestrade, pinning the unfortunate boy beneath him.

'Er . . . nothing,' smiled Gainsborough, sensing the delicacy of the situation. 'I thought there was someone with you.' He exited.

'Now.' Lestrade pulled Dollery's arms as the boy snatched the air for the rabbit's foot, and hauled them across the desk and resumed his position in the chair. 'I don't usually resort to violence, young Dollery, but you know something. What?'

Dollery twisted his fingers in Lestrade's grip so that his thumb was erect between them.

'What's that?' The Inspector asked.

'A fig,' hissed Dollery, 'to ward off the evil eye.'

Lestrade let him go. He allowed the boy to sit up again and to blow his nose. Then he ostentatiously lit a cigar and held his lucifer to the rabbit's foot.

'No!' Dollery lunged again, but Lestrade whirled away and held it at arm's length.

'Who put Singh Minor's body in the library?' he rapped.

'I don't know,' sobbed Dollery. 'I swear, I don't know.'

'He was missing for three days. You know where he was, don't you?'

'No.'

Lestrade applied the flame, hoping Dollery would crack before his fingers roasted. The smell of burning rabbit and burning Lestrade were both reaching his nostrils.

'All right!' Dollery crumpled into a heap on the floor. 'All right.'

Lestrade blew out the match gratefully and waited, facing the window and dipping his fingers surreptitiously into a vase of flowers.

'Ask Hardman,' Dollery whispered. 'Please, I can't say any more. Ask Hardman.'

Lestrade riffled through George's depositions on Gainsborough's desk. 'Hardman, O.G.W.,' he checked.

Dollery nodded.

Lestrade threw the foot to the pathetic heap whimpering in the corner. He leaned over the desk and blew smoke into the young man's face. 'All I know about superstitions,' he said, 'is that if you tread in shit, that will bring you good luck. But it must be your left foot and it must be by accident.'

Dollery nodded, momentarily impressed with Lestrade's sagacity, despite his fright.

'A lot of people round here,' said Lestrade, stepping over him, 'appear to be wading through their own.'

Evening descended early on the Gothic turrets of Rhadegund,

made even more irregular now by the weird charred columns that marked the library, black and gaunt against the stars. Lestrade stood before the fire, careful of course not to stand too close, in the Senior Common Room. Before him was ranged an odd, ragbag collection of misfits, a jumble of those who, in the phrase of a young Irish playwright totally unknown to Lestrade, could not and had therefore taught. A few the Inspector recognised. He had talked to them already. Tucked away in a corner, embarrassed by the yardage of academic gown, overawed by the presence of pedagogy, sat the three wise men: George, Derry and Toms.

'Gentlemen, I believe that Inspector Lestrade has something to say to you,' bellowed Nails, thereby reducing the room to silence. 'In view of the seriousness of the situation I have allowed him to address you. Inspector.'

Lestrade took a pace forward. 'Gentlemen. It will come as no surprise to you, I feel sure, that my men and I are investigating what began as one murder – that of Margaret Hollis the laundress, found drowned in the school laundry at the end of September. That inquiry developed into a second – the death of your colleague Anthony Denton . . . '

Saunders-Foote began sobbing quietly.

'I'll take him out, Headmaster,' said the Bursar, helping the little old classics master to the door.

'Cherak Singh Major was then found in a boat on the lake, followed by his brother, whose corpse Dr Nails and I discovered in what was left of the library. Only this morning, Mr Gainsborough came across the body of Major Bracegirdle.'

The room was stunned into a silence at once academic and electric.

'That makes five deaths in as many weeks, gentlemen.'

'Bravo!' shouted a voice from a corner.

'Sir?' Lestrade turned to face it.

'Honeycombe, mathematics master,' the florid little man announced. 'Your addition is admirable, Inspector, but what of your detection?'

'We are making some headway, sir,' Lestrade bluffed.

'What?' Clearly Honeycombe was not a man to mince his words.

Lestrade tried a long-shot. He crossed pensively to Gainsborough. 'You found Major Bracegirdle?' he asked.

'You know I did,' said the Second Master, wondering to what depths of idiocy Lestrade was descending now. 'You just told everybody.'

'While out for a morning walk?'

'Yes.'

Lestrade turned to the colleagues. 'Gentlemen, please raise your hands if you were aware of the fact that Mr Gainsborough habitually takes morning walks.'

Colleague looked at colleague. One or two tentative hands rose.

'Look here— ' began Nails, but Lestrade raised a hand to silence him.

'How many, George?' he asked.

The Sergeant stood up to get a good vantage point. 'Are you voting, sir?' he asked, and instantly regretted it as Lestrade's hand fell and his eyes raked him, ripping the metaphorical stripes off George's sleeve. 'Six, sir.'

'Six.' Lestrade spun round to Gainsborough again. 'Six, out of . . . '

There was a pause while George counted again, during which there were murmurings and shufflings and cries of 'Oh, really!'

'Twenty-nine, sir,' said the Sergeant, refusing to be hurried.

' . . . twenty-nine,' Lestrade repeated. 'Odd, Mr Gainsborough, that so few of your colleagues know of this habit of yours.'

'What are you trying to say?' Gainsborough demanded, steam beginning to hiss from his ears.

'That you are not an habitual walker. That the very least likely time the Second Master of a school would walk out for fresh air and relaxation is after a night of horror in which his library burned down and a boy died.'

'I explained that.' Gainsborough was shouting.

'Yes, and not very convincingly,' Lestrade shouted back. 'What you did not explain was that you saw Bracegirdle leave the buildings last night in search of the Fire Brigade. You saw your chance. Alone in the darkness you followed him, but not before you took the opportunity of implicating someone else – Ruffage, the Head Boy – by stealing his sword. You overtook Bracegirdle in the darkness and ran him through.'

'Overtook Bracegirdle?' Gainsborough laughed. 'He may have been the wrong side of fifty, Lestrade, but he was a fitter man than I. And what was my motive?'

'Stop it, Gainsborough,' Nails interrupted. 'Lestrade, you go too far.'

'Oh no, Headmaster,' Lestrade turned on him. 'Not nearly far enough.'

Sergeant George recognised the signs. Lestrade with his dander up, going for the throat.

'This is eighteen eighty-eight, Dr Nails,' the Inspector said.

'Indeed it is,' the Headmaster replied. 'So what?'

'So I am surprised that Rhadegund Hall does not have a telephone machine.'

'I must take the blame there, Inspector.' Mercer the Bursar had returned from comforting Saunders-Foote. 'The infernal cost of the thing, you see. Astronomical.'

'So must I,' another voice sounded. 'Rutherford, science master. They are not good for one. The resonance in the earpiece can cause deafness. That's been scientifically proven. The speaking tube has a tendency to harbour bacteria thereby rendering the speaker open to infection.'

'And what is your reason, Headmaster?' Lestrade asked.

'Newfangled nonsense, that's what. Lestrade, where is all this getting us?'

'It got Bracegirdle murdered,' Lestrade said flatly. 'If

you'd had a telephone installed you could have rung the Brigade last night. And Bracegirdle and Cherak Singh Minor would both have been alive.'

'Stuff and nonsense,' argued Nails. 'You're clutching at straws, Lestrade.'

The Inspector circled the carpet a few times. 'Then, of course, there was Denton, strangled by Saunders-Foote . . .'

'What?' The whole room was on its feet.

'How dare you, Lestrade?' Nails thundered. 'The old fellow may be slightly . . . how shall I put it? . . . not as other men . . .'

'Avuncular, Headmaster,' Mercer suggested.

'Quite so. Avuncular. And it is true I may not have strictly approved of his avuncularism, but to suggest that Saunders-Foote is a murderer is preposterous. What would be his motive? You've seen how devastated he is.'

'Oh yes, thereby making the motive all the more obvious. Why did he not report the matter to anyone? Denton died at lunchtime. The first person Saunders-Foote told was me – in the evening,' said Lestrade. 'Sit down, gentlemen, I beg you, and let me ask you to picture the scene. Mr Denton arrives from Oxford, fresh faced, bright eyed. He falls into the . . . avuncular? . . . clutches of Mr Saunders-Foote whose advances the young man rejects. Saunders-Foote is hurt, devastated even, to be rebuffed. In a fit of jealous rage, he strangles Denton and throws his body into the river.'

'Jealous rage? Advances?' Nails was purple. 'I won't have it said— '

'Come now, Headmaster, we are all men of the world.' Lestrade glanced at Spooner. 'Or at least I am. Words cannot frighten us.'

'How could Denton have been overpowered by Saunders-Foote?' Gainsborough asked. 'Any more than I could have outrun Bracegirdle?'

'What's your point?' Lestrade asked.

Gainsborough closed to him, then took his place, centre

carpet. 'Headmaster, gentlemen, I don't say this lightly. God knows, it goes against all I've ever stood for, but, Lestrade, look to the boys.'

'Any boys in particular?'

Gainsborough looked at Nails, who slowly raised his head. 'Ovett could outrun Bracegirdle,' he said.

'And Eaden had a grudge against him,' Gainsborough said. 'I shouldn't say it of a departed colleague, but Bracegirdle was a beast.'

'Unlike Temple of Rugby,' nodded Nails, half to himself, 'just a beast.'

'And he didn't like Indians,' Lestrade said, in the same contemplative tone. 'But then, Reverend Spooner, neither do you.'

'Eh?' The Chaplain shot up off his chair.

'When we first met, you told me you disapproved of Dr Nails introducing our brethren of the Empire to Rhadegund.'

'Spooner? Is this true?' Nails lowered.

'Only in the broadest sense, Headmaster. I am, as you know, coyal to the lause of education. And the honour of the school.'

'I see,' said Nails, which mystified Lestrade still further.

'And, of course,' the Inspector said, 'two of the victims were black. Then again,' he patted the Chaplain's ample shoulder and admired the bull neck above the dog-collar, 'it would have taken a powerful man to deliver that sword thrust through Bracegirdle's body and to strangle young Denton. I suspect Maggie Hollis and the boys were rather easier. Muscular Christianity I think you called it when you pole-axed Mrs Shuttlecomb the laundress. How is she, by the way, George?'

The Sergeant consulted his book. 'A vegetable, sir,' he said.

'Thank God she's recovered,' sighed Spooner. 'Headmaster, I must protest. Faunders-Soote is innocent. He kept the death of Denton to himself because he feared your wrath. He panicked. Knew not which way to turn.'

Nails held up both hands. 'I will do the protesting, Chaplain. Lestrade, had I known that the purpose of this little charade was to harangue and hound my staff, I would never have allowed it. You have falsely accused several of my colleagues tonight, not to mention sullied the honour of the school.' He controlled himself with the experience that came of years of dealing with children infinitely more stupid than he was. 'You have my word for it that your head will roll. I do not need a telephone to get you off this case. I will merely point my head in the direction of London and shout.'

Lestrade could believe it. With Nails and Gainsborough at their head, one by one and two by two the Rhadegund Senior Common Room filed out, all except Mercer.

'How is Saunders-Foote?' Lestrade asked him.

'Inconsolable,' the Bursar said. 'You know, Lestrade, I'm not like the others. I'm not a master, you see, so I view things perhaps in a different light.'

'If your light is any brighter than mine, Mr Mercer, I'd be grateful to share it,' Lestrade sighed.

The Bursar got up. 'I was in the library last night,' he said.

'Indeed?' Lestrade's ears pricked up.

'In fact I entered by the west door as you gentlemen left by the east.'

'May I ask what you were doing there at that hour?'

'I couldn't sleep, what with all this business. I think we're all a little on edge recently. I came to get a book.'

'And?'

Mercer produced a slim volume from his pocket. 'While browsing, I came across this. It sounded familiar.'

He handed it to Lestrade, who read the embossed letters: ' "The P . . . Proc . . . " '

'Proximae Accessit, for the best all-rounder in the Upper Fifths. Won, I seem to remember, by Timothy Porpoise in that year,' Mercer said. 'Not the prize, the title. On the spine.'

Lestrade flipped the book over. '*Thuggee. Its Practices and Incidence*,' he read.

'Page five,' Mercer told him.

Lestrade stiffened, causing his neck to lock again.

'What is it, sir?' George asked.

'Mr Mercer has told us how Margaret Hollis, Anthony Denton and Cherak Singh Major died,' he said. 'They were killed by a thuggee knot. "The thuggees",' he read, ' "were a fraternity of murderers and robbers who strangled unsuspecting travellers with a noose, turban or handkerchief. Their secret jargon was called *Ramasi* and their patroness was Kali, the Hindu Goddess of Destruction".'

'Does that help you, Mr Lestrade?' Mercer asked.

'Er . . . I feel sure it does, Mr Mercer, yes. But just now I'm not quite clear how.'

'Yours, I think.' Lestrade threw the Rhadegund Sword of Honour onto the floor where it clattered and then lay still.

'The Devil, copper,' snarled a young man by the fire.

'It's all right, Partridge. I've been waiting for the Inspector to call.'

'You're Ruffage?' asked Lestrade.

'I am.'

'I'd like to talk to you. Alone.' He lashed Partridge with a look that was guaranteed to freeze blood. Even so, the boy did not move until he got the nod from Ruffage.

Lestrade sat down uninvited. 'So you're the Bearer of the Sword?' he asked.

'For this year, yes,' said Ruffage. 'I go up to Cambridge next October.'

'Or down from the Drop,' said Lestrade.

Ruffage raised an elegant eyebrow. 'I know the Sword ended up through old Bracegirdle,' he said. 'The whole school does, but what I don't know is how it got there.'

Lestrade looked hard at the handsome young man before him. Arrogant, clever, athletic, loaded with honours.

'I know you're arrogant, clever, athletic, loaded with honours,' he said. 'What I don't know is if I can trust you.'

'It's true I was Victor Ludorum,' smiled Ruffage, 'but I don't know about the clever bit. As for arrogance, you're probably right, it's in the blood of the Ruffages. My great-grandfather was first into the breaches of Badajoz, you know.'

Lestrade was unprepared for the change of name. He'd get George to check on this Ludorum back at the Yard. But he really wasn't interested whose trousers Ruffage's great-grandfather had worn. He leaned forward and offered the Captain of the School a cigar.

'Havana?' Ruffage asked.

'Of course.'

'Then I will.' He popped it into his blazer pocket. 'Better smoke it later, when the oiks are in bed.'

'I'll be frank, Mr Ruffage,' said Lestrade. 'Five people are dead at this school. I need an ally before there are six.'

'And you've chosen me.'

'Among the boys, yes.'

'And among the staff?'

'That's my business,' smiled Lestrade, lighting up.

Ruffage nodded. 'I hope you've chosen well,' he said.

Lestrade leaned forward again. 'So do I,' he said.

Ruffage looked at the papers spread on his desk. 'What do you know about Tacitus?' he asked.

'Would that be Tacitus of the Remove?' Lestrade couldn't really remember the name from George's depositions.

Ruffage smiled. 'All right, Mr Lestrade, you need help. What can I do?'

'First,' Lestrade pointed to the sword, still lying where he had thrown it, 'I want to clear up that little matter. When did you last see it?'

'Thursday,' Ruffage told him. 'Corps Parade is every Thursday morning, from reveille until luncheon.'

'You wear the Sword every Thursday?'

'Yes.'

'And where is it kept?'

'In the Corps Hut. Hardman brings it to me.'

'Hardman?' Bells began to tinkle in Lestrade's ears. 'I was told only Major Bracegirdle, the Headmaster and you had access to it.'

'Perfectly true, Inspector, but I give my keys to Hardman at reveille who fetches it from the Corps Hut.'

'Why?'

Ruffage chuckled. 'One of our rather silly traditions. Rhadegund must seem a little quaint to outsiders . . . oh, meaning no disrespect, of course. You see, next year's Bearer of the Sword within the Corps is always chosen a year in advance. When I'm gone, it will be Hardman's turn. He will be senior cadet under . . . whoever they appoint. As such, it is his duty to bear the sword to the Bearer. Silly, isn't it?'

'And is it also his duty to return it?'

'At luncheon, yes. I give him the key again.'

'And this happened as usual this Thursday?'

'Yes, of course.'

'So you have no way of knowing whether Hardman actually returned the Sword?'

Ruffage frowned. 'Well, no, I suppose not . . . Look here, you don't suspect Hardman, surely?'

Lestrade leaned back in his chair. 'Why not?'

Ruffage thought for a moment. 'The sword is circumstantial, surely? It's not hard evidence, as you chappies say.'

'I thought you were my ally.' Lestrade blew blue rings to the panelled ceiling.

'So I am,' said Ruffage, 'but not to the extent of ratting on a friend.'

'Hardman is your friend?' Lestrade had been at Rhadegund long enough to form some idea of the tangled web of relationships that characterised the English public school.

'Not exactly,' Ruffage admitted. 'Call it the honour of the school if you like.'

'Ah, you've been talking to the Chaplain,' said Lestrade. 'On second thoughts, perhaps you haven't. You pronounced it properly.'

'You can't expect a chap to peach on his fellows, Lestrade. This is a public school. More than that, it is St Rhadegund's. Anyway, if I had the slightest shred of evidence of any involvement – by Hardman or anyone else – I'd tell you, believe me. But I cannot and will not deal in tittle-tattle.'

'Spoken like a true Rhadegundian,' Lestrade applauded. 'Careless talk may cost lives, Mr Ruffage; it can also save them. If you reconsider, you know where to find me.'

There was a knock at the door and a little boy stood there.

'Well?' said Ruffage.

'Sorry, Ruffage,' the little boy said meekly, 'I've a message for Mr Lestrade.' He handed the Inspector an envelope, and left.

'Well, well,' mused Lestrade, 'so Dollery was right. A letter.'

'What?' Ruffage asked.

'Nothing.' Lestrade opened the envelope. It was the sort of invitation he couldn't resist. 'It appears Hardman wants to see me. In the gymnasium at midnight.'

Ruffage stood up and crossed to Lestrade. 'If you'll take my advice you won't go,' he said.

'Why?' said Lestrade ingenuously.

'Because Hardman won't be alone,' Ruffage told him.

Lestrade smiled. 'Neither will I,' he said.

'Oh, yes,' said Ruffage. 'I'd forgotten your men.'

'No,' Lestrade chuckled. 'Six great plates of meat tramping all over the late Major's floors. That would be unfair to the fabric – and no doubt the honour – of the school. Even so,' he patted his pocket in a gesture Ruffage didn't understand, 'I shan't be alone.'

Lestrade turned left at the top of the stairs. Prefectorial eyes followed him from the photographs on the walls. The 1st XI and the 1st XV were silent witnesses to his approach, clandestine, in the dark. He knocked on the door, below which shone the glow of lamplight. And the lady of the lamp opened it to him.

'Matron,' he said and felt himself being hauled inside.

'Madeleine,' she smiled, 'when I'm off duty.'

Lestrade admired the transformation. The starched apron and winged cap had gone and her long chestnut hair swayed as she moved. Perhaps Carman had better taste than Lestrade have given the under groundsman credit for. She sat him down on an upright chair and eased off the regulation tweed jacket. Next came the regulation tweed waistcoat and his braces twanged to one side.

'You poor man,' she murmured, easing her fingertips along the seam of his shirt and probing for the spine. 'Oh, how tense you are! Has a doctor seen this neck?'

'I did go to the Police Surgeon,' Lestrade told her. 'He told me that's what came of sticking my nose in other people's business.'

'And your neck out, I suppose?' she soothed.

Lestrade felt his arms getting heavy and when Madeleine the Matron unhooked his regulation tie and pinged out his collar studs, who was he to resist?

'Would you like some brandy, Inspector?' she asked. 'I have a little put by for medicinal purposes.'

'Not while I'm on duty, Matr . . . Madeleine, but now would be fine. Thank you.'

She poured them both a glass and invited him to sprawl on the ottoman. 'I'm not really sure . . . '

'Oh, tut, tut,' she scolded. 'I've had medical training. Besides, this is a boy's school. I've had more males lying there than you've had hot dinners.'

Looking at her now, tightly bodiced and full lipped, Lestrade could believe it.

'Tell me,' he said, easing his back into the cushions, 'do you have a theory on these murders?'

She sat beside him, crossing one voluptuous thigh over the other under the taut satin of her dress. 'It would be rather unprofessional of me,' she said, 'Sholto. May I call you Sholto?'

'You may,' said Lestrade, a little irritated to find that all and sundry knew his Christian name.

'Well,' she sipped her Napoleon, 'for my money it's Adelstrop.'

'Adelstrop?'

'Yes. You remember Adelstrop? The head groundsman?'

'Ah yes. Why him particularly?'

'He's in charge of the boats at the lake. He had ample opportunity.' She slipped delicate fingers into Lestrade's shirt front and began to work her way round until she was doing things to his deltoids he had only ever dreamt about.

'Madeleine . . . '

'No, no, lie still. It'll do you good.'

There was no denying that.

'He's a cantankerous old besom, Adelstrop. Lost his leg in the Great Rhadegund Riot of 'seventy-two.'

'Riot?'

'Yes. They used to be a regular occurrence in schools such as this. Usual thing. The then Headmaster had neglected to give the boys a half holiday and they barricaded themselves in the Orlitarians.'

'Oh dear,' said Lestrade. 'What happened?'

'The Northamptonshire Regiment was called in to eject them, it proving too much for the local constabulary, I fear. All ended happily. The Headmaster expelled six, caned forty-three and granted the half holiday. Unfortunately, poor Adelstrop was pinned under debris when a staircase full of chaps collapsed. He was lucky it wasn't more serious.'

'Quite,' chuckled Lestrade, 'an inch or so to the left . . . '

'How's that?' Her fingers wove their magic.

'No,' Lestrade's eyes watered, 'that's not what I meant.'

'Lower?'

'I like your voice just as it is,' he told her and removed her hand. 'So you think Adelstrop bears a grudge?'

'He tends to blame all boys and all staff for what happened to him. Irrational, I dare say it is, but there you have it. Tell me, Sholto, are you married?'

'Er . . . no, I'm not, Madeleine.' Lestrade wasn't sure he liked this new line of questioning. 'Except to my job, of course.'

'Quite.' She looked him in the eye. 'I too, of course. And yet . . . '

'What of Maggie Hollis?' He desperately changed tack, sitting up now.

'Silly goose,' snorted Madeleine. 'No better than she should be, that one.'

'Meaning?'

'She really thought Singh Major would marry her, you know.'

'Singh Major?' Lestrade's neck caught him again. 'Was he the father of her child?'

'Of course.' Madeleine poured them both another tot. 'I thought you knew that. The talisman in her hand— '

'You knew about that?'

She looped an arm across his chest. 'My dear Sholto,' she purred, 'there is little a school matron does not know.' She whirled away and began unbuttoning her bodice with her back to him. 'Dr Nails's young lady, for example . . . '

'Oh?' Lestrade was all ears. Madeleine released her breasts and became even more expansive. 'When he pretends to be off in the Cairngorms or wherever, he is actually in a house in Balham with a certain Mrs Payne.'

'So the ropes and irons . . . ?'

'Oh, yes, he still uses those. I believe her north face is the most difficult.'

'I see you are well informed,' he said and swallowed hard as she turned to him with buttons and chemise awry.

'And well endowed.' Her voice was altogether more husky. She had gone lower after all. She pounced on him, running wild fingers through his hair and kissing him violently on the moustache.

'Matron, I . . . ' he mumbled.

'Madeleine, Madeleine,' she breathed.

'Madeleine,' he repeated, 'the talisman in Maggie Hollis's hand . . . '

'Was a love token, Sholto. Given to her by Singh, I shouldn't wonder, after a night of wild abandon. I hear these Rajputs are beasts, you know.'

'Yes,' he gasped as his shirt tails flapped free and the iron thighs of Matron gripped his waist. 'I think Major Bracegirdle was of that opinion.'

'Let's not talk of him,' she panted, smothering the struggling Inspector with kisses. 'Let's talk of ourselves. Of our needs, our passions.'

'Yes, well . . . ' Lestrade realised that Matron's powerful fingers were now making a determined bid for his regulation trousers.

'I knew it when I first saw you,' she growled.

'What?' Lestrade squeaked, suddenly darting a downward glance to ensure all was well.

'That there was some madness in you and in me that was infectious.'

'Rather like diphtheria,' he quipped only to be forced backwards and wriggled over. His hands alighted by the merest chance on the taut buttocks of his dancing partner, grinding lasciviously against him. Despite himself, he felt the familiar stirrings in his loins and his heart stopped when the door shook with knocking.

'Yes?' Matron's voice was its usual starched self.

'It's Spencer, Matron. He's not well,' a squeaky little voice called. 'Come quick.'

'It'll be the spotted dick,' she sighed. 'Making a reappearance. Some boys should never be tempted by second helpings.'

She hauled herself upright, buttoning and pinning until the siren had gone and the angel stood there. 'Get a mop,

Peartree, and don't dither. I shall be one moment.'

Footsteps scurried away along the corridor. She fastened her belt with its elaborate silver buckle and popped a humbug into her mouth. At the door she turned to the dishevelled figure, desperately searching for his studs. 'Another time,' she purred. 'There is much more I could tell you . . . And show you,' and she blew him a kiss.

The pavilion clock struck twelve as Lestrade shivered under the arch of the quad. The wind was rising, blowing the leaves of the limes in great circles across the worn stones. He made for the gymnasium, dark and bleak against the line of trees, the trees which skirted the river where Anthony Denton had died. He pushed the door gingerly with his foot and it creaked back on its hinges.

'Mr Hardman?' he said. His voice rang back at him, bouncing off echoing walls. But there was no reply. He entered the vaulted room. Dim shadows of ropes knocked and swung in the draughts. As his eyes accustomed themselves to the dark, he made out the vaulting horse, the javelins in their racks. Then one head, then two. A muttering grew in pitch-black corners. Lestrade stepped back, once, twice, then felt the cold brick at his shoulder blades.

'Mr Hardman?' he repeated, louder now as if the strength of his voice gave him courage.

The House prefect stepped into a pool of light the obliging moon had created in the centre of the floor.

'Adsum,' he said haughtily. 'Oh, I forgot. You don't have Latin, Lestrade, do you? You coppers are rather short on culture.'

'And on patience,' Lestrade said. 'The fact that you should be tucked up in your little dormitory bed by now does not concern me one jot. But I am a busy man.'

'You certainly are.' Hardman picked up a cricket bat that was leaning against a vaulting horse and cradled it in his arms. 'Quite the little socialite, aren't you? First visiting Ruffage and then popping along to Matron's boudoir.

Madeleine has quite a little body on her, hasn't she?'

'That's enough,' said Lestrade.

'Oh, no, copper,' snarled Hardman. 'It's not nearly enough. Unfortunately, young Peartree, my fag, couldn't make out the gist of the conversation through the door.'

'Perhaps he'll do better next time.' Lestrade watched with growing unease as more heads appeared silhouetted against the windows and stockinged feet squeaked on Bracegirdle's polished floor.

'Oh, there won't be a next time,' snorted Hardman. 'You see, you've snooped around here for long enough. Odd, isn't it, that whenever *you* appear someone else dies. At best you are a Jonah, Lestrade . . . '

'Sholto,' smiled the Inspector. 'Sholto Lestrade.' He counted thirteen heads in the moonlight and as many cudgels and bats.

'And at worst you could be a murderer. Well, after tonight it won't really matter.'

Rumblings grew from the others. 'This is St Rhadegund's,' someone muttered. 'We don't like strangers here.'

'Up school,' shouted someone else and they rushed at him.

It was true – and as well – that Madeleine's ministrations had loosened Lestrade somewhat. He rolled to one side, pushing one boy away and catching a second in the groin with his boot. The lad squeaked and hit the floor. Lestrade ran the length of the room, boys hot on his heels. He bounced off the wall and shoulder-barged two of them, then felt a sickening crack as a bat caught him on the shoulder. He crouched as another crunched into the plaster above his head.

'Get him low, Rhadegund,' screamed Hardman. 'Come on Beaumont, you're a prop forward; behave like it.'

Hardman's wish was Beaumont's command and the giant hit the Inspector amidships and sent him sprawling. Before Lestrade could roll upright, he was pinned in a sitting position with lads at his corners and unable to move. The circle of panting boys around him parted and Hardman strode into it, tapping the cricket bat lightly on his finger-tips.

'Dear old Dr Grace gave me this,' he beamed. 'He's a family friend, you know. Toughest willow. Guaranteed to crack a skull like eggshell. Goodbye, Lestrade.'

'We call that murder,' Lestrade shouted, his wits all that was left to save him.

'Murder?' Hardman lowered the bat. 'Peartree and the others have followed your every move since you arrived. You are, I believe, what is known as accident prone. Sooner or later one of your little slips was bound to result in tragedy. You will be found at the foot of the main staircase. Eighty-nine stone steps. Your head of course will be pulp.'

'That will do, Hardman!' A powerful voice roared across the gym, rattling windows and composures.

'Ruffage!' Hardman's sangfroid showed signs of melting. A line of school prefects, whose average age appeared to be forty and whose shoulders were built like steam hammers fanned out on either side of the Captain of the School.

'Your fag gave Mr Lestrade your note at the wrong time,' said Ruffage. 'When he was with me. Something of an oversight. All of you,' Ruffage snapped his fingers, 'drop those sticks and get out. The prefects and I will be inspecting dorms in five minutes. Anyone out of his bed gets a roasting.'

'Roasting's banned,' Hardman reminded him.

'When you wear this cap,' Ruffage pointed to the tasselled velvet perched on his head, 'you can decide what's banned. Until then, I will. Now get out. Beaumont, you're dropped. You'll never play rugby in this school again. Not even for the Remnants.'

Beaumont shuffled off, crying.

'One moment.' Lestrade got to his feet. He crossed to Hardman and the switchblade knife in his pocket flashed clear in the moonlight.

'Mr Lestrade . . . ' said Ruffage.

'Don't worry,' the Inspector said, 'I'm not going to draw blood.'

He took Hardman's bat and cut the rope cording around the grip, then he folded away the knife and, swirling the bat with both hands, shattered it on the wall. 'King Willow isn't what it was,' he tutted and let the broken bits clatter on the floor.

'You bastard!' Hardman screamed and lunged for Lestrade, but the Inspector was quicker. He blocked Hardman's swing with his forearm and slapped him sickeningly across the head with his open hand. Again and again the slaps reverberated until Hardman lay whimpering in the dust of the floor. Lestrade knelt over him, yanking him back by the hair. 'What do you know about Singh Minor?' he hissed.

'N . . . nothing,' Hardman blubbered.

'Try again.' Lestrade pulled the hair harder.

'Ruffage.' Beaumont had the sense of outrage to bounce back. 'Stop this.'

'What might that be?' Ruffage turned to face him and the ex-prop forward melted away.

'All right,' shrieked Hardman. 'All right. Cherak Singh knew something. About the murders, I mean. The sneaky little blackamoor was going to tell you what he knew. He was going to peach like a snivelling little prep school oik.'

'So you killed him?'

'No!' yelled Hardman. 'No, we just . . . hid him for a while. Tied him up in the boat house until he was ready to tell us what he knew. Or until you went away.'

'And did he tell you?'

'No. The little bastard was stubborn. It had something to do with his brother and with Whitechapel, but he wouldn't say what.'

'So how did Singh Minor die?'

'I don't know.' Lestrade tugged on the hair again. 'I swear it! This is police brutality, you know,' Hardman whispered.

'Ten out of ten,' Lestrade congratulated him.

'When we went to see him on the night of the fire, he'd gone. We thought your men had found him and the game was up.'

'Oh no, Mr Hardman.' Lestrade stood up. 'The game is not up yet. I doubt whether, as a certain acquaintance of mine would say, it's even properly afoot.'

'W . . . what will happen?'

'To you?' Lestrade called as he walked into the darkness. 'Nothing. As long as you don't join the Army.'

'The Army?' Ruffage asked as Lestrade passed him.

'Why, yes,' Lestrade stopped. 'Surely Hardman has told you all about his father the Field Marshal?'

'Oh, yes,' grunted Ruffage, 'many times.'

There were murmurs of assent from the school prefects.

'One of the advantages of belonging to Scotland Yard,' smiled Lestrade, 'is that one has miles and miles of shoe-boxes crammed full of information. Most of it is useless, of course, but now and again a snippet proves of value. Like the snippet that mentions Corporal Hardman . . . '

'*Corporal* Hardman?' Ruffage sniggered.

' . . . of the Army Pay Corps,' Lestrade finished.

Corporate sniggers now.

' . . . lately cashiered.'

Gales of laughter.

'Something to do with stolen wages. Which might, of course,' Lestrade continued for the door, 'explain young Hardman's sojourn at this expensive school for the sons of gentlefolk . . . and cashiered pay clerks.'

Rapturous applause and whistles.

Lestrade stopped. 'I could charge you with kidnapping, grievous bodily harm, obstructing the police in the course of their enquiries and attempted murder,' he said to the broken Hardman, 'were it not for the fact that I am in a jovial frame of mind tonight. Mr Ruffage, I may well owe you my life. I think I chose my ally well. Goodnight.'

'Goodnight, Mr Lestrade.'

*

Not only did Lestrade prove Dollery right by receiving a letter; he also received a telegram. An urgent summons from the Yard. Whatever he was doing, he must leave it, nay, drop it and go to London at once. He left instructions with George and his constables, impressing on them the need to watch closely any reactions among the staff to his deliberate needling of them the previous night and above all to stay away from Matron.

He arrived at the Yard mid-morning, having snatched forty winks on the train, and hurried by hansom to Hyde Park where, in the grey fog of an October morning, Assistant Commissioner Rodney of the Uniformed Branch was calling through a loud-hailer.

'Er . . . '

'That sounds like Mr Rodney over there, sir.' The uniformed constable pointed through the swirling mist.

'It certainly does,' Lestrade agreed and collided with Sergeant Woodhouse, the dog handler.

'Have *you* seen 'em, sir?'

'Who, Sergeant?'

'Barnaby and Burgho, sir. My bloodhounds.'

'No, I'm afraid not.'

'Oh, Lord. I'll be forrit. Mr Abberline's around somewhere an' 'e's 'oppin' mad as it is.'

'Got out of the right side of the wrong bed again, then?' beamed Lestrade.

'Er . . . ' Rodney's echoing dither seemed to come from all sides at once.

'What are you doing here, Sergeant, you and your dogs?'

'Oh, it's not just me, sir. There are thirty-eight coppers in the park somewhere. Mr Abberline's idea. I gave Barnaby and Burgho the scent of the Whitechapel murderer. Some blood-stained linen thought to be his.'

'And?'

'And they led us 'ere, sir. To the park.'

'And then?'

'And then we lost 'em, sir. If anything's 'appened to them dogs, I'll never forgive myself.' He blew his nose, like a foghorn in the morning.

'Don't take on, Woodhouse, we'll find them. Dry your eyes, there's a good fellow.'

Lestrade groped his way forward, tangling with gorse and briar as he did so. There was a female shriek off to his left.

'Chief Inspector Abberline?' he called, but there was no response.

'Er . . . ' The grey figure of Rodney loomed out of the grey mist. No wonder he had been so difficult to find.

'Mr Rodney, sir, I came as quickly as I could.'

'Er . . . ' Rodney deafened Lestrade by bellowing through his loud-hailer at him. 'Oh, I'm terribly sorry. It's . . . er . . . '

'Lestrade, sir,' the Inspector said resignedly.

'Ah, yes, of course. I telegrammed you, didn't I?'

'Yes, sir.'

'Let's see, now. You're on a case in Nottingham.'

'Northampton, sir.'

'Yes, I thought it was. In a hospital. Patients being murdered.'

'A school, sir.'

'Quite so. Well, I must take you off it, Gregson.'

'Lestrade, sir.'

'Yes. I must take you off it because we have a new chappie . . . ' He pointed skyward.

' . . . hiding in the trees?' Lestrade did his best to be helpful.

'Upstairs in the Yard,' Rodney confided.

'In Special Branch?' Lestrade tried to follow the drift.

'You're obsessed with trees, Jones.'

'Lestrade, sir.'

'Anderson.'

'What, sir?'

'His name is Anderson. Dr Robert Anderson. He takes over from . . . er . . . '

'Sir Charles?'

'Who?'

'Sir Charles Warren?'

'Yes. Quite. He's in Switzerland at the moment.'

'Sir Charles?'

'No, Dr Robert. Really, Abberline, do try and concentrate. Life is difficult enough as it is. Dr Robert is in Switzerland for the good of his health. Dicky lungs.'

'Who's that, sir?'

'No, no. That's his complaint. Asthma. Anyway, he's moving to Paris shortly to be nearer the scene of the crime. Any questions?'

'Er . . . '

'What?' Rodney did not suffer fools gladly.

'Why have I been summoned, sir?'

'Where?'

'Here.' Bearing in mind the night he had had, Lestrade was a model of patience.

'Dr Robert wants all the men he can get. The City's in hysterics, Gregson. It's pandemonium. Abberline has arrested over a hundred men.'

'He thinks it's a conspiracy, does he, sir?'

'No need to be flippant, Jones. Her Majesty Herself has asked for you.'

'Really?' Even Lestrade was impressed.

'But don't let it go to your head. She'd be bound to remember you. Abberline is an unusual name.'

'Isn't it?' Lestrade hoped Rodney wouldn't notice his knuckles whitening in the morning air.

Horrible howls and savagings echoed through the swirling fog.

'I believe the dogs have found Chief Inspector Abberline, sir,' said Lestrade. 'I'd know that strangled cry anywhere. Shall we?'

In another part of the field, two gentlemen, one in

a Donegal and wide-awake, the other in tawdry harlot's rags, crouched in the bushes.

'Did you have to scream like that, Holmes?' one of them asked.

'I must stay in character, Watson,' the harlot answered. 'It is essential to the very core of my being.'

'But you've been dressing as a lady now for nearly a month,' Watson hissed. 'I believe you're secretly enjoying it.'

'Nonsense, Watson. I scarcely feel any thrill at all at the tightness of my bodice. Besides, I fear we are wasting our time here as surely as Abberline is.'

'I fancied I saw the footprints of two gigantic hounds,' muttered Watson.

'You've been drinking,' commented Holmes, and marched into thin air.

The Russian Agent

The fog did not lift all day and so it was that Inspector Lestrade stumbled and groped his way through the bricks and planks of the builders' yard in Alderney Street, the premises of George Lusk, whose card now read 'Builder, Roofer, Joiner and Chairman of the Whitechapel Vigilante Committee Est. 1888'.

'It's in this parcel,' the truculent Cockney told the Yard man. 'Wrapped in a mysterious way.'

Lestrade watched while his constable wrestled with the string.

'It's a box, sir,' was the man's verdict. No doubt about it, Lestrade observed, the calibre of the Force was improving. 'Oh, gor blimey!' The constable all but dropped it in his revulsion, but Lestrade was faster and peered inside.

'It's a kidney,' said Lusk triumphantly.

'Is it?' said Lestrade, who had obviously missed that lecture and never examined the contents of Mrs Lovett's pies at the Yard canteen very carefully. 'When did it arrive?'

'Two days ago – evenin' post. This was with it.' Lusk gave Lestrade a crumpled piece of paper and he read to himself, '*Sor I send you half the kidne I took from one women prasarved it for you tother piece I fried and ate it was very nise I may send you the bloody knif that took it out if you only wate a whil longer. Signed Catch me when you can Mishter Lusk.*'

This was not the handiwork of Cherak Singh. The letters sloped this way and that, without rhyme or reason, but Lestrade did not need the Yard boffin to tell him the obvious. An illiterate man would not spell 'knife' with a k or 'while' with an h. Clearly this was another hoax, like hundreds the Yard had received, yet the kidney could not be ignored.

'Have you other letters?' Lestrade asked.

'Lor, dozens,' Lusk spat into his own woodshavings, 'an' I've 'ad a prowler around 'ere.'

'Anything missing?' Lestrade asked, though by the look of the yard that would be impossible to tell.

'Nothin',' Lusk assured him. 'I'd know if so much as a nail 'ad gorn.'

'Did you see anybody?'

'The ovver night, yeah. Tall bloke. Natty 'tache. Proper gent.'

'What did you do?'

'I shot at 'im wiv me over an' under, didn' I?'

'You carry a gun?'

'Who don't?' Lusk was truly astonished by the question. 'Wiv blokes like you chasing yer own bloody tails. How many people 'as Mr Abberline harrested now? 'Underd? 'Underd an' ten?'

'Do you feel like a walk, Mr Lusk?' Lestrade ignored the question.

'All right. Where are we goin'?'

'To see a friend of mine at the Pathological Museum of the London Hospital.'

'Museum? Do me a bloody favour! I 'ad enough of that when I was a kid. Gotta get some learnin', my old man said. Used to drag me kickin' and screamin' to the bloody Crystal Palace. Then 'e used to levver me for cuttin' up rough. I vowed to meself the day I put the old sod in the ground I'd never go near a bloody museum again.'

'Suit yourself,' said Lestrade, 'but I'll need these for evidence.' He took parcel, box, letter and kidney and bade Lusk good day. 'Constable,' he stopped at the gate, 'get this letter back to Mr Wensley, at Leman Street. See what he makes of it. And, Constable . . . '

'Sir?'

'On no account are you to show it to Mr Gregson of Special Branch. What with "Sor" and "Mishter", he'll be arresting every Irishman in sight!'

'Very good, sir. Mind 'ow you go.'

'Lestrade!' The man in the muffler and white coat croaked through the steam and the thickening throat.

'Dr Openshaw?' The Inspector peered through the swirling fumes.

'Come in,' he croaked. 'I've got a touch of the vapours.'

Lestrade had sensed that.

'You don't look well,' he said.

'Watch out for the— '

Lestrade leapt backwards as the searing pain burned through his ankle.

' —mustard poultice. I must have dropped it somewhere.'

'Oh, it'll turn up sometime,' Lestrade said through gritted teeth.

'To what do I owe the pleasure?' Openshaw collapsed under his towel in a paroxysm of coughing.

'This.' The Inspector placed the open box under the oil-lamp's glare.

'Good Lord!' Openshaw peered at it. 'Not yours, is it? Oh, no, of course not. Where did you get it?'

'I didn't. A man named Lusk got it. Through the post.'

'Tut, tut.' Openshaw shook his head. 'Circulars! I get lots of those.'

'Can you tell me anything about it?' Lestrade groped for a chair and sat in the impenetrable gloom like a trapper in a mine, fanning himself with his bowler.

'It's a kidney,' said the Doctor after some consideration.

'Human?'

'Just a moment.' Openshaw reached across the table and set up an elaborate microscope. He adjusted lenses, twiddled wheels and knobs, estimating the Almroth Quotient and the Angle of Dangle. 'That's better,' he sighed at last. 'I've been meaning to do that all day. Now, what was your question?'

Lestrade had almost forgotten. 'The kidney,' he remembered, 'is it human?'

Openshaw sniffed it, squinted at it, held it up to the light. 'Oh, yes. It's also been preserved in spirits.'

'Really?'

'Left kidney, I'd say. Removed quickly. And by someone not very skilled.'

'Not a surgeon, then?'

'I said someone not very skilled, Lestrade,' Openshaw reminded him. 'That leaves you with all the medical students in the land, about half the army surgeons and I would estimate seventy-four per cent of the Royal College.'

'I see.'

'It also had Bright's Disease.' The doctor disappeared under his towel again.

'Whose?' asked Lestrade.

'It drank, Lestrade.'

'The kidney?'

'*Mutatis mutandis*, yes.'

'Now for the big one, Doctor. Was this kidney, in your opinion, ripped from the body of Catherine Eddowes?'

'God knows.' Openshaw reached for a phial of cloudy liquid, sniffed it and drank it. 'Worth digging her up, do you think?'

Lestrade shook his head. 'I doubt if she'd be able to tell us much now,' he said and bid the Doctor adieu.

Inspector Fred Wensley was more than interested in Mr Lusk's letter and he sent Lestrade's constable back to him almost by return of post.

'He said to come to Leman Street quick, sir. He's got a lead,' the Constable reported.

'Dogged as ever, I see,' mused Lestrade and hailed a hansom. The Constable was paying.

'We've met before today, haven't we?' Lestrade asked

as they jolted through the night, past sleeping St Paul's and into the City.

'Yes, sir. Dew, sir. Constable H342.'

'Ah, the old H Division. Sergeant Pepper still there? It must have been twenty years ago today . . . before I joined.'

'Dead, sir,' said Dew.

'Old Pepper, dead?' Lestrade lifted the blind to check their whereabouts.

'It was his ticker, sir, apparently. Died with his boots off, he did.'

'It'll come to us all one day.' Lestrade was philosophical at this hour. The cab rattled up the Cornhill and left through Bishopsgate, the growler punctuating the night air with his whip and cries not fit for a decent policeman to hear.

'Got any views on the Whitechapel murders, Dew?' Lestrade asked.

'Views, sir?' The Constable was shocked. He had never been asked that before.

'You've been working with Mr Wensley, haven't you? And today with me? Come on, man, out with it.'

'Well . . . Mrs Dew has a theory, sir.'

Lestrade looked at the earnest young constable, cape and helmet still dripping in the hour before dawn.

'*Mrs* Dew?' Lestrade raised an eyebrow. 'How long have you been married, Constable?'

'Six months, two weeks and four days, sir,' Dew beamed, then caught Lestrade's appalled look, 'give or take.'

'I understand there has to be a lot of that in marriage,' Lestrade ruminated.

'Never been smitten yourself, sir?' Dew asked.

'Smitten?' asked Lestrade. 'Oh, once or twice. A few lads with cudgels the other day for instance . . . oh, I see. *Smitten*. No, never.'

'Ah, one day, sir,' Dew smiled, then realised his place and crawled back under it.

'So you and Mrs Dew spend your hours of connubial bliss discussing the Whitechapel murders, eh?'

'Oh, no, sir.' Dew shuffled his feet and grinned inanely at something in his lap. 'It's just something she happened to mention.'

'Well, don't keep us all in suspense, Constable. If Inspector Wensley is being over-optimistic, I may have reason to be grateful for Mrs Dew's crumbs.'

'Oh, no, sir. My lady wife is spotless, sir. Spotless.'

'Yes, I'm sure she is,' sighed Lestrade. 'What is her theory?'

'Well,' Dew looked from side to side to make sure no one was hanging outside the cab. 'you know how we haven't caught any man leaving the scenes of the crimes?'

'Yes.' Lestrade was with him so far.

'Why is that, do you think?'

'I thought Mr Abberline had arrested several people . . . '

'Oh, he has, sir. But he's had to let them all go, hasn't he?'

Lestrade looked at him, shrewdly. 'You'll go far, Constable,' he smiled. 'Go on.'

'Well, I turned to Mrs Dew and I said, "Well, Mrs Dew, what do you make of it all?" And she said . . . you'll never guess it, sir . . . '

Lestrade yawned ostentatiously. 'No, probably not, perhaps you'll tell me, will you?'

' "Well, Mr Dew," she said to me, "Why haven't they found a blood-stained man? Because they ought to be looking for a blood-stained woman." And I said to her— '

'A woman?' Lestrade broke in. 'A sort of Jill the Ripper, you might say?'

'Beg pardon, sir?'

'You interest me strangely, Dew.' Lestrade ignored him. 'Or rather your wife does.'

'Beg pardon, sir?' The tone was more assertive, territorial.

'A woman,' Lestrade repeated.

The hansom lurched to a halt. 'Einer leiner,' snarled the cabbie.

'You probably speak the language better than I do, Dew. Where are we?'

'Spitalfields Market, sir.'

Lestrade alighted, landing perfectly in the middle of a midden, steaming freshly in the night. Dew paid the growler and the hansom sped away. The policemen clattered through the glistening cobbled streets that flanked the market. Lestrade's ancestors had settled here centuries ago, when the weavers had come all the way from Huguenot. Such was the extent of his grasp of family trees. A few roughs tumbled, carousing mournfully, from the lighted door of The Britannia, whence a small, sallow-faced figure much the cut of Lestrade's own beckoned the policemen across.

'Shouldn't this place be shut up, Fred, or am I being over-zealous?' Lestrade asked.

'I won't tell Mr Gladstone if you don't,' said Wensley. 'Dew, is that you?'

'Evening, sir!' Dew saluted.

'Sssshhhh!' Wensley flapped his arms about. 'How long have you been on the Force, Dew?' he asked.

'Three years come Christmas, sir.'

'Well, Christmas won't come, Dew, not for you, not for any of us, if you clump around in that fancy dress using a loud-hailer. On your Raleigh. You're too conspicuous. Mr Lestrade and I can handle this. I'm sure you have reports to write up.'

'Very good, sir,' Dew whispered, saluting again, though he was secretly hurt at the charge of being conspicuous. He didn't think politics came into it. He slunk into the night.

'Talking of loud-hailers,' Wensley led Lestrade through a dimly lit passage, the walls peeling and brown, 'is it true about Abberline and those bloodhounds?'

'As I live and breathe,' said Lestrade. 'Savaged his inside leg something cruel.'

'You don't think *he's* the Ripper, do you?' Wensley chuckled.

'Woodhouse, the dog handler, is moribund,' Lestrade told him. 'There's talk of putting them down.'

'Who? Abberline and Woodhouse?'

'No levity, Fred, please.'

'Sholto.' Wensley was suddenly serious; he caught Lestrade by the sleeve. 'Beyond that door is Puma Court.'

'I see.'

'No, you don't. The lead I've got is somewhere through there. Rupasobly.'

Lestrade stumbled in the corner. 'Rupasobly?' he repeated.

'Makes your blood run cold, doesn't it?' Wensley nodded. 'Makes the gangs in the Nichol look like choirboys.'

'No wonder you sent Dew home. They say the sight of collar numbers unhinges him.'

'Are you armed?' Wensley asked.

Lestrade patted the brass knuckles in his pocket. 'Sort of,' he said. 'You?'

Wensley pulled a coiled chain from his pocket from which two iron balls dangled.

'Who did they belong to?' asked Lestrade, pointing at the spheroids.

'The last person to ask that question,' said Wensley blandly. 'After the operation he had no further use for them. Will you lead?'

'Oh, it's a policeman's excuse me, is it?' Lestrade slid the bolt.

'Sholto?'

'Yes, Fred.' Lestrade slid it back again.

'That smell . . . '

'Yes, it is me. I trod in something. And frankly, just at the moment, that's the very least of our troubles.'

Gingerly, like a man on thin ice, Lestrade crept into the total darkness of Puma Court. A gate swung in the rain to his left, sending shivers up his spine.

'Why Rupasobly?' he hissed to Wensley.

'Tip-off,' the Inspector of that name answered; 'enemy of an enemy, that sort of thing.'

'I'd heard he'd gone to ground in Clerkenwell.' Lestrade peered into the gloom, trying to make sense of the dim shapes in the corners.

'I'd have been happier if he'd gone to ground in Abney Park,' Wensley muttered.

'Now, don't be ungrateful, Fred. If anything comes of this, it'll be a feather in your cap. Just think, you'll be the man who caught Jack the Ripper. Tell me, was your tip-off a usual nark or anonymous?'

Wensley did not reply.

'Come on, Fred. This is Sholto, your old mate. No need to be coy. Fred? Fred?'

But Wensley had gone, vanished into the shadows, merged with the dark. And he had made no sound.

Lestrade turned slowly, sensing eyes everywhere. The hairs on his neck stood on end. This was no child's play with cricket bats and vaulting horses. Chubb Rupasobly played for keeps. He edged the brass knuckles forward so that the switchblade clicked out and gleamed in the faint light still streaming from The Britannia behind him. There was no sound but the thump of his own heart and the tiny scream growing inside his brain. Don't shiver, he told himself. They're watching. Don't give them the satisfaction.

'Chubb Rupasobly!' he suddenly shouted.

Silence.

He slid sideways like a crab, feeling the rough brick at his back and a wall of fear ahead. A click in the darkness. Another. Then the unmistakable sliding of bolts and a shaft of light slashed across his Donegal. In the doorway the diminutive figure of Chubb Rupasobly shrugged. 'Now, now, Mr Lestrade,' he lisped, 'no tricks, please. I've done you the favour of opening the door for you myself. Believe me, that's an honour.'

Lestrade ostentatiously folded away the blade. 'No tricks,' he said.

'Come in.'

Lestrade followed the swaggering little figure up a staircase to a candlelit room. The dwarf scrambled over a table with the agility of a mountain goat and sat in the huge, gilded chair. He picked his teeth with a gold pin and clicked his fingers. An enormous lackey poured two large brandies in the half-light.

Rupasobly quaffed one, shooting the cuffs of his frilled, white shirt, the stubby little fingers glittering with diamonds. He clicked them again, and the lackey crossed to Lestrade, obliterating him with his shadow. Lestrade took the glass.

'Where is Inspector Wensley?' he asked the dwarf.

'Mr Vensel?' Rupasobly gave him his Chosen name. 'When you leave here, Mr Lestrade, assuming we can do business, Mr Vensel you will find chained with his balls to the railings along Thrawl Street. Just a little precaution.'

'Precaution?' Lestrade said.

'Come now,' the dwarf chuckled in an Eastern European sort of way, 'I know you, Mr Lestrade. And I don't forget. I could have been Mr Big around here.'

Lestrade looked at the rings, the cut glass and he sniffed the brandy. 'You're doing all right,' he said.

'Perhaps,' Rupasobly shrugged, 'but I could have done better.'

'Wensley said you could help.'

'With the Whitechapel murders, yes.'

Lestrade sat down uninvited. Rupasobly clicked his fingers and a second lackey provided him with a footstool.

'Cigar?' The Inspector produced two from his pocket.

'No, I only smoke Turkish.' He clicked his fingers and a third lackey lit up for him, then for Lestrade.

'What's the deal?' Lestrade asked.

'No deal.' Rupasobly shook his head. 'I want this bastard caught. He's queering my pitch.'

'So you'll give me his name *and* Fred Wensley back – for nothing.'

'Let's just say I'm a public-spirited citizen.' Rupasobly's eyes sparkled in the candlelight. 'Besides, this man's a Jew.

And I'm a good Methodist. Ask General Booth if you don't believe me.'

'I might just do that,' nodded Lestrade, savouring the cigar. 'I didn't know there were any Polish Methodists.'

'Polish?' Rupasobly almost choked on his brandy. He clicked his fingers and a lackey hurled an empty glass to the floor. 'How dare you, Lestrade!' he snarled. 'I am Hungarian!'

'Yes, of course you are,' the Inspector beamed. 'I apologise.'

Rupasobly bridled, adjusting the white tie and flicking down the diminutive tails.

'The man's name, then?' asked Lestrade.

'Oh, no,' Rupasobly dissented, 'I'd planned to give you his head.'

Lestrade froze. He looked at the dwarf, the distorted features a livid white in the flickering light. He knew he meant it.

'That won't do,' he said. 'If you give me his head on a plate, we'll never know, will we?'

'Know what?'

'If he was the Whitechapel murderer. If he was Jack the Ripper.'

'So?'

'So,' Lestrade leaned forward. 'Just imagine it. No one will ever know for certain who the Ripper was. What will future generations say of us? That we couldn't catch a cold? But what if future generations record the name of Chubb Rupasobly for all time?'

The dwarf sat upright slowly. 'For all time?'

'Yes.' Lestrade nodded through the smoke. 'A hundred years from now. In . . . let's see, nineteen eighty-eight somebody or other will write a book about you. You. Chubb Rupasobly. You will be . . . immortal.'

'Immortal,' repeated the dwarf in a rapture of vanity. He looked at Lestrade. 'What's in it for you?' he scowled.

The Inspector leaned forward. 'Read your papers, Chubb,'

he said. 'You can't have failed to notice what a load of Charlies we've been made to look recently? I don't like that. I want this bastard nailed to a wall. But I want to nail him.'

There was a silence. Then Rupasobly smiled. 'His name,' he said, 'is Kosminski. He lives here in Whitechapel and is a Polish Jew.'

Lestrade stood up. 'Thank you, Mr Rupasobly,' he said. 'Can I have the Inspector back?'

'You'll find him as I said,' the dwarf told him. 'No tricks. Goodnight, Mr Lestrade.'

And there weren't any tricks. Though by the time Lestrade had reached Thrawl Street there were two policemen near the railings. One was hanging there like something in Smithfield Market, the other, solicitous, flapping, was about to blow his whistle to summon aid. Lestrade stopped him.

'Good of you to hang around, Dew,' he said. 'Oh, you too, Fred.'

The Inspector grunted something basic in Yiddish or Dorset. He was capable of either.

'But I don't think we want the whole neighbourhood alerted to Mr Wensley's position. There could be talk,' and the laugh he had been stifling in the collar flaps of his Donegal erupted. 'Of course,' he screamed, in an effort to become serious, 'I don't like these things.' He examined Dew's whistle. 'When I started, you had a wooden rattle or you bashed the pavement with your truncheon. Well, that's progress, I suppose.'

'Talking of progress, Inspector,' Wensley hissed through gritted teeth, 'could you possibly get me out of these chains?' He rattled them, for all the world like a Gothic Horror. 'I assume that was what Constable Dew here had in mind when you stopped him.'

'Ah, but you see, the embarrassment, Fred,' smiled Lestrade, striking a lucifer on one of Wensley's chains. 'Constable Dew blows his whistle, the whole of Whitechapel comes running. Mr Lusk and his charmers, armed to the teeth; that tall, rather masculine judy he's been looking for. Not to mention the eighty or more blokes who've had their collars felt by Abberline over the last six weeks. As it is, I shall have to report all this to Rodney. Who'll probably pass it on to Anderson, assuming Sir Charles has actually vacated his premises by then. I hear he's loth to go.'

'What do you mean, report?' Wensley asked, struggling now.

'Come on, Fred, you've written as many of them as I have . . .'

'All right,' sighed Wensley. 'What do you want?'

'Ah,' Lestrade smiled. 'The address of one Kosminski, here in Whitechapel.'

'Kosminski? Kosminski? Hanbury Street, I think. Yes, Number thirty-six.'

'A few yards from Annie Chapman's murder.'

'That's right. Is he our man?'

'I'm not sure. Rupasobly seems to think so.'

'That was the lead?'

'Yes, as you'd have found out if you'd stayed with me.'

'Sholto!' Wensley shouted, then, calmer, 'I didn't have a lot of choice in the matter. All I knew was I had a sack pulled over my head and I was carried here.'

'Any injuries?'

'None,' fumed Wensley.

'Ho, ho,' chuckled Lestrade. 'Wait till the lads hear about this.'

'Sholto . . .' Wensley was beside himself.

'All right, Fred, keep your combs on. It's a chilly night.'

He worked the point of his switchblade in Rupasobly's padlock. 'You can always tell one of Chubb's,' he said. He heaved against a link until his eyes stood on stalks and his face turned purple. 'It's no good, Fred. It won't budge.'

'You're just not trying, Lestrade!' Wensley snapped, growing more embarrassed and more uncomfortable by the second.

'Dew,' said Lestrade, 'lean on that railing, will you?'

The Constable obliged, cursing and swearing. 'Oh, shit a brick . . . begging both your pardons, sirs.'

There was a crack and a railing broke free of the others, releasing Wensley with it.

'Tut, tut,' said Lestrade, 'look at the workmanship in that. I don't know about the slums of tomorrow. We're looking at the slums of later on today. Come on, let's hop it before someone insists we pay for the breakages.'

Wensley shuffled along behind them.

'I didn't mean it literally, Fred,' Lestrade said.

'Dammit, Sholto, Dew may have broken the rail away from the fence, but he hasn't separated me from this particular one.'

'We'll do that at Leman Street,' said Lestrade.

'You must be joking!' Wensley stopped. 'I'll never live it down. Can't we find a smithy somewhere?'

'All right, but Kosminski first. It's funny how attached to things you can get, isn't it?' and Lestrade skipped away as Wensley aimed a blow at him.

Tadeusz Kosminski lived in a common lodging house, typical of thousands of its type. Grey washing hung limp in the dawn drizzle, strung across the narrow courts, as Lestrade and Dew climbed the fire escape, negotiating rubbish and sleeping down-and-outs, perched perilously on the rusted rungs. In the street below, the carters began to emerge on their way to work, tying scarves and straightening caps. Any one of them, Lestrade told himself, could be the man he was after. Below him too, pressed into a doorway, trying to keep his railing out of sight, huddled Fred Wensley. People were already giving him funny looks.

Lestrade peered in through the grimy window at the third floor. He could make out a bed, a table, a chair and little else.

'Now!' he shouted to Dew and lashed out against the glass and wood with both feet. He landed badly, rolling hard against the far wall and it was left to Dew to handle the understandably miffed figure in the nightshirt who sprang onto the Inspector's back. The Constable hooked his truncheon under Kosminski's chin and hauled him upright, only to jacknife seconds later as the Pole's foot caught him in the necessaries and he went down. But it had given Lestrade a breathing space and he drove his knee hard into Kosminski's groin and cuffed him around the head with his forearm. It was only a playful tap in the great scheme of things, but Kosminski huddled on his bed, crying inconsolably.

'Is your name Kosminski?' Lestrade asked.

A sob in reply.

'Tadeusz Kosminski?'

Another sob.

'Sob once for yes and twice for no,' muttered Lestrade. 'Dew, are you all right?'

'I think so, sir.' The Constable was looking for his helmet.

'Nothing Mrs Dew can't put right, eh?' Lestrade smiled, watching his constable turn crimson.

'All right, Kosminski.' Lestrade climbed onto the crawling bed and turned his man over. 'Give me your bull's-eye, Constable.'

Dew complied and Lestrade shone it in the Pole's eyes.

'I am Inspector Lestrade of Scotland Yard,' he said. 'I'd like to ask you some questions.'

'It about them women,' sobbed Kosminski. 'Them judys.'

'That's right. I'd like you to tell me where you were on the nights in question.'

'I work,' said Kosminski, blowing his nose in his bedsheet. 'All night.'

'Then why are you here now?'

'I sacked,' sobbed Kosminski, 'because of my habits.'

Lestrade looked at Dew. 'Habits?' he asked.

'Habits.' Kosminski repeated.

'Tell me, Kosminski,' Lestrade stood back from the bed, just in case, 'do you like women?'

Kosminski spat copiously into a corner. 'I hate them' he growled; 'filthy, disgusting, that's what they are. They are not fit to live.'

Lestrade circled the room a few times. It did not take him long.

'Is that why you killed them?' he asked.

'Kill?' Kosminski had stopped crying now and was staring hard through the shattered window pane whence his visitors had entered. 'Oh, yes, I could kill. Women. Any women,' and he spat again.

Lestrade threw the man his trousers and shirt. 'Get dressed,' he said, 'you're coming along with me.'

'I under arrest?' Kosminski retreated again into his huddle.

'No,' said Lestrade, 'I just want to ask you a few questions, that's all.'

And he came meekly as a lamb.

Tadeusz Kosminski had a string of convictions, it turned out, for assault and grievous bodily harm. He had broken the jaw of one woman who had looked at him funny, and kicked several prostitutes quite hard while they plied their trade against various walls in the Whitechapel area. What he did to their surprised clients was not recorded. But Lestrade was not happy. On no occasion had Kosminski used a knife; his shaven head and squat appearance fitted none of the eye-witness accounts of men seen talking to any of the deceased shortly before their deaths and, above all, he had a watertight alibi for two of the murder nights. He was in the cells at Cannon Row for punching temperance marchers and a lady Salvationist. Two other factors weighed heavily on Lestrade. The first was that Kosminski was raving mad. The second, that if he went around arresting every foreigner in sight he would be branded with Gregson's reputation. If he arrested every misog . . . myssog . . . everybody who hated women, he would be linked indelibly with Honeybun, who had now told the *News of the World* that he had been ordained by God to rid the world of vice. If he arrested anybody at all, people other than Rodney would start calling him Abberline.

'So why did Chubb Rupasobly finger him in the first place?' Wensley asked one morning after a gruelling session in the Charge Room.

'Kosminski's bad for business,' said Lestrade, sipping his tea as though his life depended on it. 'Quite a sizeable portion of Chubb's income comes from poncing. You know, he's probably the biggest cash carrier in London.'

'And Kosminski was a threat?'

Lestrade nodded. 'As Rupasobly said, "he's queering my pitch." His girls are going in terror of their lives.'

'But they're still there, Sholto,' mused Wensley, 'on the streets. They're still good natured, dearie – and they may still be killed.'

'You don't think Kosminski's our man, then?' asked Lestrade.

'No, I don't. Any more than you do.'

'There is another name I'd like to follow up,' said Lestrade. 'Kosminski gave it to me in one of his more lucid moments.'

'Who?'

'I'll tell you on the way.' He snatched up Donegal and bowler and made for the stairs. 'Time for Bedlam.'

'Mr Lestrade, is it?' asked the man in the white coat.

'It is,' he answered. 'This is Inspector Wensley, also of the Yard.'

'Gentlemen,' he shook their hands. 'Walk this way, would you?' and he clumped off down the darkened corridor, swinging his leg wide. After a few paces he stopped. 'Gentlemen,' he said quietly, 'one thing which is vitally important in the treatment of the deranged is that they obey, quickly and implicitly. There must be absolute trust, you see. I wonder . . . I hate to ask it of you, but could you walk this way as I asked. Not to do so would weaken the position of authority I hold. You will notice some of the inmates,' he gestured to the wrecks of human beings who wandered the halls, giggling or in solemn silence. 'They appear not to observe you, but they do. Please . . . ' and he swung on as first Lestrade then Wensley did likewise, until all three of them were hobbling along the corridor like so many war veterans.

A large, suited figure emerged suddenly from a side door, flanked by two more men in white coats. 'Thank you, Dick, I'll have my coat back now.'

The man with the limp spun round. 'No, you promised,' he screamed.

'Tomorrow,' the big man beamed, patting him on the head. 'Now, go with Harry and Bert. Time for the water treatment.'

Dick gripped the man's lapels. 'Oh, Doctor, can I hold the hose?' he positively slavered.

'Well . . . ' the Doctor began, 'oh, very well.' He patted Dick indulgently and the little man limped off, swinging his leg wide, while Harry and Bert did likewise, all of them craning to the left simultaneously as they staggered back down the corridor.

'I'm sorry about that, gentlemen,' he said, ushering them into an office. 'I really am Dr McGregor.'

'Who was that?' Lestrade asked, taking the proffered chair.

'That was Dick,' McGregor smiled. 'That's the third time this week he's pinched my coat.'

'He had an authoritative air,' commented Wensley. 'Not that we were fooled, of course.'

'You should have been.' McGregor adjusted his pince-nez. 'He was my predecessor here at the hospital.'

The Yard men looked at each other, wondering in their silence whether all doctors at the Bethlehem Hospital ended up as patients.

'What's wrong with his leg?' Lestrade asked.

'Absolutely nothing,' said McGregor, 'but . . . I couldn't help noticing your neck . . . '

'Oh, it's nothing either . . . or, rather, it is something . . . ' said Lestrade quickly, anxious to be allowed to leave the place at some point.

'Dick's leg has become an obsession with him. He thinks he has to limp and he thinks everybody he talks to must have the same affliction.'

'What exactly is the matter with him, Doctor?' Wensley asked.

'He's mad,' said McGregor, 'which brings me to the purpose of your visit. Michael Ostrog. He's a different kettle of fish entirely. Is it vital you see him?'

'Yes,' said Lestrade.

McGregor put his spectacles down on the desk and sat back, patting the gold chain of his hunter. 'I warn you, sir, the man is unhinged. He is cunning, he is ruthless and he has definite homicidal tendencies. He nearly killed a warder only last week.'

'Why?' Wensley asked.

McGregor shrugged. 'If I knew that, we could probably shut this infernal place down,' he said. 'The mind is a dark place, Mr . . . Wensley, is it? All medical science can do is to strike the odd match here and there to light that dark. Some of the shadows are frightening.'

'Will Ostrog talk to me?' Lestrade asked.

'He might,' nodded McGregor after a moment's consideration, 'but I shall be obliged to lock you in the cell with him. It's padded. If he closes that grille in the door – and he has the strength to do it – it would be minutes before we heard your screams. In those minutes, Mr Lestrade, I promise you, you would be dead. Tell me,' McGregor leant back again, 'are you armed?'

Lestrade nodded.

'Whatever weapon you are carrying, leave it here. Now. If he finds you're armed, he'll kill you.'

Lestrade stood up and dropped the brass knuckles with the concealed blade onto McGregor's desk.

'Sholto, this is madness,' said Wensley.

'Never a truer word . . . ' said McGregor. 'Welcome to Bedlam, gentlemen.'

The three of them left the office by a side door, McGregor

leading the way. At the bottom of a flight of stone steps, a girl met them.

'Annie.' McGregor stopped her, lifting up her chin. She was pretty, perhaps twenty-one or two. 'You've been crying,' he said. 'How's the baby?'

'Alice is fine, thank you, sir.' She curtseyed and scurried away.

'I think I know that girl,' said Wensley.

'Annie Crook,' said McGregor. 'A sad case.'

'Crook.' Wensley chewed the name over. 'No, I can't place it.'

'How long has Ostrog been here?' Lestrade asked.

'This time, six days,' McGregor told him.

'So he was at large at the time of the Whitechapel murders?'

McGregor raised an eyebrow. 'So that's what all this is about?'

'You'll keep this under your coat, Doctor, of course?' Lestrade checked.

McGregor nodded and mounted the stairs. At the top, a burly warder stood aside and slid the heavy bolts on a studded door.

'Humour him, Lestrade,' was McGregor's final advice as the Inspector disappeared inside the cell. Wensley offered a silent prayer and leant against the wall. A few seconds of this and he was pacing up and down. Suddenly aware that McGregor and the warder were watching him, he stopped, folded his arms tightly and stared at the floor. It was altogether the least neurotic thing he could think of doing.

There were no corners in the room where Lestrade found himself. And it was a radiant white. Neither was there any furniture. When he glanced round to check the door, he couldn't find it at first, so tightly did it fit. Only the tiny grille high in the wall gave a hint of its presence. But he couldn't miss the black, bearded figure in the far corner, whose dark, hypnotic eyes bored right through him.

'Mr Ostrog?' He found his voice.

The Russian stood up, with difficulty in his strait-jacket, and bowed. 'Doctor.' The voice was deep enough to shake the furniture, had there been any. 'Doctor Mikhail Ostrog, at your service.'

He hopped across to Lestrade, pinioned together as his legs were. He peered intently into his eyes, then a broad smile appeared on his face. 'Tovarich,' he said, 'it *is* you.'

Lestrade blinked. Then he remembered McGregor's advice – 'Humour him,' he had said.

Tears welled in Ostrog's eyes and he gabbled something incomprehensible.

'Speak English,' whispered Lestrade, pointing upwards. 'That's most important. They' – he glanced left and right – 'must not know I am Russian.'

'My dear friend,' beamed Ostrog, 'I would embrace you if I could.'

Lestrade hugged the bearded man in what he hoped was a Russian gesture, just as long as he didn't have to start rolling around on the floor like a Cossack.

'Do you have any wodka?' Ostrog asked.

Lestrade shook his head. 'They searched me,' he said.

'So . . . you're not armed?' Lestrade did not care for the glint in the man's eye. He opened his Donegal flap to show that he was not.

'That's a wery good disguise, tovarich.' Ostrog nodded his approval. 'What is that?'

'It's what the well-dressed Englishman is wearing this year,' Lestrade lied. Actually, no *well*-dressed Englishman would have been seen dead in it, even ten years ago.

'How is Dragomilov?' Ostrog asked.

'Well, well,' Lestrade bluffed through a gritted smile. He could sense the white walls of the room closing in on him.

'And Gorbachev?'

'He sends his love.' Lestrade grew bolder, but froze as he realised a look of horror appear on Ostrog's face.

'Anastasia Gorbachev is a woman,' the Russian said, 'or she was when I saw her last.'

'Ah, you know these Ukrainians!' Lestrade laughed. It was the only part of All the Russias he had heard of. It would have to do.

A silence. Followed by a smirk. Then Ostrog broke into a steady, rhythmic guffaw. 'These Ukrainians!' he chuckled. 'That's good tovarich. Wery good. It's the way you tell them!'

'But you,' said Lestrade, delighted to change the subject, 'how have you been?'

Ostrog shrugged to indicate his position, about the only gesture of which he was capable. 'But my report. You have come for my report.'

Lestrade nodded. Ostrog lowered himself into the corner where the conversation had begun and Lestrade thought it best to do the same.

'As you know, I arrived here two months ago, on the merchant-man *Ulyanova*. I jumped ship in their Albert Docks and made my way to their Whitechapel.'

'Why Whitechapel?' Lestrade hoped he wasn't showing too much ignorance.

'I would not be noticed, tovarich,' Ostrog explained. 'Ah, the number of foreigners in this country. It's worse than a Kiev bazaar.'

Lestrade laughed with him and was still doing so when Ostrog fell silent. 'I forgot to ask,' he said solemnly, 'His Imperial Majesty the Tsar . . . '

'Er . . . as well as can be expected,' Lestrade hedged.

Ostrog nodded grimly. 'It's all that caviar,' he sighed ruefully. 'That or the nihilists.'

Lestrade, of course, was woefully unfamiliar with either dish. 'Go on with your report, Mikhail,' he said, hoping the pronunciation was approximate.

'I lived in their Berners Street,' Ostrog told him, 'and took a job as a butcher's assistant. A family firm of old standing called Prentiss. That gave me access to the sharpest of knives.' Lestrade's heart began to ascend to his mouth. This was *it*. 'It also allowed me to pass unnoticed through the streets in the early hours.'

'You had no trouble?'

'Well,' Ostrog shrugged, 'not really. Not until an idiot called Lusk began to chase the Jews around. Not that that is a bad thing in itself, of course. His Imperial Majesty has done it all his life.'

'Of course,' Lestrade found himself agreeing, as though he and the Tsar were bosom pals.

'But Lusk made it difficult for me to operate . . . '

'Operate?' Lestrade repeated.

Ostrog chuckled. 'Ah, I can't remember when I operated last . . . ' he mused.

'Whitechapel?' Lestrade jogged his memory. 'September the thirtieth – a lady named Catherine Eddowes.'

Ostrog looked puzzled. 'Tovarich,' he said, 'either you've been drinking or one of us is mad.'

Lestrade chuckled. It was the civilised form of the scream he really wanted to give vent to. 'Tell me, Mikhail,' he said 'didn't the police bother you in all this?'

Ostrog guffawed. It was no more than Lestrade had expected. 'Isn't that the whole point of the exercise, tovarich?' he laughed. 'Why I was brought here in the first place? Tut, tut. You haven't read the Okhrana file, have you?'

Lestrade smiled sheepishly.

'My duty was to slip unnoticed into London, commit an atrocious crime so as to embarrass the British police and slip away again.'

'I see,' said Lestrade. 'Well, Mikhail, I must admit you've done a splendid job. We . . . er . . . the police are embarrassed, all right. Did you choose the four women at random? Or were there more? What about Martha Tabram? Was she the first?'

Ostrog looked at him oddly. 'Tovarich, I don't know what you are talking about. I chose the target which would embarrass their British Police more than anything else.'

'Oh?' Lestrade had lost this conversation entirely.

'I killed Their Majesty Queen Victoria.'

'Ah,' said Lestrade after the inevitable pause.

'Well, she's the next best thing to a mother-in-law to his Imperial Majesty,' Ostrog chuckled. 'What man does not wish to be rid of his mother-in-law?'

'What . . . er . . . what did you do?' Lestrade asked.

'I cut her throat, the fat little cow,' said Ostrog with some relish.

'I see. So the . . . Prince of Wales will become King now?'

'Not before time,' said Ostrog as though he was discussing the onset of a shower in August. 'I read their London Illustrative News. I know how the poor man is suffering. Well, there it is, I have inadvertently given him his chance. But, more importantly,' he sat upright with a light in his eyes, 'I have done my duty.'

'But you've been caught, Mikhail,' Lestrade reminded him.

Ostrog looked at him, darkly, then staggered to his feet; his face changed colour, his shoulders heaved and the warder at the grille began unbolting furiously, aided and abetted by the frantic McGregor and Wensley. There was a ripping sound as Ostrog's straps and buckles flew in all directions and he peeled the jacket off.

The door crashed back and three men rushed in. But Ostrog was serenity itself. 'Goodbye, my dear fellow.' He shook Lestrade's hand warmly. 'It has been fun. Thank you for calling.' He leaned close to Lestrade and whispered, 'Don't worry, tovarich, I've got out of here before. Twice. Allow me to congratulate you, by the way, on your English accent. Most impressive.'

McGregor took charge. 'Well then, Doctor,' he beamed, 'perhaps a quiet game of chess later?'

Ostrog looked at and through him. 'I think I'd rather watch a girder rust,' he said blandly, and sank into the corner again.

McGregor gestured Lestrade and Wensley out of the

cell. 'It's turned rather cold, Tom,' he said to the warder. 'Perhaps Dr Ostrog would like to put another jacket on,' and he nodded furiously in the Russian's direction as they left.

Lestrade flattened himself against the right side of the door.

'God, Sholto,' said Wensley, 'you're white as a sheet.'

'It's just the reflection from the walls,' gulped Lestrade. 'Do you know a family called Prentiss?'

'Butchers in Spitalfields? Yes, I do.'

'He works for them.' Lestrade gestured through the wall. 'Sharp knives. Leather aprons. Bloodstains. It all fits.'

'You mean the Ripper's a Prentiss?' Wensley was incredulous.

'That's not what I said, Fred. The Hand and Gavel's near here, isn't it? They're on you,' and they thanked the good Doctor and fled the building, careful to swing their legs wide as they met Dick on the way out.

M. J. Druitt

The visitor fumed and paced the corridor again.

'He shouldn't be long now, sir,' said Sergeant Dixon.

The visitor looked at his watch again. 'Yes, so you've told me,' he said, tapping the glass for the umpteenth time.

'We're in for a change, I shouldn't wonder,' Dixon stirred his cocoa dreamily with his thumb. That gave him the problem of having nowhere to put the skin.

'Oh, this is ridiculous. I can't wait any longer!' and the visitor snatched up his hat and made for the door. It was his misfortune – and Lestrade's – that the two men should arrive at the same point simultaneously. There was a crack of crania and Lestrade rolled steadily sideways, dunking his elbow neatly into Dixon's cocoa. The Sergeant steadied his superior and in doing so found a useful repository for the cocoa skin.

'Are you all right, sirs?' the Sergeant asked.

Lestrade groaned in reply.

'I think so,' said the other man, and for the first time caught sight of Lestrade's neck. 'Good God, did I do that?' he asked.

'No, no,' Lestrade assured him; 'a combination of things, really.'

'Even so, I'd see a doctor if I were you.'

'Allow me to introduce you gentlemen, now that you've run into each other,' said Dixon. 'Inspector Lestrade, this is Dr Druitt.'

'Ah, Lestrade,' Druitt extended a hand, 'I've been waiting for you.'

'Dixon, get on that blowing machine and order two teas – my office, double quick.'

'Very good, sir,' Dixon straightened behind his desk, 'and mind 'ow you go.'

The doctor and the policeman struggled together in the tiny lift, Lestrade's bowler rim pinned under Druitt's nose, and it was with relief that they spilled out onto the first floor.

'What I have to say,' Druitt moved confidentially close to his man, 'is for your ears only.' He leaned back, eyes flicking from left to right to check for eavesdroppers. 'Actually, it was originally intended for Chief Inspector Abberline's ears, but he told me he couldn't be bothered.'

Lestrade clicked his tongue and shook his head. 'Have a seat,' he said.

'I shall be filing a complaint against him, of course.'

'I'll get you the forms,' Lestrade offered, perhaps a touch over-eagerly. 'Ah, tea.'

He wrapped his hands gratefully around the steaming mug, then bawled to the retreating Constable who had brought it, 'I thought today we might have had handles!' He smiled at Druitt. 'Now, sir. May I have your name again, please?'

'Druitt, Lionel Druitt.'

'Mr Druitt . . . ' Lestrade began to write down the details.

'*Doctor*,' Druitt thundered. 'Look, Inspector, I have been passed down the line, ignored, kept waiting, ridiculed, walked into and wrongly addressed . . . '

'What *is* your address, sir?' Lestrade asked, blandly.

'Eighty-four, the Minories. I have a practice there.'

'I see. And how may I help you, sir, if Chief Inspector Abberline could not?'

'I am only here under duress,' Druitt said. 'If you hadn't arrived when you did . . . I came at the suggestion of a colleague of mine. Dr John Watson.'

'Sometime of 221B Baker Street?' Lestrade looked up.

'I believe so. We were at medical school together. We share the same club and dine occasionally.'

'And why did Dr Watson suggest you come to see me?' Lestrade asked.

'He didn't. He suggested I see Abberline. And all he did was point to a list of names as long as your quadriceps femoris and say, "Wait your turn". Apparently, he was working his way through a few hundred foreign sailors . . .'

'Oh, dear,' tutted Lestrade, 'that'll be a new one for Mrs Abberline.'

Druitt stood up. 'I can't help thinking you're not taking this very seriously, Lestrade! People are being horribly murdered in Whitechapel, the police are clearly at a loss to know what to do and you're being flippant.'

'I'm sorry,' said Lestrade. 'What is it you have to tell me, Doctor?'

Druitt paused in mid-rant and sat down heavily. He looked at Lestrade, then whipped out a silver hip flask and poured its contents into the tea. 'Medicinal, of course,' he said. 'I just can't stand Darjeeling straight.'

Lestrade was unfamiliar with the sexual practices of the Hindu and let it pass.

'The Whitechapel murderer,' said Druitt, staring at Lestrade. 'I know him.'

Lestrade leant back, pausing for the first time to take off his bowler. 'Go on,' he said.

'My cousin, Montague John Druitt,' the doctor said. 'I believe that he has been killing these women.'

'These are serious allegations, Doctor,' Lestrade warned him.

Druitt nodded. 'I know, but they must be made.'

'Tell me about your cousin.'

Druitt took a deep breath. 'Monty is thirty-one. All the right things in life: Winchester, Oxford, that sort of thing. We are an old family, Lestrade. There have been Druitts in Dorset for centuries.'

Lestrade wrote in his black book: 'Descended from the ancient Druitts.'

'He obtained his degree – in classics – in . . . let me see, eighteen eighty, it would be.'

'And then?'

'Then he had a yen for the theatre, Lestrade.'

'He became an actor?'

'No, a surgeon,' scowled Druitt. 'The operating theatre, man. He joined me for a while at my Minories practice and assisted in various minor operations. He was surprisingly good at wielding the knife . . . '

Their eyes met across a crowded room.

'Then, I never really knew why, he switched to Law; joined the Inner Temple. He was called to the Bar three years ago, shortly after his father died.'

'Go on.'

'It's not going well for him. He's had perhaps five briefs in all this time. Consequently, he took to teaching at a school in Blackheath.'

'Not Mr Poulson's Academy?' Lestrade cried.

'No, it's some appalling crammer,' said Druitt with some distaste. 'They'll be abolishing fees next. I don't know what the world's coming to. He's not happy in that post either. He's not experienced, you see. Only taught in one school before, and then only for a few weeks.'

'I don't see the connection between your cousin and the Whitechapel murders.' Lestrade was frank.

'I suppose it's what you chappies would call circumstantial,' said Druitt. 'He knows the area like the back of his metatarsals – his time in the Minories. He is also a natural with a knife. I read somewhere that these poor women were mutilated, possibly with a surgeon's scalpel.'

'Have you any missing?'

'You can buy them over any shop counter, Lestrade,' Druitt told him. 'My favourite I got secondhand from a butcher in Smithfield. Honed to perfection.'

'Was he? As you say, Doctor, circumstantial,' said Lestrade.

'So far, yes. But what I have not told you, Inspector, is that cousin Monty is deranged.'

'Mad?'

'Raving.'

'His mother, God rest her . . . '

'Dead?'

'No, in Chiswick.' They both knew it amounted to the same thing. 'They put her away three months ago.'

'Certified?' Lestrade checked, for the record.

Druitt nodded. 'Monty is exhibiting distressingly similar tendencies. Knitting without wool, you know the sort of thing.'

Lestrade nodded wisely.

'He's never liked women,' Druitt went on. 'Broke all the teeth of his first nanny . . . '

Lestrade knew a school chaplain like that.

' . . . still, I suppose she shouldn't have left them on the sideboard; it was asking for trouble really.'

'Do you have a likeness of your cousin, Dr Druitt?' Lestrade asked.

'Not on me. Oh, wait a minute.' He rummaged in his wallet and produced a sepia photograph of a darkly handsome face with sad eyes and a five o'clock shadow. 'No, that's my wife. I haven't one of Monty.'

'Perhaps you could describe him?'

'He's of medium height, swarthy. Hair parted centrally. Small moustache.'

'Is he in the habit of wearing workmen's clothes, Doctor? A flat cap? A red scarf?'

'Certainly not!' Druitt was horrified. 'He may be deranged, Inspector, but he still dresses to the Right!'

'Quite, quite,' nodded Lestrade.

'I am not a crank, Inspector,' Druitt said, rising to go. 'I leave for Australia in a very few weeks; I cannot answer for what happens in my absence. Believe me, I have come here with a heavy heart. The shame of it! A Druitt! But murder will out, Lestrade, or so I've heard it said.'

'So have I,' muttered Lestrade, momentarily at a loss to know where.

'Take it from me, Lestrade, unless Monty is stopped he will kill again.'

'Where can I find him?' Lestrade asked.

'Either at the school at Blackheath or at Number nine, King's Bench Walk, in the Temple. I'll see myself out.'

Lestrade had always hated the monthly inspectors' meetings with the Head of the Criminal Investigation Department. He hated them even more now that they had become weekly. And with the Autumn of Terror in full swing, and cartloads of suspects being sorted and shovelled every day, he was driven to doing his own paperwork. He longed to bring back George from Rhadegund. Even Derry and Toms would be better than nothing. But he must keep the lid on that particular kettle of fish a while longer. What he feared most was that the day would come when he would have to make his own tea.

'We are very privileged this morning,' Rodney was dithering, 'to welcome the Acting Commissioner of the City Police Force, Major Henry . . . er . . . er . . . '

'Smith,' the Acting Commissioner filled in for him.

A likely story, thought Lestrade, but Fred Wensley seemed to know him and Fred virtually lived in the City, despite his working for the Yard.

'Quite.' Rodney leaned back, stirring his tea with an air of complacency odd in a man whose city was on the verge of panic. 'Gentlemen, this morning I want to hear your theories. Dr Robert Anderson is poised to take over the case at any moment. The latest report is that he's reached Gobelins.'

Athelney Jones of the River Police, the most droning bluebottle of them all, broke into applause. Thirteen eyes stared him into silence. The fourteenth, Major Henry Smith's glass one, obstinately refused to swivel, though it had cost him an arm and a leg.

'Inspector Gregson,' said Rodney, looking at Jones, 'you will have your turn shortly. First, Chief Inspector Abberline.'

Abberline pulled his nose from his decidedly dog-eared gardenia. 'Gentlemen, I shudder to think of the man hours we've expended on this case. The miles walked, the boots worn out. But now, at last, I am able to name names. The Whitechapel murderer, the man we've all come to know as Jack the Ripper, is none other than George Chapman.'

A ripple ran round the room. 'Who?' Lestrade thought he'd better ask, as nobody else seemed likely to.

'Chapman,' beamed Abberline triumphantly. 'He's a hairdresser living in Whitechapel.'

'Knows the area,' nodded Jones.

'Access to sharp scissors,' Gregson observed.

'But these women haven't been killed with scissors,' Wensley felt bound to comment. 'The coroner's reports in all the cases . . . '

'We don't know what they were killed with,' said Abberline. 'We don't know if the murderer was right or left handed, tall or short. Whether he had sex with his victims first or not.'

'What of George Chapman?' Lestrade asked. 'Is he right handed?'

'He is.' Abberline leaned forward, wagging an enthusiastic finger. '*And* he's tall. Something of a ladies' man too, I understand. Large ears, you see. And the sort of moustache that drives women wild,' and he twirled his own with pride.

'I know that sort of moustache,' Wensley said. 'Is your man fair haired, rather striking appearance? Dresses carelessly on omnibuses?'

'I believe so . . . ' Abberline was bluffing.

'Severin Klosowski,' Wensley said.

'What?' Abberline asked.

'That's his real name. He's a Polish Jew. Along with Louis Diemschutz, Joseph Lawende and the hundred and twenty or so others you've interrogated!'

Wensley, in uncharacteristic mood, jumped up from his chair and swung backwards to the window where the rainy grey of a November morning bounced off the pane.

'That will do, Gregson!' Rodney felt he ought to assert himself.

The inspector of that name opened his mouth to protest, but Rodney swept on, 'Do you have anything specific on this Chapman?' he asked Abberline.

'Not in so many words,' the Chief Inspector was forced to admit, 'but I'm working on it.'

'Mr Lestrade,' said Rodney. 'We'd like to hear from you . . . '

'Well, it's . . . ' Lestrade began, only to be silenced by an unusually forceful Rodney.

'No, Jones. You'll have to wait. It's Lestrade's turn now,' and he turned to Honeybun.

That Inspector produced a page from the latest edition of the *Charivari*. 'There, gentlemen,' he said, 'The Nemesis of Neglect.' He held up the gaunt spectre, shroud-draped and staring with blood-crazed eyes, the long knife flashing in the shadows. 'The lid has been lifted off the stinking kettle of the East End,' he shrilled, rising to the occasion with the fervour of the Evangelist. 'Quit yourselves like men, and fight.'

'Fight whom?' Smith asked.

'Let no man's heart fail because of him!' Honeybun stabbed his finger into the air. 'My little finger,' he went on, 'shall be thicker than my father's loins.'

Doesn't say much for his father, thought Lestrade to himself, but it wasn't his place to say so.

'Do you have somebody in mind, Honeybun?' Abberline demanded. He was always a man on the edge and the problems of the past weeks saw him teetering dangerously.

'Thou art the man!' shrieked Honeybun pointing at him. Smith and Rodney, sitting nearest to Abberline, moved away a little. Thirteen eyes now fixed the Chief Inspector, who sat open-mouthed.

'I know thy pride,' Honeybun ranted, 'and the naughtiness of thine heart.'

'He's got you there, Chief Inspector,' Lestrade beamed hugely.

'Shut up, Lestrade!' Abberline snarled. 'I'll see you later. Assistant Commissioner, I insist this maniac be taken off the case. He's deranged.'

'Lestrade?' Rodney asked for clarity.

'Honeybun!' Abberline roared.

'I think you'd better explain yourself, Honeybun.' It was a rare moment for Rodney; he'd got the right man. 'Are you implying that Abberline here is the Ripper?'

'Any one of us,' asserted Honeybun. 'All of us. Don't you see, sir, that we are all to blame? We have allowed that sink of iniquity in Whitechapel to exist. It is an abomination unto the Lord.'

'Deranged!' sighed Abberline in exasperation.

'Can you come to particulars?' Rodney asked him.

'Very well,' Honeybun said. 'A social worker. One who has seen too much suffering, too little hope. He has killed these degenerates to awake the conscience of the nation.'

'Who *is* he?' Smith's eye began to rotate unnervingly. Lestrade wasn't sure whether it was the glass one or not.

'Er . . . ' Honeybun began to sound depressingly like Rodney. 'I'll find him,' he promised.

'Not good enough!' Rodney said. 'People are dying, Inspector, and you're babbling. See me afterwards.' It might have been Dr Nails talking.

Honeybun looked abashed, perhaps for the first time in his life. 'Behold,' he muttered, eyes downcast, 'I have played the fool and have erred exceedingly.'

Now he *did* sound like Rodney, Lestrade thought.

'Amen to that!' Abberline growled. They all looked at him.

'Now, Inspector . . . Gregson?' Right again. 'Your views?'

'A foreigner, obviously,' the Inspector replied. 'At first I thought the Jews – the clue on the wall which . . . sadly . . . disappeared. The Jews are the men that will not be blamed for nothing . . . '

'And now you don't think so?' Smith asked.

'I still think it's the Jews, sir, but not a local man.' Gregson began to light his pipe with an air of authority. '*Somebody* would know him and would give him away. Even in the Yid community, somebody would crack. The reward's high enough.'

'So where have you been looking?'

Under the beds, mused Lestrade.

'The ports,' said Gregson. 'Chief Inspector Abberline and I have been going over all foreign merchantmen, looking for a pattern.'

'And?' Rodney edged forward.

'There isn't one,' Gregson said sheepishly. 'There is no one ship that was here on all the nights in question.'

'Even so,' said Jones, 'eye-witnesses said the man talking to Catherine Eddowes looked like a sailor.'

'So does everybody in the East End,' Wensley chimed from the window. 'I think you'll agree, Major Smith?'

'Hmmmm? Oh, yes, quite, quite.' Smith hadn't a clue what East Enders looked like owing to his natural aversion to them. Besides, his view of them, by definition, was a little one sided. But he knew Fred Wensley's reputation and thought it best to agree.

'What about a hop-picker?' Jones ventured. 'Someone the workers picked up in Kent? That would make him an outsider.'

'All the more reason for someone to shop him,' said Lestrade. 'If these murders are ghastly enough to turn chavim against chavim, as the Jews have it, then surely they'd be wary of a stranger.'

'Yes,' said Smith. 'The lodger.'

'Lodger?' Rodney looked at him.

'Think for a moment.' Smith had centre stage. 'The man we are after knows the area. He kills on clear nights. He has no fog to help him. The women he has killed have all been reasonably strong and ought to have been on their guard, especially after the death of Annie Chapman. He strangles them, rips them open and vanishes into the night. He knows those courts and alleyways. But I'm inclined to agree with Gregson,' Rodney looked at Jones; 'he's not local, not in the true sense. The only sort of person who is not local but who knows the area is a temporary resident – a lodger.'

'The whole place is crawling with lodgers, sir,' Wensley reminded him. 'Every tenement has hundreds.'

'Druitt,' muttered Lestrade.

'No need to be offensive, Wensley,' Rodney reminded him.

'What?' Abberline was more astute.

'Nothing,' said Lestrade, anxious not to have his theories tested too closely, too soon.

'We haven't heard from you, Jones,' Rodney said to him. 'Out with it.'

'We've eliminated two important inquiries, sir,' Lestrade told him: 'Kosminski and Ostrog. They're both insane, but they're not the man we're after. But I've been thinking . . .'

'Well, there's a first time for everything,' beamed Abberline.

Lestrade ignored him. 'Something one of my constables said.'

'Constables!' Abberline snorted.

'Go on,' ordered Rodney in a dithery sort of way.

'What if the man we're after isn't a man at all, but a woman?'

There was a silence in the room.

'What's your motive?' Abberline asked.

'What's yours?' Lestrade countered. 'If the murderer is mad, we don't need a motive, do we?'

'Are you asking me or telling me, Lestrade?' Abberline snapped. 'In all my years— '

'Gentlemen, gentlemen,' Rodney tapped his Waverley on the desk top. 'Why a woman, Lestrade?' He really was getting better all the time.

'Because no one has reported a blood-stained man,' was

the answer; 'because whenever a woman is attacked, we automatically suspect a man.'

There were nods and murmurs of agreement.

'Let me try a theory on you, gentlemen,' said Lestrade. 'One which, I admit, has just come into my head. What if, *if*, mark you, the murderess is experienced in the business of her sex?'

'What?' Honeybun was on surprisingly alien ground here.

'An abortionist,' explained Wensley.

'Thank you, Fred,' Lestrade said.

'No time for delicacy, Lestrade,' said Smith. 'Get on with it.'

'What if these women, the four – or is it five? – who've died, were pregnant? What if they went to this woman, whoever she is, and she botched the operation?'

'It's common,' nodded Abberline, as the one with the most experience of these things.

'And to disguise the botch, she cuts their throats and makes it look like the work of a madman?' Smith had caught the drift.'Yes, yes,' he said with some verve, 'you may have something.'

There was a murmur of approval, even from Abberline, and Honeybun was still pleased to think that the Scarlet Sisterhood could be blamed.

'Of course,' Lestrade was less euphoric than the rest, 'there are two problems with that.'

'Oh?' said Rodney.

'First, none of the coroners, Wynne Baxter and the others, mentioned a pregnancy – remember these women were in their forties – and second, the timescale. *Four*, perhaps even five women, *all* pregnant and in need of the services of an abortionist, in one tiny area within *five* weeks. No, gentlemen, it defies belief.'

The bubble of expectancy burst. 'More hot air, then, Lestrade?' Abberline growled.

There was a knock at Rodney's glass-panelled door.

'Come!' the Assistant Commissioner bawled.

A uniformed constable entered. 'Excuse me, sir,' he said. 'Telegram for Mr Lestrade.'

Rodney tapped again with the Waverley. It was one of his least annoying habits.

'I'll have to go, sir,' Lestrade said. 'My sergeant calls.'

'Er . . . what's afoot?' Rodney asked.

'Trouble at Rhadegund Hall,' Lestrade explained. ' "Unexpected developments" George calls them. I am to go at once.'

'Yes, yes,' said Rodney, 'of course. Your hospital case in Nottinghamshire. You mustn't keep Sergeant Arthur waiting.'

It was already dark as the trap rattled into the quad at Rhadegund. It was the flogging hour and Lestrade heard the swish and whistle of Nails's cane as he climbed numbly down. Constable Derry was waiting, a mistake as it turned out, as he found himself rummaging in his pockets to pay the growler.

'What are these developments, then?' Lestrade asked him and he was answered by an ear-piercing scream which shattered the evening. Lestrade and Derry looked at one another.

'Dr Nails a little heavy handed tonight, I see,' observed Derry, uneasily.

'Heavy handed be damned,' said Lestrade. 'Taken to flogging women now, has he?' Then he remembered Matron's words on the Headmaster's paramour in Balham and felt his comments less unlikely.

'Came from over there!' Toms had arrived at the bottom of L staircase and the three Yard men scuttled through the shrubbery in search of the scream.

It was Lestrade who found it first, stumbling headlong over something protruding from the rhododendrons. Despite his cry, he was followed immediately by Derry who landed heavily beside him.

'I just did that,' said Lestrade, a little dazed.

'You couldn't have, sir,' said Toms, the only policeman still on his feet. 'You've only just arrived.'

They followed his gaze to the shaking figure of Matron, cloaked and white-aproned against the night. Her face was a livid mask under the moon and she stared at what had brought the policemen low.

'Feet,' said Derry. Clearly his years on the Force and in the Yorkshire Light Infantry had not been wasted.

Lestrade kicked the nearest one with his own. 'And one of them is made of wood,' he said.

'Adelstrop,' they all chorused.

'Yes, I remember him.' Lestrade clambered upright, helped by his Constables. 'Head groundsman and boat-keeper.' He crossed to Matron and held her heaving shoulders. 'Madeleine?' he whispered.

'Oh, Sholto.' She turned and sobbed into his neck, while the Constables shifted from foot to foot, whistling.

Lestrade glanced down. In her hand she held a rope, knotted in an odd way. 'Madeleine?' he said again. 'What happened?' She cried silently, clinging to him like a cricket-pad, unable or unwilling to speak.

'Toms, where's George?'

'Asleep, sir.'

'Asleep? But he sent me a telegram. "Unexpected developments" he said . . . Wait a minute. He couldn't have meant Adelstrop . . . '

'Indeed not, sir,' said Toms. 'The Sergeant was referring to— '

'Lestrade!' An echoing shout rang around the inner quad, bouncing off chapel and policemen. 'Put that woman down!'

'Oh!' Matron leapt away and the Constables stood to attention.

'Good evening, Dr Nails,' said Lestrade. 'I trust you are well?'

'Well? Well? What is the meaning of this? Matron, was that you screaming?'

'Yes, Headmaster,' Madeleine whispered.

'Carman?' Nails raised a disapproving eyebrow.

'Adelstrop,' she told him.

'Adelstrop?' The Headmaster turned purple in the dusk. 'Not your type, is he?'

'Past tense, I fear, Headmaster,' said Lestrade.

'Don't argue syntax with me, Lestrade,' snapped Nails. 'You haven't the background for it.'

'I mean, Headmaster,' Lestrade explained, 'that you will have to advertise for a new head groundsman. Mr Adelstrop is dead.' He pointed to the boots jutting from the bushes.

'Good God!' Nails stared in astonishment, 'and he was no age. Matron, this is rather delicate, but were you and he . . . ?'

'I don't believe Matron had anything to do with this, Dr Nails. Derry, Toms, I want him in the gymnasium now. This area to be roped off and patrolled.'

'All night, sir?' Toms groaned.

'Naturally,' answered Lestrade. 'Headmaster, if you heard the scream, so have others.' He looked beyond him. 'I can see torches emerging as we speak. Please turn them back. There may be valuable evidence here.'

'What are you saying, Lestrade? Do you mean Adelstrop is another . . . ?'

'Victim, Headmaster, yes I do. The sixth to be precise. May I suggest you close the school?'

'Close the school?' Nails roared. 'Unthinkable!'

'This happened,' Lestrade kicked Adelstrop's good leg, 'with three policemen on the premises. I cannot be held responsible— '

'Obviously not!' snapped Nails. 'But someone shall be. I've given it out to the press that we have diphtheria here. The whole place is in quarantine. That means we have no option other than to assume the murderer is one of us.'

'Unless of course the murderer is illiterate, does not take the local paper or has had diphtheria.'

'Lestrade!' Nails roared.

'Sorry, Headmaster, you are of course quite right. A conclusion I came to long ago. We shall talk in the morning.'

'We shall indeed!' and the Headmaster crossed the quad to drive his inquisitive school back to their dormitories.

Lestrade turned left at the top of the stairs, steadying Matron as he went. In her rooms, he poured them both a medicinal brandy and flung his bowler on the sofa.

'No,' she stopped him as he was about to remove his Donegal, 'leave it on. Please.'

'Perhaps I should be going?' he suggested.

'Oh, no,' she held the glass steady in both hands, 'it's just been a bit of a shock, that's all.'

'Of course. Do you feel like telling me what happened?'

She crossed to the window and looked down on the scene below – the clutch of constables working by a bull's-eye to rope off the bushes, and, stretching beyond them, the night.

'You can see the spot clearly from here.' Lestrade joined her.

'I wasn't in my rooms,' she told him. 'I'd just come from the san. Young Spencer and that custard. Well, cook did warn him.'

'What time was this?'

'I don't know, about half-past five, I suppose.'

She shivered and turned from the window. Lestrade glanced down to see Sergeant George, now in charge below, give him a cheeky salute in the lamplight. He drew the curtains.

'What happened?' he asked her.

'I felt like a stroll. There's been an atmosphere here, Sholto, ever since Maggie Hollis died. Like a shroud hanging over the school, heavy, suffocating. I needed to breathe.'

'So did Adelstrop,' murmured Lestrade. 'What then?'

'I walked to the lake first. I like to watch the mallards on the water.'

'Did you see anyone else?'

'Ruffage and his prefects were doing the rounds.'

'Is that usual?'

'Yes. Especially now. They patrol under the auspices of Dr Nails.'

'Anyone else?'

'Mr Mercer.'

'Where was he?'

'Going to his office. He often works into the night. He's a lonely man now his wife's gone.'

'His wife?'

'She died.'

'Did he see you?'

'No . . . I don't think so. Then I came back.'

'Via the shrubbery?'

'What do you mean?' She sat down suddenly, with the look of a startled hare.

'I mean, did you come back via the shrubbery?' Lestrade didn't know how else to put it.

'Yes.' She stood up. 'It was then that I . . . found him.'

'Adelstrop?'

She nodded. Then flung herself suddenly into his arms, sobbing into his neck. He put the glass down and stroked her hair.

'Who's next?' she whispered. 'Sholto, I'm so frightened.'

He held her at arm's length. The oil-lamp glowed warm on her tear-stained cheeks. He undid the silver clasp and her cloak fell away. Then the braided hair cascaded across her white bodice. She closed to him, looking up into the steady, sad eyes.

'We'll get him,' he said, 'and it will be soon.'

He pressed hard on her trembling lips and they sat together on the sofa.

'I wasn't out there to meet Carman,' she said.

He smiled. 'I didn't say you were,' he said.

'There are those who will. Cruel tongues, hostile eyes.'

'It isn't true, then?' he asked.

'It was,' her eyes lowered as she unlaced the apron and belt, 'but it's over. I'm my own woman now.'

He nodded and made to remove the Donegal again.

'No,' she said urgently, 'make love to me, Sholto, and leave the Donegal on.'

He blinked, but this was no time to ask questions. She loosened his tie and opened the waistcoat, her warm fingers tracing patterns under his shirt.

'Is it so awful of me to want you?' she breathed. 'After all, this is eighteen eighty-eight.'

'That's progress for you.' He kissed her again. 'Watch out for the . . . arrgghhh!'

'Oh, I'm sorry.' She sat up.

'It's all right. They're brass knuckles. Quite useful at times. No! For God's sake don't touch that catch. There's a concealed blade. I wouldn't be much use to either of us, I'm afraid.'

'Oh.' She smiled coyly. 'I don't believe that,' and she breathed in to allow him access to her stays. Slowly she lowered herself backwards. Praying his neck would not click again, he moved with her until he felt the skirt fall away and the chemise ride up. He hadn't expected the garter in Rhadegund House colours and wondered momentarily what she had been awarded them for, but thought it best not to pry too closely. Expert medical fingers released his braces and his hopes soared. In a moment his hands were roaming freely over Madeleine's naked body. She shuddered as he brushed her breasts full and proud in the lamplight, and she clamped her mouth on his. The sweet scent of her hair, warm and rich, tumbled over him. His neck was forgotten, his case was forgotten. Even dead Adelstrop in the gymnasium. Then he hesitated for a moment. The old doubts and fears returned. He was a Yard man and he was on the job.

'Don't stop now.' Her voice was barely recognisable. 'A little more. That's it. Aahh!'

'Sorry,' he apologised, 'I keep meaning to get that tear mended.'

She began to move under him, slowly, rhythmically,

the springs of the battered old sofa groaning with them both. Faster and more urgently as the folds of the rough Donegal fell like a tent over her heaving hips. A knock at the door shattered the moment. Lestrade's neck locked on an upstroke.

'Mr Lestrade, sir,' he recognised Derry's voice, 'can you come right away?'

The Matron and the Inspector looked at each other. 'Not now, Constable, I've got my hands full,' he said.

'Sergeant George's compliments, sir,' Derry went on. 'Something's come up.'

'Yes, I know,' muttered Lestrade. 'Cut along, Derry. I'll join you directly.'

'Very good, sir.' They heard Derry salute and the steel shod boots clatter away down the stairs.

'First Hardman's fag, now George's,' Lestrade muttered. 'It's moments like these I start to believe in conspiracies.'

'Oh, Sholto,' she moaned. 'Don't stop. Come back to me.'

He raised himself up, kneeling over her, then rummaged for his trousers. 'Duty,' he sighed, then closed to her. 'Madeleine. It wouldn't have worked. Believe me. I was . . . weak tonight. Tired. I shouldn't have— '

She stopped him with a kiss, rising with him and twining her strong legs around his. 'Yes,' she said, 'yes, you should. I understand. It's the case. These terrible murders. Your men. You've got too much on your mind at the moment. It's not fair of me. It's just that I was so frightened. So very frightened.'

'And now?' He wrestled with his tie.

She stepped back so that the light fell full onto her jutting breasts and the curve of her thighs. 'Not now,' she said. 'Not any more.'

She passed him back his bowler, a little out of shape now with their weight. 'Come back to me soon.'

He smiled, twisting his neck. 'I will,' he said.

By the light of the bull's-eye, Lestrade broke the circle

around the head groundsman. Adelstrop had been a man of indeterminate age, silver hair and beard.

'Apparently he lost his leg in a threshing accident,' Toms said, his voice echoing around the darkened gymnasium.

George looked at Lestrade. 'Terrible thing, threshing,' he said, 'especially about.'

Lestrade ignored him. 'That sounds like one of Dr Nails's attempts to rescue the honour of his school. He lost the leg in a riot, here at Rhadegund. All right, gentlemen,' he said, 'Time you won your spurs. Derry, cause of death?'

'Strangulation, sir.'

'Why?'

'Ah, we're on to motive now.'

'No, I mean how do you know he was strangled.'

'The lips, sir – and the ears – blue. Look at his tongue.'

'I'd rather not,' muttered Toms.

'Tell it to the Marines,' snapped Lestrade. 'This is a murder inquiry, man.'

'What was it that Matron had in her hand?' George asked.

'When?' Lestrade blurted, so quickly that only Adelstrop did not look at him.

'When she found the body, sir,' George explained innocently.

'Ah, I see. You mean this.' Lestrade produced the hemp from his pocket. 'The same knot, gentlemen. The same one we found around the necks of Singh Major and Anthony Denton.'

'At least our man's consistent,' said George.

'Yes,' said Lestrade. 'It's one of his most endearing traits, isn't it? I want that ground measured, sketched, eaten if necessary, but in the morning I want clues. Do I make myself clear?'

'Crystal, sir,' the three policemen chorused.

'I shall be with the Bursar if you need me,' Lestrade called as he walked into the tangle of ropes before finding the door.

* * *

'Good evening, Constable!' was Mercer's merry greeting at Lestrade's appearance in his office.

'You're working late, sir,' said the Inspector.

'Can't sleep.' He slammed down a photograph on his desk. 'Drink?'

'No thanks. Never on duty,' Lestrade lied. 'Matron says she saw you earlier.'

'We see each other cons . . . consistently, Inspector. When do you mean?'

'This would be about five-thirty. She was taking the air.'

'Yes. I was on my way here.' He waved vaguely to the darkened room.

Lestrade sat down uninvited, and shook the contents of the half-empty bottle. 'In need of consolation, Mr Mercer?' he asked.

The Bursar looked at him, nodding anything but soberly. 'Feeling sorry for myself, I suppose,' he said, lifting his glass. 'I don't drink much often, Mr Lestrade, but when I do I make up for the fact.'

Lestrade poured him another and threw his bowler onto Mercer's ledgers.

'Did you know Dr Nails had a mistress?' he asked the Bursar.

Mercer guffawed. 'Has he now? Some floosy on the tiles, eh? Well, I can't say I'm surprised. Have you taken a good look at his lady wife recently? Rather less interesting than the south face of the Eiger – and virtually the same colour.'

'Sir?'

'A mountaineering metaphor, Inspector dear; Dr Nails's other love.'

'She lives in Balham,' Lestrade said.

'Ah, you've been hobnobbing with Matron again.'

Lestrade denied it hotly.

'Women!' Mercer suddenly roared. 'What a waste!'

'Oh, they have their place, sir, surely,' Lestrade suggested.

'Misogyny, Lestrade,' Mercer said. 'It's mankind's only hope.'

Lestrade leaned forward. 'Let's not bring religion into this,' he smiled, topping up Mercer's glass. 'You've been here a few years. You must have known Dr Nails a while.'

'Ah,' Mercer wagged a finger. 'You haven't been reading your depositions, Lestrade. If you had, you would remember that I have been here for precisely two years. I don't know Nails much better than I know you.'

'Of course, you were in the Civil Service, weren't you?'

Mercer chuckled. 'In a way,' he said. 'God, the bottle's empty.' He whirled away to a metal locker in search of another. While his back was turned, Lestrade picked up the abandoned photograph Mercer had been holding when he'd arrived. It was a portrait of a woman, thirty or so, beautiful in a chubby sort of way. Scrawled in untidy copperplate across the bottom he read the name 'Martha' and below that 'For the old times'.

'Your wife, Mr Mercer?'

'Mmm?' The Bursar turned, bottle in hand. 'Yes,' he sighed. 'Martha, my wife.'

'It was my mother's name. Is she . . . gone?'

'Yes,' he straightened and studied his hand as he poured another brandy.

'I'm sorry,' said Lestrade. 'To lose a loved one— '

'Oh, I didn't lose her, Lestrade. I lost an umbrella once. That I regretted. It was a good umbrella. It's probably still travelling round and round on the underground trains.'

'I don't understand,' Lestrade said.

'I left it at Baker Street,' Mercer explained.

'No, I mean your wife, sir.'

'Oh, her.' Mercer swigged back his brandy. 'She left me, Lestrade. For another man. Or, to be specific, several other men.'

'Oh, I'm sorry,' Lestrade said. 'I thought— '

'That she was dead?' Mercer chuckled. 'I sometimes think she is.'

'You haven't heard from her?'

Mercer shook his head. 'Inspector, as you say, it's late.

I have two new members of staff to see tomorrow to sort out their finances.'

'New staff?' Lestrade repeated.

'Replacements for Denton and Bracegirdle. I thought Nails was wrong to open the place up just at the moment. But he insisted we carry on as normal.'

'Apart from diphtheria?' Lestrade reminded him.

'This is St Rhadegund's,' Mercer reminded *him*. 'A little thing like a fatal disease is not going to keep good teachers away.'

'But a little thing like murder might?'

Mercer shrugged. 'I've a feeling these two can take care of themselves,' he said. 'One of them has a revolver.'

'Does he?' Lestrade didn't know many gun-toting teachers. But he did know first hand how beastly some boys could be. Had it come to this?

'There's one thing,' Mercer said, suddenly sober and steady.

'Yes?' Lestrade retrieved his hat.

'I too saw someone tonight. On my way here.'

'Who?'

'I don't know. He was hurrying away across the First Eleven Square. I didn't think anything of it at the time, of course. Then I heard about old Adelstrop.'

'What did this person look like?' Lestrade asked.

Mercer shook his head. 'It was dark,' he said. 'I couldn't see his face, but . . . '

'Yes?'

'Oh, I'm sure it's nothing . . . '

'Yes?' Lestrade worried him like a terrier with a rat.

'He wore a gown.'

Lestrade reached the door. 'Well, at least that eliminates a few of us, doesn't it?'

'Does it, Lestrade?' Mercer said. 'Does it?'

Lestrade was on the carpet shortly after breakfast. He had checked the corpse of Adelstrop again, by daylight, and had paced the ground cordoned off by his stalwart constables. They had been unable to find any rope and had been lent some blue tape by the cook. One of the language masters had seen it and made some reference to cordon bleu which Derry found pointless. The language master had gone off chuckling. Toms thought it in bad taste.

Lestrade had also finished wrestling with the Rhadegund toast and had slipped yet another inedible piece behind the sideboard. He had watched the boys cross the quad in the morning frost on their way to morning prayers. He heard Ruffage's bell summon them and the thunder of Spooner's huge organ berating their ears while they were inside.

'This is insanity, Lestrade,' Nails roared, whirling like a caged panther in his academic black, circling and snarling, the whiskers flaring as he harangued his man. 'Adelstrop died under the noses of your men! This is absolutely the last straw. You accuse my staff, bully my boys and get precisely nowhere. Let me make it clear,' he pulled himself up to his full height, '*I* do the bullying around here. I am paid for it. It's what I do best.'

'You must close the school, Dr Nails.' Lestrade remained stock still while the Headmaster whirled this way, then that.

'And let the culprit get away? Come, Lestrade, you can't have become an inspector with naiveté on that scale! It defies belief. Ruffage's prefects keep vigil on the school bounds, the House prefects patrol the lawns. The staff have eyes in their backsides. If I close the school, whoever has perpetrated these foul deeds will walk out of that gate. As it is, he's here. Somewhere. He can't get out. And all you have to do is catch him. Good God, man, it isn't too much to ask.'

A knock at the door broke the silence that followed.

'Well?' Nails bawled.

'It's only me, my dear.' The diminutive, bird-like Mrs Nails appeared around the oak panelling.

'What do you want?' The Headmaster snapped affectionately.

'The two new members of staff are here to see you, Theophilus.'

'Lestrade, get out. I have a school to run.'

'Dr Nails— ' he began.

'Another time, Inspector, please. Ah, gentlemen, come in.'

He grasped the hands of his acolytes. The first was a tall, hawk-eyed man with a deerstalker and a neurosis. The other was shorter, more florid, grey-haired and moustached, bordering on the human. They both gawped at Lestrade.

'Thank you, Lestrade,' said Nails. 'That will be all.'

'Aren't you going to introduce us?' Lestrade smiled icily.

'No,' said Nails flatly.

'Inspector Lestrade, Scotland Yard.' He extended a hand.

'Wilson,' said the shorter man, blustering. 'Games and the Cadet Corps.'

'Charmed,' beamed Lestrade. 'And Mr . . . er . . . ?'

'Sherrinford,' said the other smoothly. 'Classics.'

'Classics, Mr Sherrinford?' Lestrade probed.

'*Si fueris Romae, Romano vivito more*,' beamed Sherrinford.

'Bravo!' Nails slapped the taller man's shoulder.

'Careful,' he winced.

'Aren't you well?' Nails asked.

'My bow arm,' he explained.

'Ah, an archer to boot? I don't remember that in your curriculum vitae.'

'Violin,' said Sherrinford.

'What?' Nails wasn't sure he had hear correctly.

'I play the violin. I do not shoot arrows.'

'Ah.' Nails's face fell. 'Pity. The world is full of violinists, eh, Lestrade?'

'Yes, Headmaster,' the Inspector agreed. 'Everybody's on some fiddle or another.'

'Well, well, I mustn't keep you.' Nails all but pushed him to the door.

Lestrade allowed himself to be ushered out and lit a post-prandial cigar while he waited. After a few moments, the new members of the Senior Common Room emerged, wreathed in smiles. The sight of Lestrade caused those to vanish.

'All right, Lestrade,' said Sherrinford. 'What do you want?'

'Want, Mr Sherrinford?' Lestrade was ingenuousness itself.

'What are you doing here, Lestrade?' Wilson asked.

'I was about to ask you the same question, Dr— '

'Sshh!' Wilson flapped his arms like an albatross taking off into a headwind.

' —before I go in to see Dr Nails.'

'No, no!' Wilson fumed. 'Holmes . . . er . . . I mean, Sherrinford, what shall we do?'

'We shall remember, Watson, that we are grown men and one of us at least has a brain. Lestrade, in here.' Holmes ducked into the doorway beside him only to duck out again at the sound of a scream.

'The ladies' cloakroom,' explained Lestrade. 'Shall we?' He shoulder-barged another door and nearly flattened Saunders-Foote against the wall. There was a tinkle of glass as the contents of his pocket collided with the urinal. He bobbed and sobbed as he went out.

'Who was that?' Holmes asked.

Lestrade slammed the door. 'All right, gentlemen. You have precisely one minute to explain your presence. After that, I call a policeman.'

'Very well, Lestrade, since you offer us no alternative,' said Holmes. 'You will know enough of my methods, I think, to know that I am not given to chasing shadows or following flights of fancy – especially Watson's flights of fancy.'

'Steady, Holmes,' Watson bridled.

The door clicked open and all three men whirled to the urinals, shaking various parts of their anatomy for authenticity's sake.

'Morning, Lestrade.' The Second Master swirled in, shook part of his anatomy and left.

'Who was that?' Holmes asked.

'I repeat,' Lestrade ignored him, 'what are you doing here?'

'Tell him, Watson.' Holmes began to light his meerschaum.

'Wait,' said Lestrade. 'It's a little obvious here. Into the cubicles.' He made for the nearest.

'Lestrade,' Holmes reminded him, 'Watson is a married man.'

'Not the same cubicle,' Lestrade explained and the sleuths amateur and professional took up their places on their separate blue-flowered pedestal pans, each one ominously called 'The Deluge'.

'Very fine early Crapper-ware in here.' Holmes admired the porcelain, before relaxing back, eyes closed and arms folded.

'Well, Dr Watson?' Lestrade had caught his jacket on the object which held the wad of newspaper. He checked the headline. It was *The Sun*, needless to say. Apparently, Mr Peel had just reintroduced income tax.

'It was a tip-off, Lestrade,' Watson whispered, his voice echoing around the sewerage system, 'from an old medical chum of mine, Lionel Druitt.'

'Yes, I know,' Lestrade said.

'You know?' Watson was on the edge of his seat.

'He came to see me. But what has mad Montague to do with Rhadegund?'

'Quite!' snorted Holmes. 'My point exactly.'

'But he taught here for a term,' Watson explained. 'Surely Lionel told you?'

Lestrade remembered. 'He did speak of one other school where he had gained experience, other than the one at Blackheath, I mean.'

'Precisely,' Watson beamed, though its smugness was lost through green tiles, plaster and brick. 'Rhadegund.'

'And imagine our surprise,' Holmes blew pensive rings to the cistern overhead, 'when we discovered a little nest of violent death in Rhadegund's own right.'

'Ah, yes.' Lestrade toed the party line. 'The diphtheria. Terrible, isn't it?'

'Diphtheria be damned!' snapped Holmes. 'You have a mass murderer on your hands, Lestrade, and as usual you haven't a clue what to do with him.'

'I have plenty of clues, in fact,' Lestrade corrected him, 'but my job would be considerably easier if I wasn't constantly hampered by amateurs.'

'How dare you!' retorted Holmes.

'I say!' An alien voice interrupted the conversation and it stopped abruptly. 'Will you chaps be long in there?'

Lestrade put an experienced eye to the knothole in the door. Since Mr Labouchere's Buggery Bill, this had become *de rigueur* for constables on the beat, especially in the Mary-Annes' Mile between Jermyn Street and the Houses of Parliament. Never ask a constable to do something you couldn't do yourself. Lestrade recognised the blurred outline of a white coat. Had they caught up with Holmes at last or was this Rutherford, the science master?

'Haven't you a lesson to go to?' Lestrade heard Holmes rasp and recognised the clench of enamel on meerschaum.

'Er . . . yes, I have,' answered Watson. 'The First Fifteen. See you later H . . . Sherrinford.'

Watson tugged on the chain to be powdered lightly with plaster and rewarded with a metallic clank. He decided to brazen it out. 'It . . . er . . . doesn't work.' He grinned broadly to Rutherford as he came out of the closet.

'I'll get Carman on to it. You can't get plumbers nowadays, can you?' Rutherford said. 'Mr . . . er . . . ?'

'Wilson,' Watson remembered. 'Captain Wilson. New Corps Commandant.'

'Ah, yes, poor Bracegirdle's replacement.'

'Yes.' Watson sensed a lead. 'What happened to him, by the way?'

'He was found one morning,' said Rutherford, 'with the Rhadegund Sword of Honour . . . '

' . . . beside him as he lay.' Lestrade emerged from his

cubicle. 'Terminal diphtheria.' He stared hard at Rutherford who, unusually perhaps for a scientist, caught his drift almost at once.

'Yes,' he said. 'Diphtheria. I assume an old army man like you has already had it. What service have you seen?'

'No,' Lestrade intervened again. 'Captain Wilson is not the Chaplain, he's in charge of the Corps. And games. The First Fifteen, wasn't it, Captain?'

'Hmm?' Watson was lost. 'Oh, yes. By the way,' he rummaged in his pocket, 'how do you wear this thing?' He placed the webbing straps on his head. 'Seems to be too big for my ears. Probably fit you, Lestrade, what?' and he guffawed inanely.

'Probably,' said Lestrade, 'but only if I wore it down here, Captain,' and he lowered the straps to groin level, 'where it does more good. Good morning, gentlemen.'

The coroner worked in the gym in the presence of Lestrade and George. Derry and Toms were stationed outside to prevent the prying of the new classics master and the new Corps Commandant. He pronounced Adelstrop dead, which gave Lestrade some hope as to the man's abilities. When he pronounced him dead from strangulation by ligature, that hope was confirmed. That afternoon, in a simple ceremony, with Nails, Gainsborough, Lestrade, George and Carman present, they laid the groundsman beneath the sod. The Reverend Spooner officiated and did his best with the long words.

'For man that is born of woman hath but a lort time to shive.' No one could have put it better.

'Is that really Sherlock Holmes, sir?' George asked under his breath as the rain drizzled from a heavy sky.

'Of course,' said Lestrade. 'I thought he was one of the unexpected developments you telegraphed me about.'

'No, it was the fact that the other one carried a Webley that worried me. I had no idea who they were. Are you going to stop them?'

'For the moment, no, but I want them kept busy. They're here on a possible link with Whitechapel. They don't know – or at least they can't be sure – about what's going on here. You, Derry and Toms are to shadow them. Wherever they go, I want a peeler at their elbows. Understand?'

George nodded. 'He had no family, then?'

'Adelstrop? It appears not. Nobody remembered him in the end.'

Remember, remember, the Fifth of November,
Gunpowder, Treason and . . .

'Clot!' A thunder broke through the evening. 'Really, Wilson, are you totally unaware?' Nails strode through the undergrowth. 'Other way up, man.'

'Sorry, Headmaster.' Watson struggled with the taper against the prevailing wind.

'How long have you been with us now?' Nails asked, straightening his mortarboard.

'Three days,' Watson told him.

'I wasn't happy with your handling of the loose ruck.' Nails was to the point.

'Er . . . the . . . er?'

'Not to mention that débâcle with the Corps yesterday.'

'Débâcle?' Watson thought he'd performed quite well.

'You were *in* the Army?'

'Indeed I was,' Watson blustered truthfully. 'Afghanistan.'

'Well, clearly the words of command in the Afghan Army differ a little from ours. If Ruffage weren't an excellent subaltern in his own right, B Company would be bivouacking in Peterborough tonight – no one's idea of a good time.'

'I'll try and do better, Doctor,' Watson fumed.

'Good. See that you do.'

The school massed around and behind him, forming a hollow square in the darkness on Ruffage's hoarse commands. Lestrade wandered at the back, with George on his flank, watching for something, anything. The chattering of excited boys stopped as Nails snatched the taper from Watson and strode into the centre of the square.

'It is fitting,' he bellowed, 'that on this, the fifth day of November, Rhadegund Hall should once again, as it has on this day for these two hundred and eighty years, follow the tradition of Guido Fawkes.'

He held the taper aloft, illuminating briefly the huge bonfire of timber and boxes and debris assembled over the last week. Whatever else may have befallen Rhadegund, the finest traditions must go on. Lestrade saw Holmes stalking behind the line of boys, the eagle eyes flashing in the flames that began to crackle and spit at the base of the pile. He seemed particularly suspicious of the Remove, but then who wasn't?

A cheer rose from the Lower Fourths, always the least disciplined on these occasions, and, stamping and chanting in the cold night air, the Houses took it up. First Chaucer, then Shakespeare, then Milton, battling with the roar of the fire that died a little on Lestrade's left, then burst upwards like a rocket. And the cheering broke into the school song, ripping lustily from eight hundred lungs, 'Rhadegundia, Rhadegundia, Floreat Rhadegundia.'

'Sing, Wilson.' Nails roared in Watson's ears. 'Silence is rank high treason.'

And Watson found himself bumbling along.

Then the sopranos cracked among the Lower Fourths. It was not puberty that had struck, but terror. Fingers pointed skywards, screams and shouts. The basser notes foundered and Ruffage's orderly lines broke.

'Water! Water!' someone shouted.

'Not again,' muttered George and he and Lestrade leapt forward, elbowing children aside. While most staff ushered their various charges away and cleared the field, Holmes and Watson ran forward too.

'That's better, Wilson,' Nails shouted, observing Watson flinging himself on the heaving, panic-stricken bodies in his way, 'but is this really the moment to instruct the First Fifteen?'

'What is it?' Lestrade was first through the cordon.

The four men looked up to the top of the bonfire where the flames licked and roared. A sudden gust of wind took the sparks sideways, curling outwards to singe Holmes's deerstalker and narrowly miss Lestrade's head. They looked up in horror as the guy tottered and appeared to stand for a moment as the flames consumed it. Then it fell, crashing forward and landing in a burning heap too close to Watson for his liking.

'Who is it?' he gasped, holding up his arm to spare his face from the heat.

'It's not Guy Fawkes, Doctor,' Lestrade said. 'Water! Water here!' and he turned too slowly to avoid the first bucket which hit him with full force. 'Perhaps not here, exactly,' he dripped.

When the flames were smothered and while the prefects kept their Houses in check in a wide, shivering arc, Watson bent over the body.

'It's a man, Holmes,' was his medical opinion.

'Well done, Watson,' the Great Detective commented. 'Who?'

'Can't tell. Ouch!' He withdrew his probing fingers from the charred wreck. 'But I fear he's done to a turn.'

'Well, Lestrade?' Holmes looked up. 'Do you recognise him?'

Lestrade looked at the blackened skull, the shrivelled skin dropping from it like autumn leaves. He shook his head.

'Could he have got up there by himself?' George asked. The others looked at him.

'Well? What's going on?' Nails had joined them.

'May I suggest . . . ' Holmes began.

'What, Sherrinford?' Nails asked. 'Out with it, man.'

'A roll call,' Lestrade finished the sentence. 'If you'd be so kind, Dr Nails.'

Three people had missed the Rhadegund bonfire. One was Spencer Minor. He had been in the san, the hapless victim of cook's stewed prunes. The second was the luckless Dollery, cowering in bed in his dorm because he had dreamt the previous night of water, that he was drowning. And that, to him, spelt death. The third not to answer the roll call was Mercer the Bursar. But he had not missed the bonfire at all. And his charred cadaver, the legs entirely burned away, was scraped off the field by Derry and Toms later that night.

Mary Kelly

Lestrade pulled his collar up against the cold. It was a crisp, raw dawn that Friday and the Inspector kicked the frosted soil that marked the grave of Adelstrop. Beside it, another lay waiting for the mortal remains of Charles Mercer.

'So you've lost one of your allies, Lestrade.' Sherlock Holmes wandered into the little cemetery that housed umpteen school cats, one groundsman and soon one bursar.

'Who told you that?' Lestrade asked him.

'Your other ally.'

'Ruffage.'

'You shouldn't blame him, Lestrade. A lot has devolved on his shoulders recently. He didn't know it was Mercer specifically; I merely deduced – you know my methods.'

'No, I don't,' Lestrade said flatly.

'But this is a curious thing,' Holmes went on. 'Watson and I come on a fool's errand, as I now believe, in connection with one case and stumble on another. I certainly move in mysterious ways.'

'If you'll excuse me— '

'Not so hasty, Lestrade,' Holmes stopped him. 'There have been times when you and I may not have seen eye to eye, but I've always acknowledged that you and what's his name, Gregson, are the best of a bad bunch.'

'Thank you, Mr Holmes.' Lestrade tugged his bowler in mock deference.

'Lestrade . . . '

The Inspector turned to him. 'We're not jealous of you

at Scotland Yard. No, sir, we are totally bored by you, and if you come down tomorrow there's not a man, from the oldest inspector to the youngest constable, who wouldn't be glad to shake you by the throat.'

'Sir! Sir!' George came at the gallop across the white-coated lawns. 'A telegram.'

Lestrade risked exposure by ripping open the envelope. His face fell, but it gave Holmes time to read over his shoulder.

'Ah, the Ripper has been busy again,' he said. 'You'll be going south. Mind if I tag along?'

Lestrade turned to him again. 'Regrettably, it's a free country, Mr Holmes. But if you get under my feet again I'll wipe you all over the mat.'

George, Derry and Toms had their instructions to stay where they were, to watch, to wait. Watson received similar orders. Nails fumed at the sudden disappearance of Mr Sherrinford on urgent family business, but he fumed to himself, smashing Gwendoline's mother's best china with his deadly cane. He couldn't remember when a member of his staff had defied him last, but he thought it was 1868, when one of them voted for Gladstone. He hadn't stayed long after that.

'You have to hand it to Nails, Lestrade.' Holmes breathed on the frosted window in their first-class carriage.

'Must I?' Lestrade's comment was sourer than usual. Holmes had insisted on the first-class compartment which had bitten deep into the Inspector's pocket; it was cold and another victim of the Whitechapel murderer lay awaiting inspection, as though on a rack at Smithfield.

'The way he's kept that school going. "Business as usual", I suppose. Odd, though, that no parents have complained after . . . how many murders is it?'

'Cases of diphtheria,' Lestrade corrected him.

'Oh, come now, Lestrade,' Holmes rummaged for the meerschaum. 'What sort of idiot do you take me for?'

'What sort of idiot would you like to be taken for?'

The train jolted into life, hissing and clanking as it gathered speed.

'Shame about the bloodhounds, however,' Holmes smiled, peering at the discomfited Lestrade through the pipesmoke.

'You knew about that?'

'Oh, yes,' said Holmes. 'Watson and I were there at the time. Of course, I had hoped for more from the chalked slogan on the wall.'

'You knew about that too?' Lestrade was even more incredulous.

'Naturally.'

'Ah, yes,' Lestrade remembered. 'The Professor of London University – not to mention the Sandhurst lecturer.'

'Not to mention, ducks,' Holmes fluttered his eyelashes and flicked out his tongue, 'Mog Cheeks.'

'The tall, male-looking prostitute.' Lestrade clicked his fingers in recognition.

'The same,' Holmes beamed. 'Not one of my most convincing disguises. Those damned stays were murder. And as for the beds in Fashion Street . . . Frankly, Lestrade, I don't see how our great British unfortunates make a living. I made precisely three and twopence in seven weeks.'

Lestrade pressed himself rather harder into his seat. 'I could of course arrest you for that.'

'It was all done in the best possible taste, Lestrade. Besides, it was all in the cause.'

'The cause?'

'Of justice, Lestrade. Can there be any higher cause?'

'So what did *you* make of the chalk scribblings?' Lestrade was prepared to try any port in a storm.

'Elementary, my dear Lestrade.' Holmes blew smoke rings to the panelled ceiling. 'Freemasons.'

'What?' Lestrade edged forward a little.

'The Juwes,' Holmes said.

'The Jews are all Freemasons?'

'No, no, the spelling, man. J-U-W-E-S. Jubelum, Jubela,

Jubelo, the three masons convicted in antiquity for the murder of their Grand Master.'

'I don't see the connection.'

'Of course you don't, Lestrade,' Holmes smiled. 'You're a policeman. According to masonic ritual, the offending masons had to be killed in a certain way.'

'What way?'

'They had to be strangled first. Read the coroners' reports again on Mary Ann Nicholls, also known as Polly, Annie Chapman, Liz Stride and Kate Eddowes.'

'Which you've seen, of course?'

'Of course. Then, they, the Juwes, were laid on the ground and their throats were cut. Does any of this sound familiar?'

'Horribly,' confessed Lestrade.

'Between the feet of Annie Chapman, some coins, am I right?'

Lestrade nodded.

'In a neat line, carefully placed, not scattered by a maniac in a hurry.'

'I see.'

'Another masonic symbol. Finally, the ghastly mutilations. Disembowelling, Lestrade, entrails carefully draped over the shoulder – all masonic.'

Lestrade stared at his man. He was still staring at Peterborough when a man got on, struggling with canvasses, brushes and palettes.

'Assuming all this is correct,' Lestrade and Holmes both ignored the newcomer, 'do you have anyone in mind?'

'Ah,' Holmes clamped his pipe between his teeth, 'I really don't know why I'm sharing all this with you, Lestrade, but I suppose you need all the help you can get. Reflect for a moment – who is the most senior man on your force?'

'Er . . . Charles Warren, I suppose, but he's going.'

'Because of public pressure, yes. And quite right, too. The man's an idiot. But he is also a mason.'

'A mason?'

'To be precise, Past Grand Sojourner of the Supreme Grand Chapter. One of the most powerful masons in the world.'

'Are you saying,' Lestrade closed to him, 'that Sir Charles Warren, Commissioner of the Metropolitan Police, is Jack the Ripper? You'll be accusing Rodney next.'

'Ah, no,' Holmes chuckled; 'besides, he's gone already.'

'Gone? But I was with him only days ago.'

'And days ago he resigned.'

'How can you possibly know that?' Lestrade hated to be impressed in this man's presence, but events had got the better of him.

'I have my irregulars.' Holmes tapped the side of his hawk-like nose.

There was really no answer to that.

'Excuse me?' A voice in the corner broke the moment.

'Yes?' Holmes and Lestrade chorused.

'Aren't you the Great Detective?'

'Yes,' they chorused again.

'No, not you,' the interloper ignored Lestrade. 'It *is* Sherlock Holmes, isn't it?'

'Excuse me, Lestrade,' Holmes preened, 'this happens to me all the time. It is, Mr . . . ?'

'Paget.' The man fumbled in his Ulster for his card. 'Sidney Paget, the artist.'

'*The* artist?' Holmes enquired.

'I wonder . . . oh, this is joy indeed. I wonder if I may impose on you and Dr Watson here to make a few sketches . . . '

'I am not— ' Lestrade began.

'Worthy?' Paget interrupted. 'Oh, Doctor, do not, I beg you, undersell yourself.'

'Go on,' Holmes gave his royal assent, 'but anything you may hear, Mr Paget, which passes between us, is not to be divulged to a living soul. Do you understand?'

'Of course, Mr Holmes, of course.'

But it was not with living souls that either of them was concerned.

The train rattled into Liverpool Street a little after lunch. Paget finished his sketches and promised to send copies to Holmes at Baker Street, Watson at his practice and one to the *Strand Magazine* for whom he occasionally etched.

'You'd better send one to Inspector Lestrade at Scotland Yard,' Holmes called to the artist, struggling with his impedimenta through the station smoke. 'Modesty forbids me to admit it, but I am, for my sins, one of his heroes.'

Lestrade's comment was drowned by a sudden burst of steam from the locomotive.

'Where away, Lestrade? I caught the drift of your telegram, but not its gist. Whitechapel, obviously, but where precisely?'

Lestrade suddenly ducked under a barrier and flattened himself against a wall, beckoning Holmes to him. The Great Detective hurried over, eyes swivelling left and right, wondering what was afoot and whether it was game.

'Here, Mr Holmes!' Lestrade suddenly lashed out, clamping his man with his handcuffs to the brass bar that ran near the pistons. Too late, the Great Detective lurched forward, succeeding only in scattering the contents of his Gladstone the length of the platform.

'Damn you, Lestrade.' Holmes rattled the metalwork in his fury.

The Inspector beamed, tipped his hat and scuttled off through the gawping crowds. On his way, he hailed an employee of the railway company. 'There's a madman who's chained himself to your engine.' he told him.

' 'As 'e now?' the employee croaked. 'Well, 'e'd better shift 'isself. It'll be movin' off in ten minutes,' and he hurried to the scene, rolling up his sleeves ominously.

Further on his way, Lestrade found a constable of the City Force. 'A madman has chained himself to an engine,' he pointed to the smoke, 'and an employee of the railway company is about to do him violence, I fear.'

' 'Is 'e now?' The constable adjusted his helmet and whipped out his trusty truncheon. 'We'll see about that,' and he rushed off to enjoy the fray.

'Mind 'ow you go,' chuckled Lestrade and hailed a passing hansom.

'Morning, Dew.' Lestrade turned into the cesspit that was Miller's Court to find the Constable shivering, pale-faced, in a corner.

'I think to be accurate, sir, it's afternoon,' he said.

'So it is. Had your lunch?'

Dew shook his head.

'Breakfast?'

'That's it behind me, sir.'

Lestrade glanced at the mess on the cobbles. 'You don't remember eating any of it, I suppose?' he said. He turned to face the man. 'You were first on the scene?'

'In a manner of speaking, sir.'

'All right, Dew. Got any loose change?'

The Constable fumbled in his pocket. 'Yes, sir.'

'Get yourself a drink. You need one.'

'But . . . I'm on duty, sir.'

'I won't tell Mr Wensley if you don't,' Lestrade said.

'It's not Mr Wensley who worries me, sir. It's Mrs Dew.'

'That's an order, Dew,' Lestrade said.

'Very good, sir.' The Constable saluted gratefully and left.

Lestrade turned to the door of the aptly numbered thirteen. He tapped it with his foot but it stayed put. He saw the window pane smashed to his right and, angling himself gingerly to avoid the glass slivers, eased himself in. It was a slaughterhouse. The walls and floor were daubed with blood, dark and dry now. What was left of a woman lay on the bed, her head turned grotesquely as though to see who had entered her window with so little ceremony. Lestrade suddenly understood why Dew and his breakfast had parted company and why he had not partaken of lunch. The Inspector had seen the Sights before – the threshing machine in the Hard case and the garotte in the garret – but this reached out and snatched his stomach like the prunes at Rhadegund. There was no nose – it and both breasts lay on the rickety table beside the bed. Entrails were draped around the picture rails left and right. And a line from the Bible came into his mind, he didn't know why: "For we have a little sister; and she hath no breasts",' he said quietly. Honeybun would have been proud of him.

'Sholto?' The sound of his name made him jump.

'Fred?' He peered through the rags and the filthy panes.

'I've got a photographer here. The Chief Inspector's on his way.'

'Is he?' Lestrade slid the bolts on the door. 'Then we'd better make this quick.'

'God.' Wensley stepped back from that terrible room. 'Do I look as awful as you?' he asked.

'You always did.' He stopped the police photographer. 'Had your lunch, Lichfield?'

'Yes, sir,' the Sergeant answered. 'Why do you ask?'

Lestrade patted his shoulder. 'You won't have it long. Don't touch anything, there's a good fellow.'

He led Wensley to the rather less putrid corner of Miller's Court and together they strolled along Dorset Street, through the crowd kept back by the constabulary. 'What do we know about this one, Fred?'

'Name's Mary Kelly, also spelt Marie. She was twenty-four. A doxy. Lived until recently with a Joseph Barnett.'

'Fancy-man?'

'Looked plain enough when I saw him.'

'When was that?'

'This morning. About an hour after Kelly had been found.'

'Who found her? Not Dew?'

'No, he was the first policeman on the scene. The bloke who found her was the landlord, or, to be precise, his assistant, one Thomas Bowyer.'

'She owed rent?' Lestrade asked.

'Don't they all? Which reminds me . . . ' He fumbled in his wallet. Lestrade swore he saw moths fly out.

'Do we know how much?'

'Thirty-five bob, I think. Does it matter?' Wensley asked.

'God knows,' Lestrade shrugged. 'I've clutched at more straws in this case than a gleaner at harvest time,' he confessed.

'Sir! Sir!'

'Yes?' Both Inspectors replied instinctively and turned to find Constable Dew hurrying along the road towards them with a man's ear between his thumb and forefinger. The rest of the man was muttering and grumbling about police brutality.

'Well, well, Constable,' said Wensley. 'What have we here?'

'George Hutchinson, sir. I met him in the Stoat and Salamander. He knows something.'

'Indeed?' Lestrade signalled Dew to bring the man into a nearby alleyway.

' 'Ere, I'm not goin' in there wiv no coppers,' but Dew's boot in his kidneys changed his mind.

'Now, Mr . . . Hutchinson.' Lestrade leaned his back gratefully against a wall and lit a cigar. 'What is it you know?'

The labourer decided to try bravado. 'I know 'ow many ounces in a pound,' he said.

Lestrade blew smoke into the man's face and smiled at Wensley. 'Ah, a comedian,' he said and leaned forward. 'I'm tired, Mr Hutchinson. And my colleague here is tired. And my other colleague has had no lunch. And he didn't have much breakfast. So let's stop wasting time, shall we?' The smile vanished. 'Or I'll kick your head around this court like a cabbage.'

Hutchinson swallowed hard and straightened his hat. 'Well, of course, since you ask so nicely,' and he took a deep breath. 'I 'ave known Mary Kelly for free years. I met 'er in Frawl Street at about two o'clock vis mornin'. She said, " 'Utchinson, 'ave you got sixpence?" An' I said "Yes, fanks",' and he began to laugh.

'We'll do the jokes,' Lestrade and Wensley chorused.

' "Will you lend it me?" she says and I says, "I can't, I spent all me money goin' down to Romford— " '

'Where?' Lestrade stopped him.

'Romford,' Hutchinson repeated with what little dignity it merited.

'What did Mary Kelly do?' Wensley asked.

'She said she 'ad to get the money some'ow and off she went.'

'Is that it?' Lestrade was impressed by neither Hutchinson nor Dew.

'No. She walked on towards Flower and Dean an' met this bloke. I 'eard 'er say to 'im, "All right", an' 'e said, "You'll be all right for what I've told you", an' they larfed an' that.'

'And that?' Wensley was beginning to lose the thread.

'And then?' Lestrade put him on the right track.

'They come back past me. An' I saw 'im.'

'This was two in the morning,' Lestrade reminded him. 'How clearly did you see him?'

'Very clear,' Hutchinson maintained. ' 'E was standin' under the Queen's 'Ead.'

Lestrade looked to Wensley for explanation.

'It's got a light,' he said.

'All right,' said Lestrade. 'What did this man look like, the one you saw with Kelly?'

' 'E was about my age . . . '

'How old is that?'

'Er . . . ' Hutchinson began to work out on his fingers, ' . . . firty-free,' he managed at last.

'Go on.'

‘ ’E was abaht five and a ’alf foot tall. Yiddish, I’d say. Small ’tache, long coat, dark, pale vest an’ a gold chain. ’Is boots was buttoned wiv gaiters an’ ’e ’ad a ’orseshoe tiepin.’

‘Inside leg measurement?’ Dew chipped in.

Lestrade and Wensley looked at him. ‘Constables,’ Lestrade tutted; ‘they’ll be showing signs of intelligence next. Is that it, Mr Hutchinson?’

‘No indeed.’ Hutchinson was strutting his hour on the stage with relish now, enjoying the crimelight. ‘Vey went in ’ere, along Dorset Street an’ I ’eard Mary say to ’im, “All right, my dear. Come along, you’ll be comfortable”, an’ they kissed an’ went into Miller’s Court.’

‘What did you do?’

‘I went ’ome. Well, it was obvious ’e was a live one an’ I guess Mary ’ad ’er money.’

‘That’s not all she had,’ murmured Lestrade.

‘What? Oh yeah,’ Hutchinson sniggered. ‘Good ’un on ’er back is our Polly.’

‘Polly?’ Lestrade asked.

‘Yeah. Polly, Mary. She answers to bofe.’

‘She doesn’t answer to either now,’ Lestrade told him.

‘Watchya mean?’

‘She’s dead, Mr Hutchinson.’

The labourer literally staggered against the wall. ‘The Ripper,’ he whispered, ‘it’s the Ripper, ain’t it?’

‘Dew,’ Lestrade turned to the Constable, ‘take Mr Hutchinson to Leman Street and get his statement, will you? Fred, can I possibly drag you to the Yard?’

The lamps at Great Scotland Yard burned late that night. Sholto Lestrade and Fred Wensley sat slumped in their respective chairs, wreathed in smoke and surrounded by cigar butts. For the umpteenth time they scanned the wall, covered from ceiling to floor with fluttering pieces of paper.

‘So,’ Lestrade coaxed his burning eyes to focus, ‘Marie Kelly was twenty-four. Twenty years between her and the others.’

'Except Martha Tabram,' said Wensley. 'Only . . . what . . . eleven years between them.'

'Martha Tabram, Martha Tabram.' Lestrade circled the room, twisting his back and neck as he went. 'Yes, I keep coming back to her as well, Fred. And yet . . . '

'Yet?'

'Yet does she fit?'

'Why not? She was a doxy. East End. Throat cut.'

'But no mutilations, Fred. No other wounds.'

'Neither were there on Liz Stride.'

'Because our man was interrupted.'

'Who's to say he wasn't in the case of Martha Tabram?'

'Who indeed?' Lestrade stared at the wall, chewing the ends of his moustache absent-mindedly. 'Come in!' he shouted to the knock at the door.

'Your cocoa, sirs,' Sergeant Dixon appeared with the steaming cups, 'and a letter from Dr Macdonald, sir.'

Lestrade took the envelope and left the tray to Wensley, who began stirring with his pencil stub.

'Well,' Lestrade said, 'here's a novelty, Fred. Lends some substance to Mrs Dew's theory.'

'What's that?'

'The Doctor says Mary was pregnant. About three months gone, he reckons.'

'Is that right?' Wensley wrestled with his cocoa skin, a recurring problem for moustached men.

'He's not running true to form,' was Lestrade's conclusion.

'Macdonald?'

'The Ripper. Mary Kelly was younger than the others. She was expecting. She died indoors. Macdonald estimates it took over two hours to carry out the mutilations.'

'But he's down on whores,' Wensley reminded him.

'He is that,' Lestrade nodded. 'So far down that this one was all but skinned. And the bastard nips in and out of police patrols like he owns the place. What *is* it about him, Fred?' Lestrade thumped the wall. 'Between Chubb

Rupasobly, George Lusk and us, you'd think *somebody* would have seen something.'

'Somebody has, sir.' It was Constable Dew at Lestrade's door.

'Don't you knock, Constable?' Wensley snapped, irked by this insubordinate behaviour in one of his own men.

'Come in, Mr Dew.' Lestrade was more generous. 'What have you got for me?'

'A bloke, sir, in the Truss and Ratchet in Cleveland Street. Sergeant Thicke advised me to find you, sir.'

'Thicke?' Lestrade groaned. 'It had to be. H Division?'

'Wasn't he the one who arrested Leather Apron?'

'Yes, Fred, yes. Johnny Upright. All right, Dew. And this had better be something. My cocoa's ruined.'

'Lead on, Macduff,' yawned Wensley.

'Dew, sir. Constable Dew,' Constable Dew reminded him.

'Of course,' sighed Wensley. 'How could I forget?'

It was long past the closing time as laid down by Mr Gladstone, but now that Lord Salisbury was at the helm nobody asked too many questions. Lestrade and Wensley entered the tap room among the smiling doxies, the piano accordion rattling out its manic tune in the corner and the smoke and the noise. They sat down next to a squat figure in rags near the door.

'God, Bill, you smell like a sewer,' Lestrade observed. 'Whose round is it?'

'It's all right for you people,' Sergeant Thicke muttered, wiping his lips with his forearm. 'You aren't undercover, are you? You know I was pissed all over last night?'

'Tut, tut,' Lestrade shook his head, 'Abberline on your back again, was he?'

'Oh, ha, ha . . . sir,' Thicke snarled.

'Cheer up, Bill,' Wensley beamed. 'Constable Dew says you've got something.'

'Must have something,' Lestrade muttered under his breath.

'It's all right for you blokes, gentlemen,' Thicke said again. 'You're not looking at a pension for years yet. What a way to go out! Thirty years I've been in this bloody job. Man and boy. Do you know what I had for breakfast this morning?'

'What about this fellow?' Lestrade prompted him.

'What fellow, sir?' Thicke growled. 'Oh, him! He's over there. By the fire. The one with the bloody topper. Stuck up toff. It'd take me six years to buy a waistcoat like that.'

'What have you got on him?'

'Well, I'm taller. And I've got my own hair.'

'No, I mean what do you know about him?' Lestrade tried to reason with the man. 'Why do you suspect him?'

Thicke flicked a little black book from his sock and passed it under the table to Lestrade, who flicked the fleas off it and began to read. His eyes widened. 'Where did you get all this?' he asked.

Thicke tapped the side of his black nose. 'Schtumm, guv'nor,' he broke into the Yiddish patter. 'It's all bloody Kosher, innit?'

'All right, Bill. Well done. Where are you tonight?'

'Third arch along, Blackfriars bloody Station,' he told them as they left his table. 'Don't bloody ask in future. It's all right for you buggers . . . '

But the buggers had gone, twirling among the dancers briefly to emerge the other side of the room. But Wensley did not emerge. A slip of a thing with wild red hair had hooked him in her shawl and the last Lestrade saw of him was his ferrety features disappearing under a hundredweight of female pulchritude in the form of the Madame who presided over the rooms on the first floor.

'Business must be bad,' Lestrade smiled, nodding in his direction and sitting down beside the toff. 'Lister.' He extended a hand.

The toff raised himself from his arm and frowned at the interruption to his thoughts. 'Stephen,' he said. He was a darkly handsome young man, perhaps a year or two

Lestrade's junior, with rich blonde hair, of which Thicke was suspicious, falling in unruly splendour over his collar.

'May I join you?' Lestrade sat down, roasting his backside a little on the firedog on which he squatted.

'If you must.' Stephen sank back into his solitude.

'Come, sir,' Lestrade kept up the bonhomie, 'this is not a night to be alone. Nor indeed to be abroad. Gentlemen like ourselves venturing in these mean streets at this hour of the morning. What if the Ripper were to strike?'

'The Ripper?' Stephen raised himself again. 'Why do you say that?'

Lestrade leaned closer. 'They say he struck again last night.'

'I read the papers,' Stephen scowled. 'I wonder none of these wenches has turned him in. A hundred pounds reward, I understand.'

'Ah, he's too clever for them,' Lestrade confided. 'Runs rings round the police, of course.'

'Yes.' Stephen almost smiled. 'I particularly liked *The Charivari*'s cartoon of the game of blind man's buff.'

Lestrade hadn't seen it. But, then, blindness apparently went with the job.

'What's your theory?' Lestrade asked. 'This Ripper chappie? How's he got away with it so well?'

Stephen stared into the flames. 'He's mad, they say,' he said. 'A mad doctor. Ha, ha, what tiny minds these policemen have.'

'Indeed,' Lestrade played along, 'but we know better, don't we?'

'Do we?' Stephen scowled at him, pouring the last of his champagne. 'This stuff is warm, Mr Lister.' He hurled it at the fire and it shattered into a thousand pieces on the hearth.

' 'Ere!' Mine host, a rather less-than-jovial landlord, lurched towards him. Good, honest high spirits were one thing, but wanton destruction he would not tolerate. His tolerance took on a more liberal air, however, when Stephen suddenly whirled to face him with the deadly blade of a sword cane glittering at his throat.

'Scum!' Stephen hissed. 'One more step and I'll drop you where you stand.'

The landlord retraced his steps, grovelling, leaving Lestrade to calm the quivering swordsman.

'That's a natty little thing,' he said. 'Yes, indeed, very natty.'

'Tell me, Mr Lister,' Stephen slid home the concealed blade, 'are you looking for a new companion, perhaps?'

'Er . . . perhaps,' said Lestrade, looking with growing desperation for Wensley in the mêlée. 'Who did you have in mind?'

Stephen smiled, his even teeth flashing in the firelight. Lestrade felt a hand on his knee and his neck clicked. 'Me,' said the toff; 'I have lodgings not a stone's throw from here.'

'Well, then,' Lestrade said, standing up, 'shall we?' and he was careful to allow Stephen to go first. Twice as they crossed the floor, he spun round, gesturing wildly to Thicke, who merely sat there, scratching himself. 'I know,' muttered Lestrade, 'it's all right for us blokes.'

'What?' Stephen asked.

'It's a good night for blokes,' Lestrade said and winced as Stephen linked his arm with his.

They left the noise and light and warmth of the Truss and stepped out gaily for the square ahead. The morning air was crisp and cold. Lestrade got funny looks from the pair of bobbies tramping their beat up Thrawl Street. Turning into Goulston Street, under the green of the gas lamp, George Lusk clumped past, bulging with his armoury of weapons, and behind him, whistling casually to the last of the stars, four men, built like outside privies. None of them noticed Lestrade and his friend.

'Have you ever had a friend?' Stephen asked him.

'Well, I . . . er . . . yes,' Lestrade bluffed, completely out of his depth.

'I mean a real friend, a true friend.' Stephen's grip on his arm became more earnest.

'Er . . . yes.'

Stephen suddenly stopped, turning to face him. 'And has that friend ever hurt you? Abandoned you for another?'

'Er . . . ' It was a line Lestrade had learned from Assistant Commissioner Rodney.

'I had a friend,' Stephen unlocked a door and led Lestrade up a flight of stone steps, 'who loved me with a love that surpasses the love of women.'

'Ah.' Lestrade sought safety in monosyllables. That too went with the job. He was shown into a single room, dominated by a large four-poster bed. Stephen threw down his silk hat and his gold-topped cane.

'But tonight,' he sniffed back his tears, 'I intend to forget him.'

'Oh,' Lestrade felt an unaccustomed panic rising within him. 'Is that wise? Your true love?'

'True love?' Stephen snapped, unbuttoning his frock coat, 'Here!' He snatched up a silver-framed photograph of a young man in the uniform of the 10th Hussars.

'Isn't that . . . ?' Lestrade peered through the lamplight.

'Yes,' Stephen said, nostrils flaring. 'The Pet of the Tenth. His Highness, Edward Albert Victor, the Duke of Clarence. My Eddy . . . ' His voice trailed away and his shoulders began to heave.

'You are . . . ?' Lestrade prompted gently.

'His tutor. I taught him all he knows.'

Lestrade glanced at the bulge in the Royal tutor's combinations. 'Yes, I'm sure.'

Stephen did not take his eyes off the photograph.

'Oh, but he's not worth it,' Lestrade pouted, entering into the part now; 'his neck's too long, too thin. His eyes are too poppy . . . '

Stephen's face silenced him. The eyes burned with a fierceness that caused Lestrade to step backwards, and not just because the tutor was down to his kicksies.

'He is perfection,' Stephen said.

'Oh, well,' Lestrade blustered, altering the angle of the photograph, 'I see it now. It was the light. Perfection, of course. Yes, I see it.'

'*She* saw it too.' Stephen peeled off his combinations and lay on the bed. 'You're not undressed.'

'Er . . . no,' Lestrade was facing his moment of truth, 'it's a little chilly.'

'Is it?' Stephen smiled quietly. 'Well, bring it over here, I'll warm it for you.'

'Who was she?' Lestrade desperately tried to cling to the conversation.

Stephen was silent. 'I don't want to talk about it,' he said after a while. 'Come and lie beside me.'

'I . . . haven't been well,' he said.

'If it's the pox, Mr Lister, fear not. I have it myself. Probably Eddy too . . . ' He suddenly sat upright. '*She* gave it to him! That bitch!' He hurled the photograph across the room to smash in a dark corner.

'She can't have meant much to him,' Lestrade soothed. 'A passing fancy, surely?'

Stephen's face was a livid mask of hatred. 'He *married* her, didn't he? They had a child.' His lips could barely frame the words. 'The bastard king of England.'

'He married her?' Lestrade repeated dumbly, not remembering the event in the *Illustrated London News*.

'A flower girl, Lister, a filthy little trollop conceived in a gutter. Well, we've done for her now.'

'Done for her?' Lestrade's heart leapt.

'Annie Crook. He won't see her again. No one will.'

After a while Stephen's anger subsided and he looked up, a new eagerness on his face. 'Now, enough of that, let me warm you up, you gorgeous . . . '

But he was talking to himself. The Inspector had vanished.

In his haste to vacate the premises, Lestrade, going west, collided with Wensley, hurrying east.

'What happened to you?' they chorused when the stars had cleared.

'I asked first,' Lestrade insisted.

'Well, you saw at the Truss, I was unavoidably detained.'

'By a girl with red hair?'

'And her mother, the Madame.'

'And?'

'Before I knew where I was I was flat on my back upstairs, the girl with the red hair astride me.'

'What did you do?'

'I told her I was a policeman.'

'What did she do?'

'Charged me double. Now it's my turn. What happened to you?'

'Ah, well.' Lestrade pulled up his collar against the raw of the morning and waved his arms like a windmill to attract a hansom or prevent frostbite. 'I went in a different direction.'

The same two bobbies who had eyed him suspiciously minutes earlier now passed again, patrolling. They looked at Wensley, whose shirt tails were still hanging out from his close encounter at the Truss, raised their eyebrows disapprovingly and walked resolutely on.

'I went to bed with a man,' they heard Lestrade say, and they quickened their pace.

'Sholto!' Wensley was horrified.

'Don't upset yourself, Fred,' Lestrade grabbed the door as the hansom stopped. 'He wasn't my type. Get in. Got any change?'

'Of course,' sighed Wensley.

'Bedlam, driver,' said Lestrade.

'You can say that again,' the growler growled. 'Always the bloody same this time of mornin',' and he cracked his whip.

'Do you think he's related to Thicke?' Lestrade asked.

'Talking of whom,' Wensley discovered the extent of his dishabille and put himself away. 'What did that book say that he passed to you?'

'Enough.' Lestrade mechanically checked the trap in the cab's roof to ensure they were not overheard. 'The toff at the Truss was none other than James Kenneth Stephen.'

'No!' Wensley threw up his hands.

Lestrade checked his half-hunter. 'It's too early for the jokes, Fred. Stephen, since you clearly don't know, is tutor to the royal family. In particular, to His Royal Highness, the Duke of Clarence.'

'Old Collar and Cuffs? You don't say!'

'Yes.' Lestrade mused, struck by a new thought. 'Old Collar and Cuffs, a man in his late twenties, with dark hair, a small brown moustache and a pale face.' He was remembering Stephen's photograph of the Pet of the Tenth.

'So?'

'Cast your mind over about three hundred shoe-boxes, Fred. The description fits. The man talking to Annie Chapman, alias Sievey; and to Polly Nicholls . . . '

'The bloke Hutchinson saw with Mary Kelly . . . '

'Too Jewish, but otherwise all right.'

'Wait a minute.' Wensley looked at Lestrade. 'Are you saying the Ripper is the Duke of Clarence?'

'Eddy? No, I don't think so, but I'm not sure I'd leave him alone in a room with someone I cared for. Stephen told me something about him.'

'Oh? Don't tell me, he dresses to the left.'

'Now, Fred,' Lestrade sighed, 'what is it that tells me you aren't taking all this very seriously?'

'I'm sorry, Sholto,' Wensley chuckled. 'But what was the tutor of the heir presumptive doing in a dive in Cleveland Street?'

'Drowning his sorrows, same as Thicke. You see, Mr Stephen is not as other men.'

'If he picked *you* up, he can't be,' commented Wensley.

Lestrade ignored him. 'He had an affair with Eddy and Eddy threw him over.'

'For another man? They can put you in the Tower for this, Sholto.' Wensley found himself whispering now.

'No,' Lestrade shook his head, 'for a woman. A flower seller called Annie Crook.'

'Annie Crook?' Wensley leapt so high in the seat that the hansom lurched and they heard the growler complaining long and loud, frozen on his perch.

'Come on then, Fred, let's have it.'

'Er . . . that girl, that girl . . . ' She was clearly on the tip of Wensley's tongue. 'Bedlam!' he shouted.

'I know!' they heard the growler shout, 'I heard you first time!'

'I *knew* I'd seen her somewhere before. She worked, part time, I believe, in a tobacconist's in Cleveland Street. I occasionally bought my *Pickwicks* from her.'

'Did you ever see her in the company of Eddy? Or any smart young man?'

'Only some artist chappie who had a studio across the road. Stickler or Stilton or something like that.'

'Moustache?'

'Clean-shaven.'

'Dark?'

'Blond.'

'Hey ho,' sighed Lestrade.

'But what's she doing in Bedlam?'

'That's what I intend to find out. But I'm dropping you at the Yard first.'

'Why?'

'I want to know *everything* on Eddy and Stephen. Especially Stephen.'

'Right down to his inside leg?' Wensley asked.

'No thanks,' Lestrade grimaced. 'I think I know that already!'

Dr McGregor of the Royal Bethlehem Hospital was less than pleased to see Lestrade that Saturday morning. He had been up all night conversing in classical Greek with a patient who believed himself to be Aristotle, and the cave had been damp and draughty. Neither could he help a great deal, for Annie Crook and her baby, the infant Alice, had gone. They had been taken away two nights earlier. No, it was not clear by whom. The sister on duty was not at one with paperwork, but she would never have allowed anyone other than a doctor to take a patient away. Who was the doctor? She wasn't sure, but it sounded like Herring, or Glaucous, she couldn't be sure which. And where had Dr Herring taken his charges? Who knew? There were sixteen asylums south of the river alone, not to mention private institutions and upstairs rooms. Surely the police could find out. Or perhaps the Salvation Army? But, then, no, for Annie Crook was a devout Catholic girl and weren't General Booth's men of the Methodist persuasion?

The Highest in the Land

Captain Wilson, Corps Commandant and Games Master Extraordinary strode manfully across the rocky promontory that Saturday morning, swinging his stick as he went. His Donegal flew behind him in the biting east winds. But today Captain Wilson was wearing another hat, not the old Medical Corps cherry with the badge carefully removed but the bowler of a general practitioner with a Poor Law surgery on the side. What, he asked himself, would Holmes be doing in this situation? And what a feather it would be in either of his caps if he, John Watson MD, could solve the spate of Rhadegund murders. For murders they were, he now knew. He had spoken to Ruffage, honest to the last. He had spoken to Matron, who had insisted he undergo a massage before he left. He had spoken to Spencer Minor, who had been very forthcoming. And he had spoken to the Reverend Spooner, but had come away none the wiser. What a curious school this was. Nails had given out to the local press that diphtheria gripped the place, so all the tradesmen deposited their wares at the gates and armies of boys trundled them around the grounds. The parents had seemed quite content to accept this situation. After all, the Michaelmas Term had by no means ended. There was no reason why any of the young charges should go home in the meantime. Only a Field Officer of the Household Cavalry wrote to ask why his son was not being taught the facts of marital life as, in his words, forewarned is forearmed. Over a battery of steaming kettles each night, Dr and Mrs Nails prised open envelopes and censored letters. Dr Nails was in his Heaven and all was well with the world.

'Good Morning!' Watson saluted with his stick the little solitary figure of Saunders-Foote sitting like a Cornish pisky on top of a tussock. 'Fine day!' Watson shouted, assuming the old boy to have misheard him on the wind. In the end he gave up and began his descent to the sweep of the Rhadegund fields below. It was his misfortune to coincide with Dr Nails, striding manfully in the same direction.

'Ah, Wilson, out for a stroll, eh? Nothing like fresh air, what? I see the First Fifteen are out below. Let's see what they're made of. Last one to the touch line is a cissy!' and Nails gathered up his gown and sprinted forward, the drizzle clinging to his whiskers as he ran. Watson had no option but to do likewise and, bearing in mind that Nails must have been fifteen years his senior, it narked him to end up gasping and wheezing in the great man's wake and to know he was after all a cissy.

'That's the way, Ruffage!' the Headmaster shouted. 'Tackle him low, Rhadegund.' He began to prowl the line. 'You're walking, Ovett,' as the wing three-quarter of that name hurtled past him at the speed of light. 'Wilson, the pack are a shambles. Get in there and sort them out, will you?'

'But, Headmaster, I am not properly attired.'

'Footling excuses!' Nails rounded on him. 'Get in there, man. By the way,' Nails snatched off the bowler and began unbuttoning the Donegal, 'any news of Sherrinford?'

'None,' Watson confessed. It was no more than the truth. Holmes had not been in touch since he had left Rhadegund. They were not generous with the mail in Bow Street nick and the Great Detective had been denied bail pending medical reports. Anyone who would voluntarily clamp himself to one of the LNER's locomotives and then punch an employee of the same company in full view of a police constable could be little other than deranged. Thus deprived of mail and bail, Holmes was less than communicative.

'Off you go!' Nails pushed him into the mêlée and the greasy ball caught him full in the groin.

'Mark!' he shouted hopefully before the pack buried him.

'Use your feet, man,' he heard Nails bellow as studded boots bit into his Norfolk jacket from all directions. Watson fumbled in his pocket and managed to get the whistle to his lips. Feeble though the result was, the hacking, gouging pack obeyed it and broke.

It was a muddied oaf who struggled upright in the mist.

'Right,' he croaked. 'Not bad, Rhadegund, but you're not putting your hearts into it. Ruffage, take over, there's a good fellow . . . ' and he staggered to the touch line.

'You're a wreck, Wilson,' Nails sneered and threw him his gown, jacket and mortarboard with a magnificent flourish.

'Rhadegund.' He raised a finger and Ovett passed the ball, which the Headmaster proceeded to spin on the erect digit. 'On me,' and he ran towards the far line, the pack closing on him. He elbowed the reinstated Beaumont in the jaw, kicked Ovett in the stomach, ducked, dodged and weaved. His fingers jabbed into Hardman's eyes and he kicked the ball high, cracking two skulls together before jumping over the bodies to which they were joined and sailing heroically over the line, tripped headlong by a magnificent tackle from Ruffage.

'Well played, Ruffage,' Nails turned to his captain of games and brought his boot up sharply to jab him in the vitals.

'And that, Wilson, is how it should be done.' Nails bowed. 'Play on, Rhadegund,' and he marched off for an early bath.

Sergeant George had joined the throng and blew on his frozen hands in the drizzle. 'So that's how it's done,' he said. 'Morning, Dr . . . er . . . I mean, Captain.'

'Been for your constitutional, Sergeant?' Watson asked.

'No, sir, I've been walking.'

'By the river?'

George nodded.

'Pleasant there, isn't it? Even on a day like this. Any news of Lestrade?'

George shook his head. 'He keeps his cards pretty close to his chest. How about your guv'nor?'

'My guv . . . oh, you mean Holmes?' Watson bridled a little at that. 'Holmes is not my guv'nor as you so quaintly put it, George, he is my companion.'

'Well, did you get any orders from your companion?'

'Orders? Dammit, man. Haven't you been listening? What sort of orders?'

'Oh, I don't know, like what to do should another one happen.'

'Another one?' Watson became arch. 'Do you mean another murder? I thought Lestrade was trying to give the impression everyone was dying of diphtheria. Maggie Hollis, keeling over as she scrubbed, Anthony Denton succumbing to the Klebs-Loeffler bacillus while relieving himself, Major Bracegirdle, a positive martyr to fibrinous exudates. What Lestrade forgets, of course,' he said with some dignity, 'is that I am a doctor.'

'Well, I'm not Lestrade,' George admitted. 'I call a spade a spade. And I freely admit I need all the help I can get.'

Watson looked at the man, dripping there in his Scotland Yard black, and felt vaguely sorry for him. He also recognised a fellow traveller. He admitted to himself, though never to George, that without Holmes he was rudderless.

'Very well,' he said, 'I'll help if you think you need it, but I don't think we'll have any trouble for a while.'

'Well,' said George as Beaumont was pounded into the mud with a squelching grunt inches from him, 'looks peaceful enough this morning.' He waved up the hill. 'Especially Mr Saunders-Foote. He hasn't moved for over an hour.'

As he said it, he froze. So did Watson. They turned slowly to each other, gaping like frogs in the mating season.

'Derry! Toms!' George found his voice first and four men broke from the touch line, scrambling up the slope with assorted boys watching them in amused bewilderment.

*

'How long has he been dead, Doctor?' George asked.

Watson was patting the man's concave chest and loosening the rope ligature at this throat. 'About two hours, I'd say. He was all right at breakfast.'

'Was it the kedgeree, do you think?' Toms asked, not feeling very chipper himself.

'Kedgeree may poison one,' Watson told him, 'but I've never known it strangle before.' He stood up, propping the dead man against his chest with difficulty. 'What'll we do?' he asked George.

'We'll get those kids away. Derry, Toms, get them back. Then . . . ' he marshalled all his years of experience, his powers of deduction, 'we'll send a telegram to Mr Lestrade.'

Watson positively sighed with relief in spite of himself. 'Good thinking, Sergeant. I'll send one to Holmes.'

In the case of Holmes, it was not to be. The desk sergeant at Bow Street opened the telegram and for the umpteenth time that week denied any knowledge of the Great Detective to the worried, hand-wringing lady who hovered at the door, claiming to be his housekeeper. The problem for Mrs Hudson was that the master was in the habit of adopting disguises, all of which fooled her completely and any one of which he might be wearing at any given moment. For all she knew, the desk Sergeant himself might be he. But if he were, he was giving nothing away. Besides, she felt sure that the master would never take a disguise to the length of picking his own nose.

In the case of Lestrade, there was another complication – Chief Inspector Abberline. There was no Commissioner of Metropolitan Police in the November of 1888. Sir Charles Warren had gone. Sir Robert Anderson was issuing directives on the length of truncheons, the width of cravats and the cuts of jibs now that he had left the eminently handy vantage point of Montmartre, where he was carrying out a criminal study of can-can girls and short, bearded artists. There was no Assistant Commissioner of the Criminal Investigation Department either, although rumour had it that some coffee-planter called McNaghten was tipped for the job. Rodney of course had had one final dither, unsure of his direction at the top of the stairs, and he too had gone. Whatever else the Ripper had achieved, the toll in terms of senior policemen was astonishing.

'No, Lestrade,' Abberline shouted. 'Out of the question.'

'But a man's dead,' Lestrade reminded him, waving George's telegram under his nose.

'What's one man to five women?' Abberline asked, 'or is it six?'

Lestrade had never been strong on ratio questions and he let it pass.

'I simply can't spare you, Lestrade. The City's in a panic. Policemen are actually turning themselves in as the Ripper just to get a night's sleep in the cells. I can't have you gallivanting off around the countryside, to Nottingham— '

'Northampton,' Lestrade corrected him.

'Wherever!' snapped Abberline, reaching for his pills and his glass of water with trembling hand. 'By the way, I understand you've got this fellow Sherlock Holmes locked up at Bow Street.'

'None of my doing, sir,' Lestrade was wide-eyed. 'I gather he was arrested for loitering with intent.'

'He could sue for wrongful arrest, you know.'

'He could try,' smiled Lestrade, 'but I think I can slap enough charges on him along the lines of interfering with police officers to keep him inside for ever.'

'Interfering with police officers?' Abberline raised an eyebrow. 'I didn't realise *that* was the nature of the offence. Even so, you'd better see he gets out in a day or two. But first, I've had a telegram from Dr Robert Anderson.'

'Who?'

'Yes, yes,' sighed Abberline. 'I know. It's postmarked Montmartre – that's Paris to you, Lestrade.'

'He isn't getting any closer, then?'

'He's due in tomorrow. He suggests we pay a visit to Mr Lees.'

'Lees?'

'The sensitive.'

'The sensitive what?'

Abberline swigged again from the glass, grimaced and poured a large amount of amber-coloured liquid into it. 'Please Lestrade,' he winced as the whisky bounced off his ulcers, 'it's last straw time.'

Lestrade took the telegram and the address.

'Lees is a sort of human bloodhound, Lestrade. Take anything you can to do with the Ripper case and let him sniff it.'

'Very good, Mr Abberline,' Lestrade humoured him, though they both remembered the fiasco of Barnaby and Burgho. 'Please don't get up. I'll see myself out.'

The Spiritualist Centre at Peckham was not difficult to find, even for someone without any gifts. The main hall was empty, apart from a piano and a bunch of arum lilies. A man slightly older than Lestrade sat in the middle of the floor, cross-legged, his arms outstretched. His eyes were closed, his bearded head thrown back. He was groaning quietly, probably, Lestrade surmised, because he had cramp sitting like that.

He suddenly came to, the cold blue eyes sparkling as they took in the tired, battered man in the Donegal. 'You are from Scotland Yard,' he said.

'How did you know?' Lestrade was secretly impressed.

'Never mind,' said Lees. 'You are troubled and need my help.'

'Perhaps,' said Lestrade.

'Come closer.'

The Inspector did so, crossing the pale sunbeams that fell on Lees and the polished floor around him. 'And who is this with you?' he asked.

Lestrade glanced round. There was no one.

'Yes. She's smiling. Wrinkled hands,' he said in a matter-of-fact way, 'a washerwoman.'

'Mother?' Lestrade blinked.

'She has a message for you,' said Lees, smiling inanely at the aura he saw hovering around Lestrade's head. The smile vanished. 'Where's that five bob you owe her?'

'Mr Lees— '

'Wait,' Lees held up his hand, 'there's something else.' He blushed a darker shade of crimson. 'Another question,' and he whispered in Lestrade's ear.

Lestrade blushed too and stood up sharply. 'Not since I was seven,' he said with firmness. 'This is not why I came, Mr Lees.'

'But I came to you.' Lees stood up and showed Lestrade into an ante-room. 'Weeks ago, I came to the Yard.'

'I didn't know. Who did you see?'

'Some brainless lackey. Abberline, I think his name was.'

'Oh,' chuckled Lestrade. '*That* brainless lackey.'

'I should point out, sir, that I am at the height of my powers. Her Majesty has been pleased to consult me on several occasions, to reach the Prince Consort on the Other Side.'

'Was he in?' Lestrade asked.

Lees spun round. 'Sir, I detect a note of disbelief. I was after all a close friend of the late Earl of Beaconsfield.' He hastily turned a photograph of Mr Keir Hardie to the wall. 'We still commune of a quiet evening.'

'Is he . . . well?' was all Lestrade could think to ask.

'Hardly, he's dead,' sneered Lees. 'Those who have gone over do not retain their earthly vestments. Benjamin's gout has gone. He is in perfect peace.'

'Oh, good,' Lestrade smiled. 'Now, Mr Lees, to the purpose of my visit.'

'Before that, Mr . . . er . . . ?'

'Lestrade, Inspector Lestrade. Yes?'

'I came to the Yard the day the double event took

place – hours *before*, you understand. I had a presentiment, Inspector . . . I didn't feel well.' He turned pale and began to mop the brow, suddenly bedewed. 'I went to my doctor. He advised rest. I went abroad.'

'Where?'

'Ventnor.'

'Ah.'

'On my return,' Lees' eyes shone with a new intensity, 'I was riding on an omnibus with my wife, when . . . '

'Yes?'

'I had the same strange sensations. Sensations, Mr Lestrade, such as I never had before in such intensity. Such as I cannot describe to you. We were in Notting Hill . . . '

'Ah, well.' It all became crystal clear.

'A man got on. I turned to my wife and I said, "Mrs Lees", I said, "*that* man is Jack the Ripper".'

'What was your wife's reaction?'

Lees shuddered. 'I fear Mrs Lees is not of the persuasion, Mr Lestrade. She scoffed and told me not to be foolish.'

'What did you do?'

'I determined to follow the man. He got off at Marble Arch and I followed him. He was in a state of agitation until he hailed a cab in Piccadilly. I even told a passing constable of my suspicions.'

'What did he do?'

'Offered to run me in for wasting police time.'

'Yes,' Lestrade sighed, beginning to recognise the feeling.

'I could take you to the very house,' Lees whispered, as though the walls had ears.

'All right,' Lestrade said. 'But first, have a look at this.' He handed Lees a bloodied apron, stiff and brown with the life essence of Annie Chapman. Lees looked at it, sniffed it as Abberline said he would and held it gently in his fingers, moving it slowly between them.

'A lady of the night,' he murmured. 'Forty or so. She died slowly. In pain. I see . . . no . . . the name Ann or

Sylvie . . . it's distant . . . Do you have anything else?'

'Of hers, no. What about this?'

Lestrade handed the crumpled piece of envelope with the crest of the Sussex Regiment he had been handed long ago near the corpse of Mary Ann Nicholls. Lees held it to the light. 'The Sussex Regiment,' he said. 'I see blood, much blood . . . '

'Oh?' Lestrade lowered himself uneasily onto a chair, so that he straddled it, resting his elbows on the back.

'Oh, no,' Lees' face fell. 'That's Quebec. The Regiment fought there. Nothing to do with this case at all.'

'How about this?'

Lees took the grape stems a constable had found near the body of Liz Stride. 'Yes,' his face became ashen grey, 'they shared these. Another lady of the night. Some of her teeth were missing. I see . . . a camera. No, there was a second.'

'Yes.' Lestrade was impressed again. 'Photographs were taken . . . '

' . . . of the eyes of the second,' Lees said suddenly.

'Right again,' Lestrade admitted. 'She shared the grapes with whom?'

'The man on the omnibus,' he said.

'What about this?' Lestrade gave Lees the cashew nuts still in their bag as on the day Fred Wensley gave them to him.

Lees held them against his cheek, rocking slightly. 'These too,' he said. 'I see a medical man,' he whispered, 'skilful, trained fingers. They've been all over these.'

'The mad doctor,' Lestrade said, half to himself.

'Madder than you know.'

'And lastly, this.' He gave the sensitive a piece of Martha Tabram's dress, faded and torn.

Lees' eyes widened. He looked confused, and frowned at the material. 'No,' he said. 'This doesn't fit.'

'Not our man?' Lestrade asked.

'Not the *same* man,' said Lees. Lestrade was not surprised. Martha Tabram had never quite fitted the pattern, somehow. 'Edmund. The name Edmund?' Lestrade looked blank. 'Wait. There's more.' He beckoned Lestrade closer. 'I see boys.'

Lestrade looked around. 'Boys?' he repeated.

'A school. I see a gown. A rope . . . It's you!' he suddenly snapped, jabbing a finger into Lestrade's eye. 'Oh, I do apologise, Inspector,' he said.

Lestrade glared at him through his tears. 'Quite all right,' he hissed. 'Are you accusing me of being Jack the Ripper?'

Lees stood up, his face ashen in the morning sun. 'No,' he said, holding up the tatters of Tabram's dress, 'but you have met the man who did this. You know him, Inspector.'

The Inspector and the sensitive took an omnibus at the corner. Lees was paying. They alighted at Brook Street a little after lunch and stood before the imposing classical façade of Number 74.

'Lestrade,' Lees gripped his arm, 'I can't . . . I don't feel well . . . ' and he slumped against the portico.

'All right, Mr Lees.' Lestrade supported him. 'This is my business now. You can go home. And thank you. Thank you very much. If I need you again, I'll know where to find you.'

A sour-faced maid showed Lestrade into a plush lobby and here he was asked to wait. He took in the opulence, the power, and yet he was struck too by a hint of sorrow, deeper and more haunting, as he paced the black and white tiles.

'Inspector Lestrade?' a lady called from the grand sweep of the staircase. 'I am Lady Gull. How may I help you?'

Gull. The ornithology which had been so vital to Lestrade in the El Guano Affair came to his rescue now. The doctor who had removed Annie Crook from Bedlam had been called Herring or Glaucous. Both of them types of *gull*.

'I am here to see your husband, madam, if he is the master of the house.'

Lady Gull floated downwards. 'Peggy, some refreshment

for the Inspector – in the library, I think. Shall we?' She showed him into the oak-panelled room, with wall-to-wall anatomy tomes and a large globe, draped with a velvet cloth with curious symbols, a pair of dividers woven in gold thread.

'I'm afraid my husband isn't well,' she said, inviting him to sit down. 'He's been under rather a lot of strain recently.'

'You must forgive me, Lady Gull, but I am unaware who your husband is.'

'You have come to see him, Inspector, and you do not know who he is. Isn't that rather odd?'

'Not really, madam. You see, I am from Scotland Yard.'

'Well,' Lady Gull spread her satin dress to cover most of the chaise longue, 'he is Physician in Ordinary to Her Majesty.'

'That must indeed be a stressful occupation,' Lestrade agreed.

'It's not just that.' Lady Gull looked anxious. 'My husband has been followed, Inspector. Here, to this house.'

'By a bearded gentlemen with blue eyes and a wild look?' Lestrade asked.

'Why, yes, how did you know? Ah, Peggy.' The maid arrived. 'Will you take tea, Inspector?'

'Thank you, yes.'

'I'll do it, Peggy.' The maid bobbed and left. 'Cream and sugar, Mr Lestrade?'

'Thank you.'

'This man who followed William. Was he a policeman?'

'No, madam. He is a medium.'

'A medium?' Lady Gull was astonished. 'Do you mean a spiritualist?'

'A clairvoyant.'

'I don't understand.'

'Lady Gull,' Lestrade burned his tongue horribly on the tea but tried desperately not to show it, 'I should tell you that I am investigating the Whitechapel murders.'

Lady Gull's response was to drop her cup onto the Chinese carpet. 'Then you know,' she said.

Lestrade felt the hairs on his neck creep. 'Perhaps you'd like to tell me?' he hedged.

Lady Gull walked to the window. 'My husband was not home on the nights of the murders, Inspector,' she told him, 'not any of them. At first, of course, I paid no attention. William is a busy man. He lectures, he tends the royal family, he attends lodge meetings . . . '

'Lodge meetings?' Lestrade interrupted.

Lady Gull waved her hand towards the velvet pall with the gold devices. 'My husband is a freemason, Inspector. Rather a senior one, I believe.'

Bells were clanging in Lestrade's head. Surely Sherlock Holmes couldn't be *right*?

'Go on,' he said.

'On the night that that poor Chapman woman met her end, William came in late – three, perhaps four in the morning. His shirt was covered in blood . . . ' Lady Gull's voice trailed away.

They both jumped at the slam of a door. Lestrady duly allowed the contents of his cup to join Lady Gull's on the carpet. A heavy, fearsome man with deep-set eyes and a centre parting stood there, hands thrust into his pockets by the thumbs, gold fob swinging at his waistcoat.

'Hilda. Who have we here?' he growled with some distaste.

'Dear,' she fumbled with the brasswork on the bureau, 'this is Inspector Lestrade, of Scotland Yard. Mr Lestrade, my husband, Sir William Gull.'

Lestrade stood up. 'I am here concerning the matter of . . . '

'The Whitechapel murders, yes, I heard. What have they to do with me?' He brushed past Lestrade and poured himself a brandy from the tantalus.

'I was hoping you'd tell me, sir,' Lestrade said.

Gull spun round. 'What the devil do you mean?' he asked.

'Lady Gull has told me you were out on the nights in question.'

Gull glowered at his wife, who shrank back. 'William,' she whispered, 'I had to.'

'So was half London, I'll wager.' Gull maintained his defiance. 'The nights in question!' He quaffed the brandy and poured himself another. 'How pathetic your jargon is, you flatfeet. I had my fill of coppers on the Bravo case— '

'William!' Lady Gull exploded, then retreated as his eyes lashed her. 'William, it's no use. This gentleman knows.'

'Knows? What?'

'The blood-stained shirt,' she said, tears running the length of her pale face.

'A nosebleed,' he dismissed it. 'Nothing more.'

'Jubela, Jubelum, Jubelo,' said Lestrade. 'The Juwes are the men that will not be blamed for nothing.'

Gull's glass dropped from his hand, falling to the ground to lie alongside the two cups already there. He dropped near them, on his knees in the Chinese pile. Lady Gull rushed to comfort him, sobbing as the huge man knelt there in silence, as though poleaxed. When he looked up at Lestrade again the fight had gone out of him. 'I haven't been well,' he said. 'On the night Annie Chapman died I found myself sitting upstairs in my room. How I'd got there or where I'd been, I haven't the faintest idea.'

'Do you know the Whitechapel area, sir?' Lestrade asked.

Gull shook his head. 'My coachman, Netley, does.'

'Do you like grapes, Sir William?'

The Great Physician looked at him. 'Why, yes. Why do you ask?'

'And cashews?'

'I'd do something about that cold,' Gull said, dully. He hauled himself upright. 'I haven't been myself for some time,' he said. He crossed to Lestrade and looked at him directly with those piercing dark eyes. 'Lestrade, am I the Whitechapel murderer? Am I Jack the Ripper?'

But before Lestrade could answer, the maid appeared again. 'Begging your pardon, sir, mum, there's some doctors to see Sir William.'

'Mr Lestrade,' Lady Gull took his arm, 'we must obviously talk further. I wonder, however, if you would allow William to see these men? They are colleagues of his. I asked them to come. It is most urgent they see him.'

Lestrade hesitated for one long, dangerous moment, then he relented. 'I shall call back tomorrow, Lady Gull,' he said. 'Sir William,' and he left the library as a dozen, black-coated, top-hatted gentlemen trooped past him through the lobby. As Lady Gull made her exit, before the door closed, Lestrade saw the arrivals one by one hook their left knees over their arms before shaking Gull's hand. He did likewise.

When Lestrade returned to Number 74 Brook Street, Mayfair, as he promised he would, the house was in darkness, shutters closed and locked. Furious with himself, he ran round it hammering maniacally on every door he could find. At last, the maid appeared at the French windows at the rear.

'Where is he?' Lestrade demanded. 'Where is Sir William Gull?'

'Oh, sir,' the maid blew violently into her apron, 'he's gone, sir.'

'I can see that,' snapped the Inspector. 'Where?'

She pointed skyward and, slowly, the light dawned. He gripped the girl's bony shoulders. 'What? Do you mean he's dead?'

'As a dodo,' she said.

'But yesterday he was as fit as a fiddle. Swigging brandy to the manor born.'

'I know,' she sobbed, 'but right after those gentlemen left he was took queer. A stroke, it was. He had one a year back. Missus was ever so brave.'

'Where is Lady Gull?'

'With friends, sir, until the funeral.'

'What friends? Where?' Lestrade shook her.

'I don't know, sir, honest to God, I don't. Missus didn't say. I was to lock up the house and go home. I was doing just that when you come round. Whatever he's done, sir, it's all over now, isn't it?'

Lestrade tilted his bowler back and sighed. 'No, my dear girl, not by a long chalk it isn't.'

What with the pressures on the Metropolitan and City Forces that November, Abberline refused to spare a copper on chasing the dead. Convinced that the late Sir William Gull was not as late as all that, Lestrade combed London's undertakers from Jay's to the Seven Dials Emporium and not one could be found who would admit to laying out the Physician in Ordinary, nor indeed anything else. Several of them were impressed with Lestrade's parchment skin and sour expression, however; eight of them gave him their cards in case he needed them in the near future and two of them offered him a job. The burial grounds and cemeteries were no more use. He wobbled perilously on planking above a new and yawning grave at Kensal Green, brought a funeral at Highgate to a standstill, insisting on viewing the corpse, and got himself locked in a vault at Abney Park after the cemetery was closed. Twice during the night he was reminded of the old police joke; he distinctly heard a voice beside him on the shelf saying, 'Cold in 'ere, ain't it?' He put it down to exhaustion.

In the morning, after the inevitable altercation with the turnkey, he stumbled numbly in a different direction – to King's Bench Walk in the Temple, in search of his other quarry, Mr Druitt. After all, if Gull *was* dead, and if Lestrade leapt to the wrong conclusions, another East End woman might die. No stone must be left unturned. But Mr Druitt was not there. And other members of his Chambers said he had not been for some time. He was in the habit of frequenting his cousin Lionel's surgery in the Minories – had the Inspector thought of trying there?

In the Autumn of Terror, the busy face of a great city became greyer and older as Lestrade travelled east. The gaiety of the costers, the shouts of the street vendors were somehow duller, somehow less. The bobbies had always patrolled in twos in those mean streets, but now so did the recruiting sergeants, and the harlots were in knots of three and four. Even the old flower seller who offered Lestrade a bunch of heather for his lucky face carried a brick in her basket. From the banner headlines of the *Standard* and *News*, the press screamed for vengeance and police action. Lestrade turned his collar up against the cold of hostility and rang the surgery bell of Dr Druitt. It was opened by a man a few years his junior, with sad, dark eyes, a small moustache and a centre parting, not unlike the photograph of the Duke of Clarence Lestrade had seen smashed recently. And not unlike the eye-witness accounts of men seen talking to the various deceased near Buck's Row and Hanbury Street and Berners Street and Mitre Square and Dorset Street.

'I was looking for Dr Druitt,' Lestrade lied.

'I'm sorry, the surgery is closed; I am Montague Druitt, the Doctor's cousin. May I help?'

'I am Inspector Lestrade of Scotland Yard.'

'Ah.'

Lestrade noted the reaction. 'I am making enquiries into the Whitechapel murders. We have reason to believe that your cousin may be involved.'

'Lionel?' Druitt visibly rocked back. 'Surely not. Can I offer you something, Inspector?'

'Well . . . ' Lestrade would settle for almost anything.

'Iced coffee?'

His face fell. 'No thank you,' he said. 'Do you have access to your cousin's instruments, Mr Druitt?'

'Why, yes, there was a time when I toyed with going into medicine, Inspector. I spend quite a bit of my time here.'

He deftly unlocked a cabinet and slid out several drawers of glittering steel. Lestrade positively blanched at some of them – the ones he had only ever seen before in a knacker's yard.

'This is his favourite,' smiled Druitt, holding up an ebony-shafted knife.

'Single edged,' muttered Lestrade; 'about an inch wide.'

'What?'

'Nothing. Tell me, Mr Druitt, from your knowledge of anatomy, would it be possible to cut through bone with this?'

'No. You'd probably need a saw. This,' he held one up; 'or, for anything more elaborate, this,' he held up a fret saw. 'Inspector,' Druitt closed the drawers, 'you can't really suspect Lionel?'

'Why not?' asked Lestrade, looking for a chair to sit on. 'He knows the area, he has the weapons and he has the skill to carry out the appalling mutilations.'

'But these women were . . . unfortunates, Inspector. Lionel would have nothing to do with them.'

'What if it's not unfortunates he's killing, Mr Druitt?'

'I don't follow you.'

'What if your cousin is deranged? If in his mind, it's . . . oh, I don't know . . . his mother he's killing? Or yours?'

Druitt turned pale and had to steady himself against his cousin's skeleton, which rattled as it felt his weight.

'My mother?' he whispered. 'Why do you bring my mother into this?'

'Oh, no reason.' Lestrade watched his man intently.

Druitt stared at him. 'No reason. That's very apt, Mr Lestrade. You know of course that Lionel *is* mad, don't you?'

'Really, Mr Druitt? Could you explain?'

The failed lawyer slumped into a chair, the one Lestrade had been unable to find. 'It's the little things that give him away.'

'For instance?'

'For instance, his telephone calls from this surgery to friends in Edinburgh.'

'No telephone machines in Edinburgh?' Lestrade guessed.

Druitt shook his head. 'No telephone machines in this surgery,' he said. 'Then there's Australia.'

'What about it?'

'He wants to go there, Inspector. Can you think of a more obvious symptom of insanity than that? No, I fear cousin Lionel is going the way of his mother.'

'*His* mother?'

Druitt nodded sagely. 'My aunt. Before she died she accused him, in her ravings, of being Spring-heeled Jack. Little did the poor old thing realise he was actually Jack the Ripper.'

'I'm not actually accusing your cousin, Mr Druitt,' Lestrade said.

'Oh? But I thought . . . oh, well, no matter. Would it help to see Lionel's operating theatre, Mr Lestrade?'

'Thank you, it might.'

Druitt fumbled in his pocket for the keys and a black phial fell out and rolled across the carpet to Lestrade's feet. He stooped to pick it up, blinking in disbelief. 'What is this, Mr Druitt?'

'It's a talisman,' he told him. 'It contains writings— '

' —from the Dharam Ganth,' Lestrade finished for him.

'Yes. How did you know?'

'May I ask where you got this?'

'Certainly. It was given to me by a Sikh boy to whom I was once tutor.'

'A pupil at Blackheath?' Lestrade asked.

'You are remarkably well informed, Inspector.' Druitt was for the first time suspicious. 'Do you always check so minutely the backgrounds of cousins of your suspects?'

'Always,' Lestrade beamed.

'Actually, Cherak Singh attended a school in the Midlands – Northampton, I believe.'

'St Rhadegund's?' Lestrade asked.

'Why, yes, how did you know?'

'Perhaps you could tell me about Cherak Singh, Mr Druitt?'

'He and his brother – a boy of about seventeen, I believe – were visiting London one weekend last year. I met them in the Temple and we got talking. It transpired that young Cherak was struggling with his history so I offered to help. In the vacations from Rhadegund – I knew the place slightly as I had taught there for a term myself – they would stay at the Castle and Falcon in Aldersgate Street and each day when I was here we would do the Medes and Persians.'

'Time somebody did,' mused Lestrade, whose ancient history rarely ventured beyond Hammurabi. 'So that's how they learned to voker Romeny,' said Lestrade.

'I beg your pardon? Inspector, do you know the Singhs?'

'I knew them, sir. They're both dead.'

Druitt gasped. 'Dead? How?'

'One of them was strangled. The other may have been, but his body was so badly burned it was impossible to tell.'

Druitt closed his eyes. 'Dear God, how? Has the world gone mad, Inspector? What has happened to St Rhadegund's?'

Lestrade reached for his hat. 'I think, Mr Druitt, I am just beginning to find out.'

Leman Street was not Lestrade's favourite nick. The desk Sergeant on the afternoon watch had a St Bernard who posed as an undercover rug, just inside the door. He was docile to all the felons who fell over him, but plainclothes policemen brought out the wolf in him and he went for Lestrade in no uncertain manner that November afternoon.

'Who did you wish to see, sir?' the Sergeant asked, wrestling with the beast. 'Down, Phaidough, down.'

'Inspector Wensley,' Lestrade yelled over the monster's baying.

'It's the hat, sir,' the Sergeant yelled; 'take your bowler off, or he'll have your throat out. Phaidough, put the gentleman down, Phaidough!' The Sergeant's boots beat a tattoo on the cur's flanks. 'Would you mind, sir? Give him your hat. I'll see the lads all chip in for a new one. Phaidough! Heel!'

The dog obeyed instantly, causing Lestrade to yelp with pain. 'Not his heel, you bloody idiot!' the Sergeant yelled. 'Phaidough!'

Lestrade flung his bowler to the ravening beast who snatched it in his slobbering jaws and retired to a corner, where he proceeded to eat it with all the relish of a gentleman.

'Now, Sholto,' Wensley appeared at the bottom of the stairs, having heard all the commotion, 'put the dog down, there's a good fellow.'

Lestrade staggered across to him, dragging what was left of his foot. He hauled up his trouser leg.

'No time for a Lodge meeting now, Sholto. What did you want?'

'Anything new on the Ripper case?'

'No. Oh, one thing. Did you know Kenneth Stephen's brothers had rooms in the Temple? King's Bench Walk, in fact?'

'No, I didn't,' said Lestrade, really past caring about tangles like that.

'And something else. We should have found this earlier.'

'What?'

'Catherine Eddowes was also known as Anne Kelly. Odd, isn't it? Anne Kelly and Mary Kelly. Almost as if— '

'That's it!' Lestrade toyed with clasping Wensley to him, but thought perhaps Phaidough and Kenneth Stephen would misunderstand. One would be mortified anew at the rebuff. The other might conceivably kill him.

'What?' Wensley was confused. 'Sholto, what is it?'

But the Inspector had gone north.

Train of Events

It was as he turned into Tenter Street that Lestrade became uneasy. He was aware of two figures, tall, square, immaculately dressed, narrowing the gap that lay ahead, driving him to turn left, away from Whitechapel High Street. Then he realised there was another one behind him. The top hats began to crowd in on the bare head and in a moment Lestrade would have to ask them to pass along there. If they hadn't got to him first, of course. If they were Lusks's men, he'd probably get away with it. If they were Rupasobly's, he probably wouldn't.

'Mr Lestrade?' A fourth gent loomed out of the shadows before him, barring his way.

'Who wants to know?' Lestrade could be as obtuse as the next man, but the next man had cocked a pistol and was jabbing him in the kidneys with it. As he didn't particularly want those parts of his anatomy held up to the light by Dr Openshaw of the Pathological Museum, he said, 'Alternatively, yes, I am.'

'This way,' said the spokesman and Lestrade was hurried to a waiting barouche, gleaming in its opulent black, harnessed to four bays. As he tumbled inside, he recognised the figure already sitting on the seat opposite him.

'Your irregulars, Mr Holmes?' he asked as the top-hatted gentlemen flanked them both.

'I thought at first they were yours,' said Holmes archly. 'Then I realised they couldn't be policemen. They were far too well dressed.'

'What is the meaning of this?' Lestrade asked the nearest, ensuring first that he had put his pistol away.

'I've tried all that, my dear fellow,' said Holmes. 'They don't respond.'

Lestrade ignored him. 'Did Rupasobly send you?' he asked.

No response.

'Lusk?'

Nothing.

'You may as well give up, Lestrade. They're mute as far as you and I are concerned. Which gives me plenty of opportunity to remind you of the fact that I have spent a very uncomfortable few days in Bow Street Police Station at your recommendation. The beds were hard, the linen infested and the breakfasts indescribable. Needless to say, my gratuity was small.'

Lestrade had heard that, but he didn't want to embarrass Holmes still further.

'Sorry,' was all he said and lunged for the door. Four burly arms grabbed him and he found himself sprawling, with his head under the iron thigh of one of the gentlemen.

'That's pointless, Lestrade. I deduced that logically fourteen minutes ago.'

'Really?' Lestrade's voice was oddly muffled, what with his mouth pushed into the upholstery and all.

'These gentlemen outnumber you four to one. Given those odds, the result is inescapable.'

At a signal from the spokesman, the two released the Inspector and he sat up gratefully, wrenching his neck vaguely into position and crossing his legs. Holmes executed the same move simultaneously and their knees cracked together.

'We're going north,' the Great Detective deduced.

'Good,' said Lestrade. 'I'd planned to anyway.'

The rest was silence.

It was dark by the time the lathered horses took the gentle slope by the Eight Bells. Under the arch of St Ethelreda's

Church they clattered over the cobbles and the six occupants of the coach lurched as a man as the growler reined in.

'Forgive me,' Lestrade said to him as he was hauled down. 'No change,' and he waggled his pockets.

'Really, Lestrade,' moaned Holmes, 'have you no sense of occasion? Remember where you are, man.'

Lestrade could not remember where he was. As far as he knew, he had never been here before in his life. Before him, forming a gigantic letter 'E' and black against the frosty night sky, was a vast Elizabethan house, half-timbered and crumbling. Its many chimneys and turrets swirled and snaked starward, and there was the bark and yelp of dogs and the unmistakable sound of music coming from the central hall, whose long windows radiated the light of many chandeliers.

'Ah,' sighed Holmes, 'a Galliard. Dowland, I believe.'

Lestrade hadn't a clue who the architect was. What concerned him more was why he was here at all.

'You must forgive our manners, gentlemen,' said the spokesman. 'I assure you we have our reasons. Walk this way.'

Lestrade checked to make sure there was no sign of Dick from Bedlam and followed the apparent undertakers through a low door into a walled garden. This was laid out in perfect symmetry, with neatly trimmed hedges forming a herringbone maze that stretched out before them.

'What topiary!' Holmes was impressed.

'He *has* apologised.' Lestrade was altogether more magnanimous in these matters.

They were shown into an ante-room and then into what appeared to be a laboratory. Retorts, racks, tubes and liquids of wondrous hues rose everywhere. Holmes was fascinated and clucked around it all, periodically wringing his hands in rapture, tapping, sniffing, chuckling as he went.

'Germanium!' he shouted.

Lestrade couldn't see a flower anywhere.

'Here, Lestrade. Winkler's process – the eka-silicon of Mendeleev's table.'

To Lestrade the table looked humdrum enough. Clever of Holmes to know it was of Hungarian manufacture.

'And this.' He bounded across the room in a single stride, 'How quaint! It's titanium, Lestrade. Most people imagine this to be rare but of course it is the eighth most abundant element in the earth's crust.'

Holmes was clearly insane and, as if to prove it, a pink-eyed rat in a nearby cage winked at Lestrade.

'Gentlemen!'

A large, slightly stooping man with a bald head and full beard stood at the top of the stone steps to one corner of the room.

'Isn't that . . . ?' Lestrade whispered to Holmes.

'Precisely.' Holmes's great nostrils filled with pride. 'Robert Arthur Talbot Gascoyne-Cecil, Third Marquess of Salisbury. Your Prime Minister . . . and mine.' He all but stood on tiptoe.

'Mr Holmes,' Salisbury descended the steps. 'So you're the Great Detective?'

Holmes bowed as though Winkler's process had suddenly erupted in his groin at an alarming rate.

'I've heard so much about you. The Study in Scarlet – particularly fine.'

'I am honoured, my Lord.'

Salisbury held the man's hand with both of his own. 'Thank you. Thank you for coming . . . oh, and you, Lestrade,' and he whirled to a high desk, the sort used by clerks forty years ago, or chemistry masters at Rhadegund Hall.

'Gentlemen, pray be seated. Not there, Lestrade!'

The Inspector blanched as he realised how near to the rat's incisors he had come. He leaned gingerly against a rack of chemicals. They appeared stable enough.

'I must be brief,' the great man said. 'I have many guests at the house tonight. Representatives of the East

Africa Company. Her Majesty has been pleased to bestow Charters upon them. We're having something of a celebration. Oohh, one moment,' he bent to adjust his clothing below the left knee, 'my Garter's killing me. Now, where were we?'

'Brought rather unceremoniously from London,' Lestrade reminded him.

'Quite, Inspector. And I do apologise. What I am about to tell you, gentlemen, is of the utmost import. It must never be divulged to a living soul. And I must have your word to that before I continue. Mr Holmes?'

'You have my word, my Lord,' said Holmes, solemnly.

Lestrade presumed that telling Watson didn't count. After all, Salisbury had specifically said a *living* soul.

'Lestrade?'

'Sir, my position is not the same as Mr Holmes's.'

'Amen to that.' Holmes shifted gratefully.

'I appreciate that, Lestrade, but I must have your word, sir.'

Lestrade looked at them both. He crossed his fingers behind his back. 'My word.' He bowed.

'Gentlemen, you have both been engaged recently on a case which has come to be known as the Whitechapel murders. The Ripper case.'

'We have,' they chorused.

'Would it be true to say, Mr Holmes, that one of your principal suspects in this unfortunate matter is Sir William Withey Gull, Physician in Ordinary to Her Majesty?'

For a second, Lestrade swore he saw a look of total bewilderment darken Holmes's face. It was a look of which Watson would have said Holmes was incapable. His eyes flickered across to Lestrade and he straightened, saying, 'It might, my Lord.'

'And I understand that you have visited Sir William's house in Mayfair?' Salisbury said to the Inspector.

'That is correct.' Lestrade felt the edge for a moment and relished it.

'And I also understand that while you were there a number of Sir William's colleagues arrived?'

'They did.' Lestrade's eyes narrowed. He had noticed, draped over a carboy above the Prime Minister's head, a velvet pall, embroidered with gold. It carried the device of the dividers he had seen in Gull's library.

'What did you make of that?' Salisbury asked him.

'It was an inquisition, my Lord,' said Lestrade. 'There were twelve of them. They were a jury whose job it was to sentence him to death.'

'For what crime?' Salisbury did not bat an eyelid.

'For the murders of five women in and around the district of Whitechapel between August and November of this year.'

'Where is your proof?' Salisbury asked.

'He all but confessed,' Lestrade said.

Salisbury sighed. 'Yes, I know.'

'Where is Sir William Gull, my Lord?' Lestrade asked.

'Dead,' bluffed Salisbury.

'So those jurymen executed him as well as found him guilty?' Lestrade asked.

Salisbury nodded slowly.

Lestrade walked forward, narrowly missing one retort only to make another. 'I don't believe you, Prime Minister.'

'Lestrade!' Holmes snapped, but Salisbury held up his hand. It was nothing Gladstone and Chamberlain had not said to him countless times.

'Very well,' the old man said. 'As it happens, Inspector, you are quite right. William Gull is alive. In body at least.'

'You mean . . . ?' It wasn't often Sherlock Holmes was lost for words.

'He is mad, Mr Holmes. Unhinged.'

'Where is he?' Lestrade asked.

'Safe,' said Salisbury. He caught Lestrade looking at the velvet pall. 'Yes, Mr Lestrade, we masons look after our own.'

'That won't do, Lord Salisbury,' said the Inspector.

'Why? Because the man has a sense of honour? That is the stuff of England, Mr Lestrade, its lifeblood.'

'And what of the lifeblood of Mary Nicholls, Annie Chapman and the others?'

'Is it justice you want, Mr Lestrade?' Salisbury challenged him, 'or revenge?'

Lestrade shrugged. 'Perhaps both,' he said.

'You've got the wrong man with Gull,' Salisbury told him, 'and I can prove it.' He rang a little bell on the desk and the spokesman with the immaculate silk topper appeared from nowhere.

'Tell these gentlemen who you are,' he said.

'I am John Netley, my Lord, coachman to Sir William Gull.'

'And?' said Salisbury.

'Private Secretary to Mr Henry Matthews.'

'The Home Secretary?' Lestrade's jaw dropped.

'Brilliant, Inspector,' hissed Holmes.

'Tell them about Sir William, Netley,' Salisbury said.

'Sir William is under the impression that he may have killed these unfortunates. In fact, he is innocent of all five murders.'

'Why should a Home Office private secretary drive for the Queen's doctor?' Lestrade smelt a rat, probably the pink-eyed one that had winked at him.

'My Lord?' Netley turned to Salisbury.

'Gentlemen. Dear friend though he is, William Gull is not my main concern. This matter concerns the Highest in the Land.'

While Lestrade was wondering how Ben Nevis featured in the matter Salisbury swept on. 'It concerns His Highness the Duke of Clarence.'

'Old Collar and Cuffs,' mused Holmes.

'Quite.' Salisbury's impression of the Great Detective was dwindling all the time. 'The Duke is a headstrong young man, given to wild fancies. I have to tell you that he met, fell in love with . . . and *married* a shop girl.'

'Annie Crook,' said Lestrade.

Salisbury *did* blink this time. 'You know?' he gasped.

'And she and the child of the marriage, Alice, were abducted by Sir William Gull from Bedlam. Yes, I know. What I want, my Lord, is a reason why I shouldn't arrest this man.'

'He hasn't done anything,' said Netley. 'He merely arranged for the transference of Annie and her child from one asylum to another.'

'Why?' Lestrade asked.

'It's standard practice,' said Holmes.

'When the patient is deranged, yes,' said Lestrade. 'What about Annie Crook?'

There was a silence.

'You're right, Lestrade.' Salisbury's impression of the Lesser Detective was growing all the time.. 'She is not deranged. Grief-stricken, perhaps. She had to be parted from His Highness.'

'Did she?' Lestrade persisted.

Salisbury may have been impressed by him but he was also irritated. 'Of course!' he thundered. 'A shop girl, Lestrade! And a Catholic to boot! He may as well have married a schoolteacher! The man is heir to the throne of England, not to mention the Empire. It cannot happen. The King of England's isolation must be splendid indeed.'

'So you unleashed the madman Gull on her? And the others? What of them?'

'As Netley has told you, Lestrade,' said Salisbury, 'he is innocent.' He came down from his perch among the mortals. 'It all began as a casual chat really. You are familiar of course with Henry II and the knights?'

Was that a pub, Lestrade pondered?

'Will no one rid me of this turbulent priest?' asked Holmes, as though he and Salisbury were enjoying a private historical joke.

'Quite. His Royal Highness the Prince of Wales knew

of course of his elder son's indiscretion, but was at a loss to know how to cope with it. William Gull simply said, "Leave it to me, sir."'

'By which he meant?'

Salisbury looked at Lestrade. 'He took Annie and her child away. Put them in Bedlam under Dr McGregor's care. It then transpired that she had a friend who knew of the secret marriage.'

'Who was that?' Holmes asked.

'Ah, well, there some confusion crept in. Annie refused to tell him. She spent most of her time in tears, apparently. Well, understandable, I suppose . . . Her name was Polly, we thought.'

'Polly Nicholls and Polly Kelly,' said Lestrade.

'Quite so,' Salisbury nodded. 'But confusion doubled on confusion. We also thought her name was Kelly . . . '

'Catherine Eddowes alias Anne Kelly; and Mary Kelly,' said Lestrade.

'Even so. Poor Sir William's mind couldn't find its way through a tangle like that.'

'So he killed all three – and two more for good measure,' Lestrade said.

'No, he bought off Polly Nicholls and then she died. When I read the news and realised it was the same girl I assumed she was killed for her money. Sir William made frequent visits to the East End in search of some clue as to who stole the money and indeed whether she had been its rightful recipient in the first place. He had come to the conclusion that he had found the wrong Polly and went in search of a girl called Kelly . . . '

'Each time he went, I drove him,' said Netley. 'His confusion grew worse. He could barely find the door of his house, much less an East End doxy in a sea of doxies. They all looked the same to him. Mr Lestrade, if my word as a civil servant means anything to you, Dr Gull killed no one. At least, not outside a hospital ward.'

'What of the blood-stained shirt?'

'His nose bled on the night Annie Chapman died. I had been with him, as usual, the whole time, making our search.'

'He is the most loyal of men, Lestrade,' Salisbury said. 'He had promised to help his Prince and he did his best.'

Lestrade looked at the Prime Minister and his civil servant. 'So why did these women die? Even Lady Gull suspected her husband.'

'Of course,' said Salisbury. 'Circumstantial evidence against him looked black. You thought so yourself. Lady Gull is now in our confidence, as you are. It was cruel not to tell her, but the risk to security was immense. It still is. As to who has been traipsing those mean streets with knife at the ready, I really haven't the faintest idea, Mr Lestrade. Gull's colleagues, his fellow masons, came to him that night to take him away. Poor soul, he is no longer fit to practise medicine. A sad end to a great and distinguished career.'

'I repeat, Lord Salisbury,' Lestrade looked at him levelly, 'where is he?'

'For the moment, in Bedlam. Netley here thinks he has not long to live.'

'He's a broken man, Mr Lestrade,' Netley said, 'but he saw the wisdom of his fellow masons and knows it is for the best.'

'We thought it advisable to feign his death,' explained Salisbury. 'A sudden stroke – he's had one already. It's for the best indeed.'

Lestrade looked at Holmes. He'd almost forgotten him in the last ten minutes. Wishful thinking, of course.

'Gentlemen, I called you here privily because you were getting close to the truth, each in your different ways.'

The detectives looked at each other.

'I could not – and cannot – risk all this becoming public knowledge. If it were known that the Duke of Clarence has made this unwise marriage, if Papacy were openly connected with the English throne . . . '

'Yes, of course, my Lord,' Holmes said. 'We understand

fully. It's almost as though the heir to the throne had married an American divorcée . . . '

Salisbury turned pale and clutched himself. 'Please Mr Holmes,' he muttered, 'I am not a young man myself.'

'Your secret, sir, is safe with us,' said Holmes. 'Isn't it, Lestrade?'

'Er . . . oh, yes,' Lestrade frowned, 'of course.'

'Thank you, gentlemen.' Salisbury shook their hands, and a tear welled in his eye. 'God bless you.'

Netley saw them out and a cab took them to the station.

'Where away, Lestrade?' Holmes stopped him as he walked in the opposite direction.

'I have unfinished business, Mr Holmes,' he said, 'at Rhadegund Hall.'

'Rhadegund?' Holmes chuckled. 'Small beer indeed, Lestrade. Should you see Watson, send him to Baker Street, will you?'

'Back into retirement, Mr Holmes,' asked Lestrade, 'until the next case comes along?'

'Retirement?' Holmes closed to him. 'My dear fellow, you can't have been taken in at Hatfield House?'

'What?'

'Come, come, man. It stands out a mile. Gull is the Ripper. He kills the whores with his considerable anatomical skill. Netley drives him to and from the scenes of the crimes, which is why you chappies – not to mention George Lusks's – didn't find a blood-stained figure going homeward. And, of course, they'd need a lookout man.'

'Who?'

'Salisbury.'

'Salisbury?!' Lestrade was non-plussed.

'And that unholy trio will strike again, Lestrade, believe me. By the end of the week, there'll be another slaying. Only this time I shall be there.'

'Of course,' Lestrade said a little sheepishly, moving inexorably away.

'You, of course, were taken in with all that jingoistic

clap-trap about England. I was not. Clarence marrying a shopgirl! Preposterous! It's thin, Lestrade, but you fell for it. As Salisbury knew you would. Luckily, some of us are made of sterner stuff. Goodbye.'

And the detectives, not for the first or last time in their careers, parted company.

It was a strangely tense Rhadegund Hall at which Lestrade arrived early that morning. He toyed with finding Sergeant George to see exactly what fate had befallen Saunders-Foote, but then he suspected he knew. The telegram had been short and sharp, though hardly a shock. And the body count was grimmer. Maggie Hollis, Anthony Denton, Major Bracegirdle, Adelstrop, Charles Mercer and the Singhs, all of them mouldering now with the ancient, avuncular, sobbing classics master.

In the corner of a quad, Lestrade saw an outline he recognised. 'Watson.'

'Aarhhh!' The good Doctor leapt upright from his dozing position. 'Lestrade, you might have given me a coronary,' he gasped.

'There wasn't time,' Lestrade explained. 'I'm in a hurry, Doctor. What are you doing here?'

Watson flattened himself against the wisteria, pointing maniacally upwards. 'Gainsborough,' he whispered. 'He's our man.'

'Oh? How do you know?'

'He was out walking on the morning they found Bracegirdle, you know.'

'Yes, I do.'

'And Saunders-Foote . . . ah, of course. You haven't been here.'

'George kept me posted. What has Gainsborough to do with that?'

'Saunders-Foote was found strangled on a hillock shortly after dawn. The hour of Gainsborough's constitutional.'

'What's his motive?' Lestrade asked.

'What? Ah, well . . . Have you heard from Holmes at all?'

'As a matter of fact I have. He sends his compliments and asks you to join him at Baker Street.'

'What? Now? But I can't. The game's afoot!'

'I fancy Mr Holmes is after bigger game still, Doctor.'

'Lestrade? Where are you going? I've been here all night. I'd appreciate some help.'

'I'm sure you would, Doctor, but regrettably I have a murderer to catch.'

'A . . . I . . . ' and Lestrade left Watson gesturing emptily to the wisteria.

The Inspector turned left at the top of the stairs. He knocked softly. No response. He checked his half-hunter in the flickering gaslight. No expense had been spared, he noticed, now that Mercer had gone. He sighed and turned to go. It was late. Perhaps too late.

'Sholto?' Madeleine appeared sleepily in the doorway. 'Is that you?'

'It's late,' he said. 'I didn't mean to disturb you.'

'You haven't,' she said. 'Won't you come in?'

He smiled, stepped towards her, then saw a black serge coat and bowler hanging on the sofa. It was the serge coat and bowler of Sergeant George. 'No,' he said, 'I just called to say goodbye.'

'Goodbye?' She held his hand in a sudden, impetuous gesture.

'My work here is finished.'

'Will I . . . see you again?' she asked.

He shrugged, smiling. 'Who knows? Take care of yourself, won't you?'

She nodded, her eyes larger and wetter than he'd remembered them. He stared at her for one long, long moment, then turned to go. 'Oh, by the way. Should you see Sergeant George, tell him I'd like to see him and his constables at the Yard. When they've finished here.'

He smiled again.

'Yes, Sholto,' she whispered. 'I'll tell him . . . if I see him.'

*

He crossed the larger quad, past the shell of the library where Cherak Singh Minor had been found. He heard the mallards calling on the lake where Cherak Singh Major had died. And he was already on the upper staircase, under the eagle gaze of dusty headmasters and rows of gilded names, when he saw him. The mortarboard and the billowing gown striding manfully for the Rhadegund trap in the courtyard below. But there was no Carman on the perch. He leapt up himself and slapped the horse into action.

Lestrade hurtled back down the stairs, Donegal flying in the morning. He hit the wall at the bottom, slicing the skin off his cheek, but ran on unchecked until he fetched his length on the cobbles, wet in the mist rising over Northamptonshire in November.

Longing for the legs of Ovett and the lungs of Bracegirdle, he threw off the Donegal, ripped away the tie and ran at a steady lope through the archway and along the drive. At the gates he paused to give his thumping heart time to catch up with the rest of his body. There'd be no one passing along these roads at that time of night. And the station was nearly a mile away. There was no choice. He couldn't risk losing him now.

That mile seemed like fifty. Lestrade tried to make his mind a blank, an easier task for him than for some. Somehow he must keep his thoughts off his tortured lungs and the useless lumps of lead that pounded up the road. He swerved off the track and up through the woods, where the brambles caught him and the saplings whipped back. Like a man who has run the gauntlet, he staggered onto the platform, his boot studs striking sparks in the dark as he skidded to a halt. He was just in time to see the last of the train disappearing south.

' 'Ere!' A railway employee hailed him. 'You gotta 'ave a ticket 'ere, mate!'

'When's the next train!' Lestrade gasped.

The employee consulted his watch, shaking his head. 'Not

till half-past ten,' he said. 'But it don't go from 'ere.'

Lestrade tore away from the idiot and heard him shout. 'But we're getting there.'

He skidded into the forecourt and collapsed on the flank of the Rhadegund pony.

'You!' he shouted to a figure nodding on a stand of barrels. 'The man who drove this here? Did he get on the train?'

' 'Ow should I know?' he answered. 'I only work 'ere.'

Lestrade clambered aboard and applied the whip. He had about as much expertise on the running board of a trap as a Greek prince, but he did his best. Lashing the animal, he hurtled through the gathering dawn, skirting the great medieval forest of Rockingham. How he missed Queen Eleanor's Cross at Geddington he never knew, but he spared the whip at Benefield, in case sleeping Oundle should hear the repercussions of the scandal at Rhadegund.

At Thorpe station he crashed into a bollard in the centre of the road only to see the train pull out. Hanging on by his finger nails, the battered Inspector ran right over a policeman. Luckily, the man was sleeping at the time and didn't notice. Lestrade wondered momentarily if it was Sergeant Thicke, undercover again.

With the coming of the grey dawn, Lestrade's luck at last changed. Before him loomed the Killington tunnel, all mile and a half of it and the signals of the LNER were against the train. He hauled the trap to a halt and gratefully dropped the leather which had raised great weals on his fingers. He scrambled up the slope, slipping on the shale of the embankment, and caught himself a nasty one on a protruding sleeper. The vagrant mumbled something Northamptonshire and turned over, nursing his empty bottle.

Lestrade vanished into the total darkness of the tunnel, bouncing up and down every now and again to peer into the carriages. Those passengers who were awake and whose blinds were up commented on the escaped lunatic tapping on the windows and gesturing inanely. What were the police doing to allow it? And when would the train move?

The Inspector found a carriage shrouded in blinds. He wrenched the handle only to hear a scream.

'I do beg your pardon, madam.' He reached for his bowler, realised he hadn't got it and tugged his forelock instead. Whistles jarred the tunnel and the steaming, snorting engine began to jerk into life. A lantern swung from somewhere down the line and Lestrade leapt at the nearest carriage door and jumped up. He'd have to wait until the next station to find his quarry.

'Hello, Lestrade, what kept you?'

The Yard man blinked, fighting for breath as he was. Slowly his eyes became acclimatised and his blood froze.

'Dr Nails.' He'd know that mortarboard and those whiskers anywhere, silhouetted against the far window. 'What a coincidence.'

'So you were the idiot in the Rhadegund trap? I caught sight of old Jem once or twice in open countryside. I thought I recognised those markings and that curious way of going. I recognised the horse, too, of course.'

'There are some other curious ways of going I'm more interested in,' said Lestrade, 'and I think you can help me with them.'

'Why me?' Nails bellowed. 'Why always me?'

'It was too obvious at first,' Lestrade told him. 'The mountaineer's rope. You were prepared to take that risk because it was a common enough type of hemp. Unfortunately, Charles Mercer in his innocence pointed me in your direction. You'd climbed in the Himalayas. You were familiar with the customs of India.'

'Ah, yes, the thuggees. Indeed I was.'

'It was you who opened your school to the natives – the Singh boys. As Headmaster you had access to the laundry tower, the Sword of Honour, the boat house, all the locked little places.'

'Quite so,' chuckled Nails.

'You also left a trail of false clues. You stripped the

elder Singh knowing it would be Carstairs and Channing-Lover who found him. You hoped I'd assume they were involved.'

'Ah, yes,' mused Nails, 'the love that dare not speak its name.'

'You also hoped to confuse me with three methods of murder. The thuggee rope. Water. And fire. All three designed perhaps to make me think there was more than one murderer at Rhadegund?'

Nails laughed. 'There is murder in the heart of everyone, Lestrade. And in a place like Rhadegund, a hot bed of passions, jealousies, pride . . . you could have had four hundred murderers. Clever of you to whittle it down to little old me.'

'Before the train moves off, Dr Nails,' said Lestrade, 'would you like to tell me why.'

'Tut, tut, Lestrade,' scolded Nails as only he could. 'Scotland Yard's finest and you haven't guessed it! Go on, as I tell my boys hesitant on meeting Livy for the first time, jump in, man! The dead don't bite.'

'It was a friend of mine who gave you away,' Lestrade said. 'We were working on another case entirely and he pointed out that two of the victims had the same name. There was some confusion, you see, in the murderer's mind. That was what confused me for so long. I was trying to work out what, apart from Rhadegund Hall, your victims had in common. Then it dawned on me. Nothing. You only wanted one person dead. And that was Cherak Singh Minor. The others were merely blinds.'

The second series of whistles up the line saw the whole train jolt and shudder and it began to roll forward. 'Clever of you not to begin with Singh, of course. And risky. If you'd been detected after the death of Maggie Hollis, Singh would have lived. So of course would the others. And whatever secret Singh held would have been revealed to the world.'

Nails chuckled again as the train gathered speed. 'And why do you suppose I wanted young Singh to die? Did I share Bracegirdle's hatred of little niggers for what they did at Chilianwala and Cawnpore?'

'No,' said Lestrade. 'It's something altogether more personal. And it has to do with Mrs Payne, your mistress. Matron helped me there . . . '

'I'm sure she did.' The features, shrouded in darkness, betrayed a smirk.

'Only it wasn't Balham, was it? It was Whitechapel.'

'No, it wasn't Balham, Lestrade. And you're quite right about young Singh. The little black bastard was blackmailing me. He had a knack for writing lurid letters.'

'I know; I read one of them.'

'But Balham wasn't the only mistake you made. There are two more . . . '

'Oh? And what are they, Dr Nails?'

The carriage slid into the light of a grey morning and Lestrade blinked as the sky broke again. He sat there with his mouth open as the Headmaster peeled off his whiskers and threw the mortarboard on Lestrade's seat.

'This is your first,' he said. The voice had changed.

'Mercer?' Lestrade angled his head to be sure of what he was seeing.

'The Bursar,' Mercer said. 'At your service. Cap size, boy?'

Lestrade continued to sit there.

'What's the matter, Lestrade? Got it wrong again, have you? Tut, tut. If I *were* Nails I'd flog you rotten for this. You see, you played the hand I dealt you every inch of the way. Yes, I set up the Headmaster, hoping you'd put him in the frame sooner. The mountaineer's rope, the reference to the Himalayas. What you missed, of course, was dear old Theophilus's retort that I knew the Himalayas too. I prayed you'd missed it. You had. And, as Bursar, I had all the keys I needed – access to the laundry room, the Sword of Honour, the boat house. In the confusion of the library fire anyone could have slipped out to follow Bracegirdle. Mind you, I had to run some to catch him.

You should have seen the look on his face as I ran him through.'

Lestrade had not moved.

Mercer chuckled. 'Actually, none of them was difficult. Maggie Hollis, of course, I dumped in her own bleach. What with the water *and* the noose, she had no chance. Anthony Denton's hands were full of other things at the time. I didn't even have to use a noose for that one. His spectacles chain was ideal.'

'What about the elder Singh?'

'I sent him a note to meet me in the boat house. Such trysts are common, Lestrade. Singh was Maggie Hollis's lover. I knew that and I pretended to be a member of her family who had some information relating to her death. I did. I'd killed her. The thuggee noose, especially in the dark, is a match for any Sikh. The disciples of Kali proved that in India thousands of times. What I enjoyed most was laying false trails for you. The suggestion of untoward practices between Denton and Saunders-Foote, the muscular Christianity of Spooner. I didn't need to do anything to involve an overt pig like Hardman. And, of course, the bestiality of Nails spoke for itself.'

'And you a former civil servant.' Lestrade shook his head.

'Ah, yes,' Mercer smiled. 'But it was the *Indian* Civil Service. That's where all my training came in. The need for strict accountability, precision, everything to the letter. I even put the elder Singh's clothes back in the pile in the store for reselling,' he chuckled. 'I wonder if the luckless Dollery realises whose blazer he's wearing?'

'Talking of blazers,' Lestrade went on, 'your own "death" was clever.'

'If hard,' Mercer sighed, leaning back with a picture of Skegness behind him. 'Not only did I have to resurrect old Adelstrop, not the easiest or the most pleasant of tasks, but I shaved off his beard just in case. I knew his eyes would go and his features would blur, but stubble can be so stubborn, can't it?' He looked with some distaste at the grey shadow around Lestrade's parchment features. 'His leg of course was no problem. I knew that would disintegrate along with his real one. Getting him up there, on top of that bonfire, was the worst of all. I had to hide the straw guy in the stack itself. When all that was done, of course, I watched the whole thing from a safe distance. Splendid show, wasn't it?'

'But that was nearly three weeks ago,' said Lestrade. 'Have you been at Rhadegund all this time?'

'I reckoned without Ruffage and his prefects. He'll go far, that lad, you mark my words. They'd ringed the grounds pretty tightly. Then there was Hardman and the House prefects, not to mention the three brass monkeys you'd left behind.'

'And of course Captain Wilson,' Lestrade reminded him.

'Who? You perhaps remember, Lestrade, when we first met. Young Singh appeared in my office through a panel in the wall. Rhadegund is full of such panels and corridors of course. It's a veritable rabbit warren. I merely laid low there and crept along to the kitchens after lights out. I am really quite fit after three weeks of cheese and prunes. Cook has had a field day with her traps, but I fear she'd have to invent a better one entirely to catch me.'

'Why Saunders-Foote?' Lestrade asked. 'Surely, once we were all convinced you were dead . . . '

'Call it bravado if you like. I didn't think anyone would be looking for a dead man as a murderer. It would be fun to risk it. Anyway, it was a kindness, really. Saunders-Foote had been genuinely fond of young Denton. He was a nice old boy. He didn't suffer unduly.'

'And so tonight . . . last night . . . was the first chance you had to escape?'

'It occurred to me the only way was to pose as someone else. Who better than Nails? The stride and swagger, the booming voice. All the boys can take him off. Why not me? All I needed was the gown and mortarboard and they're ten a penny at Rhadegund. The whiskers I'll grant you were a little theatrical, but they served their purpose. At night. In the dark. No one would query them. They certainly fooled you.'

Lestrade had to admit they had. 'And Balham?' he said.

'Ah, yes, Balham. You were right on that point of course. It was Whitechapel. I confess I didn't know of the dear Headmaster's peccadillo in that district. But then I suspect Matron was not as forthcoming with me as she appears to have been with you.'

'Life has its ups and downs,' observed Lestrade, swaying now as the train reached top speed.

'Cherak Singh *was* blackmailing me. And the terrible secret?' Mercer smiled. 'You know, after all that's happened, it doesn't seem so terrible now. Was it chance or design that brought the little Sikh into that yard that fateful night?'

'Yard? Night?' Lestrade was not following.

'It was George Yard,' he said, 'and the night was August the seventh.'

Lestrade's eyebrows knotted in a frown. 'Martha Tabram!' he shouted.

Mercer nodded. 'Martha,' he said.

'So Lees was right,' Lestrade muttered.

'What?'

'A clairvoyant friend of mine,' the Inspector told him. 'When I handed him a portion of Martha Tabram's dress he said . . . what was it . . . ? "I see boys. A rope. A gown." And he said I knew the murderer.'

'Well, that wasn't much help, was it?'

'He said something else,' Lestrade remembered. 'He said the name "Edmund".'

Mercer leaned back as the grey fields sped by, the train rattling and lurching over the points.

'Oh, Lestrade, Lestrade. You really haven't grasped this at all, have you? It's funny really. When you first came to Rhadegund, I talked to Spooner. He's a garrulous fellow, once you've learned to translate for him. He told me why you'd come – looking into the death of Edmund Gurney. You could have knocked me over with a cassock when I realised Spooner was a friend of his.'

'You knew him too?'

'Indirectly. You see, Lestrade, Martha Tabram was not her real name. She was once Martha Mercer.'

Pennies dropped loudly in Lestrade's tired brain.

'Your wife? Who left you?'

Mercer's smile vanished for the first time on the journey. 'Yes, she left me, Lestrade. Oh, we were happy once, in India. Then the flirtations started. With my colleagues, with officers in the local garrison. There was even talk of regimental bhistis . . . Imagine the shame, Lestrade. My wife was prepared to sleep with natives. We had a row – lots of rows – and she walked out. For good. I learned she'd come home, to London, and I followed her. I discovered she was living with a man named Edmund Gurney, a spiritualist and philosopher. I found her, tried to talk to her, asked her to come back. She fled from me, Lestrade, and from Gurney. I spent months searching for her. Whenever I could take leave from Rhadegund I did so. Always coming south, always combing the hotels.'

'And you found her again?'

'Yes, I did. The hotels got seedier and seedier as she moved east. I realised that Gurney was looking for her too. He must have loved her, Lestrade. Ironic, isn't it?'

'Ironic?'

'That I found her first. In George Yard on the night of August the seventh. Oh, I suppose I wanted to ask her to come back one last time. In the shadows she didn't recognise me any more than you did, earlier. All she saw was the top hat, the cape. She said to me, "Are you good natured, dearie?" and lifted up her dress. She'd become a common whore, Lestrade. An East End doxy. I'd picked up some new equipment for Nails earlier in the day. I had a crampon in my hand. A sort of . . . red mist rose before me and I swung out. I remember her look of disbelief as her throat spouted all that blood.'

Mercer sat there in the carriage, shaking a little and pale. 'Then I turned, leaving her lying on the stairs, and I came face to face with Cherak Singh. He had noticed me earlier, he said, by chance. He was intrigued to know why I had been there in that place, at that hour. I suppose it would have been easier if I'd killed him there and then but I didn't. When I returned to Rhadegund, the blackmail started. Oh, he was open about it. And he wasn't greedy. But I couldn't live like that, Lestrade. He knew about Martha, you see. I don't think I'd have minded the world knowing I'd killed her, but the hideous thought of everyone knowing about her, what she had become. No, that I could not stand. And Cherak Singh I could not trust.'

'So it became an academic exercise?' said Lestrade.

'It did. When Spooner told me that Gurney was dead I couldn't believe it. Had he contacted Martha? Had they arranged to meet? Did her failing to keep their appointment drive him to suicide? Or had he too found out the depths to which she had descended? I don't know.'

Lestrade began to take stock of his situation and Mercer sensed it.

'Don't worry, Inspector. There aren't any stops on this line now until King's Cross. You forget, I know the route well. Which gives me a chance to capitalise on your second mistake.'

'Which is?' Lestrade asked.

'To ride alone in a carriage with me,' and Mercer leapt forward, twisting a rope around Lestrade's neck as he did so. Instinctively, Lestrade grabbed for the brass knuckles in his Donegal pocket, only to remember that he had flung that somewhere in the Northamptonshire countryside and he was in fact unarmed. With the sinewy arms of a practised mountaineer and strangler, Mercer forced his man round and down, so that Lestrade was kneeling on the floor with Mercer's knee jammed into his back. The Inspector was powerless to move. All he could do was to make odd clicking noises with what was left of his larynx and claw convulsively at the hemp biting deep into his throat.

'Goodbye, Lestrade,' Mercer hissed. As a numbness spread over the Inspector there was a crash of glass and a splintering of wood and Lestrade was thrown forward, face down on the upholstery. When he managed to scramble to his knees, desperately freeing the noose and fighting for breath, he saw the far carriage door swinging open and felt the wind of the Essex countryside whipping through it. The other side of the carriage was all but caved in, as though a meteor had hurtled past. Lestrade leapt to the open door and looked back. Lying yards below the line, like a bundle of rags in the field, lay all that was left of Charles Mercer, his head beaten to a pulp by the quarter-past six from King's Cross which continued to whistle and rattle its way north.

Lestrade turned to the other occupant of the carriage.

'Is it really you this time, Dr Nails?' he asked.

'Of course!' the Headmaster bellowed. 'Did my eyes deceive me, Lestrade, or was that Charles Mercer with a rope around your neck?'

'It was,' Lestrade croaked, slamming the door and falling back exhausted into the seat. 'Tell me, were you just passing or . . . ?'

'I've been following you since Rhadegund,' Nails told him. 'I saw you running like the very devil after the Rhadegund trap. Since no one had orders to leave the premises I knew something was afoot. Unfortunately, I couldn't get a cab for a while – uncivilised hour and all. I realised you'd caught the train, and I followed on somebody's bicycle. Bounder didn't want to part with it, but he came round in the end. Or at least he probably will.'

Lestrade pointed at the wrecked door. 'But . . . ?'

'I got to one of the bridges and jumped on. Must say, it's quite exhilarating. I've never been on a *moving* mountain before.'

'You could have been killed,' Lestrade growled, rubbing his neck.

'So, it seems, could you. I was clumping around up there for quite a while. By the time I reached the right compartment it looked nearly up for you. Look, oughtn't we to pull the alarm cord or something? I mean, that's my Bursar back there, who appears to have caught the quarter-past six.'

'I don't think there's much point, Headmaster. I'll contact the Essex Constabulary when we get to King's Cross. In the meantime, there's a little story I'd like to tell you . . . '

The Inspector and the Headmaster alighted at Platform Three. In the steam and noise of a great station, they shook hands.

'I owe you my life, Dr Nails,' Lestrade said.

'And I owe you my school, Inspector Lestrade. I believe that makes us quits.'

'Perhaps,' said Lestrade, hailing a police wagon as it passed the entrance way, 'but if I can ever repay you . . . '

'Well, as a matter of fact, you can. Could you ask your chappie here to give me a lift to Balham?'

Assistant Chief Constable Melville McNaghten, the ex-coffee-planter, sat at his new desk and admired his new carpet. He checked his new calendar, the one that marked the new year, 1889. He twirled his faintly waxed moustaches and adjusted his cravat.

'Come!' he called as the door responded to an Inspectorial knock.

'Inspector Lestrade to see you, sir.' The Constable saluted and left.

'Ah, Lestrade, is it?' McNaghten shook the man's hand. 'I've just read your report on the Rhadegund business. Good work. Good work.'

'Thank you, sir.' Lestrade brushed his new bowler with a

hint of smugness and adjusted the Donegal, returned to him by ex-Sergeant and Mrs George from Northamptonshire.

'So we've resolved the case of the unfortunate Martha Tabram. But what of the Ripper murders, Lestrade? Did Mercer commit those too?'

'I think not, sir.'

McNaghten looked at him. 'Then who did, Lestrade, who did?'

'Er . . . It's Chief Inspector Abberline's case, sir.'

'I am well aware whose case it is, Lestrade— '

A second knock interrupted him. 'Come!' he bellowed.

A large young lady with long dark hair and dancing eyes swirled into the room. 'Papa, I've just bought this darling little board game called "How to Catch Jack" . . . Oh, I'm sorry, I didn't realise you were busy . . . '

'That's all right, my dear.' McNaghten was clearly a little embarrassed. 'This is Inspector . . . '

'Lestrade,' he said.

'Lestrade,' McNaghten repeated. 'My daughter, Miss McNaghten.'

'Arabella,' she said, pulling him gently to her with a gloved hand. 'I look forward to seeing much more of you, Inspector.' She stroked his sleeve while her father fidgeted with his cravat. And then in lowered voice she said, 'I do so love men in Donegals . . . '

Sir William Withey Gull, Physician in Ordinary to Her Majesty, died in an asylum for the incurably insane on 27 January, 1890, supposedly of a cerebral haemorrhage. His Royal Highness, the Duke of Clarence – Eddy – died of influenza in the bitter January of 1892. Montague John Druitt was found floating in the Thames near Chiswick on 31 December, 1888, with small change and a bus ticket in his pocket.

And Jack the Ripper, he haunts us still . . .